Japanese Roses

A Novel of the Japanese American Internment

Theresa Lorella

Lorella Rose Publishing
Seattle, Washington

Cover artwork by Alexandre Rito.

Paperback Edition: ISBN-13: 978-1484849798
ISBN-10: 1484849795

DEDICATION

For my mother and all the Roses. And for the Nisei and their families.

CONTENTS

It should be noted, to begin with, that all legal restrictions which curtail the legal rights of a single racial group are immediately suspect. That is not to say that all such restrictions are unconstitutional.

Justice Hugo Black, Supreme Court majority opinion, *Korematsu v. United States*, 323 U.S. 214 (1944).

ACKNOWLEDGMENTS

Japanese Roses is a work of fiction, but it would not have been possible without the first person accounts of the *Nisei* who lived through the internment and the scholars and historians who have compiled some of the excellent anthologies of the lives of the Japanese and their children in America from the late nineteenth century through World War II. For full thanks and recognition, as well as acknowledgement of the work that has gone into this novel, please see the list of references and further reading at the end of this book.

I have to thank all the people throughout the years who have encouraged me, this book, and who reminded me that this was an important story to be told. First and foremost, my thanks goes to my mother, Arlene Rose, for always believing in me, for reading numerous editions of this novel, and for working as publicist, agent, and moral support. For my husband, Brad, who has endured me escaping to my world of books for years, and whose help and encouragement led to the actual publication of this book. For my father, Pete, for always reminding me that anything is possible, for my sister-in-law, Kelli, for being an early reader and giving input throughout, and to my sisters Jennifer Rose and Christina Rose for their input throughout the publishing process. Thanks to my brother for always having faith. Special thanks to Christina for editing the second edition and helping get this book out there.

I would also like to thank the ladies of the Tam O'Shanter book club, who encouraged, throughout. Thanks to Sue for reading an early draft. Finally, a special thanks to Mary and Joan, two *Nissei* women who have taken the time to remind me that it is important to tell the story of the internment.

Issei – 1st generation
Born in Japan, ineligible for
U.S. Citizenship under U.S. law

Nisei – 2nd generation
American born Japanese
with U.S. Citizenship

Sansei – third generation
Children of Nisei

FORWARD

THE WOMEN IN MY family did not speak at all about the war years. You wouldn't have even thought they had lived through the Second World War except that the mathematics of their ages puts my mother and my aunts definitely and certainly on Planet Earth during that conflict. In fact, the math also puts my early childhood comfortably within the same timeframe, but I was too young to really remember and whenever I pressed for stories I was always dismissed. "No, no," they would say, "don't worry about the past." I didn't understand; I was there too and I wanted to know, to understand what had happened. I didn't realize that people didn't speak about the interment at all for many years.

What I didn't understand at the time was that it was considered unpatriotic to protest the camps, even years after the last camp closed. Frustrated, I just stopped talking about it altogether, thinking that maybe there wasn't that much to say at the end of the day. Besides, the reaction I would get for even mentioning Camp Harmony or Minidoka made me feel like I had something to be ashamed of and I couldn't figure out why.

In fact, when I was a child, the only person who would ever refer to the internment was my paternal grandmother who would say, rather cryptically, that when she thought of the war, of the camps, she was proud of her roses. I thought she meant the flowers that she grew in her garden behind her home, the ones that she cultivated and insisted that each of her daughters and granddaughters take and grow in their yards as well. Her bushes had survived even in her absence, ready to be cared for by her expert hand when she returned home from Minidoka and so I always assumed that was what she meant.

The roses were very important to my grandmother, but she didn't know enough English to explain exactly why to me and I never learned her native Japanese. Mama had wanted to send me to Japanese school when I was a child, but Auntie Maggie said that I would hate her forever if she forced me to go and it would only make my life more difficult like it had for her and her sister, my Auntie Kimiko. Auntie Maggie always seemed to be a little upset with my grandmother and her inability to speak proper English and her funny, sort of old fashioned ways. Not really embarrassed, but uncomfortable, like she was being watched by unseen eyes whenever Grandma said something in Japanese. Still, it was Auntie Maggie who made sure to transplant the rose bushes from Grandma's house to her own yard when Grandma passed away and the home was sold.

It was nearly fifty years after the bombing of Pearl Harbor and the notices for internment were posted that I finally discovered what my grandmother really meant when she said she was proud of her "roses." In November 1994, my mother called me up and asked me to drive her down to the Wing Luke Museum in Seattle's International District. She said she had to be there on December third at precisely eight-thirty in the morning. I thought that maybe she was a bit confused as she was getting on in age at the time. "Are you sure, Mama?" I asked her, "Do you want to go today instead?" I was trying to be accommodating and if she wanted to tour the museum, I was fine with going that day and not waiting a couple of weeks.

"Rose," she said, clearly and inexplicably frustrated with me, "I have an interview on the third and I want you to come, too." Funny, that was the very first time that I ever made the connection with my name and my grandmother's plants. "In the meantime," she continued, "I have been holding onto a couple of things that I would like you to read before we go because I am going to donate them to the museum."

My mother has always found a way to astound me: An interview that I had to prepare for, of all things! Still, I could sense that she was nervous about this. "It's about the camps," she continued, presumably reading my mind as I couldn't figure out for the life of me what she was going to say in an interview at a museum. As soon as she said this I could hear the sadness in her voice. The war, the camps; it all reminded her of my father and that was one of the reasons that I thought she never talked about it.

"Of course I'll take you." And of course I would, and did, give my mother a ride that day. What I heard, and what I read before going finally answered all the questions that I had about the internment and why I spent nearly three years of my life imprisoned before I was even old enough to start school. And I learned that my grandmother had never meant to say that she was proud of her roses. She was proud of her Roses.

Rose Lundstrom Miramoto
Seattle, June 2009

4

1 ROSE MARIE

Transcribed from archived interview given at Wing Luke Museum, Seattle, Washington, on December 3, 1994.

IT'S FUNNY THE THINGS that seem important before everything changes. One minute you are worried about what people think about you or whether you have enough butter or milk at home, and the next moment, bombs are ripping apart your life. I was not in Hawaii on December 7th, but my life changed as certainly as if I had been there when the naval base was attacked. Funny thing was, I had just been thinking about how my life would have been different if I had not married a Japanese American. It was as if I had a premonition of things to come.

I had just gotten out of the church I attended on Seattle's Capitol Hill. Akio hadn't gone with me that day. In fact, he usually did not come along. We had learned that it was easier to just do things separately and avoid the unpleasant stares and rude comments, not unlike the things my father had said to me when I told him that I was going to marry Akio. It was that memory which I was inexplicably rehashing as I sat in my car following the morning service on December 7, 1941. There was no reason for me to be thinking about hate. I loved my husband and I loved our daughter; I didn't have any regrets about choosing to marry Akio. Besides, regrets or not, I was in a hurry to get back to our home on Beacon Hill where I was having Akio's sister, Maggie over for lunch and I certainly had no time to feel sorry for myself.

I was late and feeling rushed, as usual. I had to go to pick up butter from the grocery store on the way home. I couldn't serve dry rolls and I had used up my extra supply on the cake that I had been up half the night making. Now I was worried that I wouldn't make it back to the house in time to greet my teenage sister-in-law. Even though she was younger than me, I was fond of Maggie and I really wanted her to like me. I wanted to have a family again and since my own family was less than receptive to Akio, I wanted more than anything to impress the Miramotos. As I hurried out of the church's parking lot, I worried that Maggie would be sitting at my front door before I arrived, no doubt presuming that I didn't think she was important enough for me to actually arrive to my own luncheon on time.

If only I had not been so frazzled the day before, scrapping the cake I was making more than once and starting over to make it perfect. On top of my worry about the food and my timing, I was feeling guilty that I had left my small daughter at home with her father that morning so that I was not slowed down by her usual request to go up to the park and visit with her great-grandmother—the only member of my own family still talking to me. Thinking of my grandmother only reminded me once again of my father's comments and the cycle of guilt continued. I was so wrapped up in my own head that morning that the territory of Hawaii was the last thing that would have ever crossed my mind.

When I think back to the moments before I heard of the attack, I am struck by the smallness of my problems. Really, on that morning in December, I was happily married to a good man. We had a healthy child and a cozy little home. That's all that really should have mattered—not butter, not the opinion of others, not even being a few minutes behind. But that was before things changed in an instant and so on the way to the store nobody could drive fast enough to comply with my all-important schedule. With each passing moment I grew more irritable and impatient. When I finally arrived at the grocery store at the bottom of Beacon Hill, I glared from my position in line at the owner, Mrs. Lewis, when she did not immediately ring up my butter, but instead engaged in a conversation with an acquaintance of hers who was before me in the line. It wasn't my usual manner to be so impatient and rude, but my thoughts of doubt and shame had made me even more intent on getting home in time to make up in displays of love for the horrible thoughts I had been thinking in my head. The fact is, my father's words had not just sprung to mind for no reason at all: Life had never been easy for Akio and I—1941 was a time period long before interracial couples were accepted or even common, and it didn't help that the Japanese along the West Coast had been disliked for years before tensions related to the war had increased that sentiment. I could feel the distrust in my neighbor's eyes when they looked at my husband and it was starting to concern me. Maybe because of this, or maybe it was just a coincidence, we had also been stretched very thinly with our finances lately and I just wasn't seeing much hope. My worries were starting to show through my usually calm façade and I was increasingly irritable and self-concerned with my own problems.

This bad attitude on my part was certainly apparent as I stood in the unending line at Mrs. Lewis's grocery on December 7, 1941. I tried to distract myself and not be so restless and mean by listening to the radio that was droning on in a corner behind Mrs. Lewis. Nothing too important or entertaining seemed to be happening, which, at the time, only made me more impatient—I couldn't even be entertained while I was forced to wait endlessly. As I stood there contemplating whether to just interrupt the woman in front of me, the voice on the radio announced that it was twelve noon. Great, I thought to myself, Maggie is probably already at my house now. That was it, I decided, I was just going to cut in on Mrs. Lewis's animated conversation when the announcer's voice became suddenly frantic. I had actually started moving closer to the counter, planning my own little verbal attack when the words hit me: I stopped moving and we all fell silent (even the talkative Mrs. Lewis). The words came at us almost too fast to catch: The Japanese had succeeded in pulling off a "sneak attack" on our naval base at Pearl Harbor in Hawaii. Thousands were dead.

"Those damn Japs!" the man in line behind me exclaimed under his breath. I have to admit, that was my first thought, too. I don't exactly remember what happened next. I must have left the line, walked out the door and gotten into my car. I believe that I sat in my car for several minutes, maybe even half an hour. I was still holding the butter, but only noticed it when I realized that the sticks were slowly beginning to soften in the heat of my hands. As I began to come to, I noticed that I was also still clutching the coins that I had taken out to pay for the butter while I was in line. First an attack on the country and now I was a thief! I tried to coach myself to get out of the car and go back into the store to pay for the item I had taken in my state of astonishment, but I couldn't do it. My legs didn't seem to work. I must have been in complete and utter shock.

I sat there for a few minutes more before I began to cry. During those moments I told myself that I had misheard. After replaying the announcement back in my head I realized that I had not. Next, I reasoned that the report must be incorrect. Hawaii was far away and it was very possible that we were getting bad news. Europe was in the midst of a war and so was China— maybe a false report had been given. Maybe the announcer meant to say Hamburg but accidently said Hawaii, Japanese instead of German. But no, that didn't make sense at all. Or maybe, I thought, maybe the news came from Japan itself as a means to frighten us. But why would Japan want to frighten us? Then, slowly, I could feel my body come back to life as I accepted the fact that Japan had in fact bombed our navy in our territory. Suddenly I felt vulnerable and unprotected. What if the mainland was next? What if I was sitting in a parking lot at a grocery store and my home—with my child in it—was about to be bombed? Even now, thinking about, it amazed me how I quickly I went from worrying about groceries to worrying about bombs. In the span of just minutes, my life had changed drastically.

Once the tears came, they showed no immediate sign of ceasing. I cried for the sailors, I cried for the fact that this surely meant war. But I also cried for my family, for myself. My father had warned me to not make the choice, to not choose a "Jap." Back then he, and all his friends in the Bellevue Anti-Japanese League, had no real reason to dislike the Japanese or their children. What would happen now? What would happen to my daughter? It was while I was crying over my fear for Rosie that I realized that someone was knocking on my window. I had to roll down the driver's side window to see who it was; my crying had caused the car's windows to steam up. The window-tapper was Mrs. Lewis.

"Oh, Mrs. Lewis," I slobbered, trying to regain my composure, "I apologize for not paying. Here is some money." I struggled to pick up the coins that I had dropped on the seat next to me. I had to get home; I didn't have time to be arrested for stealing.

"Money?" asked Mrs. Lewis, perplexed. She looked at the butter in my lap, now starting to leak out of its wrapper, a complete mess. She smiled kindly. "No, keep the money...and the butter, on me. I came to see if you are alright, Mrs. Miramoto." She looked genuinely concerned. This made me cry even harder. I had been so angry with her just minutes before and, although I appreciated her kindness, I wish that I could go back to that moment in the line and have the radio report never happen. I wish that I could still be perturbed with Mrs. Lewis because that would mean that life was still normal. But I certainly couldn't say that. I was clearly confused.

"I'm sorry," I said, hoping that she had no idea what was going on in my mind. "I'm so sorry. I'm just," I struggled for the right word. "I'm just really upset."

"Yes," she continued to smile, but seemed to be trying to assess my state of mind. "Can I call your husband or someone to help you?" she asked eventually. Clearly I was not doing my best.

"No," I responded. I took a couple of deep breath. "No, thank you. I will be fine. I'm going to go home." I paused for a moment. "And Mrs. Lewis," I called to her as she started to walk back towards her store. "I am sorry." She waved. "We're all sorry, Mrs. Miramoto."

I sat there a moment longer watching the owner walk back into her store. What a shame that it took something so terrible to bring out a small kindness in her and me, at least for that one moment. Someday, I thought, I will make it up, be a nicer person in general. Someday this war would end, even if it had just begun.

2 MAGGIE

From the previously unpublished memoir, "The Roses of Minidoka."

I'VE ALWAYS THOUGHT IT was a shame that what started as a day full of such promise had to be forever ruined by the dropping of bombs. December 7, 1941 really started off wonderfully. The weather was crisp and clear with blue skies. In fact, it was unusually clear and bright for December in Bellevue, Washington. No rain, not even a cloud to be seen. Many people have described that morning in hindsight as if it were almost magical, sparkling. Maybe they think of it as the last good day before life was turned upside down, interrupted. I think, though, that it wasn't that much different or better than any other morning in all honesty. It just helped that it was dry and it was Sunday. Sunday meant no school and no chores—which was rare for those of us who were the children of farmers. That Sunday I was going to visit with my brother and his wife and baby downtown Seattle. And going downtown meant a chance to spend time with Henry, my very first boyfriend. To me, that made the morning of December 7, 1941 a very good one indeed.

As excited as I was to meet with Henry—who remained a secret to my family—I was also looking forward to an afternoon with my Akio and Rose Marie and my little niece, Rosie.

Coincidentally, Akio had married a "Rose." All of us Miramoto women were all called "Rose" in some form or another. My big sister was Kimiko Rose, I was Megumi Rose, and Akio married Rose Marie, and they named their daughter Rose. My mother had started the tradition to remind her of the rose bushes that her own mother had cultivated in their garden in Japan. We were her "Japanese Roses," she always said. When Akio first told my parents that he was going to marry a *hakujin*, a Caucasian, he said that they shouldn't worry since he was just marrying another rose and somehow managed to convince them that Rose Marie's name was a sign that it was meant to be. I don't think they necessarily agreed (especially since they could barely actually say the word "rose" in English despite putting it on our birth certificates). But Akio was happy and Rose Marie was always trying to please my parents—unlike a certain youngest daughter of theirs that only seemed to defy their wishes at all times.

Honestly, it didn't matter who I was going to see once I got there, I loved going to Seattle. It was exciting to cross the new bridge over Lake Washington and into the city. Even though Seattle was less than ten miles away from Bellevue, back then it felt like I was leaving one world and entering another. Not only was Bellevue still a sleepy little country town in those days, but in Bellevue our community was small and confined. The Japanese were isolated enough that we *Nisei* had a very hard time asserting our independence from our *Issei* parents. Oddly, though, in retrospect we rural Japanese were less isolated as a group in regards to other members of the town—the Caucasian members I mean--than the Japanese in the city. In small communities we had to work and live together whether we wanted to or not. In the city, though, the Japanese community was large enough that it could sustain itself within its own ranks and so it remained insulated from other members of the city.

However, one thing both the country and city had in common was that neither was quite ready for my brother and his Caucasian wife. Even though I know that it bothered Akio and his Rose Marie, they put on a brave face and would say, "We're both Americans and that's all that matters." Well, we soon learned that "American" sometimes is just another word for "white," so actually only one of them was "American" enough. Anyway, whatever the case, Akio and Rose Marie were the only interracial couple that I had ever seen—or even heard of. I thought they were terribly brave and romantic. I was seventeen at the time so I was very romantic myself. Funny though how, unlike my brother and sister-in-law, I almost let adversity get the better of my love. But before the attack that changed everything, I would have done just about anything to go and see Henry— even sneak around behind my parents' backs.

Henry Fusaka lived in Seattle. I met him while I was watching Akio play in a baseball game between the Bellevue and Seattle all-Japanese teams. Henry played shortstop on the Seattle team with Akio. He was nineteen, a student at the University of Washington and, I thought, absolutely wonderful. I knew that Henry and Akio were friends from the team, but I had asked Henry to keep the relationship secret for the time being. My father did not believe that I should see anyone, however innocent the relationship, until I had graduated from high school. I didn't like to go behind my family's back, but I just couldn't help myself. Henry thought my parents were pretty strict, but he had grown up with *Issei* parents himself, so he understood what I was going through. "A proper Japanese boy/girl doesn't (fill in the blank)," was a common refrain from each of our childhoods.

I was supposed to be at Akio and Rose Marie's house at noon for lunch that day. I remember this because Rose Marie never let me forget how frantic she was to get home to meet me only to discover that I wasn't even there on time. Of course, on the day itself, we didn't have time to argue about who was on time. (In fact, I doubt that even she was there at noon knowing her!) However, despite my lunch plans, at about quarter 'till twelve I was still in Japantown with Henry. I knew that I should have left earlier since I was traveling by bus, but I was having a hard time tearing myself away from Henry. We had met for the morning at a teahouse on Sixth and Main. I was just having tea because I did not want to ruin my appetite. I loved eating at Rose Marie's because she was a great cook and, more importantly, she cooked American food. I have always loved eating anything that was not pickled or made with seaweed! I told Henry that I really should catch the next possible bus so that I would only be a few minutes late, but Henry kept saying "just a bit longer." He offered to drop me off at my brother's house. I figured Rose Marie would appreciate a few extra minutes to get ready since she was likely coming from church so I stayed. I thought I would just have to come up with a good excuse, say the bus was late or something. I didn't worry too much about it; I stayed with Henry at the teahouse until noon.

We heard the commotion in the street outside before we heard the actual news. Our waiter had disappeared into the kitchen. We could hear the radio, which was suddenly turned up quite loud. We could not make out what the reporter was saying, but we could hear that it was just breaking and the news seemed to be urgent and bad. Straining to hear the radio I heard the sound of glass, a plate probably, shattering and several voices gasping. I heard a voice cry, "No, it cannot be!" Henry put money on the table—I remember that we did not have the check. We just put money on the table and left. We went out onto the street to try and get some information.

People were already running through the street, speaking animatedly to friends and family. We were still in the core of Japantown and most people were speaking Japanese. I spoke only the basic Japanese that I had been forced to learn at Saturday Japanese school and even with that knowledge, I could not understand the franticly fast way that everyone was speaking. Henry had studied at Seattle's Nihon Gakko Japanese School, and unlike me, had actually paid attention to his teachers so he understood what was being said better than I. "Oh my God," he muttered under his breath. "What, what is it?" I kept asking him. With a firm grasp on my arm, he directed me towards his car and answered only with, "Keep your head down, I'll tell you in the car." "But what, please, what is it?" I persisted.

As we approached the car, we left behind Japantown and entered into what was then Chinatown, really just one street over. Now the whole area is known as the "International District." On this street the voices were less frantic and more angry than over on Main Street. Since many people were speaking in Cantonese, I was at an even greater loss to understand. I saw a man approach Henry and I; I thought he was going to tell us what was going on. But as he approached he looked first at me and then at Henry. He lifted his finger, pointed, and yelled that word that will haunt me for the rest of my life: "Jap!" I am not Japanese. I am an American. I am not a Jap.

While people back in the forties were not as politically correct as they are now, I didn't really grow up being called names. Sure, there was plenty of discrimination, but it was often subtle and my parents insulated me, Akio, and our older sister Kimiko from hate whenever they could. I wasn't used to being called an ethnic slur. But from that moment in December 1941, that word would follow me wherever I went: Jap. It was like the bombing in Hawaii had opened a floodgate of hatred towards the Japanese. We hadn't even left Chinatown when I heard it again: As Henry and I reached the car an old Cantonese woman came up to us. "You filthy Japs! Can't you keep out of other people's countries?"

Rather than respond, Henry pushed me into the car. I still had no idea what was even going on. We were in such a hurry that he pushed me into the driver's side and I had to scoot across the seat so that he could get in. "Henry, what is happening, why are they saying those things?" Henry didn't answer at first. He turned on the car and backed up so quickly that he made his tires peel. "Let's get out of here," he said.

We drove in silence for a few minutes. Finally, after what felt to be an eternity, Henry pulled over and put his head in his hands. He had understood the words people were saying as we left the teahouse, but he hadn't understood the meaning at first. As he told me what he had heard, I realized that I had understood better than I had thought: Attack. Sneak. Bombs. Killed. And over and over: Japs. I knew it immediately then—the lives of us *Nisei* would never be the same.

To this day I separate my life into two distinct parts: The years before the attack on Pearl Harbor, and the years after.

Even before the bombing in Hawaii, life had been difficult for us second generation Japanese Americans, and worse for our parents, the *Issei*. While our parents had always been hated and feared, we *Nisei* caused confusion to other Americans. We were Americans, but we looked Japanese. Although we felt completely American, our fellow, non-*Nisei* Americans, treated us like outsiders. No matter where I went, I felt like I stood out. I was always explaining that I spoke English just fine, that I was born and raised in Washington State, not some small village in Japan. I always felt like I had to prove my Americanism and myself.

Maybe it was this inferiority complex about my own identity that caused my gut reaction to the news of the Pearl Harbor attack: Guilt. Of course, that's crazy—I had nothing to do with Japan or their military or any bombing. But I had the same face as the people who had bombed our ships. I looked like the enemy. I knew that people would see that and think that I was just another "Jap," their new favorite word. I know that I shouldn't have let other people make me feel guilty, but I did. I think that many *Nisei* did. I think that the *Issei* felt worse—they were conflicted between their country of birth and their country of choice. I wondered what my own *Issei* parents must be thinking as I sat in Henry's care absorbing the news.

Henry brought me up to Akio's and we didn't even worry that he was supposed to be a secret: Let me tell you, if you have a secret boyfriend, tell your family about him during a national emergency and, absent extreme circumstances, I can almost guarantee you won't even get a shrug. Not even Mama and Papa were that upset when I told them where I had been when I heard the news. I have to say that Papa did say something to effect of "another *hakujin* like your brother?" Papa loved Rose Marie, but I think he felt that his daughters in particular should be good little Japanese girls. For once I didn't disappoint. "Fusaka, Papa," I told him. "Henry Fusaka." At least there one ray of sunshine for my father on December 7, 1941.

I didn't see my parents until the evening of the seventh, however. Once Henry and I got to Akio's, we hurried into the house, where the blinds were drawn and Akio and Rose Marie

16

were huddled together, listening to the radio for further news. Little Rosie could see that something was wrong, and sat in the corner, playing silently with her doll. She seemed blissfully unaware that life had changed dramatically just hours before, although she must have known that the adults were acting funny; we were too quiet. After I called my parents to tell them I was with my brother and Henry called his, we all sat at the table, with the radio planted firmly in the middle, like a talking centerpiece. Finally, after hearing various commentators speak about the burning ships and going to war with Japan, we turned it off and sat looking at each other.

"This is going to be bad for the *Issei*," Henry said, breaking our exhausted silence. "They are not U.S. citizens. They are still citizens of Japan, technically."

"But that is only because they cannot become citizens here," countered Akio. "Most *Issei* like our parents," he pointed to me and back to himself, "have lived over half their lives in America, they have American children, and they would never go back to Japan. They would become citizens if they could."

"But don't you see, Akio? That is the problem. Americans hate the Japanese so much that they denied *Issei* the right to naturalize as citizens. As you know, they aren't even allowed to own land. It's only going to get worse now. Our parents are in trouble," said Henry. He seemed to contemplate before voicing his next thought. "*We* may not even be safe."

"But we are citizens, we were born here," said my brother, optimistically stating what seemed so obvious at the time. "We are just as American as everyone else."

"American but with Japanese faces and names and customs," responded Henry. "And I don't know about your Japanese school in Bellevue, but at Nihon Gakko we bowed to a portrait of the emperor in celebration of his birthday—us American *Nisei*. Surely the government will not look kindly upon that." We had done that, too. "But we only did all that to make our parents happy," I cut in. "None of us care about the emperor of Japan!" I was well known in my family for my dislike of going to Japanese School, even back then. I could barely carry a conversation in my parents' language.

As my brother nodded his agreement, Rose Marie spoke up. "I don't understand. What could possibly happen to the *Issei*? This is America, whether they are citizens or not. We have rights here. You have rights. They have rights. What could the government possibly do?" Rose Marie had told me once after the internment that she had come to see that "What's right isn't always right." Back then, though, she still had faith in rights.

"In theory, I agree," said Henry. "But the truth is that the government has been watching the *Issei* for years now for no other reason except for the fact that they are Japanese. We all know that the government has never liked the Japanese, but ever since Japan began taking over every other country in Asia they have had a supposed justification for their suspicion of the *Issei* here at home."

"Do you think they have been watching my father?" I asked, completely disbelieving that anyone could find my middle-aged farmer father to be a threat.

No one answered. No one had a good answer. Responding to Henry instead, Rose Marie said quietly, "Well, isn't that a reason to be suspicious, all that invading and conquering that has been going on? I'm not agreeing with the suspicion, but isn't there a bit of a justification for it?" She looked around at the three of us. When we remained silent she added, "I'm sorry, I don't mean to offend. I just mean that Japan's bombing of our naval station is worrisome, to say the least. While there may not have been a reason for suspicion before, I can somewhat understand why the government would be looking at the Japanese now. I'm sorry." Rose Marie seemed uncomfortable; she averted her eyes and looked down at her hands.

"No, it's okay," said Akio, breaking the tension and reaching for his wife's hand. "It's true, if another nation is acting as an aggressor and citizens of that nation are in your country, there's fair cause to be concerned. But only if there is a real reason, I think. The problem is that having a Japanese face shouldn't make your government think that you are a secret agent for the enemy. It's frustrating for us *Nisei* that we arouse suspicion and hatred whenever we go out of our houses. We are American—citizens of this country. But you're right, our parents are not."

"But the thing to remember about the *Issei*," Henry said, continuing the thought and repeating his point, "is that they are not *allowed* to be citizens. They aren't just a bunch of tourists. They have homes and lives here. Why would they spend years and years posing as Americans just to turn on their adopted country? Does that make sense?"

"Does any of this make any sense?" Rose Marie sighed, pushing up from the table and standing. "Well, keep trying to figure it out. I'm going to serve some lunch. I made sure to have butter for the rolls and, by God, we're eating them."

*****

After we ate and were too tired to try any harder to make sense of the chaos of the day, Henry and I went onto the porch to say goodbye. He was going to go home to his parents' apartment to make sure they were okay and Akio and Rose Marie were going to drive me back to Bellevue to check on our parents. Neither of us actually wanted to say out loud what we were thinking. Finally, I just couldn't help it.

"Henry, I'm really scared," I blurted out, my eyes tearing up with the power of the emotion that hit me as the words escaped.

Henry took my hands in each of his. "No matter what, Maggie, I'll take care of you. I love you."

It was the first time that he had said that he loved me. It was the first time he said that he would take care of me. It was overwhelming—too much had happened in one day. What had happened to the morning where I was sneaking out to meet a sweetheart before coming to eat American food and play with my niece? Now people were trying to take care of me. What was going to happen that I needed to be cared for?

"Henry…"

"It's okay, you don't have to…" The look of disappointment in his eyes only made me cry harder. What a mess I was making of this!

"Henry!" I cut him off, trying to reassure him. "Let me speak! I love you, too. I do, I love you."

He squeezed my hands and smiled, but something had gone terribly wrong with this conversation.

*****

After promising to call as soon as I arrived home, I watched Henry drive off until his car disappeared from sight. I could have stood there all night, just watching him leaving, but I felt a hand gently squeeze my shoulder. My brother told me it was time to go. All four of us—Akio, Rose Marie, Rosie and me—piled into the car. Rose Marie said she didn't want to be left home alone after such a bad day, but I think she didn't want Akio driving around by himself. I remember thinking that I hadn't worried about Henry in that same way. As I sat in the car, I stared out the window into the growing winter twilight and thought about being a wife. Rose Marie was so good at it; I didn't think I could compare.

It was already dark when we finally rolled up to my parents' small farm in the Midlakes area of Bellevue, so dark that I could barely make out their tidy little house or the strawberry fields behind it. My father was so proud of his little "truck farm," a small farm where we put our daily harvest onto the backs of trucks for my father or his workers to drive to markets in Everett or Seattle. Back then there were so many truck farms in Bellevue that many people referred to it—derogatorily—as a "Japtown." The farmers had even gotten together to form a co-op that sent their produce on trains all around the country, even, my father would say, to New York City. Of course, I was neither interested nor proud of any of these things at the time. That night, however, I was incomparably happy to be pulling up to our family farm. Well, technically it was Akio's farm since my parents, as *Issei*, were barred by law from owning land in America.

As we drove up to my parents' house, I was struck by an immediate feeling that something was wrong: The lights in the usually bright and welcoming house were extinguished and the whole house was completely dark on the front side. The only sign of life occurring behind the dark façade was a faint trickle of smoke coming up out of the back chimney that rose out of the kitchen fireplace. When I stepped out of the car, still feeling like something was off, I noticed immediately that there was something strange about the smell of the smoke coming out of the chimney; a smell of something other than wood burning.

"Ma, Pa, we're back," Akio announced our arrival as we walked onto the porch. He tried the door, but it was locked. This was the first time in my memory that my parents' door was locked. Akio and I made eye contact briefly, wordlessly agreeing that something was not right with this situation.

"I hope they're all okay," said Rose Marie behind us as Akio knocked at the door tentatively.

"We see Grandma and Grandpa?" asked little Rosie who was holding her mother's hand, standing on the porch with the rest of us with a look of confusion on her face. Even my young niece could sense that this was an odd way to come and visit our house.

After a few tries with our light knocking, my mother appeared at the door and we were shepherded through the small front room and into the kitchen in back. As we walked in, we saw my father bending over the fire, prodding something in the fireplace.

"Papa-san, what is that, what are you burning?" I asked, immediately concerned by my father's actions. As soon as I got close I knew immediately what was in the fireplace.

"Megumi-chan, I met with the other members of the co-op after hearing the news," said my father, turning back to the fireplace to prod the embers. "We all agreed. We must destroy anything that would implicate us as allies with Japan."

I saw that my fears were correct. My father was burning his most prized possession—a collection of classical Japanese poems that his mother had given to him when he went off to university in Tokyo. He had carried it from Japan to America, and to each place that he had traveled until he settled in Bellevue. When we were children, he would read us poems from the book and tell us stories about growing up in *Hiroshima-ken*. Even though the book was probably not that valuable, or even that hard to replace, it was the fact that it was from my grandmother that made it so special. And now it was gone, turning to ashes in our fireplace.

"Papa-san, no" I screamed, lunging into the fire, coming close to burning my hands in the growing flames. "You have nothing to hide! Why do you have to destroy the things that you love?" I turned towards my mother to get her support. I noticed an empty crate at her feet. Jolted by the continuing shocks of the day, I turned my attentions to my mother.

"Where are your dolls?" I gasped in disbelief. The empty crate had held the special dolls used to decorate for the Day of the Dolls. In Japanese tradition, these special dolls were displayed once a year. They were beautiful, with ornate costumes and exquisitely painted faces. My mother had saved up and ordered them from Japan the first year that the farm had turned a profit. She had left her set behind in Japan when she came to America as a young picture bride and had waited many years to be able to replace them.

"It is fine, all is fine, Megumi-chan," my mother said, comforting me despite the fact that it was her possessions that had been destroyed. "Your father is right. We must not appear to be holding onto Japan. We are in America and must not arouse suspicion. These times will be trying for us Japanese."

"Arouse suspicion? How could you possibly arouse suspicion and of what, Mama? You are the wife of a strawberry farmer. You and Papa are not suspicious!" It was breaking my heart to see my parent's destroy their few beloved possessions, their only real memories of their childhood and youth. They had not done anything wrong. This was so obvious to me that I could not believe that nobody else seemed to be jumping up and agreeing with me. Not getting support for my plight from either of my parents, I turned next to Akio. "Please stop them," I pleaded with my brother.

He thought about it a minute, there was a hesitation before he responded. "No, Maggie," said Akio firmly. "They are right. We need to find anything that is Japanese or that could be considered questionable and get rid of it."

I was outnumbered. For the next hour or so, Akio and my parents went through the house searching for anything else that was "too Japanese." I—the person who hated Japanese school and couldn't bear the thought of going back to Japan--could not bear to take part and sat with Rose Marie and helped with Rosie who was clearly showing the signs of being up past her bedtime. As we sat there and watched, my parents and Akio burned our old Japanese school texts, the ceremonial kimonos that we had worn on holidays, an old framed photograph of the emperor (which is the one thing that I myself would have volunteered to throw into the flames and was happy to see go), a watercolor print of Mount Fuji and everything that could be found that was written in Japanese characters, including newspapers that were printed right in Seattle.

I was happy to see that there were a few things that even my mother could not bear to burn despite my father and brother's wishes including the pictures she had from the one trip we took to Japan as a family when I was a child. She also refused to burn her Japanese-language Bible. Those things Akio put into a box and then into two burlap bags and buried them beneath the big tree behind the house.

When my brother came back into the house, looking like even he might have been crying, Rosie was asleep in her mother's arms and my parents, who had joined us at the table, were discussing my sister Kimiko with Rose Marie. As my brother took a seat, Mama pulled a stack of letters from her apron pocket. The letters were those that had been sent home by Kimiko before the mail service stopped. My mother had been carrying the letters around with her for months to "keep her daughter close." None of us had the heart to burn these letters. Besides, even if Papa or Akio had suggested it, it was clear that my mother would not have parted with Kimiko's letters for anything in the world. I knew that her heart was broken for her oldest child who had been gone for almost two years, first just studying in Japan and then, seemingly, marooned there.

Perhaps I shouldn't have chosen that time to ask, but I

couldn't help but nod towards the letters and ask, "What do you think will happen to Kimiko now?" We knew from our sporadic communication with my sister that things had been increasingly difficult for Kimiko before the bombing. We couldn't imagine how conditions would be for an American in Japan now that they had declared war on our country. Poor Kimiko had never even wanted to go study abroad. Now she had been gone so long without word, it was almost as if she had disappeared altogether. But my mother had never given up hope that word would come from her oldest daughter any day.

"I do not know, Megumi-chan," said my mother. My parents never called me by my American name, "Maggie," but always by my given name, Megumi. "My hope is that she will go and find your father's family in Hiroshima. Perhaps they could help her to get back home."

My father's family in Japan did not know that Kimiko was not my father's biological child. Rather than trying to explain the situation to his family, my father simply introduced Kimiko as his oldest daughter to his brother and the remaining family when we visited their home in Hiroshima years before. Although we knew about it, Kimiko, Akio and I had been raised to believe that the fact that Mama had been married before her marriage to Papa, or that Kimiko was the child of that first husband, was just not that important. She was our sister, no matter what. To my father, she was his daughter, no matter what. Oddly, in some ways, Kimiko was always my father's favorite child.

"But do you think that she'll be able to come home anytime soon?" asked Rose Marie. "Especially now…" She let the words drift off, seeing that her question had done more to upset my mother than she would have ever intended. Poor Rose Marie— when she saw that Mama was upset I thought that she was going to cry herself; she was so worried that she had done something to make my family dislike her. Truly my parents always adored that girl.

Thankfully, Papa came to his daughter-in-law's rescue. "We hope so, Rosemaru-chan," he said in his accented English, trying his hardest to pronounce Rose Marie's name. I could tell that my father was also very concerned about my sister, probably more concerned than he even let on. Besides missing Kimiko, my parents were having a hard time feeling guilty about how they had insisted that their children go back to study in Japan to prepare for the so-called Pacific Era that people began talking about after Japan was successful in China. When Akio flat out refused—and it was determined that I was still too young, thank God--Kimiko volunteered. She packed up her favorite clothes, books, and keepsakes into a steamer trunk, put on a brave face, and set sail for Japan. You should have seen the look of pride on my parents' faces as Kimiko's ship left the docks. You should have seen their faces that night two years later, realizing that Kimiko's homecoming was becoming less and less of a reality.

The last time I had seen my sister, as she waved from the deck of her ship, I was just happy that I was safe at home and not the one who got stuck going to Japan for "heritage training," as my mother called it. After my one trip to Japan as a child, I had vowed to never go back at all let alone for any sort of training. That trip had been a terrible disappointment to me. It seemed that everything that I did or said only offended people or gave them reason to laugh at me. I had thought it would be wonderful to go to my father's home in Hiroshima and—finally—look like everyone around me. I thought that I would fit in. I was wrong.

While our relatives were excited to see us at first, the three of us (but especially Akio and me) seemed unable to communicate and what words and gestures we did get across only horrified people. Not only did we not speak very well, but our language skills were learned primarily from speaking with our parents and our *Issei* neighbors—all people who had left Japan decades before. This included our teacher in the Japanese school we attended. In the ensuing time since these people had left Japan, the language had changed with the times. There we were, little children using the colloquialisms of the elderly. We had terrible accents, we had tiny vocabularies, and we sounded like old ladies (even poor Akio!) when we did manage to speak in complete sentences. Besides the language issue, we were forever offending our Japanese relatives with our "brash" American habits and mannerisms. Besides the "unladylike" manners of my sister and me while on our tour of our parents' homeland, Akio kept forgetting to take his shoes off when he entered buildings. Everywhere we went, it seemed that we Miramotos offended and scandalized. But Kimiko, probably the most traditional of the three of us, had gotten on that ship in Elliot Bay years later without a single complaint.

"We will try to speak with Kimiko tomorrow," my father cut into my thoughts. "I have tried calling again today, but the lines were down or blocked. Maybe we can get through tomorrow. She is smart, she'll be fine." For months my parents had been saying, "She'll be fine, she'll be *fine*." I think that they were trying to convince themselves that everything would work out. But we had all known instinctively for weeks what now seemed certain: Kimiko was in trouble.

Adding our worries about Kimiko into the mix of an already terrible day had exhausted us. Besides, it was getting late. We had been listening to the radio softly all evening. Things seemed to be settling down for the night as the nation came to terms with the fact that we would be at war come morning. It had been a long day. After getting together a late night snack to make up for our lack of a dinner early that night, Akio rounded up his wife and daughter and they set off for Seattle. My mother made them call when they got home, just as I had finally called Henry after my parents had finished burning their goods. Henry said that his parents had been doing the same thing. Finally, after a day that would truly live on in my mind forever, my parents and I tumbled into our beds and gave in to unsettled dreams.

3 KIMIKO

From FBI confession regarding charge of treason against the United States during a time of war, 1954.

I AWOKE FROM A deep sleep, confused about where I was; often I dreamed of home so vividly that it took me a moment to register the extreme disappointment and confusion that settled into my brain upon waking to find myself still in Tokyo. Perhaps that is why I had hardly been sleeping at all. I had been exhausted the past couple of weeks trying to find ways to get back home and the night of December 6, 1941 had been one of the first in which I allowed myself to get a full night's sleep. I had tried to forget about my predicament for just one night and finally get some much needed rest so that I would be re-energized the next day. I was hoping to go speak to the embassy once more and maybe scrape together enough money to take the train down to Yokohama to see if there were any ships that would take me with them—I almost didn't even care where they were bound. I just knew that time was running out: It was a bad time to be an American in Japan.

Of course, even though it was possible to enter Japan when I did without an American passport, I had refused to travel overseas without all my papers in order. Unlike many of my Japanese American counterparts in Japan, I had my passport; not only did I think it would speed up the process to go home, but it gave me a reinforced sense of identity. I was proud of that passport and all that it implied. However, when it came time to use the document to buy passage out of the country, it was gone. Naturally, I assumed that I had somehow misplaced it or that it had been temporarily lost. I had been so careful with it, so proud of it that losing my passport was a blow to my psyche in and of itself. The day that I realized the little book was gone was the day that I felt my ties to America loosening just a little.

Desperate to get out of Japan, I had spent about twenty hours a day for the past several weeks searching for it. Japan had been very successful in their campaign in China and they were setting their sights on the Unites States next. It was getting ugly and American companies, diplomats, and students were starting to retreat from the country faster than the ships could carry them. Of course, along with the Americans and Europeans trying to leave were many Japanese with ties to the outside world—many Japanese without any papers. Suddenly that little unnecessary document that only a few of us had become one of the most precious commodities on the market.

Still, I just didn't see how or when my papers could have been stolen and so I had searched and retraced my steps, thinking that I would certainly find the booklet at the school, at my friend's house, even at the teahouse where I had bought a daily little snack. Eventually I had started going to embassies—not just U.S, but European as well--trying to get help and trying to get through to my family in Bellevue and Seattle. By that time in early December 1941, I was quickly becoming penniless; I didn't have enough for the passage to America even if I could have found my passport. You see, the Japanese had made it illegal for people who were not Japanese to work in their country. The irony! I didn't have the papers to be allowed to live in peace, but I didn't have the papers to be allowed to leave. What was I to do? I was nearly hopeless. And then it got worse.

I had been in bed, getting the sleep that I needed so badly. As I lay in my bed in Tokyo, my mind had drifted back to my parents' farm in Bellevue. I was home! They were having a party for me! I couldn't see my family yet, but I could see their little house and I could hear the cheers coming from—where? Behind the house, maybe. But that didn't make sense. Why would people be cheering if they couldn't even see me yet? Perhaps they had forgotten me, I felt in my dream. Perhaps they were cheering for somebody else and I was just standing here watching the scene as an outsider.

The pain of the feeling of rejection that I felt in my sleep jolted me awake. As I sat up, customarily confused, but now with an aching heart, I realized that the sound of the cheering crowd had not stopped when I opened my eyes. It seemed that the crowd was real but it was not cheering for my arrival back to America. The crowd was cheering because Japan had bombed America. I went to the window and slid open the paper windows. People were milling about in the streets, clapping each other on the back, smiling and laughing. It was a distinctly un-Japanese display that these usually reserved people were putting on. It reminded me, oddly, of Fourth of July celebrations back home, especially because I saw some people holding what looked to be American flags. As I ducked my head back into my room, I didn't yet know about the specifics of Pearl Harbor, but I did know immediately that something was very wrong. And that Japan was quite pleased with itself.

4 MAGGIE

From "The Roses of Minidoka."

I WAS AWAKENED IN the early morning hours of December 8th by a flash of light that passed over my face and startled me into a confused state of half-sleep. My bedroom was in the front of the house; I thought that perhaps a car had driven down the road in front of our home. But that couldn't be right. What kind of car headlight would shine right into a second story bedroom window? Dreading what I might see, I swung my tired legs onto the floor and padded over to the window. Pulling the curtains aside, I peered into the road, but saw no cars driving off. I thought about going and getting my parents, but they had had a long day and it seemed that I was imagining things. I got back into my bed listening to every sound with the heightened hearing of the paranoid. I decided that I would lay there listening extra-hard for a few moments longer and see if I heard anything. If not, I would go back to sleep and be rested to face the next day. After laying there for a few minutes longer, I must have dozed off again because at some point shortly thereafter I was jolted back awake by the sound of the front door being pounded on and hitting the wall as it was slammed open. I was so scared that I nearly fell out of the bed. And then I froze.

I was paralyzed with fear for myself, for my parents. "Oh

God," I prayed into the darkness, "Please don't let them hurt us." I didn't know who was down there or what they wanted, but I knew it couldn't be good. After what felt like a lifetime, but must have only been minutes—maybe seconds—my refrain of "Please God, please God," was interrupted by my mother, who had come into the room to find me still lying in bed, the covers over my head. Like a baby.

As my mother held me, telling me that it was going to be okay—clearly a lie to make me feel better—I could hear my father's voice down in the front room demanding to know what was going on, what the men wanted. I could hear the shuffle and bangs of things being knocked over, furniture being overturned. I looked up to my mother, my eyes asking the question that I still could not get my mouth to form.

"Megumi, it is the FBI," my mother whispered. I'll be honest: I'm not exactly sure what my mother said to me. Maybe she said it was the police or something about federal agents, I don't know. I don't know if she knew what the FBI was or how she would have even translated it into Japanese. But, whatever she actually called the men who were currently in our home, they were agents of the Federal Bureau of Investigation and they were looking very specifically for my Papa.

"What! What have we done wrong?" I screamed in a whisper at my poor mother, who had no better answer to that question than I. She and I looked into each other's eyes for a moment, each of us silently categorizing all the things we had destroyed the night before (or earlier that same night), wondering what we had forgotten. I knew that I would need to go down and help my father since his English wasn't very good; I was worried that I wouldn't be able to do it. Reading my mind, my mother said to me "You will be fine, Megumi-chan," as she pulled me to my feet. I was beginning to lose faith in this constant assurance that all things would be "fine."

My mother and I held hands as we descended downstairs. We saw my father sitting in a chair at the table where we had been sitting together earlier that evening. Two large Caucasian men were standing around him, clearly blocking his ability to get up or leave. Stacked on the table were many household items that we hadn't even considered earlier. In the FBI agent's hand were the letters that my sister had written from Japan. My mother had left them on the kitchen table last night.

"Things in Japan are rough right now, Papa," the agent closest to my father read from the letter he was holding in one hand. He raised the letter he was holding in his other hand and continued, "I visited Mount Fuji today. It was nice to get out of the crowded streets of the city for the day, but I am learning much in school. My Japanese is almost fluent now, but I still have a hard time reading and writing." And finally back to the first, "I am practically ready to be a 'bridge over the Pacific' as you and Mama wanted of me." Without knowing my sister, there was no way for the FBI agents to hear the hidden sarcasm in that phrase. The last thing that Kimiko really wanted was to be a bridge to anything. If there had been a bridge over the Pacific back to Seattle, she probably would have been willing to walk back home. She was hoping that Mama and Papa would think that the mission was completed and would send her a ticket to come back to Washington, purportedly to use her new skills to live a more Japanese life.

"They are from my daughter," my father struggled to say in English. He seemed weary, almost resigned to the fact that his answers were in vain. Even though he had said it perfectly the first time, I translated by repeating the sentence. "They are from my sister," I added, barely above a whisper. The agents looked me up and down, then at each other before turning back to my father.

"She is studying in Japan, Mr. Miramoto?" asked the agent on the other side of Papa, the one not holding the letters. "That must be convenient for you." When my father was silent, the agent pressed on. "Is she connected to your co-op as well?" Something about the way the man said the word co-op made me realize that they were accusing my father of something far more sinister than sending lettuce to Detroit or strawberries to Manhattan.

I don't think that my mother could understand exactly

what was happening, but hearing that the men were talking about Kimiko, my mother brushed past me and approached them. "Please," she nearly pleaded, "my daughter is stranded in Japan. Can you help us?"

The agent with the letters looked at her as they had at me, but with more malice, as if sizing up her potential threat. He threw the letters into the heap on the table that now included our shortwave radio, our kitchen knives, and my father's hunting rifle—a rifle that I don't think had ever been shot, let alone used to harm or kill anything. All farmers had one, in case a wild animal came and threatened the crops, but my parents were Buddhists at heart even though they often attended an Episcopalian church and Papa was not one to resort to killing if he could help it, even if the season's harvest was at stake.

Apparently determining that, like myself, my mother was not sufficiently dangerous enough to pose an immediate threat to the United States, the agent turned his attention from my mother back to the letters and once again to my father. He did not answer her question about Kimiko, but his silence on the matter was answer enough. "Mr. Miramoto, you will be coming with us." I rushed to my mother's side; her knees had given out and she nearly hit the floor. I don't know at what point we had switched roles from her comforting me to me supporting her. I looked to my father to see if he had understood; in my rush to catch my mother I hadn't translated for him. He had.

"May I change?" asked my father, not an ounce of fight left in him. What was he to do? This was the FBI. He was wearing his pajamas.

"No." And with that, one agent herded my father out of the house while the other heaped our belongings, including Kimiko's letters, into a big canvas bag. In hindsight I realized that we had never seen a warrant, there had never been any mention of what exactly my father was being arrested for doing. They just came, took our things, and took my Papa.

"Hiroshi!" cried my mother as each agent took one of my father's arms and hoisted him from the chair. She looked stricken, at a complete loss.

My father remained calm. "Take care of the children and yourself," he said in his forced English, no doubt to not arouse any further suspicion with the agents by speaking in Japanese. Confused, I found myself translating his words into Japanese for my mother. But she understood what he was saying. "Reiko, I love you."

"I will take care of them. I love you," she answered. It was the first time I had heard my traditional parents say these words to each other. In any language.

As my father was being dragged out his own front door, I was having no problem translating for the other people in the room, but I myself was speechless. I wish I had said, "No, this isn't right!" or in the very least, "Papa, I love you." But in my state all I could muster was a feeble, "Papa!" as I watched the guards drag him towards the car they had parked behind a bush, hidden from view. As they carried him, one of his slippers fell off on the front walkway. The agents did not stop to let him put it back on. Mama and I stood in the doorway and watched until the taillights of the agents' car had disappeared.

My mother did not cry. She did not show her sorrow or fear. Once the car had gone and we were enveloped by the silence of the night, she turned to me and said, simply, "Megumi-chan, please help me straighten this mess." Without speaking we set about putting our remaining things back into their places and righting furniture that had been overturned or pushed askance. The little house was now almost completely bare, all of my parents' belongings burned, buried or confiscated in the matter of hours.

"Shall we call Akio," I asked, wishing that my brother was there to tell us both what to do next. As he had gotten older, we had all come to rely on Akio when Papa was not available. I was surprised when my mother said, "Let him sleep. We will call him in the morning." At first I was angry; I thought that Mama was letting Papa go too easily when perhaps Akio could have found him and explained things to the FBI. Later, I understood that Mama was protecting her son by not allowing him to find Papa and attempt to "explain" to people who had already made up their minds.

As we straightened up, my mother sent me upstairs to try to sleep. She said she would do the same, but I heard her go out the back door so I snuck back downstairs to see what she was doing. From the kitchen window I could see her in the backyard, shovel in hand. When she came back in with the Bible she had Akio bury earlier, she said, "They can take my husband, but they cannot take my faith." Funny, I thought, it was *their* faith that she was talking about, their Bible. But, then again, it was also my mother's, just in a different language. The language was the problem, not the content.

In the days that followed, we learned that my father was taken to an Immigration Department holding cell downtown Seattle. There he stayed with other farming leaders, teachers, and prominent *Issei* men from the Puget Sound area. No formal charges could, or would, be brought against these men beyond their Japanese births while they were held there by Immigration. During the one month or so that Papa was held downtown, we were allowed to visit him only once and to bring him something to wear besides the pajamas that he had been wearing the night he was taken from his home. After this visit he was shipped to Fort Missoula, a Department of Justice prison camp outside of Missoula, Montana. He, like the two thousand other *Issei* men who were arrested by the FBI in the early hours of December 8th, 1941, were eventually charged with being "enemy aliens who were in possession of contraband that could have been used for espionage for the Imperial Army of Japan." We never had our radio, kitchen knives, or Kimiko's letters returned. They were evidence of my father's status as a threat to his adopted country.

5 ROSE MARIE

From archived interview, continued.

WHEN I WOKE UP on the morning of December 8th, for just a moment I forgot that anything out of the ordinary had happened the day before. I sat up, rubbed my eyes, and then was hit by a wave of nausea as I remembered. It was still early, not even six a.m. yet, but Akio was not in bed. Although he was an early riser, Akio was normally still in bed at that hour. Something was wrong. I jumped out of bed and ran to the kitchen. Sure enough, there I found my husband at the kitchen table, his head in his hands. I came up behind him and put my hands on his shoulders, trying not to startle him. He hadn't looked up when I had entered the room. "What is it, Akio?" I whispered. "Can I do anything?"

After a pause, my husband lifted his head and pulled me down into the chair next to him. He took my hands in his, took a deep breath and said, "Rose, my father was arrested last night by the FBI. They came in the middle of the night, ransacked the house, and hauled him off in front of my mother and sister."

"The FBI?" I was confused. As in *the* FBI, I wondered? Didn't they only go after criminals? "I don't understand—why would the FBI take your father?"

"They took Henry's father, too." Akio continued, "Maggie

called this morning—the phone didn't wake you. Henry called her after his father was taken around three o'clock in the morning. They were taken as suspected spies—men all over the Bellevue and Seattle areas were taken from their homes. *Issei* men."

That fast then; this was going to happen that quickly. "Can I do anything?" I repeated, feeling stupid for having nothing better to offer my husband. I lowered my eyes, tears coming dangerously close to spilling. How could I let my husband see me cry for my own shortcomings when his father was sitting in jail somewhere?

Akio looked at me and took my face in his hands, tilting it back up to face him. "Yes, you can, Rose Marie. You can make some coffee, please."

"Coffee?" I almost laughed. "Of all the things I could maybe do to help, that is what you want right now?" Akio did laugh, but his eyes were still troubled. "Well, you make great coffee, my dear and I have to get to work."

I froze. How could he even think about going to work on a day like this? "Are you sure that you should go?" I asked, not wanting to sound accusatory. Not wanting to say with my tone, "Who goes to work after their father is taken away?" I knew that Akio was a good man who loved his father, but I would have thought that he would have been as paralyzed by fear and confusion as me. Or by anger.

"It is Monday, Rose and war or not, father in prison or not, I need to feed my family. It'll help. I'll think about what I can do while I work," he responded. "Besides," he continued less certainly, "I think I need to put on a good face right now, show that I'm not hiding or..." words seemed to fail him. "Being suspicious?" I asked, whatever that even meant anymore. He just nodded.

"What about the farm?" I asked. Mr. Miramoto was the lifeblood of his fields and even though the rest of the family knew the business, I wasn't sure if they could do it without Hiroshi. At least not so suddenly.

"My mother will see to the farm. She'll be okay—it's the

slow season and I think they have money saved up. We'll help her," he added seeing that I had a look of doubt on my face. I didn't know how to farm. "And Maggie will help." Again, I have to say that I grimaced. Maggie was a good kid, but she had never shown evidence of having inherited the farming gene. Akio ignored my facial expressions, but he sort of chuckled in agreement about Maggie. "Well, Mama can even hire some help, Rose."

"Besides, how long can they keep Papa for espionage?" he continued after a pause. "The evidence will either show that he is or he isn't a spy. And we all know that he isn't. They cannot just hold him indefinitely."

"Right," I said, not convinced, not really certain of anything anymore. "Okay, go get dressed and I'll get some coffee ready for you." What else could I do?

"Perfect," he said, starting off down the hall to our room. Before he got there he turned and stuck his head back into the kitchen. "And Rose? I love you."

"I love you too, Akio." I turned back from the cabinet where I had started to measure out coffee. "I'm sorry about all of this."

"You have nothing to be sorry about. But if you really do feel bad, maybe you could make it up by whipping up some French toast for me."

"Yeah, yeah. Go get ready," I laughed.

I watched my husband once again head off down the short hall from the kitchen to the bedroom. When he got to our bedroom door, he turned and smiled at me.

"Get going!" I joked as he darted into the bedroom.

Akio could always make me smile. That was my favorite thing about him. We had been in the same grade together in school—we graduated from Bellevue High School together. It was difficult to begin dating Akio, worse to have to tell our parents. His parents were easier to tell than my father; my mother had died when I was young. While *Issei* were not normally fond of their *Nisei* children marrying Caucasians, the Miramotos seemed to warm to the idea after time. I think a lot of it was my name: Rose Marie. All of the Miramoto girls had the name Rose for a middle name—something to remind my mother-in-law of her childhood rose garden. If I would have been called Anne or Jane, I do not think that his parents would have ever allowed Akio to marry a *hakujin*!

My father, though, he was a different story. As I stood there making breakfast, images of Daddy came to mind. Two days in a row I was thinking these thoughts! After my mother's death he changed, he became a different man. He missed my mother, but his sadness manifested itself in anger and jealousy. As I got older, my father became more and more distant, preferring the company of his nightcaps and ledgers to me.

My father had always done well, but never as well as his own father. My grandfather had made a fortune by buying up land following the Great Seattle Fire. He became a turn-of-the-century—the last century, of course—real estate mogul. My father, with the intent of following in his father's footsteps, set out in the world and made several bad investments until he had no choice but to work for my grandfather. He ended up in Bellevue, along with his new wife and child, to manage the farm lands that my grandfather owned and leased to Japanese truck farmers as well as some other investments that my grandfather had made on the east side of Lake Washington.

Maybe because he could not seem to hold on to a piece of property himself, my father grew very resentful of the *Issei* farmers who prospered through backbreaking work and were able to utilize the law's loophole and purchase land in the name of their American children. It became almost an obsession with him. "You've got to watch out for the sneaky Japs—they're stealing our land from right under our noses," he would say. He joined groups such as the American Legion who fostered this hatred. He was also a founding member of the local group started in Bellevue called the Anti-Japanese League, led by prominent community leaders and sanctioned by local government leaders. When I revealed my relationship with Akio, rather than revoking his membership in that group, my father ran in the elections to be an officer. He won.

I suppose you are doing some of that modern psychological assessing that is so commonly done now and have determined that in dating a Japanese American boy, I may have just been another teenage girl doing the opposite of what her father wants. I won't say that it didn't give me some satisfaction. But I never wanted to hurt my father; I just knew that he was wrong. Did I marry a *Nisei* to prove my point? Well, I don't know—I'm not a psychologist. But did I love Akio Miramoto? Yes, and with all my heart.

In all honesty, though, there were times that I felt like I had gotten in way over my head. It was hard to be stared at in public. Gradually, after a year or two of marriage, I had begun to run a few errands, like going to church on my own, telling Akio that he could just stay home and relax or watch the baby. While I was normally strong in the face of stares and rudeness, I had been getting anxious and tired by the end of 1941. I never wanted to leave my husband, but I wanted other people to leave us alone. Looking back, things were difficult before Pearl Harbor, but they became so much worse those first few months of 1942. As I stood in my kitchen on December eighth making breakfast, I think that I already knew that the arrest of Mr. Miramoto and Mr. Fusaka was just the beginning. But the beginning of what?

As I pondered my own fears for the future, Akio came back into the kitchen, dressed in his work clothes, hair combed, and looking like the handsome boy who had given me my first kiss behind a crate of his father's strawberries at the 1936 Bellevue Strawberry Festival. He was a good-looking man, at least to me. I do not know if my husband was handsome in an Asian or Western sense; I just knew that I liked the way he looked. He was just a few inches taller than me, about five foot seven, and he had a strong, muscular farm boy's build. His hair gleamed like black silk, and his eyes were a color somewhere between black and brown. They were shaped like almonds and literally twinkled when he laughed. But Akio's best feature was his smile. It was sort of lop-sided and goofy, but it warmed the entire room with its sincerity.

Maggie looked more like Akio than like her sister, Kimiko.

Maggie was the pretty, smaller, and more feminine version of Akio. The two were almost exact replicas of their father. Kimiko, though, she looked like their mother. She had an almost breathtakingly exotic quality about her. While she had similarities to her siblings, her build was smaller, her features more refined. I suppose she was beautiful in the more Western sense. She looked like a movie star. Her smile was more seductive and hard-won than the grin of her brother and sister who would give you a smile for nothing. Kimiko, on the other hand, was more reserved with her emotions. However, the effect of getting a smile from her was so lovely that it made you feel good just to actually see it. She was gorgeous.

And me? Well it may be hard to imagine this old woman as being anything other than a grandmother, but I had my day. I was certainly never exotically stunning like Kimiko or even cute like Maggie. Akio said that I was beautiful to him and that was all that really mattered. I was the exact opposite of him and his sisters—a Swede with blond hair, blue eyes and a bigger build. I guess it's true: Opposites attract! Or so I thought as I watched my husband eat his French toast (I never liked French toast!). After finishing the last drop of coffee in his mug, Akio stood up. "I'm off to work," he said, kissing me on the forehead.

"Be careful," I said, tears welling in my eyes once again. "Please."

He knew that I meant so much more than to just be careful in the ordinary sense. Be careful on the street, be careful with the machines, look both ways for busses when you cross the street. No, that day I meant something different: Be careful that you don't get hurt or arrested or beaten. Be careful and don't let them take you from me. "Don't worry, Rose Marie," Akio whispered in my ear, giving a last embrace before leaving. "We'll get through this."

That's what everyone kept saying right after the attack on Pearl Harbor: Don't worry. We'll get through this. It will all be okay. If everyone was so convinced of that, why was I so worried?

*****

As December 1941 wore on, the immediate fear that I had felt on the afternoon of the seventh and the morning of the eighth did eventually wear off, but the concern did not. Newspapers continued to report on "sightings" of Japanese bombs or planes looming over the West Coast. Almost all of these reports were completely unfounded, but the public opinion against Japanese and Japanese Americans became increasingly hostile, as I had feared. Nearly every time I went out with my husband I overheard the word "Jap," either whispered or shouted. Once I was even called, "Jap lover" as Akio and I walked our daughter to the park down the street from our house. Akio wanted to confront the man who had said it to me, but I managed to convince him to do no such thing. I asked my husband when we got home to explain why he had gotten so upset, especially because he always managed to remain calm when people degraded him directly. His answer astounded me. "Because *you* don't deserve it, Rose." No, of course I didn't. But I didn't say, "Well neither do you," in response. I didn't say anything at all. I didn't know what anyone *deserved* anymore.

As much as I tried to insulate myself from the growing hatred of Japan and the Japanese, it surrounded me. On the streets, in the shops, on the radio, in the newspapers. It was the reawakening of the popular fear of the Yellow Peril, the plots and conspiracies of the "Japs" to take over America. There were beatings—applauded by the press—of Japanese Americans walking home after work. There was talk that the government was going to separate the Japanese from the rest of the population "for their own protection." There was talk that the Japanese would be segregated for the protection of the rest of the population. Above all, there was talk. Eventually, people started to use the word "camps."

All this was a definite change in the way that people spoke about the Japanese almost immediately after the bombing. Before the bombing of Pearl Harbor, I knew there were laws about the *Issei* owning land or getting citizenship. I knew that

Nisei weren't allowed to live in certain neighborhoods in Seattle or get loans—that is why our house was in my grandmother's name--I knew that people had never like the Japanese or those who intermingled with them. I had gotten used to it. But now it was different, now I had to rearrange my entire life nearly overnight to deal with the open hatred that I encountered. Now a simple trip to the grocery store meant that I had to steel myself for the stares and possible insults of my neighbors, who used to be friendly to me. Were they lying before? Had they always hated me and my family? I began to avoid certain stores and parts of town, especially if I was with Akio or my daughter.

I was terrified for my daughter. One night, after getting groceries, I contemplated buying extra bleach to see if I could make my daughter's hair lighter. She had her father's coloring. I didn't know how to protect my three year old daughter from what was happening around us. The truth was that the hate was not new, but now it was blatant and unexpected in its cruelty. I sensed this, but I didn't truly understand it until one morning when I was out of milk (I had enough butter!) and I found myself at Mrs. Lewis's store. I hadn't been in to her grocery in the weeks since the attack, mostly because I was still feeling so embarrassed by my outbursts that day. I was hoping to thank her once again while she was ringing up the milk and was happy to see her behind the counter.

Once again, there was somebody in line in front of me, just like the morning of December 7th. But this time Mrs. Lewis wasn't talking to the woman in front of her. This time Mrs. Lewis stopped mid-sentence and just stared, first at me and then at my daughter. Her customer did the same. It was this woman who broke the silence. "I told you to put up your sign. If you are going to serve that Jap's wife and his little Jap daughter, you are losing a patron today."

I was stunned, utterly speechless. This woman said this about, in front of, my three year-old daughter. I looked up at Mrs. Lewis expectantly. She had been so kind on the seventh, offering to call my husband—my Japanese American husband—to help me. Please God, I thought to myself, let her make this better. I took a deep breath and, after squeezing my daughter's hand, looked up at the shopkeeper.

"Mrs. Miramoto," she said. "I'm afraid there are no Japs allowed in this store."

I didn't say anything. I gripped my daughter even tighter (I heard the poor thing say "ouch") and turned on my heel. If they didn't want us then fine, we would leave. This time I would not take any unpaid merchandise with me. I purposefully dropped the jar of milk I had been holding, hearing the glass shatter as I made my exit. I told my daughter that I had forgotten my money and we would get milk later. On the way home she was silent, clearly trying to make sense of why her mama was acting like a crazy person. But she was old enough to understand something. "Mama," she said as we drove up to our home, "what's a Jap?" "It's a bad word, baby, don't say it." I snapped at her. I realized my mistake as soon as it came out of my mouth. "Am I a bad word, Mama?" I felt a knife drive through my chest. If I was only going to hurt my daughter by trying to explain, maybe it was better that I didn't explain at all.

I didn't say anything to Akio about the milk, the store. I could have because he was there at the house when we got home. I knew immediately that something was very wrong. He was supposed to be at work and Akio, obviously, was not one to miss a day of work. Even though my husband was the first in his family to get a degree from the University of Washington—he studied business—he couldn't find any business that would hire him. Finally, desperate to provide for his young and growing family, he took a job doing manual labor in the shipyards. "Just temporarily," he had said, "until I find the perfect job." We both knew the odds of that happening were only getting more dismal.

I didn't think that I could handle any more horror stories, but I couldn't very well ignore the fact that Akio was home at ten in the morning in the middle of the week. "What?" I asked too curtly than I intended. "What happened?" I tried to smile to make up for my obvious anxiety. Akio looked up at me and winced; I had hurt him. "Heya Rosie," he hugged our daughter, "how about you run inside and get your building blocks ready and then you and your dad will build a tower to the sky!" She nodded and ran through the door, excited by the unexpected play date. Akio watched her retreat to her room and when she was out of earshot turned back towards me.

"I showed up to work this morning, Rose," he whispered hurriedly, trying to get the story out before our daughter reappeared. "The supervisor met me at the time clock. 'No need to clock-in, Miramoto,' he said. 'These ships are being built to blow the shit out of you Japs so we can't have any of you monkeys working here and sabotaging the war effort, now can we?' He had a gang of some of my co-workers standing with him. A clear sign that arguments would not be tolerated." I could see that my husband had finally hit the end of his tolerance; he looked utterly defeated. "The funny thing is, the supervisor's name is Kruger," he smiled.

"German," I said, after taking a second to process his meaning. We let it hang in the air, not admitting verbally the irony of the situation.

"Correct," Akio said, "but with a face that doesn't betray him." That was one of the first and only things that I ever heard Akio say that sounded critical. He never lost hope in people, even after what he and his family had been through. He never gave up hope in America. The next day he was out looking for a job, any job, to tide us over. I knew it was hard on him not being able to support us, but I had a little money tucked away. I also had a family with money. After Akio was out of work for a few weeks with no paychecks, and I had burned through our tiny savings, I knew that I was going to have to at least ask for some help. While I knew that it would hurt Akio to know that I was visiting my father, we were quickly running out of funds for the house payment and for food. So, while Akio was out hunting for another job (one that he would never find), I made the decision to pack Rosie into the car and drive over the Interstate 90 Bridge into Bellevue.

My father, Lars Lundgren, may have been a hate-filled man, but he was my father. He also was not alone in his hate. His racist peers esteemed him for his fervent "support of the rights of

Americans." To please his friends, my father had not attended my wedding. He had never been to my home. He refused to interact with Akio. He had met Rosie, but only because he had asked if I would bring her by his house once right after she was born and Akio insisted that it was important that our daughter know her grandfather. I reluctantly brought Rosie to my childhood home when she was just a newborn. My father took one look at her and said, "Her hair is so dark and her eyes are shaped like a Chink's. What a shame. My daughter had herself a little Jap." That was the last time I had seen my father until that day in early 1942, more than three years later.

When I walked up the porch of my father's house, I was immediately struck by memories of my mother. I missed her so much. I knew that she would have been so proud of her granddaughter. I remember thinking about how different my life could have been if my mother had lived, if my father had been a better man. I was standing on the porch thinking about all this when the front door abruptly opened. I hadn't even knocked yet. My father stood there scowling at me. He looked me up and down and then looked behind me to see if there was anyone with me. I had left Rosie in the car. I didn't want her to be called any more names by her own grandfather. I didn't plan on entering the house and I could see her playing out of the corner of my eye. I am here for my daughter I reminded myself, to keep a roof over her head, buy her food.

"Well, what do you want, Rose Marie? Have you finally decided to leave your Jap husband?"

"Please, Dad," my voice was plaintive, not strong and steady like I had hoped as I approached the house. "Akio is my family." This was already going terribly.

"Rose Marie, he may be your family, but I have no Jap family. I am not a Jap-lover like you. I love my country." He paused and glared at me. I could smell the alcohol on his breath. It was eleven in the morning. "Why are you here?"

What a great question. Why did I think that my father would suddenly become a better person when the world around him was now allowing him to be openly hateful? Still, in some ways I suppose that I had hoped that my father would welcome me with open arms and I could cry to him about the hardships that I was facing. If he had been a normal father maybe I could have asked if he could help get a job for Akio or help me make the house payment that was now long overdue. But this was not a normal father and his comments only made me angry. While I wasn't brave enough to stand up to the people on the street who called me names, I wasn't afraid of arguing with my father; I had done it before. Maybe that's the reason that I was standing there. Maybe I wanted to understand what it was that people like him were thinking that could make them so hateful. I wanted to see if love was stronger than hate.

"Daddy," I said. I hadn't called him that in years. "Daddy, I want to know why people like you are calling people like my husband and baby girl names. I want to know why they are saying they should be carted off and put in camps. Is that true? Are they going to put us in camps?" The press had been running quotes by groups such as my father's, saying that it was only a matter of time before the area would be "evacuated." But now, standing at my father's door, I realized something: My father didn't care if his granddaughter was called names, he didn't care if people like the Miramotos were put into camps.

As it hit me, as I understood the unspoken answer to my questions, I looked at the man who was my father and said nothing. I looked at him and remembered that he once loved me and that he once loved my mother. He had been a man who had had hopes and dreams and weaknesses and faults. He had been happy once. That man was gone. This man was just a shell of the man that I had loved. The answer to my question was hate. Hate was stronger than love—you let it in and it will eat you alive.

"Dad, I do not know when we will see each other again. I'm sorry to bother you." As I walked back down the walkway to my car, I still half expected my father to call out and try to stop me. I half wanted to turn and run back towards him and force him to see me, his little girl. Instead, I heard the front door of his house, the house where I grew up, slam definitively shut.

6 KIMIKO

From treason confession, continued.

ONE THING THAT I need to make very clear is that, as of December 8th, 1941, all avenues for me to get home any time soon were completely cut off. In fact, communication of any kind with the United States was severed completely, from both countries' perspectives. In the course of one day, I went from not being able to get through to America to not even being able to attempt to call or write to my family. Now, much more than I had been even prior to the attack, I was totally and utterly stranded. And I didn't know what to do. I was in my early twenties, nearly penniless, practically without friends, and too pretty for my own good. I don't say that thing about my looks because I have no humility, but because it was continually problematic for me to be attracting unwanted attention from men. I wanted to blend in, lay low until I could figure out a plan b.

In the days following the declaration of war, I was still in Tokyo, still in the housing I had obtained while I was at school.

My landlady, Mrs. Inouye, was a decent woman, although she couldn't help but show her pride in Japan's successes; she could recount the military victories in China as easily as if she were listing the names of her children. She had the good manners to not speak to me directly about Pearl Harbor and the growing number of wins that the Imperial Navy was racking up in the Pacific, but through the papers walls of her boarding house I would often overhear her and her friends chatting in the central courtyard about the great glories awaiting the emperor and his subjects. I have a suspicion—maybe a hope--that Mrs. Inouye counted the winning battles in a way to keep her own anxieties about war at bay; both of Mrs. Inouye's sons were in the Imperial Navy.

Wherever her sympathies lay, Mrs. Inouye extending kindnesses to me during the initial excitement after the attack, something that was in short supply overall when it came to Americans. After learning firsthand that it had become publically acceptable to berate Americans (one of my fellow boarders offered me her shoe—to lick like the American dog that I am, of course), I stuck to my room at all costs. Even though it was strictly against her policy (it was a boardinghouse, not a five star hotel), Mrs. Inouye started bringing me trays of food once it became apparent that I was not going to make an appearance at the communal meal table. Before the meal had been served in the dining room, she would appear at my door with my portion. She never knocked, she never said anything at all, but the meals kept coming the full week that I kept myself incubated. I was so tired, so distraught, that I just shut down completely.

In honesty, I stayed in the room for the first three days for no other reason than the fact that I was depressed and tired, my twenty hour days finally catching up with me. The next four days or so after that I isolated myself because I was afraid. I had woken up one morning soon after the attack—maybe the tenth, maybe the eleventh, I'm not sure—committed to putting on a brave face and facing the world once again. I threw open my shutters, letting the light seep into the room, which had grown stale and dreary the past few days. Eager to feel the fresh, albeit chilly, air on my face, I stuck my head out the small window and breathed in deeply. The celebrants had long since retired to their daily routines and the world seemed to have returned to normal, at least on the surface. In fact, I could even see the oil man coming down the street, on his weekly round of selling lamp oil. I had spoken to Hiro-san several times during my stay at Mrs. Inouye's boardinghouse; he had a cousin living in California and liked to practice his limited English with me, just in case he ever "made it over the Pacific." I saw him approach and stop at the front door, just below my window. While I'm sure that he must have seen me, Hiro-san did not acknowledge me that morning. That was odd.

I pulled back and, perhaps shamefully, did not close my shutters. I strained to hear the conversation between the oil man and Mrs. Inouye. I was beginning to feel foolish; they were talking about oil, after all! Just as I stated to slowly close the window—slowly so that nobody would hear it and thus know that I had been eavesdropping—I heard Hiro-san steer the conversation to the war. "Quite a victory, wasn't it Madame Inouye?"

"Of course, Hiro-san; but may I inquire about the oil? It would appear that you have given me the same amount of oil as last week and all the weeks before that for the past couple years, but charged a higher price. Have you increased your rates in honor of the emperor?"

There was something ominous in the pause that followed. "As a matter of speaking Madame, the answer is yes. If you choose to waste my oil on that American bitch that you are harboring, you will pay a higher rate. Of course you understand."

I held my breath, completely uncertain as to what to expect from my landlady. I put my hands up to my face in a silent prayer. I just couldn't deal with another blow; I had no place else to go. "Hiro-san," she said after a pause, "I will pay the same amount for the oil as last week. If you do not wish to continue our business partnership, I will find another oil salesperson in the future." Thank you, God, I thought, I had a roof over my head for another night.

But while she may have been protecting me, Mrs. Inouye was also putting herself at risk by making this decision. In my relief to hear her defend me, I didn't realize that her courage could be just as detrimental to her as an outright public declamation would be helpful. "Mrs. Inouye, are you not a loyal citizen of the emperor? Or do you cater to American students because you support America; do you wish for those yellow-haired devils to come to Japan and massacre our children?" This accusation against her loyalty was a dangerous one in wartime Japan; if overheard by the wrong person, it could lead to an interrogation—or worse—by the Imperial Thought Police.

"Hiro-san, I am loyal to our exalted emperor. I am also a meek and mild woman. Please do not come to my premises and speak of massacres, nor of my boarders. I am not strong enough to hear such talk. I would hate to have to seek assistance to ease any fears such talk might create."

Of course, Mrs. Inouye was not a meek and mild woman— she was a shrewd business woman and had supported herself and her children since the early death of her husband. Polite and quiet she was, but meek and mild she was not. She had gained a reputation in the neighborhood for being a strong ally in any disputes between neighbors and thus being well connected. Hiro-san heeded her words, left his oil, and was silent in the future when he made his delivery the following week. Still, the damage was done: I went back to bed for several more days and Mrs. Inouye knew that she was being watched.

Later that week, when I finally realized that hiding wasn't going to get me anywhere, I left my room to find Mrs. Inouye. I wanted to thank her for the food; I couldn't say anything about the kind gesture in my support since it would give away that I had been eavesdropping. It was before meal time so I went down to the kitchen where, sure enough, Mrs. Inouye was busy getting the boarders' meals together. She didn't turn around when I walked through the door and she continued dishing food onto plates. I noticed that the tray that she used to bring my food up to me was already in place, currently being loaded with my meal. Not wanting to startle her, I coughed gently to get her attention.

Without turning around, Mrs. Inouye said, "It is nice to see you out and about. You must be feeling better."

"Yes, thank you, Madame Inouye. You have been most kind. Thank you for allowing me to eat upstairs. I wasn't…myself these past couple of days." When she didn't turn towards me, I just stood there a moment longer, somewhat confused. "I can eat downstairs from now on."

"Kimiko-san, I understand that you were not feeling well and so I felt that we could bend our rules a bit." I bowed despite the fact that I was still being presented with a rather unwelcoming back. "Kimiko-san," Mrs. Inouye said, sounding almost impatient. "What are you going to do now?"

"I do not honestly know," I responded. "I need to keep trying to get home."

"But what if there is no way to get home for you, at least not for some time? Please think about what you will do."

Suddenly I understood what Mrs. Inouye was saying between the words that she was using. "Mrs. Inouye, I will be able to pay for my board, I assure you. I will find a job or work off my board around the house."

"It is not money that worries me, Kimiko-san," she responded after a lengthy pause. She still was engaged in ladling out the meal, soup now. "Although I am ashamed to admit it, I am worried for my safety having an American here. I still have my two youngest children at home with me. I have no place else to go. I cannot lose my business and home."

"Am I putting you in jeopardy?" I asked. I was confused— she had defended me. She had fed me. She seemed to like me even though we were now technically enemies.

"It is not personal, Kimiko. It is war." Finally she turned towards me. I noticed that she no longer used the respectful "san" at the end of my name. "You will need to leave as soon as possible. You understand, I'm sure."

I was dumbstruck. I understood alright: I was being evicted based upon my nationality. "I will begin looking for an alternate residence tomorrow," I replied through gritted teeth but still polite. I began to retreat through the door, desperate to get away from Mrs. Inouye before the tears fell. I would not let her see me cry.

"Perhaps you can look today," she said as I was slowly backing up. I stopped, stunned. "If you can't find anything, I may be able to make an arrangement for you." I nodded, now without words. I turned my back on her and began to leave the room, not caring if I was now being rude. "And Kimiko," she called after me. "You will continue to take meals in your room until you leave. I'm sure you understand." I understood.

I was left with two options and I didn't yet want to resort to the second: I needed to find a place in Tokyo or, as a last choice, find my way down to Hiroshima to see if the Miramoto family in Japan would help me. Although I loved my father dearly, his family here in Japan had left a bad taste in my mouth during our previous visit years before. I had been uncomfortable around many members of the family when I was a teenager. Papa's nephew, Ryuu, just kept looking at me and saying, "Funny, she doesn't look like you, Hiroshi-san." "No," answered my father, "she looks like her mother." But Ryuu wouldn't let it go. "How old are you Kimiko, you seem too big to be a little girl as you say you are," he would say when the adults had left the room. In Japan, I was told to be three years younger than I was to make up for the years of my life that my parents were not married to each other. It was ridiculous—I was never large for my age, but nobody believed that I was twelve when I was fifteen. My parents actually told everyone that in America everyone is bigger because of all the food and wealth.

Still, despite my discomfort in the past, I had recently visited the compound. I had already been in Japan for over one year, and I knew that I had to get down there eventually. Finally, when my school let out for a break, I couldn't put it off any longer. I boarded the train and made my way back to *Hiroshima-ken*. I had dreaded the visit in particular because now my aunts and uncle were all dead and Ryuu—the eldest male--was in charge of what was left of the family. Ryuu, who was only a few years older than I, was young, unmarried, rich, and powerful. He had studied in the military academy and owned several factories that were prospering by manufacturing various implements for the war effort.

While I had certainly not hit it off with Ryuu when we were younger, my reasons for disliking Ryuu grew exponentially with each day of my visit. The first few days he was simply obnoxious and entitled; by the latter part of my visit he was blatantly inappropriate and threatening. On the last night of my visit, as I was packing my bags for my early morning departure, he entered my sleeping quarters and began making suggestions to me that were decidedly not family-oriented. While he stood at the door, I kept my focus on transferring things from the bed into my small suitcase; clothing, books, a magazine, undergarments. As I picked up my silk slip, Ryuu grabbed it from my hand and, with his other hand, pulled me towards him, crushing me against his body. I could smell sake on his breath as he struggled to kiss my mouth. I managed to twist enough to have the kiss land awkwardly on my cheek. I struggled to get away as he threw my slip onto the floor and pushed me onto the bed. I landed, painfully, on top of my open suitcase.

"I know how you American girls like to be treated," he hissed in my ear.

"You are wrong, Ryuu," I panted, losing my breath in my efforts to free myself. "We are cousins. This is not proper." Of course, we were not blood cousins. However, by nature, by the way things should have been, this was wrong.

"We are cousins," he mimicked me. "I think it is just fine, my dear cousin," responded Ryuu as he pressed his body against mine. He was excited and I was scared. Ryuu could have made things very difficult for me in Japan if he had wanted; it was a very male-dominated society and he was powerful. Who would I go to, what could I say? For just a brief moment I thought that it might be easier to just give in. But that moment passed as I remembered that I was not Japanese. Please remember, this event occurred before the war, before the starvation and fear. Back then, when Ryuu cornered me in my room, I still had something to lose. And so I didn't give in; I managed to get one leg free enough to swiftly pull my knee right into his greedy crotch, sending him onto the floor in pain. I didn't wait for him to get back up. I literally swept everything on the bed into my suitcase and ran for the door without stopping to look back. Knowing that Ryuu would likely come to find me if I stayed at the train station to wait for my scheduled departure, I bought a ticket for the next train out of Hiroshima, not even caring where it was heading. I ended up adding an extra day of travel, doubling back from my unintended first night of travel, but I had avoided seeing Ryuu again.

In light of what occurred on my last visit, I just could not bring myself to go back to Hiroshima for help once the war started. So after being somewhat summarily set free from my living arrangements with Mrs. Inouye, I decided that I had to find a place to live in Tokyo. I knew that I would have to find a place where I could be somewhat anonymous since most landlords would have fears similar to those of Mrs. Inouye. I also knew that I could not afford much. So I also knew that I would have to get a job—and quick.

Since I couldn't get a new room without employment, I set out to search for a job that very day. I didn't stop to eat the food that I found outside my bedroom door as I left, nor did I eat the fresh servings that appeared when I arrived home. It was petty and rude, but it was one of the only protests I felt that I could make. Of course, after a couple of days I had to swallow my pride and apologize to Mrs. Inouye for my insolence. I was finding it to be nearly impossible to find any job at all in the crazy post-attack world I was living in. Talk about a rough employment market! I was a foreigner in a country that was at war with my own. While I could speak Japanese fairly well, my knowledge of *kanju*, Japanese characters, was still so minimal that I often felt nearly illiterate in Japanese, and I had very few, if any, skills. I had been raised traditionally, expected to find a nice *Nisei* boy to marry and then start a family. I had helped my mother keep house, so I could clean and I had helped my father in the strawberry fields, so I knew how to do hard physical labor, but nobody wanted to hire me to even scrub their toilets. It didn't look good to have an American "dog" in your house, even to serve. The only jobs that seemed to be open (particularly to me) all had something to do with the Japanese war effort and I refused to do anything that would help or assist the emperor in any way.

Not only did I have personal reasons about not wanting to help the Japanese win a war, but also I was worried about a very practical matter: My citizenship. While I didn't grasp the fragility of my situation per the laws of the United States, I knew that many *Nisei* abroad in Japan were being asked to revoke their US citizenship in honor of the emperor's glories. In those initial days of victory, many of my former friends and classmates did just that. For people like me--those of us who refused to accept Japanese citizenship--we were labeled as *enu*, or enemy. Once that labeled was applied, I may as well have been a leper.

When Mrs. Inouye heard of my troubles she urged me to claim Japanese citizenship and thus be afforded full rights—and rations. "Your parents are Japanese, Kimiko," she said, never again adding the respectful *san* suffix to my name. "Claim your birthright here and become a full citizen." In Japan, the *Nisei* were considered dual citizens with Japan and the United States, but it was no longer an automatic distinction as it had been in the past. Now, rather than passively being considered a citizen, I would have to put my name on my family's registry in order for Japan to recognize my citizenship. Even without knowing the exact consequences, I knew this would be a risky move to make and something difficult to explain when I finally left Japan. What if claiming citizenship with Japan meant I was revoking my citizenship with America? It was not a risk that I was willing to make so early on in the war. Back then I wasn't starving.

Instead, I kept trudging on, applying for any job that I could find. I even applied to be a domestic at a fancy house but the lady of the house was not interested in having the enemy work in her home. She suggested that I become a prostitute. Eventually, after nearly two weeks of leaving early in the morning and coming back to the boardinghouse without news of any progress, I arrived home to discover that Mrs. Inouye had exercised her list of connections to get me a job at Domei Press, in the English language section of the local newspaper. While I'm sure it could have caused Mrs. Inouye some grief to have to put in a good word for me, she probably determined that it was better to put her neck out to get me the position than to continue to house an *enu*. After announcing that she had procured the position for me, Mrs. Inouye told me to be out of the house by the following Monday. It was a Friday. Once I left, I never saw Mrs. Inouye again. Her boardinghouse was in a part of Tokyo that suffered greatly during the fire-bombings years later. When I went back a few years after the war, the whole neighborhood was gone, replaced by modern Occupation-era structures.

7 MAGGIE

From "The Roses of Minidoka," continued.

WHILE MY MOTHER WAS dealing with the imprisonment of my father and my brother was dealing with being shut out of work, I spent the beginning of 1942, mourning my own loss: Henry Fusaka entered the Army. He wasn't alone: In early 1942 many young *Nisei* men along the West Coast had joined up in response to a cry from leaders in the Japanese American Citizens League to show the extent of Japanese American patriotism. Desperate to "prove" that he was American, Henry joined as soon as he heard the call to arms; he left nearly immediately. While I had been concerned that things were moving too quickly just weeks before, I was devastated when Henry actually got on the bus that took him away from me. I realized that I wanted and needed him to be there, just over the bridge, waiting for me. When he left, I cried for days on end. My mother, who had just lost Papa to the FBI, hadn't shed a tear once, at least in front of me. I alternated between admiring her strength and cursing her heritage, which discouraged the open showing of emotions.

My tears for Henry, however, were short-lived. He was home just a few weeks after enlisting. The Army, he explained to us at a "Welcome Home" dinner in his honor, had re-classified

Japanese Americans from U.S. citizens to what they called Class C-IV; Japanese Americans were now considered to be enemy aliens. While I was secretly overjoyed that he was back, my brother and Henry shared many an ominous discussion how this was just the beginning. They felt that the rumors must be true: It was just a matter of time before the Japanese in America received word of their marching orders. I was more optimistic; we had been hearing rumors for months and life had continued to go on, albeit with open animosity and empty chairs at the dinner table.

I was just starting to get used to the new "normal." Now it didn't startle me to see headlines in the Seattle Times about how the Japs were a threat to the safety of the nation. Now we had Japanese curfews and we were prohibited from entering places of business, parts of town. I figured this was as bad as it would get—and it was bad. Soon, I thought, the country will come to its sense and the No Japs Allowed signs will come down, the papers will print stories about Germany instead of Japan, and the curfews would be lifted. It was just a matter of time, I thought. But I was wrong. The only thing that time brought was what was inevitable to my brother and Henry: On February 19, 1942 President Roosevelt signed Executive Order 9066.

The order did not mention the word "Japanese" anywhere in it, but we all knew that we were the Order's intended targets. The Executive Order gave the military the right to evacuate the West Coast for the purpose of national safety. The Army was to remove and relocate residents within that zone if they were perceived as a possible threat to national security. And, shortly thereafter, a threat was perceived. In the end, it was as easy as that. The government issued an order meant to protect our nation, but that in practice ended up doing a hideous injustice to the Constitution. Maybe it wouldn't have been so bad if the order had only allowed the removal of non-citizens, but it did so much more than that. Executive Order 9066 gave the government the right to remove U.S. citizens from their homes without any form of due process. So, when the evacuations began, it wasn't only the *Issei* who had to pack up and leave, but so did we *Nisei*—born and bred American citizens.

I didn't really understand all that stuff about the Constitution and Due Process rights back then. When the Order was issued, my main concerns were practical, not constitutional. It was Henry who was always talking our "rights." He spent his time with the Seattle JACL leaders speaking about the best way to handle this news. The thing that was most surprising, I think to all of us, was that the *Nisei* were included in the plans to evacuate the Coast. We had expected that the *Issei* would be seen to pose a threat because they were not citizens. My father was still incarcerated in a prison camp in Missoula, Montana. We had spoken—me and Henry, me and my brother, Henry and Akio—about what was going to happen to our parents and how we would have to help out with their farms and businesses and homes while they were gone. We had planned for just about every scenario except the one that was actually happening, that we would also be asked to leave.

I had been worried about my mother, but I had always assumed that I would still be able to carry on with my life in her absence. I thought that I would finish school, attend the university, continue dating Henry, all while helping to maintain the farm and sending aid packages to my parents of fresh fruit, sweets, and other goodies. I hadn't thought that my life might be interrupted right then and there, during my senior year of high school, when I was seventeen years old. I realized—with a selfish horror—that I was going to have to leave everything I knew and go to some unknown place while the government decided how to deal with the potential threat that I posed to my country. What if I wanted to travel to Europe, or even to San Francisco or Los Angeles? Now I could not do any of these things. I had been classified as an enemy of my own country. Now, instead of ordering a dress for high school graduation, I was waiting for instructions from the government telling me when I would have to leave my home and where I was going to go once I did so.

I am not proud of my initial reaction to the news that the *Nisei* would be evacuated. I screamed, I cried, I was angry and moody with my family. My mother, on the other hand, received the news of the president's decision with the stoicism typical of her native culture. That infuriated me; how could she not be as angry as I was? Akio also tried to remain hopeful, as was his nature, but I remember that Rose Marie was indignant that the government could do such a thing. "This just isn't right," Rose Marie kept saying whenever we started speaking of the upcoming evacuation. "This just isn't right." Once when we were together and Rose Marie went into the no right tirade, Henry, rather bravely, cut her off and said, "But now it is the law."

"What's right isn't always right," she would retort. "I read that once; now I know what the story meant," she would add, somewhat cryptically.

Once the shock of the president's order subsided, I comforted myself with thoughts of Henry and me facing this challenge together. I pictured us holding hands, walking into an evacuation center together, a unit. Perhaps we would marry during evacuation and come back to start our lives together after. There was no reason that I couldn't go to college as an old married woman, after all! And, to make things even better, if Henry was in a camp, he couldn't go and make a stupid decision like joining the Army once again. Let the rest of the country fight the war; maybe we were actually lucking out. Or so I liked to tell myself on the nights that I couldn't get to sleep wondering how many nights I had left in the bed that I had slept in every night of my life since I was a baby.

Eventually both my romantic daydreams and my anxiety began to abate as the wait for further news about the evacuation turned from days to weeks. The president had signed Executive Order 9066 on February 19th and then we did not hear anything for what felt like a lifetime. What would happen and when? After a couple of weeks with no word, some people dared to hope that the Order had been a fluke. After a month passed, people speculated that somebody had gotten some sense in their heads and realized that there was no threat to the nation within the *Issei* and *Nisei* communities. We began to relax, have hope that things were finally going to calm down. We talked about getting the spring planting done, whitewashing the walls of the home to freshen up after the winter. Life started to go on as we all let out the collective breath we had been holding for four weeks. And then, in the blink of an eye, it began.

On March 24th, 1942, Henry called my house, nearly hysterical. "It's happening, Maggie," was all he said. "It's happening." General DeWitt, the Army's West Coast commander, had announced that the Japanese community of Bainbridge Island, Washington would be evacuated on the first of April. Six days were all that were given to those people to close their farms and nurseries, sublease or rent their homes and land, pack their belongings to take with them, and find a place for all of their things. Later, years after the war, I learned that the Army chose the Bainbridge Island community as its first batch of evacuees because it was small, only about two hundred and fifty families on the island and dispersed throughout rural Kitsap County. Because of the community's small size, the Bainbridge Island Japanese were selected as a practice run for the larger scale evacuations that the Army would have to pull off in cities such as Seattle, Oakland, Los Angeles, and San Francisco where there were large Japanese and Japanese American communities. Not only were they being asked to pack up their lives, the Japanese and Japanese American people of Bainbridge Island were being treated as the government's guinea pigs. "Let's go, Maggie," Henry nearly barked into the phone receiver. "Let's go and see this for ourselves."

A few days later, against my mother's wishes, Henry and I took a ferry across Elliot Bay from the Coleman Dock downtown, to the small village of Winslow on the island. We were there to see this for ourselves, but Henry was also going to write up a story for the Japanese American newspaper, published by the local JACL office. In the small town itself, we fit in, as we had arrived on the day in which the head of all Japanese households were to report to the old ferry building to register their families. For just that once, the streets were full of Japanese faces.

Henry wanted to duck into the ferry building to see the evacuation station itself, but our attempts to do so were met by loud cries of "Get to the back of the line," and "We've been waiting all day." With all the commotion that was caused by our attempts to get into the crammed building, we were approached by an armed soldier who asked what we were trying to do and why were we not waiting our turn. As he spoke, the soldier had his hand on his gun. Although most men in Bellevue had hunting rifles, including my father's before it was confiscated, I had never actually seen one in a person's hands in a defensive stance. I certainly had never seen a gun that could at any minute be used on people. On *me*. As Henry stood there and tried to explain his newsman status to the soldier, I grabbed Henry's arm, my eyes still on the gun, and said, "No, its okay, officer. We'll go." I took Henry's hand and pulled him away from the door, the soldier, and the line of people.

"Why did you do that?" he asked once we had gotten a safe distance from the building.

"Henry," I responded, breathless from the exertion of steering Henry away from the building, "he had a gun. We were making him angry."

"But we weren't doing anything wrong, Maggie," Henry reasoned. "He had a gun because he's a soldier. I had one, too, before they discharged me."

"I was scared," I said.

"I'm sorry," Henry said after a pause. "I guess I was a little, too." I'm not sure he was. Still, he seemed happy enough to get away from the man and his weapons.

We determined that peeking into the ferry building without waiting in line was out of the question, so Henry decided to focus on the situation in general and just observe what was happening. Neither of us knew any of the families on Bainbridge Island or in Kitsap County so Henry and I started to walk towards the line, hoping that someone would be friendly despite the circumstances. We were in luck. As we walked down the line away from the ferry building, a young man not much older than us smiled and said hello. "I heard what happened with the soldier," he continued after Henry and I made our introduction. "George Fujisaka. It's nice to meet you. I lease some land over by Poulsbo." Poulsbo was a little town just over the bridge from

Bainbridge Island on the Kitsap peninsula. "You're from JACL?" he asked Henry.

"Yes," replied Henry. "I'm trying to write up what is happening, to get the word out. And so we know what to tell our families when the time comes for us. Would you mind helping us out?"

"Well, it is my pleasure to help, but the truth is, I do not know what to expect. We do not know anything more than what you know, what has been reported in the Seattle Times."

"Please, if you could tell us what it has been like for you experiencing it," I said, hoping that Henry would not be offended that I had interfered with his reporting style.

"Well," George began, "I am confused and upset." He paused. "Please do not say that in your article. I don't want to get in any trouble for criticizing the evacuation. The FBI has already taken my father and I am the only one left to take care of my wife and two children, my mother, and my three unmarried siblings. I cannot be arrested for dissidence or be separated from my family. Who will take care of them if not me?"

"Don't worry," said Henry. "I understand. The FBI also took our fathers. I am fortunate that my father was returned after just a few weeks—it seems that he was deemed to not have any ties to Japan sufficient enough to continue holding him. But Maggie's father is still in Missoula. No, I will not use your name at all."

George just looked at Henry for a moment without saying anything. After seemingly determining that Henry was trustworthy, George told us what life had been like for him since the evacuation order was signed. "When we heard about the president's mandate in February, we over here in Kitsap never thought that we would be the first to be evacuated. Last Tuesday, the twenty-fourth, the Army came and posted "Instructions" for the Japanese and Japanese Americans. On March 30th we are to be at the ferry to load and be taken to a center to hold us for the duration of the war."

"But how can you be ready so quickly?" I asked.

"You cannot," replied George. "I have just those six days to sublet both my land and home and that of my father. We also have to sell everything that we own or find a place to put it. That has been the worst—we are being offered the lowest prices possible for our furniture and other household items. It is insulting."

"What about the land?" Henry asked.

"The land is being rented at absolutely no profit to me. If I am lucky my neighbor who is taking over the lease will make good on his word and allow me to take my lease over again when I get back, whenever that might be."

"And your crops," I asked, knowing how hard it can be to keep a farm running. "Who will work the land?"

"I have asked my Norwegian neighbor to continue to work the crops and he may receive the profits from sale. My biggest fear is that all my crops will die and I'll return to nothing."

"Do you really need to sell your things? Why not bring your things with you," I asked naively, still not fully grasping what was happening.

"We can only take what we can carry," replied George. "Here, read this," he said as he handed me what appeared to be a flyer. Indeed, it was the same announcement that I had seen posted on buildings and signposts since disembarking from the ferry. It was labeled "Instructions to All Japanese Living on Bainbridge Island." I scanned it until I found the list of items that could be taken with each person. The Instructions said that each person must bring blankets and linens, toilet articles, clothing, and eating utensils, plates and cups. Everything that was taken must be securely packaged and marked with the name and number of the family. No contraband was allowed. That meant no radios, which meant no listening to the soap operas and serials that were so popular back then.

"What about books?" I asked. I had always been a bookworm and I couldn't imagine leaving behind my much-loved copy of *Wuthering Heights*.

"Can you carry them?" asked George. "Besides, I've also heard that any books taken have to pass through the censor's inspection."

"The censor," I whispered in fear. What was this world coming to? I didn't want to even think about it. "What is this 'number' that must be put on everything?" Henry asked George as I pictured men like the FBI agents who had taken my father; censors, agents, thought police.

"The number is what I'm in line for now," said George, who was just about at the front of the line to get into the ferry building. "When you register, your family receives a number. On the thirtieth, when we show up to board the ferry, we have to pin a luggage tag with our family's number to each item of luggage and to each of our lapels. A little like livestock." George looked alarmed at his own comment.

"No need to worry, friend," Henry put a reassuring hand on our new acquaintance's shoulder. That livestock bit won't hit the papers." With that, George's time had come; he was herded into the building as we exchanged our thanks and goodbyes. "We'll be on the other side on the thirtieth," I promised. Many Japanese had already made plans to watch the Bainbridge Island community arrive at the Coleman Docks to see them off. Many were also curious to see what treatment and fate awaited them. "Look for us in the crowd. In the meantime, good luck." What else was there to say?

As George disappeared into the building, Henry and I looked at each other. He took my hand and we began walking back towards the ferry. "Let's head home," Henry said.

"Don't you need more interviews," I asked, hoping that he didn't. He shook his head no. We both wanted to get out of there. There was a ferry at the dock that we almost missed because one of the workers didn't believe that we were not local. "Looks like we have some escape artists," he sneered. Fortunately, Henry had his JACL press badge and I had my high school ID. We hadn't even thought that we could get stuck in Kitsap County—we weren't used to being treated like criminals. As we sat on the ferry back to Seattle, I pulled out the Instructions that George had given to me earlier. I spent the ride across Elliott Bay scouring the document trying to figure out why this was happening to us. It didn't say.

*****

INSTRUCTIONS TO ALL JAPANESE
LIVING ON BAINBRIDGE ISLAND

All Japanese persons, both alien and nonalien, will be evacuated from this area by twelve noon, Monday, March 30, 1942. No Japanese person will be permitted to leave or enter Bainbridge Island after 9:00 a.m., March 24, 1942, without obtaining special permission from the Civil Control Office established on this island near the ferryboat landing at the Anderson Dock Store in Winslow. The Civil Control Office is equipped to assist the Japanese population affected by this evacuation in the following ways:

1. Give advice and instructions on the evacuation.
2. Provide services with respect to the management, leasing, sale, storage, or other disposition of most kinds of property, including farms, livestock and farm equipment, boats, tools, household goods, automobiles, etc.
3. Provide temporary residence for all Japanese in family groups, elsewhere.
4. Transport persons and a limited amount of clothing and equipment to their new residence, as specified below.
5. Give medical examinations and make provision for all invalided persons affected by the evacuation order.
6. Give special permission to individuals and families who are able to leave the area and proceed to an approved destination of their own choosing on or prior to March 29, 1942.

The following instructions must be observed:

1. A responsible member of each family, preferably the head of the family, or person in whose name most of the

property is held, and each individual living alone, will report to the Civil Control Office to receive further instruction. This must be done between 8:00 a.m. and 5:00 p.m., Wednesday, March 25, 1942.

2. Before leaving the area all persons will be given a medical examination. For this purpose all members of the family should be present at the same time when directed by the Civil Control Office.

3. Under special conditions, individuals and families will be permitted to leave the area prior to the date for complete evacuation indicated above. In general conditions imposed on voluntary evacuation are as follows: (a) That the destination be outside of Military Area No. 1, prescribed by Proclamation No. 1 of the Commanding General, Western Defense Command and Fourth Army, March 2, 1942; (b) That arrangements have been made for employment and shelter at the destination.

4. Provisions have been made to give temporary residence in a reception center elsewhere. Evacuees who do not go to an approved destination of their own choice, but who go to a reception center under Government supervision, must carry with them the following property, not exceeding that which can be carried by the family or individual:

   a. Blankets and linens for each member of the family;
   b. Toilet articles for each member of the family;
   c. Clothing for each member of the family;
   d. Sufficient knives, forks, spoons, plates, bowls, and cups for each member of the family;
   e. All items carried will be securely packaged, tied, and plainly marked with the name of the owner and numbered in accordance with instructions received at the Civil Control Office;
   f. No contraband items may be carried.

5. The United States Government through its agencies will provide for storage at the sole risk of the owner of only

the more substantial household items, such as ice boxes, washing machines, pianos, and other heavy furniture. Cooking utensils and other small items must be crated, packed, and plainly marked with the name and address of the owner. Only one name and address will be used by a given family.

6. Each family and individual living alone who goes to a reception center will be furnished transportation and food for the trip. Transportation by private means will not be permitted. Instructions will be given by the Civil Control Office as to when evacuees must be fully prepared to travel.

Go to the Civil Control Office at the Anderson Dock Store in Winslow between 8:00 a.m. and 5:00 p.m. on March 25, 1942, to receive further instructions.

J.L. DeWitt
Lieutenant General, U.S. Army, Commanding

8 ROSE MARIE

From archived interview, continued.

I IGNORED FOR AS long as I could the reality that my husband and his family (and possibly me) would be relocated. It was a truth that I just was not ready to face. It placed me in too strange of a position. It was not clear what would happen to me if my husband was to be sent to a camp for the duration of the war. Did non-Japanese spouses have to be evacuated? And what about my child? She was half-Japanese American. What would I say if I was told that I did not have to go? I did not want to be away from Akio, but the idea of bringing my daughter to a prison camp if I didn't have to do so seemed unthinkable. She had done nothing wrong. But neither had Akio or any of the Miramotos or Fusakas, or any of the other Japanese and Japanese American people that I knew. I dreaded the moment that I would have to make a decision, pick a side.

Before having to actually decide what I would do when the time came, I would have been perfectly content to stick my head in the sand and pretend that life was normal. It was Maggie who kept making the impending evacuation a reality for me. After her trip to Bainbridge Island, Maggie showed me the Instructions that she had brought back. Not wanting to see them with my own eyes, she read them to me as I went about tidying my kitchen as if nothing out of the ordinary were happening. "I'm sure that can't be right," I said in response. The next day, she had me accompany her and Henry as they stood watching the flock of Bainbridge Island residents disembark from the ferry and get immediately into Pullman train cars to be taken to an assembly center in Manzanar, California. As we stood in the crowd, I was struck by the odd mood. It was almost festive, as if we were seeing old friends off on a long holiday. The islanders were happy and polite and waved back to our crowd as if nothing was strange about the day's events. I looked hard though, and I could see the stoic faces of several people who seemed to be fighting within themselves to appear to be happy with their circumstances. I didn't understand; why weren't these people showing their anger? Why were they just complying? Didn't they realize that their complicity almost made it seem worse, like they were, in fact, guilty and deserving of their punishment? After parting with Maggie, I went back home to put my spinning head back in the growing mound of sand.

Still, Maggie kept hounding me, albeit unintentionally, about the logistics of the evacuation. It seemed that her main concern was how the evacuation and relocation might affect her and Henry. It wasn't so much that she was thinking about herself; the issue of the Seattle and Bellevue communities was on everyone's mind. People had spent quite a bit of time discussing when, where, and how the Japanese would be evacuated. It was not totally surprising that the Bainbridge Island community had been evacuated separately from the King County or Pierce County communities. However, there was concern about the logistics of evacuating the communities in Seattle, Bellevue, and the White River Valley. There were family overlaps in many of the communities and being evacuated together was a major topic of conversation around many dinner tables. It was hoped and expected that all of the Puget Sound Japanese communities would end up together. I know this is what I assumed and so I kept telling Maggie to calm down. Of course we would all end up in the same place, preferably right in our own homes if luck held out. In the meantime, though, all we could do was wait. Waiting had become a way of life for us since Pearl Harbor was attacked.

And then, as suddenly as the news of the attack in Hawaii had changed our lives, the wait was over. At the end of April of 1942, the Instructions went up in the city of Seattle. They were identical to the ones that Maggie had been showing me for weeks, trying to get me to see. By the end of the week two thousand five hundred people had to register their families with the War Relocation Authority and evacuate their homes. We were told to supply our own bedding and eating utensils. We were told that we could bring only what we could carry. We were told that we had just days to leave behind everything. What had seemed like the unthinkable, even after Bainbridge Island, was actually happening. But it was only happening in Seattle, not in Bellevue.

Akio's name came up in the first round of people to be evacuated. Because of the size of the Japanese community in Seattle there were several waves of evacuation of the city. The Fusakas were in the third wave. Being in the first group, we only had six days to be ready, just like the original evacuees on Bainbridge Island. However, unlike the islanders, the Seattle group was not headed for California. Word went round that the reason there had been a delay in evacuating us after Bainbridge was because the government was frantically building "barracks" in what was going to be our new home: Camp Harmony. An "assembly center" had been created at the Western Washington Fairgrounds in Puyallup. What we didn't realize at the time was that the barracks were built for the expected overflow; the first choice of housing for the evacuees was the horse stables on the Fair grounds. Anyone who couldn't fit in the barns would be living either under the grandstand or in the barracks on the parking lots.

Once we got word of the evacuation, things happened so fast that they are still a blur to me. Six days to pack up an entire life! Almost impossible, though that is what we all did. Few, if any of us, had found renters or made storage plans before the actual notices were posted. Still reeling from the shock of seeing the Seattle notices, Akio and I sat down at our kitchen table after putting our daughter to bed and took inventory of both our things and of our situation. "First," said Akio, "we need to figure out what will happen to you and to Rosie. Surely, Rose Marie, you do not have to be evacuated just for being married to me." Here it finally was then, the conversation that I had been losing sleep over for weeks. "If that is the case, I want to you stay here with Rosie until the madness passes."

"But I do not want to leave you, Akio," I responded emphatically…and truthfully. "But I'm worried about Rosie—I've heard that anyone who is at all Japanese must go to the camps." I had been trying to get as much information as possible about what constituted an "enemy alien." I continued, "I'm not going to leave my daughter if she is sent along with you. And it's not that she won't be taken care of by you or your family, but we don't know how long this will last and I just can't be away from her indefinitely. Or at all," I said, shivering at the very thought of having the military take my child from me.

"I understand," replied Akio, nodding, but with a look of concern in this eyes. I know that he was blaming himself for putting me and his child in this position. "Well I'm supposed to go down to register tomorrow. We'll find out then whether or not you and Rosie have to come with me, I guess. If you don't, then we'll take it from there. But even if you don't, we need to make some plans."

"Because how will I take care of the house by myself, with no job and you in a camp somewhere," I asked, a bit too harshly I think. This wasn't my husband's fault.

"Right," he nodded, "And how about my parents' farm? It is in my name, after all. Even though Mama hasn't been told to evacuate yet, you know it's just a matter of time. And there's no sign that Papa will be released. I can't just leave it here on your shoulders if I'm gone. I certainly can't leave it all on Maggie's plate since she's still a kid. I also wonder if there is anything that we can do for Kimiko…who knows, though? Maybe she's having a better time than we are," Akio smiled sadly. We had had many conversations about Kimiko and I think, like my head in the sand routine, it was easier to just assume that her life would go on as well as could be assumed. Especially since, in all honesty, Japan was actually winning in those days; maybe they were living like kings in Tokyo.

"We'll need to figure out where we are going to store our furniture and how to pack for the things that we need to carry to the camp," Akio continued, counting his to-dos off on his fingers. "It doesn't help that we don't know where we are going to end up or for how long."

"No, that doesn't help at all," I answered. Nor, I realized, does it help to not pretend that this isn't happening. I didn't want to pack my things; where would I put them once they were packed? Anyway, I convinced myself, it was likely that I would be staying in the house with Rosie and it would only be temporary so no need to pack up anything except some clothes for Akio. Probably, I reasoned, he wouldn't mind having a little vacation down in Puyallup without me for a couple of weeks. I could even drive down and see him, bring him food and candy. While I fantasized about President Roosevelt getting on the radio at the end of the week and saying that he had changed his mind, Akio kept right on going. "I also don't see how we are going to be landlords if we don't know how long we are going to be renting the house and the farm—not to mention that it is hard to oversee property or collect rents if I'm not here."

"If you are in prison, you mean," I said, my frustration finally getting the better of me. It has since dawned on me that pretending this wasn't happening was the only way to keep my anger at bay. When forced to confront the evacuation face-to-face, I was enraged. I was breathing funny and I'm sure I must have turned bright red. Seeing that I was upset, Akio put his hand on my shoulder and squeezed gently. "It's not like that, Rose. You know that the government is trying to keep the country safe." He shook me lightly, playfully. "Come on now, snap out of it!" He gave me that big grin of his. But it wasn't going to work this time; it actually just made me even angrier.

"I don't understand, Akio," I responded at a near yell. "How can you not be angry about this? It's not fair. It's not American what the government is doing! You haven't done anything wrong!"

"I'm not angry because anger won't help," Akio said softly as he pulled me close "It's not fair. But I can't go around saying that because it will make it seem that I'm not being patriotic. I need to show support for the government or it will look like I'm against it. And if I'm against it, then they're right—then I'm just a Jap with something against the U.S. government. Either way, they win. But if I go along with it maybe that will help them see that I am an American, that I love my country." And then the tears that I had been avoiding for weeks finally spilt. "Oh, Akio," I sobbed falling into his open arms, "What are we going to do?"

He didn't answer; he just held me until my tears stopped.

*****

Even though I thought that my husband was heroically brave—if not a bit of a martyr—I realized over the next few days that his feelings were not only common, but the JACL party line. Don't complain, don't raise suspicion. Don't cause any problems. Patriotism through compliance. The JACL leaders even volunteered to help the Army register families for the evacuation and to send members to Camp Harmony in advance to get things ready. Years later, many people accused JACL of selling out and not fighting when they should have. That was my sentiment, but I also understood that protesting didn't really get anyone very far either. Later, at Camp Harmony, people would talk about a man in San Francisco named Korematsu who did not evacuate, but stayed in the city past the date for evacuation, asserting his right to do so. He had a Caucasian girlfriend with whom he lived with and he even had surgery to have his eyelids look more Caucasian. It was to no avail. The United States Supreme Court heard the case of Korematsu at the same time that they heard the case brought by our own Gordon Hirabayishi.

I had met Gordon a couple of times in passing. He was often at the JACL headquarters and he was friendly with both Henry and Akio. Gordon was a smart boy, a student at the University of Washington with Henry. Like Mr. Korematsu in California, Gordon did not feel that what was happening to

Japanese Americans was just under the Constitution. He staged his own protest by staying out past the curfew that was put in place against the Japanese and Japanese Americans. When he was arrested, he challenged the constitutionality of targeting a group of American citizens based upon their ethnic ancestry. There was another case later in the war brought on behalf of a woman in California named Endo. In that later case, the Supreme Court came to a different decision and the camps ended up being closed. But for Korematsu and Hirabayishi, the Supreme Court came to the same conclusion: There was nothing wrong with putting American citizens in prison camps without due process if the security of the country was at stake. Of course, I'm paraphrasing, but that was the heart of the matter. Believe it or not, that is still the law, which is why many of the former internees still get so upset when they remember what Mr. Korematsu and Mr. Hirabayishi stood for. Once the Court issued their ruling, I knew that there was no more hope. The law—or the lack thereof—had spoken. No more arguing on the point would be tolerated.

*****

The line at the hastily set-up registration center downtown Seattle was terrible. It snaked on for blocks and seemed to move at a snail's pace. In hindsight, this was just one of the first in many lines that we would have to endure; the next three years there was a line for absolutely everything, be it the cafeteria, the latrine, or the water pump. It was as if the Army knew they could keep control by putting everybody in an endless line to nowhere. This was where the line began, on our own streets at home. It was demeaning to have to spend our day doing this and difficult with a three year-old child. We tried to make small talk, but many of the people around us in line spoke only Japanese. We managed to yell a few cheerful and joking words to some *Nisei* friends of ours down the way (in English) causing us all to break out into some much needed laughs, but as we did so a Caucasian man walking on the other side of the street screamed over to us,

"Enjoy your laughs now, Japs, soon you won't think it's so funny." Well, we stopped even trying to make light of the situation right then and there.

When we got into the building after an hour or two more of standing outside waiting—this time in near silence lest we cause another outburst from passersby—we were ushered up to the first available table. The young man working the table, a member of JACL helping with the registration, did not even look up as we approached. He was *Nisei*, about eighteen, and he seemed to be buried in the stack of official-looking papers in front of him. "Name?" he asked half-heartedly, his nose down.

"Miramoto," responded Akio.

"How many?" the volunteer asked.

"I don't know," responded Akio.

At that, we finally got the attention of the boy, who looked up suddenly, his rhythm interrupted. He looked from Akio to me, child in arms, and back to Akio.

"She's not Japanese," Akio said pointing to me.

"No," said the volunteer, stating the fairly obvious, still staring at me and Rosie. When more information was not forthcoming, Akio continued. "Does she have to go?" he asked.

"I don't know, sir," said the volunteer. "Does she want to go?" Did I *want* to go?

"What about my daughter?" I asked in response, cutting to the chase. Surely I was not the only person who had asked this question; while there may not have been many Caucasians married to Japanese Americans, there were certainly non-Japanese Asian people who had married Japanese spouses. Did the Army not care if they accidently caught other Asians in their evacuation net? Hadn't any of these other people come in and said, "But what about me, what about my children?" Apparently the answer was no. Stammering, clearly flustered, the young man mumbled something about "one-eighth, definitely half for sure," and then finally, "I need to get an officer" as he left in a huff to find a soldier to help. I probably already knew the answer: Rosie was half Japanese. She had dark hair, dark eyes. She looked more like her father than like me. They were going to evacuate my three-year old daughter for national security.

After a few minutes—during which time Akio and I tried to keep our tired child quiet—the volunteer reappeared, trailing behind an Army officer. The officer, of course, was Caucasian. As he approached, I braced myself to hear the news, but it seemed that the officer wasn't clear on what the problem was. The volunteer kept his eyes down. "What is going on here?" asked the officer, noticeably making a face at our daughter, who as now sniveling into her father's lapel; I had passed her off to Akio to deal with while we waited for the volunteer to return. My anxiety was starting to get the better of me.

"Sir," said Akio, being as deferential as he could, "we are confused about how to register. As you see, I am *Nisei*. I am here to register and do what the Army requires of me. But my wife is not Japanese. She is a Swede. She is an American, I mean, but Swedish. I do not know what the Army would like me to do with her here for registration. Also, there is our daughter..."

The officer cut in, clearly perturbed with our inability to complete the registration process without causing problems. "Well, only Japanese have to be evacuated," he sighed. He glared at me as if he was disappointed by me somehow. "Your wife is free to remain in the restricted zones unless further ordered to evacuate."

"You see, honey," Akio beamed at me, relief washing across his face, easing some of the lines and furrows that had become commonplace the past few weeks. "You do not have to go! You can stay and watch the houses and be here in Seattle." The officer nearly rolled his eyes. "Yes, well we *are* in a hurry here, sir. Are you registering for two then?" He clasped his hands behind his back and seemed to rock back and forth, an odd smile on his face. He was enjoying this, I thought.

For just a split second I thought this would be it, the moment that Akio finally lost his cool. The officer was being so condescending, so overtly rude. After weeks of taking abuse from random people on the streets, I worried that Akio was going to take a swing at an Army officer. "Two?" Akio asked, the one word coming out in a single staccato verbal punch. It was like a dare. The officer didn't flinch, just smiled even more broadly.

"Of course," he said with a saccharine tone. "You and the child."

Akio's stance changed; it was unclear if he was angry or begging. "But, my daughter can stay with my wife. She's only half Japanese and completely American. She is only three. She certainly does not pose any threat to the country!" At this last comment, Akio froze, knowing that his anger had finally betrayed him. This could be construed as treasonous. My husband's torrent of words stopped nearly as quickly as they had started. I, however, was too angry to be silent, treason or not.

I pushed myself around Akio, still holding Rosie. I took the child from my husband as if having her in my arms would protect her from her fate. "Please officer," I glared although my words were polite. "Who is to care for my child if she is in the camp and I am not? Who will be watching to make sure she doesn't cause any trouble, perhaps cry loudly enough to attract the enemy's attention and thus compromise national safety?" It was too much. Akio blanched, Rosie stopped whining, and the officer smiled even harder.

"Ma'am," replied the officer firmly, "it is not my fault or my problem that you married a Jap instead of an American and decided to have a little Jap baby."

The local boy working the table had been sitting next to the officer, still manning his post this entire time. He looked like he wanted more than anything to become one with the form he had been examining during our exchange with the officer. I managed to catch his eye and, pointing to the list he was keeping, calmly said, "Three. There are three Miramotos." And so it was decided then, all three of us were registered for evacuation just days later. We were given our tags—matching sets for each of our lapels and our luggage—bearing our official identification for the purposes of the government. From that point until the end of the war, the Akio Miramoto family became family number 10447.

*****

After the registration debacle, the enormity of evacuation hit me like a ton of bricks. If there hadn't been so much to do in a seemingly impossible amount of time, I would have luxuriated in the injustice of what was happening, going around complaining and causing a fuss. But instead I had just days to pack our necessary items, prepare the house, find renters, secure a plan for Mrs. Miramoto…The list was seemingly endless and the time was seemingly over before it even began. Now I had only five days. I didn't know where to begin but I knew that I needed help; I sensed that my father would not be willing to volunteer any time, let alone money, but there was the chance that my grandfather might be able to do something. I knew my grandmother would be helpful, especially since she was the legal owner of my house. Grandma had put the house in her own name (along with my grandfather since they were married), when I had told her that the bank wouldn't loan money to a Japanese person—regardless of their citizenship--nor could a Japanese person own a home in our neighborhood. She had told my grandfather that she wanted to start to make her own investments and my grandfather apparently said yes; we had been paying her back every month.

I knew that my grandfather cared for me, but he was hideously embarrassed when I announced my marriage to Akio; he wasn't as bad as my father, but he certainly wasn't pleased. He knew about the house and he hadn't completely disowned me, so that was a start. Still, he did not openly support my marriage and I felt that I had to meet my grandmother alone, without my grandfather. When Rose was born, I would arrange to meet my grandmother at places around town, usually Volunteer Park--the park close to both her house and my church-- so that she could visit with her great-granddaughter. While it was wonderful to see her, we both felt uneasy having to be so secretive about meetings that would have been joyous for any other family. However, my grandfather was not an active part of my life as he had reasoned that I would "come to my senses" once I realized that I had chosen a difficult path; it seemed that he was determined to speed that realization as quickly as possible by essentially cutting me off (except through my grandmother). I reciprocated in kind by avoiding reaching out or asking for any help unless absolutely necessary. Now, faced with very few choices, I knew that I would have to approach my grandmother to let her know that I was leaving. And I was going to have to swallow my pride and ask for some help from Grandpa. I just prayed that my grandfather wasn't as hopeless a case as my father had been.

I would have preferred to have taken some time before going to my grandparent's house unannounced so that I could send word and make it a proper visit. It would have also been nice to prepare myself mentally for whatever my grandfather may say to me upon my arrival; I had already learned my lesson with my father. But with only days before evacuation, I knew it was now or never. On April 25th, 1942, I got up early so that I could start packing and, at about ten in the morning, I told Akio that I had to go out to find some more boxes. I told him that I would be back soon and that I was going to leave Rosie with him. I got into our Packard and headed out towards my grandparents' home on Capitol Hill. If the news from my grandparents' house was good, I'd admit to my husband where I had been; if not, no need to tell him about it.

I hadn't expected to be as nervous as I was as I drove north on Broadway and the street changed to Tenth. My favorite part of town has always been the stately residential section of Capitol Hill. My grandparents lived in one of the small but impressive mansions near the entrance to Volunteer Park where I often took Rosie to see my grandmother. Not only was this close to her house, but it brought back memories of happier times for me. As a child I had often spent my weekends with my grandparents and, after church, Grandma and I would walk over to the park to look at the view, or walk through the gardens. I tried to keep these memories in mind to keep my nerves in check as I parked my car and approached my grandparents' front door.

As I neared the front door, I panicked and took the turn in the pathway towards the kitchen door at the side of the house. As I walked up to that door, I could see my grandparents' cook through the glass of the door's window. Ethel looked up and saw me almost at the same time that I saw her; seeing a friendly face caused relief to wash over me. Here, at least, was someone who was happy to see me. As she opened the door, I found myself immediately embraced in a soft hug that smelled of fresh-baked bread.

Even though Ethel had lived in America all her life, I could still hear vestiges of her Irish parents' accent as she cooed in my ear, "Hello darlin'." She let me go and gave me an appraising once-over, apparently determining whether or not I was eating enough. It seems that I was not. "How good to see you! Are you hungry? It looks like you could use some food!" She looked behind me expectantly. "Where's that precious little one? What is going to happen to all of you now?"

I couldn't help myself but laugh. I was so happy to see Ethel that her barrage of questions about me and my child was like an elixir. Unfortunately, I laughed so hard that I began to cry and once the tears started, they didn't stop. Embarrassed, I found that I was now sobbing. It was just that I was so relieved that somebody outside of the Japanese community had concerns about my family that I lost control of the stoicism that I had been attempting at home. I told her everything, even the things that I hadn't told Akio—that I was afraid of losing my home, of his family losing their farm, that I was afraid of what would happen to us when we were put into camps, and that I was afraid of what the camps would be like for me, a non-Japanese person. I didn't know that there would be others, especially in California, who would be swept up in the evacuation who, like me, did not consider separation from their husbands and wives and children as a viable option. I just knew that I was going to stick it out in the camps and I was worried. All this and I hadn't even sat down yet.

As I was blubbering on, Ethel managed to steer me to a nearby chair and literally pushed me down by my shoulders. She turned and took a glass from a cupboard, filling it with cool water before turning back towards me. She put the glass down on the table and pulled up another chair. "But do you have to go to one of these camps just because you are married to a Jap...anese man?" Ethel's look of apology at almost saying the word "Jap" was forgiven—I knew that she wasn't a racist. It just goes to show that using that word had become commonplace thanks to the media-fueled hysteria following the bombing at Pearl Harbor. I explained that I did not have to go, but that Akio did, of course, and so did Rosie.

"Ah," Ethel responded, "enough said. I wouldn't want to leave my baby either, and don't you do it—you can't ever get back that time with the wee ones." She looked distantly sad for a moment before continuing. "Besides, the whole thing seems just a little drastic to me. Seems like the Japanese around here haven't ever hurt anybody, and speaking as a cook, I can tell you that they grow some of the best lettuce and berries I have ever had. It just doesn't seem fair, war or no war."

"Thanks, Ethel," I said. "It's good to hear that not everybody thinks that my husband and child are war-mongering traitors." She studied me for a moment with a look of concern, "No, my dear," she replied. "Certainly not the child—she is only a baby still." She must have realized her gaffe because she continued, "And Akio seems like an all-American boy what with being a farmer's son and the high school's star baseball player. Without his Japanese looks, I wouldn't think that he was anything but a good American. I mean, without being Japanese, other Americans wouldn't think anything different." She paused. "I'm sorry that I seem to be unable to resist putting my foot in my mouth. What I mean to say is, it's hard because even the Americans like your husband look Japanese. And when we see a Japanese face we think of the enemy." Another pause; clearly this was not coming out as Ethel intended, but it certainly mirrored the thoughts of many people. "My nephew was on the Arizona," she said, finally, in a whisper.

"I'm so sorry, Ethel," I said. "Is he...?"

"He died that day," she replied, wiping tears from her eyes.

"I'm sorry," I repeated, not knowing what else to say.

"Thank you. But I know that isn't Akio's fault. That's what I mean to say. Even though the papers and the radio make it seem like there's no difference between a Japanese boy in the emperor's army and an American boy with Japanese parents, I'm not so easily swayed. I know there's a difference. It's just the war. Things are crazy with all the blackouts and radio messages about the troops dying in Europe and the Pacific. I'm scared, to tell the truth."

She smiled, then, and tried to change the subject. "But enough with all that; what brings you here today, Rose Marie? Do you have plans to see your grandparents for lunch? They didn't mention it to me or I would have set another place for you at the table. But no mind, there's plenty of food."

I shook my head no. "They don't know I was coming, Ethel. I didn't mean to intrude on their lunch plans. I'm here to ask for help with my house. I'm leaving for the assembly center in four days and I'm afraid that we're going to lose everything. I'm out of options and too tired to think straight, but I thought maybe they could do something…" I couldn't help but smile at the probable futility of the task at hand as I let the words drift off.

"You don't think he will help, do you?" Ethel seemed to read my mind, knowing that my grandfather had never been overly willing to assist in the past. "Why would he?" I asked, fighting back tears. "Grandma practically had to beg and lie to get the house in her name and that was before the war." The tears threatened again.

Ethel gave my arm a little squeeze and smiled warmly. "It will work out, I'm sure of it," she said as she stood up, dusting off her thighs as if she was getting to work on the issue herself. "Stay strong; you are doing the right thing. God always rewards the good." I looked up at her. I so badly wanted to believe that, but my faith in such things was quickly waning.

"Ethel, I think that God left during the last war and he has not come back yet. At this rate, He may be gone for good."

"Watch what you say Rose." Ethel was stern, "No matter where He is, God is listening to you. Don't make Him angry, you're going to need Him, especially since you probably should go and say hello to your grandparents. I do believe I hear them in the other room." I, too, had heard the floorboards creak as my grandparents, like clockwork, made their way into the dining room to be served their eleven a.m. lunch. I took a deep breath; I didn't have a lot of time left to keep on delaying.

After giving me a last encouraging smile, Ethel ushered me out of the kitchen and into dining room where my grandparents were just sitting down. They looked up expectantly as we entered the room. I could see the look of shock on their faces when, instead of being presented their first course, they were presented with me. "I have a surprise for you," Ethel announced to my grandparents as she opened the servant's door into the kitchen. "Your granddaughter is here to see you." My grandmother's face erupted first into a welcoming smile and then, looking at my grandfather, into a look of worry. My grandfather, who to his credit at least tried to look pleased to see me, greeted me with the detached courtesy of a business acquaintance. "Rose Marie, how nice to see you. Please join us for lunch." He made a sweeping gesture towards an empty chair at the table. As Ethel began setting a place for me, my grandmother got up and gave me a kiss and a hug. My grandfather stayed seated. Well, at least he hadn't asked me to leave; I hadn't even made into my father's house.

I apologized for having come without an invitation and that I hadn't intended to interrupt their meal. Ethel continued to bring out dishes and for a bit my grandparents carried on almost as if I wasn't there, my grandmother speaking of upcoming social events and my grandfather speaking of ways to make money on the war effort. There was no talk at all during the meal of the Japanese or of my family. While my grandmother kept sending me inquiring looks, my grandfather nearly ignored me altogether except for meaningless small talk. After a while, his calculated avoidance of the topic was almost worse than what my father's outburst had been; at least with my father I knew where I stood immediately.

Finally, as the meal drew to an end, I realized that I was going to have to bring up the real reason for my visit myself since no questions about my family and the evacuation were being offered at the table. As if knowing that this was my purpose—and wanting to avoid it--my grandfather suddenly said, "It was good to see you, Rose Marie, but I have to be getting back to my business." He stood up and began to take his leave. Good to see me! I hadn't even said more than two words during the meal. It was as if I hadn't been there at all as he talked to Grandma about his golf game, his business associates, and the weather. While I suppose it was obvious that he didn't want to help, this time I was not going to make it easy for him to abandon me to my situation. If that was his choice, I wanted it to be a well-informed decision.

"Grandpa," I blurted out before he had left the room. "I need your help." This is not the way that I had hoped to do this. I thought that my best chances lay in presenting a logical and business-like argument. I had wanted to minimize any plaintive words or groveling. I wanted to try to maintain some equal bargaining power with the old man. However, in the end I was reduced to the very thing that I had hoped to avoid: Begging. He hadn't turned back towards me, but he had stopped walking. It was something; I continued, "Grandpa, I am being sent to an assembly camp in four days." My grandmother gasped at the news and put her hands to her mouth in shock. I pressed on, determined to say my full piece. "I will need a renter for my house. Also, the Miramoto's farm in Bellevue will most likely be lost if it cannot be leased."

"I was not aware that the Bellevue Japanese were already being relocated," was my grandfather's response. He turned back to face me, but he did not return to his seat at the table. He clearly wanted to be near to the door. This was not to be a long conversation.

"The order has not come yet, but it is inevitable at this point. Besides, the farm is in Akio's name since he is American and his father…"

"What, Rose Marie? Will you actually say it now? His father is a Jap," my grandfather said in a matter of fact tone. "And where is Mr. Miramoto these days?"

"He was taken to a Department of Justice prisoner of war camp in Montana," I responded, already dreading the likely outcome of this conversation. I wanted to tell my grandfather that he shouldn't use that word, that it was unfair, that it was racist. What good would that have done me? What good would that have done in general? Speaking with my grandfather I realized that there was nothing that could be said, no argument that could be made; the voice of the people had spoken and that voice was repeating the words of the evacuation notices. As this dawned on me, I had almost stopped listening to my grandfather's voice. "And so you are asking me to risk my good business name in this community by associating myself with known traitors to this country during a time of war? By paying the rent on the homes of Jap traitors, Rose Marie?" When I was silent he repeated, "Is that what you want, Rose Marie?"

And so nobody was going to even extend a helping hand for fear of being seen helping these apparent traitors, these Americans with different faces. I wanted to say, "Yes," to just cut to the chase, but I had to defend my in-laws. "Grandpa, Mr. Miramoto is not a 'known traitor,' he was simply born in Japan. He is as American as anyone else in this country. In fact, you and he have a lot in common—Mr. Miramoto has taken his piece of land in Bellevue and turned it into one of the most successful strawberry farms in Western Washington. Before the war he was even shipping produce on the train all the way to New York City. If the law and people would have allowed it he would have been just as wealthy and successful as you."

My grandfather stared at me in silence for what seemed a full minute. He took a seat at the table before continuing. "Is the farm really that successful?" he asked. I knew that talking money would get his attention much faster than any attempts to tug at his heart. "What type of labor does it require?" he continued, his brow furrowed in thought.

"The Miramotos and their three children ran it primarily on their own during the non-harvest or planting seasons. During harvest you can hire laborers from the Chinatown district— usually Filipinos—to help. Also, young Bellevue children will often pick berries during their summer breaks for extra spending money; even I did one summer. The labor itself should not be difficult to find, it is the daily driving of the fruit to the markets that is the most important."

"And what is the monthly payment?" I could tell that he was doing calculations in his head, trying to figure out if this made business sense. In the least, I would have some potential good news to tell Akio about his parents' farm; I still didn't know what we would do about our house. Perhaps my grandmother would just have to sell it. "I'm sure it takes care of itself, Grandpa." He gave me a disappointed look that seemed to say, you are asking for help here, shouldn't you know these things. I guess I just wasn't the consummate businessman that my grandfather was.

He tapped his fingers on the table, a gesture that I recognized from my youth meaning that a proclamation was forthcoming. Sure enough, "I'll speak to your father," he said. "Perhaps he would be willing to overlook this little project. But I will only consider this if I am certain that I can make money. I am not interested in doing any charity work for the Japs."

I just nodded and kept my mouth shut. I was pleased that I had, rather unexpectedly, found someone to lease out the Miramoto's farm. However, the issue of my house had me worried. I made eye contact with my grandmother, willing her to make herself available to speak to me privately. She took the cue. Standing up, Grandma said, "I'm sure Rose needs to be getting back about her business." Grandpa nodded as my grandmother offered to see me to my car. I thanked my grandfather for both the wonderful lunch and his offer to "look into" the Miramoto farm. I did not thank him for his company. How far we had come from the days when he greeted me and saw me off with big bear hugs. What had I done so wrong?

When we reached the car my grandmother wrapped me in a big hug. "I'm so sorry, Rose Marie," she whispered as she held me.

"I don't know what I'm going to do, Grandma," I said, allowing myself a moment of emotional vulnerability. "I don't know how Akio and I will be able to make payments on the house. I don't want to lose it," I was crying now, "and I certainly don't want to create any problems for you!"

"No, no, not another thought about that. I'll figure something out, Rose Marie. Please try not to worry."

"I don't even have time to worry," was my reply, a little too short. "I'm sorry, Grandma. I'm not angry with you."

"No, but you maybe should be. Maybe I haven't done enough for you all these years..."

"No, don't speak like that. You have been my closest family member since Mama died."

"Then I truly am sorry. I love you, Rose Marie. Please forgive me." Assuring her that I did and that there was no reason for her to feel like that, I left in a hurry; I didn't have time to dwell on my family's issues with my marriage. I had to get back to pack—and to let Akio know that my grandfather might help take care of his parents' farm. Now, with just hours before evacuation, we would be able to—or have to—shift our focus to preparing ourselves for what was to come.

*****

Imagine that you were given less than one week to pack up your entire life into boxes. Of course, you are probably thinking, "Well, I've done that before Rose Marie, I've moved." Fair enough. But now imagine that you have had no real warning that you are going to move. And imagine that you don't really have a place to put your things. And imagine that you don't even know where you are going, let alone how long you will be there. And, worse than all the rest, imagine that you aren't allowed to bring any of your things with you, except for basic clothing, toiletries, bedding, and eating utensils. Only what you can carry.

There were no boxes to be found anywhere. That is what I remember most about the actual process of packing. There were several thousand Japanese and Japanese Americans being evacuated from Seattle alone and we were all looking for boxes. Boxes and crates. And we needed to find big, Army-style or sailor-style canvas bags to pack all of our bedding, clothing, and eating utensils. On the third-to-last day before we were evacuated, I spent the morning shopping for good wool blankets, utensils and bags at the Army-Navy surplus store. Although we were approaching summer, we were potentially going to be gone for the duration of the war. Europe had already been at war for three years. I thus assumed that we would be in camps for several seasons. Unfortunately, it is nearly impossible to find winter boots and coats in the stores in late April. Not having time to continue shopping at every store in town, I gave up and just hoped for the best later in the year.

By the second-to-last day before evacuation, we had placed just about everything we could into boxes. However, we didn't have any place to put our boxes. In Washington, we were not offered warehouses to store our items as the Army would later do in California. We could not afford any storage even if we would have had the time to find something suitable. It turned out to be difficult to move furniture and other big items in such a short time. It was also difficult to sign a contract when we didn't know how long we would be needing services. In the end, without any real alternatives, Akio and I decided that we might as well leave the furniture in the house. We had acquired a few nice pieces of furniture—an oak dining room set that my grandmother gave us as a wedding present, my mother's piano that my grandmother had talked my father into giving me. Other things, such as our living room furniture, were not as nice, but all that we could afford. We figured that if we lost the house, that would be worse than losing the furniture and so it might as well all stay together. Not necessarily the most practical decision, but the best we could come up with on short notice.

Before we left, there was some good news regarding the Miramoto's farm in Bellevue; my grandfather had actually contacted my father. Grandpa was going to pay the monthly loan amount on the farm while the Miramotos were detained. My father was going to oversee the operation of the farm with the idea being that the property should pay for itself and provide a small profit for my grandfather and father to split, even after all labor and costs were paid. When I first heard the news I was proud for the first time of my father and grandfather. Even though I knew they were doing this for their own sakes, at least I could say that my family had offered to "help." Still, I was concerned that perhaps they weren't the best choice, all things considered. My hope was that my relatives wouldn't let my in-laws or me down and came through on their word if for no other reason than because it gave them a bit of extra spending money to do so.

Finally, as the days until evacuation turned into hours, I started sleeping less and less even though we had found some solutions to our problems and I had learned to give up a little on some of the others. Still, I had to spend every spare minute packing up our belongings, making calls to creditors, the gas and electric companies, and packing the items that we were allowed to carry with us. I also had a three year-old to contend with. Rosie faced the evacuation with the curiosity and concern of a child her age. She really had no idea what was going on and Akio and I were somewhat determined to keep her in the dark as much as possible. I didn't want to scare her and I didn't want her to feel bad, like she was being punished. Akio and I told her that we were going on an adventure, or "camping." She looked forward to the experience as if we were going on a family vacation. We didn't see any need to tell her that our "vacation" was going to be at least semi-permanent. That way Rosie did not know that the toys and clothing and furniture that we were boxing up could not be played with in just a week or two. We packed her favorite doll and hoped that she would forget about the box of toys that she was leaving behind. Whatever we did seemed to work; our daughter was looking forward to leaving and asked everyday if it was time yet. Little did she know that her parents were dreading the day that we had taught her to look forward to as if it were a holiday.

And then, after the busiest, fastest and slowest six says of my life, there were no more days left; the day had arrived, the day that we left behind our homes and reported downtown to board a bus to the Puyallup Fairgrounds, now called Camp Harmony, in the hopes that the name would produce the result. The night before we left, Mrs. Miramoto and Maggie stayed the night with us to help care for Rosie and help us with any last-minute needs. They also wanted to spend time with us before we left. Although Bellevue had still not received its orders, we assumed it was just a matter of time until our family members and friends joined us in Puyallup. Because we didn't know how long that would be, or if we would ever be back together in that house, our last evening together was bittersweet and tinged with unspoken anxiety.

We spent the evening reminiscing about better times. Henry and his parents came over with a picnic dinner and we made a small party of it, sitting on boxes and crates because our furniture was already locked up and covered in the two bedrooms. Although it had been hard at first, we could now look back at the day of my and Akio's graduation from Bellevue High School, the day that we announced our plans to marry. The look on the faces of the elder Miramotos was pure astonishment with perhaps a hint of dismay. They were too polite to voice their concern or disapproval so they stood still like mannequins, without a single word issuing from their lips. Maggie and Kimiko, on the other hand, seemed surprised, but happy. Kimiko rushed up and gave me a big hug and said, "Welcome to the family, Rosemaru-chan," with a sly giggle. "Now you will have to learn Japanese." "And how to tie a kimono!" added Maggie, giggling. "And how to serve tea properly," piped in Mr. Miramoto. "And flower arranging," said Mrs. Miramoto, their surprise fading into the family's characteristic good cheer. "And how to be a nice little proper Japanese wife," said Akio. "Probably easier to learn how to speak Japanese," Maggie had countered, her and Kimiko each taking an arm and steering me away from their parents and brother. We laughed for a few more hours, me finally feeling like I was getting what I had always longer for: Sisters. Now, those of us gathered in my house laughed as if it had happened just yesterday. We did not mention the people who were not with us that evening, hoping that we would all be reunited in the near future. At least we knew where Mr. Miramoto was—still in fort Missoula—but Kimiko had essentially dropped out of existence.

We got up early that last morning; Akio and I were up at five to make the final preparations to close the house until Grandma could come up with a plan. While my mother-in-law cooked us a simple breakfast and Maggie watched Rosie, I rolled up our bedding—we had used our new camp bedding that last night because everything was already packed—and put our final items into our large canvas bags. Although the bags were of a carrying size, they were so full that I was barely able to lift them. But I had no choice; there was nothing that could be removed from the bags. Finally, even though it was late April, I dressed Rosie and me into our warmest, bulkiest winter clothes. I didn't want to take up the space in our bags with our larger clothing. When all was said and done, between the weight of the bags and the three or four layers of clothes I was wearing, I could barely move. We looked like we were going out to play in the snow. At least we didn't have to walk with those massive bags and all the clothing; Maggie was going to drive us down to the bus pickup site in our Packard. She would then drive herself and Mrs. Miramoto back over the bridge to their farm where we were going to store the car for the duration. We had thought about selling it, but the only offer was for twenty dollars from one of our less-than-sympathetic neighbors.

Before going out the door for the last time, I decided to check the home once more. I took that one last look around that little house with the little rooms, the little yard and the little garden. My mother-in-law's roses were in bloom. I couldn't bear to leave the roses. I went out the backdoor and pulled two roses off of the bush, completely impervious to the pain of the thorns. After removing the thorns, I placed a rose in my hair, tight into the pins holding my bun in place. The other I placed behind Rosie's ear when I finally made it to the car where everyone was waiting expectantly for me. "A rose for my little Rosie," I said to my delighted daughter. A rose to remember what was once our home, I thought to myself. It may be the last time we ever see it

*****

I fought back tears as we gathered to load the buses. There were probably about one thousand of us in that first group of evacuees. Despite the numbers, though, everything seemed to be happening smoothly. Of course, the presence of armed Army soldiers prevented any real misconduct, but I don't think that there would have been much bad behavior even without the guards. The community was cooperative in an effort to show their "patriotism" per the JACL mandate. Many people seemed to take this even further and, unlike me, were seemingly cheerful as they waved goodbyes to family members and shouted parting comments such as "We'll see you in a couple of weeks!" "We'll miss you in the meantime!" I try to not be stereotypical, but the lack of tears—the stoicism that I witnessed all around me—I believe is part of the Japanese culture. I think that this trait was inherited by the *Nisei* as well—an ability to perform one's duty without a show of emotion. Or, in this case, without a show of negative emotion. Maybe I'm wrong; maybe this is a just a trait of an easy-going person. Whatever the case, it was all I could do to grit my teeth and keep quiet. Sometimes silence is the safest route.

And so I was nearly mute as Akio and I heaved our bags out of the Packard at the loading station. With the help of Maggie, Akio and I dragged our big bags down to the pile of luggage where we would leave it so that it could be boarded onto the bus while Mrs. Miramoto said her goodbyes to Rosie. Later, at Camp Harmony the luggage would be returned to us after inspection for contraband such as radios, tools, or knives. After depositing our packs, we had to stand in line to board a bus, which meant the time had finally come to say goodbye to my in-laws. Henry and his parents, scheduled to leave in one week, were also there. We had said the majority of our farewells the night before, but this moment was still far more emotional than I had planned. "We'll see you soon, Mama," Akio said to his mother. After embracing his mother, he turned to his sister. "Take care of her," he said, nodding towards his mother, as he took Maggie in his arms. At that moment, we all thought it would be just a couple of weeks before we would be able to share welcoming hugs at Camp Harmony. The thought that these could be the last hugs between family members would never have crossed our minds.

As the buses started their engines and the officers told us to get a move on, Mrs. Miramoto kissed us all one last time and asked me to take care of her only son and granddaughter. "And,

Rosemaru-chan," she said, "Please take care of yourself. I will be thinking about you as well. You are my own daughter, a rose in my garden."

The tears could no longer be contained. "I love you, too, Reiko-san. I promise to take care of all of us. But you can help when you get to Harmony!" I tried to sound cheerful.

"But in the meantime, until we are all together, take care of them. You are strong, Rose Marie, a fighter, and brave." She hugged me and, up close, I thought that I could hear the whisper of tears in her voice.

"Okay, okay, my turn," Maggie pushed her way towards me. "Goodbye for now, big sis-in-law. Keep an eye on Henry for me until I get down to Harmony," she joked.

"I'll watch him like a hawk," I promised. We said our final farewells to our family and to the Fusakas and we headed for the bus, which was filling up quickly. I took a window seat with Rosie on my lap and Akio slid in next to me. After the bus was filled to absolute capacity, we pulled out. We had opened the windows and we all stuck our hands out, some of us waved handkerchiefs, at the crowd outside the bus. "Goodbye!" we cheered and the crowd yelled back, "Bon voyage!" We kept waving until the crowd was out of sight. Then we settled back for our bus trip into the farmlands south of Seattle and, eventually, our destination.

9 MAGGIE

From "The Roses of Minidoka," continued.

I WAVED TO MY brother and his family until the bus was completely out of sight, on its way to Puyallup. What was I feeling as I watched them go? I wish that I could tell you that I was thinking of the misfortune of my family or anger at the government, or something noble and profound. I hope that it isn't terribly selfish to admit that I was concerned about myself. And, honestly, I bet that deep down most people of any age couldn't help but think, "What about me?" as we faced relocation for an unknown time period and to an unknown place. I have never felt so out of control of my own destiny as at that time.

So as the bus was taking my brother and his family away from me, I was thinking about how unfair it was that the government was ruining the plans that I had made for my future. It was the end of April and I was set to graduate from Bellevue High School at the end of that year's term. I had worked hard and I was actually going to graduate one year early. I tried to focus on missing Akio, on the anticipated parting with Henry; these were the important things. But I was also worried about graduation and what was going to happen to my plans to attend the University of Washington later that year. After convincing my parents that it was appropriate (there were several other *Nisei* students at the University, including women), I had also managed to convince the school that should follow in my brother's footsteps. I didn't even care about what Akio or Henry said about the odds of me getting a job—after all, they both reminded me, I was both *Nisei* and a woman—I wanted to go and I wanted to prove everyone wrong. I was going to be a journalist or a teacher or…anything. Back then, I thought I could be whatever I wanted to be.

However, now (on top of my ethnicity and gender), I had a big problem in my path towards success: I was likely going to be unable to physically be in the part of the country where my university was located. I hoped that things would calm down, but with the rate that the Japanese were tearing up the Pacific, not to mention the increasing hatred of Japanese Americans in the United States, I had little hope that I would be a university student in the fall of 1942. But still, I had my dreams and I refused to give up on them, war or no war, relocation or no relocation. It was becoming an obsession of mine.

I was finding that my plans for school and concerns over my future were beginning to take precedence over all other thoughts. I thought about school while my family was evacuated, while my mother cried over Kimiko or fretted over the farm, while Henry spoke to me of our future together. He knew that I wanted to go to school and had even shown me around the campus and introduced me to members of the *Nisei* club, but he thought that I just wanted to get a degree and maybe write some stories along the way or teach small children until I had my own babies. He seemed to think that I would get my degree and then just settle into the life that I would have led without having gone to college—a proper Japanese housewife. I suppose I should be fair; it was the Forties. It didn't matter if I was Japanese or Caucasian when it came to being a housewife. I was in the mood for some excitement, not housework and laundry.

I was starting to think that I did not want to be a housewife, at least not right away. I loved Henry, but I did not want my life to be limited to sitting in a house all day waiting for him to come home. No, I had spent my life cooped up on a little farm in

Bellevue, Washington, working in the fields when I wasn't working at my schoolwork. I wanted to live, to see the world. Henry didn't seem to understand this, but, in his defense, I wasn't so good at telling him, either. The last time it came up was the night before Henry's family was supposed to report to their wave of evacuation. I had been increasingly irritable as the day approached and I was a mess of confused emotions that evening as Henry and I sat down on the top step of my parents' front porch, exhausted from the anticipation of what was to come. For a time we were silent, watching the sunset over the horizon, as I tapped my fingers on the floorboard beside me to the rhythm of a song in my head--a nervous tick. I knew that I had to let Henry know that things were going too fast between him and I, but that didn't mean I didn't want to continue to be with him. I was frustrated with myself for not being able to express this and I sat there frowning and tapping away at the floor.

Henry seemed to misunderstand my bad mood for sadness and anxiety. "Don't worry, Maggie, we'll be together soon." That was it, I had to say something, make him understand that I loved him, but I had to get a degree, I just had to. I opened my mouth to say it, spit it out, but before the words could form themselves, he continued, "Maybe we can pass the time in the camp getting married. By the time that we get out, we'll be an old married couple." He laughed a high-pitched nervous burst of sound. Startled, I turned towards him, laughing a little at what I thought was, at least primarily, a joke. But when I looked at Henry, he had a small box in his hand. A jewelry-sized box.

And then words—or one word—did not escape me: "No," I said decisively. And then, as he hurriedly stood up and made his way over to his parents' car. "No, Henry, come back!" I yelled after him. "You don't understand." But he did: I did not want to get married at age seventeen because we were going to be stuck together in a prison camp. There was no other way around it. What he didn't understand was that I did love him. One of my greatest regrets in life is that I did not follow Henry; I didn't run after his car, I didn't call him, I didn't show up the next morning to say goodbye to him and his parents as they boarded the bus for Camp Harmony.

I did pick up the jewelry box that Henry had thrown on the ground as he got into his car, ignoring me. Inside was a simple gold band with a single, perfect pearl. There was also a little note, carefully folded, "Someday I will buy you a proper engagement ring." Little did Henry know that this was perfect; pearls were my favorite gem. As Henry drove away, I watched him stoically, like a statue. Then I went inside and put the ring on a gold chain that my parents had given me for my sixteenth birthday. I had just finished clasping the chain around my neck and securing the ring beneath my collar when I saw in the mirror that my mother had walked up behind me. She paused in the doorway and looked at me for a moment before speaking.

"I saw Henry leave in a hurry. I hope that all is well with his family, Megumi-chan?" Her statement was more of a question: What happened, Maggie? "I'm sorry that I didn't have a chance to say goodnight before Henry left—I suppose I can still say goodbye tomorrow?" I smiled and turned towards her.

"Nothing happened, Mama," I lied. "He just needed to get home to help his parents pack, that's all. We decided that it makes more sense for us to rest and not travel all the way downtown tomorrow. We'll see them soon enough." She had been planning on going to Seattle to see the Fusakas off to Camp Harmony in the morning. I smiled and walked past her, heading for the stairs.

"Henry and I said our goodbyes tonight," I said over my shoulder, feigning nonchalance. I'm sure that I didn't fool her, but I couldn't muster anything better. In truth, I was drained, devoid of all emotion.

I fell into bed later that night and slept like a person drugged; everything that had happened in the past few months had finally caught up with me and I was exhausted. For the first time in weeks I slept without dreaming of bombs or the FBI or of busses full of Japanese faces. I didn't even wake up when my mother came into check on me and stroked my hair and sang me a lullaby from my childhood; perhaps it was this comforting gesture, which she told me about later, that allowed me to relax completely. Whatever the case, I just kept right on sleeping, through the night and unusually late the next morning. I slept well past the time that we would have left to go downtown, well past the time that the Fusakas got on their assigned bus and were carried down to Puyallup. Only once I knew it was too late did I actually get up and start my day.

*****

I tried to keep as busy as possible in the weeks after Henry left. Every day we in Bellevue played a weird game of wait-and-see. Many of us would take random walks down the street, looking around for notices to be posted. After determining that that particular day was not to be the one that would determine my fate, I would then shift my focus to trying to finish up schoolwork so that I could still graduate on time. Besides school, Mama and I spent all remaining time readying our house for the eventual Bellevue evacuation. Even though the Mr. Lundstrom was going to rent our farm while we were in the camps, we still had to pack and store our belongings for the duration. Also, in the meantime, Mama and I were trying to keep the farm going. We had stopped growing anything except for the summer's strawberry crop, but even the one crop was proving difficult for just the two of us. My mother worked all day in the fields and I helped before school, during my lunches, and after school. After dark we would spend time wrapping up and packing our few valuables. We slept less and less until about four hours was considered a good night's rest. After a couple of weeks, I believe we both came to welcome the notice of our own evacuation. In the very least, I figured that the break from the physical exertion of farming and packing would be a welcome change.

On May 15, 1942 our time finally came. On that day the Army posted notice of Civilian Exclusion Order Number 80 in Bellevue. Nearly three months after we heard that we would be evacuated, we were finally given our marching orders. All sixty or so Japanese families in Bellevue had to be ready to go by May 20th. We were being given less than five days to pack and report

100

to the Kirkland way station to board a train for a government assembly center. Funny, even though we as a community had already seen the evacuation of Bainbridge Island, Seattle, Tacoma, and the White River Valley, it was still a surprise when we saw those notices go up in our own city. As I made my daily walk down the street to the nearest light pole, I saw the poster before I could read its contents. I knew when I saw the faces of the people who were already gathered around the pole what was happening. "Hey, Maggie," shouted Horu, one of our neighbors and a brother of a friend shouted as he saw me coming, "It's finally here; we're out of here." Still, I didn't believe it until I read the words with my own eyes.

Those four days between notice and reporting to the train passed by in a blur of chaos and emotion. I had another bout of anger over my own ethnic and cultural heritage, resulting in a deep-seated guilt that would take me years to overcome. At the time, this anger manifested itself primarily in embarrassment; I had spent my young life trying to fit in, to be as American as my blonde schoolmates. I had been ashamed of my parents, my house, and my lunch food. I had even been embarrassed about my own name, insisting that I be called Maggie the moment that I enrolled in school instead of by my given name. Thus, there is no record of a Megumi Miramoto ever attending the Bellevue School District; there is a record of a Maggie R. Miramoto, however. If I could have, I would have changed my last name to something far less ethnic to go along with my Anglicized first and middle names. At a certain point, I would have done anything to have passed as a non-Japanese American. And now there was no avoiding my ethnicity; it had finally caught up with me.

While I was suffering from my own angst and generally feeling sorry for myself, my mother was in a nearly manic state of panic and activity. When not packing, planting, and cleaning, she focused all of her remaining attention on trying to make certain that my father and Kimiko would know where we were should they try to contact us or, God-willing, actually return home. This, of course, was made extremely difficult by the fact that we had no idea where we were going. We just assumed and hoped that it would be Camp Harmony. Like my mother and I, many Bellevue families had family members or friends from Seattle or White River who were already in Puyallup. However, there was always the unspoken possibility that we would be sent somewhere else; maybe California like the Bainbridge residents before us.

There were some rumors floating around that Camp Harmony was full or that they wanted to separate the communities for the long haul. But that just didn't make sense. There was a camp less than an hour away. Of course we were going there, to Camp Harmony. I chose to ignore the possibility of separation from Akio and Henry so that I did not feel the panic and could focus on getting ready to go. Not only was I packing my belongings, I had begun to compose an explanation to Henry in my head that I was hoping to tell him in person. I wanted to tell him that I loved him and that my answer was yes, but not yet. I needed to focus on that; it was the only thing that kept me going. In just a couple of days I could set right what I had so badly messed up. I could regain a bit of the control that I had starting losing over my own life the previous December.

*****

On May 20, 1942, my mother and I reported to the small way station in Kirkland, a small town just north of Bellevue, ready to board the train for an assembly center. My mother was silent, no doubt worrying still about my father and my sister and how they would find us. I was waiting in anticipation to arrive at Camp Harmony and anticipating a reunion with Akio and his family and, of course, with Henry. I was daydreaming as Mama and I boarded the train that morning. Like the Bainbridge Island and Seattle communities, those of us in Bellevue tried to put on a happy face and show our willingness to be good citizens and patriots by cooperating and not causing trouble. I was glad that we were boarding the train in Kirkland and not in Bellevue because that meant that we didn't have to do it in our own home and in front of our neighbors; I was still pretending in my own head that this wasn't quite real, that we were going on vacation. I didn't think I could handle the stares of our neighbors watching us being forced from our homes. I knew there were people in town who were happy to see us go; I didn't want to see the triumph on their faces. Ironically, though, the train would take us south from Kirkland right back through Bellevue on the way to its final destination. Fortunately, as the train jolted to a start and took us back down through our own hometown, we were apparently too nondescript of a load to attract the attention of any onlookers. For all they knew, ours could have been a train full of livestock, making its usual rounds down the coast.

We weren't supposed to be looking out the windows—an Army officer had told us to not attract any attention from people outside the train "for our own safety"—and thus the blinds were to remain drawn even though it was the middle of the day. This announcement made my mother extremely nervous so I tried to take her mind off of it by reminding her that she would soon be seeing her son and granddaughter again. I was just close enough to a window that had blind that was slightly crooked that I could sneak a few peaks of what was going past us. "Mama!" I exclaimed to her as we entered into Renton. "This is the way to Camp Harmony!"

"Yes, Megumi-chan," my mother answered distracted by her own interior thoughts. "Puyallup is to the south of Bellevue. And we are going south."

"Mama!" I scolded her, the breath taken out of me by her pessimism.

"Sorry, Megumi," she replied with that sad smile that had I had become used to seeing on her pretty face. "No desire," she said in her broken English.

I knew what my mother meant by this. It was not that she had no desire to go to Harmony or to see my brother and his family. She was referring to the Buddhist idea that, without desires, we cannot be disappointed and thus unhappy when those desires go unfulfilled. She was saying that she was not getting her hopes up. She and I were so different in so many ways. I was high on the hope that we were heading towards Puyallup. We were, after all, *heading* towards Puyallup. It was just a matter of stopping there. "But the Seattle community took a bus for the short trip to Puyallup, not a train," my subconscious told me. "No," I argued back with myself inside my head. "The Army is just more efficient now that they have already evacuated so many people. It was faster to have us get onto a train." The closer we got the more certain that I became: Puyallup, with Henry and Akio and Rose Marie and Rosie, was to be our temporary home.

The train continued south from Renton into the White River Valley. We went through the small town of Kent. We continued through the valley into Auburn. "Kent, Auburn, and then…Puyallup!" I sang to myself under my breath. Sure enough, minutes after we went through Auburn we began approaching Puyallup. I craned my head to see out the window; somebody had edged their way in front of me and I had to practically grow my neck to catch a glimpse from the slab of window. My physical feat was rewarded; I had managed a view of the large white roller coaster on the fairgrounds. The roller coaster was a beacon that had always announced the town of Puyallup when we had gone to the Western Washington State Fair.

"Mama, I can see the roller coaster!" I whispered excitedly. "That's where Akio and Rose Marie and the baby and Henry are right now! Can you believe it? They can probably hear the train. I'm certain that we are going to Camp Harmony. I can see it!" My mother still appeared unconvinced, but her lips began moving in what could have only been a silent prayer.

As we approached downtown Puyallup, the train seemed to slow. "We're going to stop!" I heard someone in the train car exclaim. "We're going to Camp Harmony!" said another. I just smiled, a huge feeling of relief washing over me. Sure, it was really bad to be evacuated from my home, but it would be so much worse to have to be evacuated separately from my family and loved ones. In fact, it would be cruel and pointless, I reasoned. "We're going to Camp Harmony," I told myself, content; I would be with my brother and his family and I would make things right with Henry. We would be together throughout the duration of the war and figure out how to get through this together. I smiled. I was going to get through this. Then, as suddenly as it had slowed, the train picked up speed again. We were passing through downtown. "What's happening?" I shouted involuntarily. "Why aren't we stopping?" Nobody answered my questions. They didn't have to. The answer was obvious: We weren't going to Camp Harmony.

*****

After days on a hot, stuffy, and darkened train, we arrived at the Pinedale Assembly Center located just outside of Fresno, California. We arrived in late May, which, as we learned, is a terribly hot time to visit the area outside of Fresno. I remember two things distinctly about Pinedale: The heat and the dust. Every day it was hot and everywhere there was dust. The rooms—if you choose to call them that--did little to protect from either. The thin, un-insulated boards of the barracks did little to block out the heat of the sun. In fact, the black tar paper roofs seemed to invite heat. On top of that, the large gaps left between the boards of the barrack walls did absolutely nothing to stop the flow of dust from coming into the small living areas. It was so bad that it was not unusual to wake up in the morning to find that your entire bed, including your body in the bed, was covered in a thick layer of the ever-present dust of Fresno. Mama and I developed a ritual of dusting each other off first thing every morning.

The mix of the heat and the cloying dust did little to improve our spirits. From the moment we arrived at Pinedale, I was struck nearly dumb with disbelief at my situation. My mother had to help guide me through the surrealistic steps of being assigned a "barrack," using the latrine, or lining up for meals. I lived with a constant feeling of regret and guilt that I could escape only through day dreaming that life was much different than my present circumstances would have allowed. I fantasized that I had accepted Henry, that I had married him before he left. Then I could have gone with him. But that would have meant that Mama would have been in California by herself…there was no winning, even in my fantasies. But fantasy was all I had. The regular day-to-day was too much for me to bear.

For the two months that we were in Pinedale, I did very little. I stood in many lines; waiting for things comprised the vast majority of my day. There was nothing to do, not even work. I knew the people in the assembly center from Bellevue, but there were also many, many families from all over California. Even in the assembly center I was a bit of an outsider! Not really feeling friendly enough to make new friends, I spoke only to Mama or not at all; I didn't have the energy to find the other teenagers from Bellevue and socialize. Sometimes I would just sit and listen to other people. Since there were no real walls between the rooms, you could hear people snoring, babies crying, couples arguing. You could even hear couples who were getting along very...well. I tried to keep my mouth shut as much as possible; I spent my days furiously imagining what could have been, compulsively checking to see if my ring was still safely around my neck. To pass the hours, and as a release to my emotions, I began to write. I eventually began to keep a journal, but at first I made several attempts at a letter to Henry. However, once I managed to get something passable on paper, I learned that the government wasn't allowing letters between the camps yet. In time it would be allowed, but only after the government censors read and removed anything they felt was inappropriate— sometimes that meant just about all the content beyond the hellos and goodbyes. After enough time had passed, I thought it was too late; I didn't know how to bridge the gap.

Overall, the time at Pinedale was fairly uneventful for Mama and me. We knew that our placement here was temporary and the only real topic of conversation that everyone had was about where we would end up on a permanent basis. By mid or late June we began to hear the words "Tule Lake." This was to be the name and location of one of the government's ten relocation centers. Built on a dried-out lake bed just south of the Oregon-California border (close to Klamath Falls, Oregon, but in California), this mega-camp was built to hold over sixteen thousand people. At its peak it held over eighteen thousand. My mother and I, along with the rest of the Japanese American Bellevue community were sent to Tule Lake at the end of July of

1942.

*****

Once again we were transported by train and once again we had to keep the window curtains drawn. In an added effort to protect good Americans from us, the train traveled only at night. This decision was made in hopes to further reduce the chances of people discovering what cargo was being transported through their backyards. This was truly a miserable train ride. It was hot and stuffy and uncomfortable. The cars were old and out-dated. We had to sit in the stifling cars all day long in the hot northern central California sun not moving. Not doing anything. We tried to keep our moods and tempers in check, but more than one argument occurred amongst internees on those long and boring days.

After two days we disembarked from the train and got onto buses to carry us to our final destination. Once again the first thing that greeted us was dust. Tule Lake, a dried out lakebed, had turned to dust and dirt. The second thing that greeted us was the barbed wire and guard towers around our new home. This was not a "relocation center;" this was a concentration camp. And the third thing that greeted us was a glimpse of our new, permanent homes. Even knowing that people were to be permanently housed in these structures had not prompted the War Relocation Authority to go to any extra pains to build anything that would have passed any sort of housing code inspection. There were still slats between the outer walls of barracks, there were still four-foot gaps between the wall and ceilings; there were still no barriers between latrine holes. In fact, the camp did not even seem to be complete when we arrived. And we were often plagued by lack of water and electricity on a daily basis. While this had all been bad at the temporary assembly center, a hard truth hit us those first days at Tule Lake: We had better get used to this.

We settled into life at Tule Lake differently than we had at Pinedale. At Pinedale we were still in shock about losing our homes, families, and futures. In Pinedale we also faced the shock of coping with our new living conditions—conditions that were inhumane and rough even for the poorest of farmers amongst us. But in Tule Lake we were here for the duration, as we would say. For the duration of the war, however long that might be. Ironically, the war with Japan ended in August of 1945, but Tule Lake did not close until 1946, so the camps didn't magically close with victory. However, by that point everything was such a mess that the camps, especially Tule Lake, could not just close.

Although my attitude in the camps was never very good, the majority of internees seemed to deal with the lack of hope with a large measure of Japanese stoicism. This was especially true with the *Issei* who set about making the camp aesthetically pleasing, and with the older *Nisei*—especially those with children. These groups of internees began creating needed infrastructure and services such as schools for the children, classes for the older people, and gardens for both beauty and to grow vegetables to supplement the starchy government diet. Thanks to these industrious people, the camps turned into cities that, if not for the barbed wire fence and barrack living quarters, would have seemed very much like cities in the outside world—albeit cities that you weren't allowed to leave.

For some of us, though, no matter how many pretty rock gardens our neighbors created, or how many workshops we did on Japanese flower arranging, or *ikebana*, all we could see was the barbed wire. This was especially true for the *Nisei* of my age—we were of an age when we were ready to start our lives and none of us had envisioned doing so in prison camps. Anger and frustration began showing itself amongst people my age all through Tule Lake. We were angry and we had nothing to do— we were too old to be forced to the schools that were set up, but too young to not have structure to our days. Many teenage *Nisei* boys joined gangs and patrolled the camp together. Many of these groups were fairly benign beyond the usual mischief that teenage boys seem to find themselves in, but some of the gangs were just that, in the true sense of the word; angry teenage boys whose parents had lost control of their children. This group of boys would become an increasing threat at Tule Lake the longer that we were interned. While the gangs grew, it became apparent that the one infrastructure that the camps seemed to lack was an adequate police force. Because of the lack of protection from other internees it became dangerous to walk around Tule Lake camp alone or at night, especially as a girl.

I knew that this was no way to live and it made me angry. My anger manifested in one goal and one goal only. I had to get out of Tule Lake Relocation Center at the very first opportunity that presented itself. Living behind barbed wire was going to kill me if I had to endure it very long. I longed for freedom, for the ability to begin my life. I was eighteen by the time that I arrived in Tule Lake. I had "graduated" high school in the assembly center and therefore could not distract myself by going to the camp high school. I was too young and inexperienced to teach. I had nothing to do all day except for a job I found as a secretary in the Caucasian administrative building doing clerical work. I had no purpose, no life inside the camp as far as I was concerned. I just wanted out.

10 KIMIKO

From treason confession, continued.

THE JOB AT DOMEI did not pay well, but it was something. I was always concerned that I would be asked to do something that could compromise my citizenship, but my job description was simply to listen to the American and English news and transcribe it. I would stay at the job for just less than a year making just enough to avoid starvation and pay my rent. As my welcome at Mrs. Inouye's boardinghouse came to an end, I was down to one option—a boardinghouse that I was certain was full of prostitutes. Fortunately, Mrs. Inouye came through once more and gave me the address of an acquaintance of hers who was looking for a boarder. The woman, Madame Yasuda, was a delightful older woman who was alone in the world. I think that she was beginning to go a bit senile, as she seemed to have no idea what was happening around her. The war, the hatred of Americans did not seem to be part of her existence. To me, this made my new landlord very pleasant indeed.

Instead of talking about the war like everyone else I came across, Madame Yasuda liked to sit in her garden and practice traditional Japanese arts such as dance, music, and the tea ceremony, which she tried to teach me. She also tried to teach me flower arranging, saying that I was a natural, although I think that she was being kind. What I really loved to do was paint the creations that she formed with flowers. I must have painted nearly a hundred watercolors based upon her arrangements. I do not know what happened to any of my paintings—most I think were probably lost later in the war when the Allies started fire-bombing Tokyo.

Besides teaching me about the tea ceremony and poetry and flower arranging, Madame Yasuda taught me many other cultural skills. She even had tips for my painting. I would think of how proud that my parents would be to know that I was finally becoming the demure and graceful Japanese maiden that they had always hoped Maggie and I would become. I suppose that I just assumed that all Japanese women possessed the skills that Madame Yasuda shared with me. I heard rumors that she had been a geisha and she purchased her home with money she saved over a lifetime of work. I was just happy to have a place to live. Being allowed to live in her home and to relax made Madame Yasuda's home almost idyllic. It was a particularly welcome change after the months of struggle that I had encountered since Japan had geared for war.

Of course, during this time, I had no success contacting my family in the United States and my only information about the war was warped by the emperor's propaganda machine. Listening to the Japanese radio and reading the Japanese press, I lived in terror that Seattle had already been bombed and fallen under the emperor's domain. With each bit of news that I received from the Japanese press, the less that I worried for myself and the more that I worried about the safety of my family in America. I started to worry for my country itself. I remember praying to God every day. "Please keep my family safe. Please let the United States Army be victorious and strong against this threat." I did not know that the United States Army was actually putting my family in prison camps even as I uttered those prayers.

Things in Tokyo were very different in May 1942 than they were in Seattle and Bellevue. America was behind in the conflict in the Pacific (and who could blame them considering that they entered the war after having their Naval fleet bombed?), and that meant that Japan was ahead in the fight early on. And I don't mean to underestimate just how ahead Japan was. All through the Pacific, the Imperial Navy was conquering and pillaging. To add to their list of acquired property—which included much of China acquired in the late 1930's—the Japanese had added Midway and the Philippines. In the reports that I was transcribing at Domei, I was learning that the Japanese were cruel and harsh in the lands that they invaded.

Hirohito's Japan was extreme. The emperor was a totalitarian leader. He created a military state that was dead set on conquering the world. His military leaders, in particular General Tojo, attempted to bring this goal to fruition. In the homeland, Hirohito kept his own people conquered by creating institutions such as the "Thought Police," who had plagued us *Nisei* in Japan since long before the war began. You would think that after the war began that these Thought Police officers would be too busy to bother one young woman from a Bellevue farm who spent her day trying to earn money by typing at a news agency and her free time practicing water color painting and learning the fine arts of fan dancing and flower arranging. However, my very presence in Japan seemed to be a problem that required an official solution. I was not to be allowed to wait out the war in peace.

I had my very own police officer, Sergeant Shin, who would follow me nearly every day in order to keep his eye on me. He would sit outside of Madame Yasuda's home and wait for me to leave. If I went down to the neighborhood market to buy vegetables, Shin was there. When I went to work, Shin. When I looked out my window in the morning or night, Shin. He was a terrible undercover agent, but I think that was part of the Thought Police's way of doing business; they wanted you to know that they were always there, always watching.

At first, Shin's presence did little to interfere with my daily life. After all, it was not as if I was doing anything questionable in the eyes of the Empire. I was, I suppose, doing something questionable in the eyes of polite society in that my landlord was possibly a retired geisha. As I said, I never asked her and Madame Yasuda never admitted it. But she would speak in abstract, third person terms about the "art people." As an American, I was fascinated and mortified by the concept of geisha. I was a rapt listener and, not wanting to cut short the stories and teachings, I took care to not insult my friend. Also, I needed any friend that I could find, "art person," or housewife. Besides, I enjoyed the things that Madame Yasuda taught me. When I expressed my appreciation of the beauty of the subtle dances of Japanese women (and admitted that I had refused to take traditional Japanese dance when I was a child in Japanese school), Madame Yasuda began to teach me. She would accompany me on instruments that she eventually taught me to play--the three-stringed *shamisen* and the *tsutsumi* and *kodaiko* drums.

Once I was able to dance and play the traditional instruments with ease—this only took a couple of months considering that I had little else to do and learning these skills helped keep my mind off of my home—Madame Yasuda asked if I would like to give a performance. Not understanding what she meant, Madame Yasuda explained that she would teach me how to dress and apply makeup like a true performer (geisha, I suppose) and then I could perform for her on the patio. She meant no harm in it and I was actually excited by the idea. There was something alluring and mysterious about the geisha life that drew me in. The idea of playing a role, keeping calm under pressure, reminded me of my own situation. I needed to put on a show, keep myself alive so that I could go home. I had to strike a fine line between pleasing my audience and losing my soul. And, when I wasn't trying to survive, why not learn a dance or two?

We chose the following Sunday as the day for our "performance." We would begin the afternoon with a traditional tea ceremony wherein I was determined to serve Madame Yasuda her tea without spilling or sloshing it all over table. Then, after our formal tea, I was to dance while Madame Yasuda accompanied me on the three instruments and then we would switch. We would dress in traditional attire and makeup. In order to do so, we had to be up early to begin the dressing process. Like a little girl playing dress up, I was almost giddy with anticipation.

Madame Yasuda's kimonos were exquisite. These were not the simple *yakuta* robes worn around the house, but fine silk robes with intricate embroidery and patterns. Even after being stored away for many years, these kimonos made your heart swell just at seeing their beauty. They were true pieces of art. I was allowed to pick any of the garments that I preferred and I remember that I chose a *homon-gi*, or semi-formal kimono, the color of the sky. Next I chose an *obi*, or sash, in a shade of blue as dark as the night. The blues reminded me of the colors of the sky and the waters of my home in the Pacific Northwest. We had worn cheap cotton kimonos at home for feast days; I had never seen anything like Madame Yasuda's collection. I almost didn't know where to begin once I made my selection.

Because a kimono is not made-to-order, a woman must go through an intricate process of tying and adjusting the robe to make it fit. This, I learned, usually requires the help of a dresser or female family member. The process can be frustrating. Even with the two of us, it took Madame Yasuda and I well over an hour just to adjust the sleeves of our kimonos to the correct length, making sure the cords keeping everything in place were tied and tight enough, and to put on the *obi* correctly. It was this process that I had despised as a child. However, the kimonos that we had in Bellevue were simple cotton frocks—nothing like the fine silk robes that Madame Yasuda tied onto me. The beauty of the material, I noticed, made the process less boring and tedious to me. Finally, after turning ourselves into classical ideals of womanly grace, Madame Yasuda and I slipped on our *zori* sandals and went out to the courtyard to begin our festivities.

The tea ceremony, or *chanoyu*, begins with the walk to the area where the tea will be had. The concept is Buddhist and is meant to create an overall feeling of relaxation and reflection. However, despite the Zen nature of my walk into the courtyard, I was worried. I had the feeling that something was not right, that something bad would happen. Maybe it was just nerves about spilling tea or forgetting my dance, but I was beginning to dread the afternoon. I also felt suddenly ashamed. There I was, dressed like a geisha, like a glorified prostitute, about to practice the new skills that I had learned.

What am I doing here? I kept asking myself through the tea ceremony. Why am I doing this, learning this? I asked myself as I danced and then accompanied Madame Yasuda. She was so proud of me. I realized how lonely her life had most likely been, how hungry she had been to have a friend. She took me in when I was the number one persona non grata in Tokyo thanks to being American. She taught me the only things that she knew how to do, the arts. She was a good friend to me and I hope that she was able to keep her little house and live in peace. Her neighborhood was one of those that received a vast amount of fire bombings once the U.S. forces had taken Okinawa and could make it into Japan. I never went back to check. I was too afraid that I would find nothing. I was afraid that it might be my fault.

You see, we did have an audience when we had our little party: Shin. What I did not know about Shin or his duties in patrolling me was that he was not only looking for any anti-Japanese behavior, but for any "unbecoming" behavior at all. One little slip up was all it would take for the Thought Police to make my life miserable. Dressing like a geisha and putting on a performance was that slip. After our final performance, Madame Yasuda and I heard a slow, sarcastic sounding clapping coming from near the garden wall.

"Well done, Miss Miramoto," Shin hissed. "You make an excellent geisha. What are you charging for a private party?" I froze. I was completely speechless, unable to think of the proper thing to say in return in either English or Japanese. Honestly, to this day I'm not sure what a correct response would have been. My only friend left came to my rescue, thus putting herself at further risk.

"Officer, Kimiko-san is my student, not a geisha. She is studying the fine arts of her ancestors," explained Madame Yasuda.

"Keep quiet, Madame, or I will have the police investigate you as well. I'm sure they would be happy to learn how you made the money for this house—this house that you use to teach

Americans the tricks of your trade." Turning to me, Officer Shin said, "You will be coming with me. You will not say a word." That was not a problem because I was too afraid to speak.

"No, let her stay!" Madame Yasuda exclaimed as she grabbed at me and tried to pull me from Shin's grasp. Shin responded with a simple, "Enough!" coupled with a blow to Madame Yasuda's face that sent her reeling backward and onto the patio floor. My last sight of her as I was dragged from the courtyard was of my friend trying to struggle to her feet, her beautiful white face stained the red of her own blood.

*****

I was transported to the nearest police station. I was numbed by the terror of what might happen to me. I thought for sure that I would be raped, beaten, and psychologically tortured by the police. To my surprise and relief though, the police let me be; my fears were not manifested in the jail. My other fear was that I was going to be sent to one of the prisoner of war camps that had been set up in Japan for Americans (and other Allies) who had been trapped like me when the war broke out. I had heard rumors of these camps and I knew that this was not a place that I wanted to be. In hindsight, the one positive thing about being sent to a camp would be that I would not have to worry about being classified as a traitor to my country. If I had survived a camp, perhaps I would have made it home. *If* I had survived. The camps were brutal and survival was not easy.

I had to sit in a cell in that Tokyo jail for over two days. I was put in the cell designated for actual prostitutes. I was not allowed to change or wash my face and I know that by that second day I must have looked like a geisha who had been to hell and back. That is certainly how I felt. I hadn't eaten or slept since I had been arrested. The other girls in the cell were fed once a day but I was told that there wasn't enough food for the Japanese let alone for an *enu* like myself. When I tried to sit down on the dirty floor and sleep, a guard would come by and poke me with a long stick and tell me to get up, that any sitting space was reserved for the Japanese, not the enemy. Did I say, "But there is plenty of space for all of us to sit?" No, I didn't. Of course I did not. What good would it have done?

On the morning of the third day, just as I felt myself losing a grasp on reality, the guard announced that I had been "rescued" by a family member. When he said "family," I had a fantasy that it was my Mama or Papa, or my brother, Akio, who had come to Japan to save me. I thought it might even have been Maggie even though I was doubtful that anything would possess her to set aside her dislike for Japan, even her big sister. Before my mind awoke to reality, the feeling of happiness that washed over me was immense, bigger than the Pacific Ocean is wide. "Finally," I thought, "finally this is over and I can go home." But of course my parents and siblings were not waiting for me in the little room that the guard had to half-drag me to since I was too weak to walk. It was my dear cousin, Ryuu.

When I saw Ryuu, I snapped back to reality. "This is it," I told myself. "This is the beginning of the end." I knew when I made eye contact with Ryuu that my choices had become drastically few. There were two, really: Accept or decline. Neither option promised much hope for me. Now you call me a "traitor," but I just wanted to live. I never stopped being an American. Never.

11 ROSE MARIE

From archived interview, continued.

WHEN I GOT OFF the bus at Camp Harmony, the Puyallup Assembly Center, I looked around and took inventory. Rows of crudely built barracks: check. Spaces between wall and floorboards: check. Mud everywhere: check. No furniture: check. I made a list in my head of all the deficiencies around me. Deep down, though, I was thinking, "What have I done, what have these people all around me done, to have to live in these shacks?" No, not even shacks—my father-in-law's shed behind his house in Bellevue was better constructed than these structures. I was mortified. I followed Akio to our assigned "apartment" in a state of shock, carrying Rosie so her feet wouldn't get muddy. I almost slipped more than once as I made my way down the "avenue" to our barracks. When I stepped into my new home and set my daughter down onto the floor, mud seeped through the boards and got all over her feet. And I started to cry.

I cried primarily for my little girl. I had tried to protect her, to keep her clean, but I couldn't hold her forever. At some point she was going to look around her and realize that we were not "camping" like she thought. She would realize that she couldn't go home when she wanted to leave; couldn't have her toys or her room. Soon she would notice that our camp was enclosed in barbed wire and an armed soldier in a guard tower was watching us twenty-four hours a day. I cried because I could not make this normal for my baby. When I stopped crying for my daughter, I started crying for my husband. What had he done? He was an American citizen. He loved America. His favorite holiday was the Fourth of July. He had been to Japan as a boy and would often talk about how that trip had solidified in his mind that America was the place for him. "I like to keep my shoes on," he would joke when asked about why he was not fond of Japan. And when I thought about that, about my husband's humor and optimism, I cried thinking about putting such a happy and funny man behind barbed wire. Finally, after shedding tears for those that I loved most, I cried for myself. I cried for the house that I had left behind. I cried for the pause that had been put into my life. I didn't want to be in a prison camp. I cried because for one brief moment I thought, "If I hadn't married Akio, I wouldn't be here."

As I sobbed, Akio put his arm around me and said, "Don't cry, Rose. It's going to be okay."

"I just don't understand," I whimpered. "I'm sorry. I'll be fine," I said trying to convince myself that I would, in fact, be okay. "Akio, aren't you upset? Isn't everyone here upset?" I had not seen anyone else cry or get angry on the bus or even as they walked through the assembly center. Surely there were people all through Camp Harmony who were incensed that they had been ripped from their homes and put into these terrible shacks. Surely they saw the same things that I saw?

"Please, Rose," he answered in a whisper, "we are just trying to cooperate. Besides, the Japanese are nothing if not survivors. We are the silent, strong, and stoic people from the East." He made a movement with his shoulders as if he could carry the weight of the world. It made me smile. Here he was being strong for me instead of the other way around. "Are you doing better now?" Akio asked quietly as he smiled back at me.

"Yes," I said as I wiped the tears from my eyes. "But why do you keep talking so softly?" In response, Akio just pointed towards the ceiling. In the darkness inside our hovel, I had not even noticed that the partition between each apartment did not go all the way up to the barrack's ceiling. There was a three or four foot space between the "wall" and the roof. A space big enough for a person to crawl through from apartment to apartment. A space big enough for every single sound from each apartment to be heard as clearly by the neighboring family as if they were living right there with us.

"I hope our neighbors like the sounds of a three year-old," I laughed as Rosie began to sing the ABC's, her new favorite song. She had already made herself at home in the corner by the cot, playing with the one doll we allowed her to bring along. "We do," came the reply through the partition, "we have our own little ones so don't blame us if they keep you up all night!" We all laughed, on both sides of the wall; there was no need to even pretend that we would have privacy for the next few years. We were in this together.

*****

I soon discovered that Akio and I were lucky in one respect with our "apartment" at Camp Harmony: We were just a couple of doors down from the nearest latrines. We would learn, however, that we had not lucked out regarding the mess hall—it was several blocks away. Not knowing what to expect using the facilities for the first time, I took my daughter's hand and we set out for our first Camp Harmony bathroom adventure. As soon as we stepped out of our door, I could see the line. Dozens of women were standing in line waiting. I noticed that many women had paper products in their hands. When I asked the lady in front of me what was going on, she just looked at me— somewhat surprised, most likely because I wasn't Japanese—and said, "No English." As I would discover, many *Issei* had lived for several decades amongst the Japanese community and had not mastered English. Fortunately, a young *Nisei* woman came up in line behind me and, sensing my confusion, handed me a couple of the napkins that she had brought along with her. "You need to bring your own paper," she said as a way of explanation.

"What do you think the problem is here?" I asked the woman after thanking her. The line seemed to either move quickly, or not at all. As we approached the latrine door, I could see many older women leaving with a look of horror on their faces.

"I've heard that the latrines are not…optimal," said my line companion. "Apparently there are no dividers between the holes. Just two rows of six back-to-back holes."

"Holes," I asked, absolutely incredulous. "Like an outhouse?"

"Like a public outhouse," said the young woman.

"That's terrible," I said. I was not very comfortable with sharing certain moments with other people.

"It is very hard for the older women," continued the woman. "Japanese women are very private in such matters. My mother has refused to use this latrine."

"Well, I understand that it is difficult for the older women, but I don't think it will be easy for us, either." I replied. She nodded her agreement and stuck out her hand to introduce herself. "Well, since we're going to get to know each other very well, my name is Toshi. My husband and I are roomed over that way," she pointed.

"You're not far from me and my husband, Akio," I replied. "And this is our daughter, Rosie." To her credit, my little girl had been a dream during this whole experience. She was dutifully holding my hand and not complaining.

"Nice to meet you, Rosie," said Toshi.

"Nice, too," said Rosie. Between speaking Japanese with her grandparents and English with Akio and me, we were still working on Rosie's speaking skills. I was about to correct her, but I saw that Toshi was delightedly shaking Rosie's hand and there seemed to be no need to dampen the meeting. I liked Toshi immediately.

"So," I could tell that Toshi was a little uncomfortable with what she was about to say, "I'm guessing that Akio is Japanese…"

"Yes, he's *Nisei*. We met in high school, in Bellevue."

"And you had to come because you had married a Japanese?" she asked. I appreciated her openness. It was much better than the looks of confusion and speculation that I would feel by the vast majority of Camp Harmony residents. If they wanted to know what I was doing in the camp, all they had to do was ask, as Toshi had.

"I had to come because my husband was being evacuated. And so was my daughter," I explained.

"I'm sorry," smiled Toshi. "I'm very sorry for your family."

"And I'm very sorry for yours," I responded. Toshi and I smiled at each other, already bound by our circumstances. "Looks like it's our turn," I said, realizing that I was now at the head of the line. "Wish me luck!"

Of course, I will spare you the details of what we encountered when Rosie and I got into the latrines. I'll just say that what I had heard was accurate: Two back-to-back rows of six holes, no dividers. The communal sinks and showers often had no hot water and, even on days when the hot water heater was working, it ran out before even a quarter of the camp could bathe themselves. It would be the same later at the permanent camp.

It was also true that many of the older women would have rather died than use such a non-private latrine. This led to some ingenious use of other items to use as shields between the holes. Large boxes, blankets—whatever we could find from the items that we were allowed in the camp. Some of the *Issei* women would bring in their daughters and granddaughters who would sing or make other noises to mask sounds that were not meant for other ears. Eventually more permanent wooden barriers were built between each of the holes by some of the men in the camp. These men, including Akio, found a pile of scrap lumber that had been left over from the building of our new community and used the wood to make all manner of barriers, shelves, and crude furniture with whatever tools could be found or improvised within the camp. After a few weeks, these simple additions helped to give Camp Harmony a little more of a home-like feel.

In the very least, the result of the men's carpentry was to create a more camp-like atmosphere than the bleak prison-like atmosphere that had greeted us upon our arrival in Puyallup.

*****

I honestly had a very hard time while we were in Harmony. I just couldn't shake the feeling of self-pity and injustice that had planted itself in my soul from the moment I stepped off the bus. I tried very hard to keep a stiff upper lip and not show my discomfort or anger. I would often spend the days wondering if I had made the right decision, if I should have stayed out of the camps. I would then spend the rest of the day berating myself for having such selfish thoughts; nobody at Camp Harmony deserved to be there—I wasn't so special. If only there were things to keep my mind off of my own misery so that I didn't have the time to dwell in pointless what-ifs.

Unfortunately, there was not much to do at Harmony at first besides laundry and standing in line at the mess hall. The mess hall line was the worst and, to add insult to injury, the food was terrible. It was practically the same thing every day, every meal: Stewed tomatoes, bread, and some other starchy food to accompany our low-protein feast. The one benefit was that I think the food was limitless (probably because nobody ever went back for seconds). So you could eat to your heart's content. And, to add insult to mealtime injury, after being served this delightful food, there was never any place to sit together, even for just the three of us. I was not interested in sitting by myself without Akio, so I usually brought Rosie back to the barracks to eat. Akio would often stay and talk to the other men in order to get information about what was going to happen to us next. After lunch or dinner, Akio would bring this information back to me. It was this group of men that almost got Henry into trouble when it came time for the vote.

I guess before I get into the administration vote, I need to back up and explain another part of the reason that I was depressed. One week after Akio and Rosie and I arrived at Camp

Harmony, Henry and his parents, as planned, joined us. We still eagerly awaited news of when Mrs. Miramoto and Maggie (along with the Bellevue community) would be evacuated to Puyallup. We had all assumed that it would happen just a couple of weeks after the Army was finished moving the Seattle and Tacoma communities into Camp Harmony. But once we were all safe and sound in the assembly center at Puyallup, we heard nothing about our friends and family in Bellevue. At first we dared to think the impossible—that, for some reason, the government had decided not to evacuate Bellevue. "Maybe they have decided to let the farmers keep growing produce," Akio ventured, hopeful. "Maybe they forgot all about little Bellevue," was my guess.

I had really looked forward to my in-laws joining us in Camp Harmony. In many ways, they were more my family at that point than my blood relatives and I wanted to be around them during this terrible and chaotic time. I also needed the support and help with my child because I honestly was just not the best mother that I could have been. I was too depressed at the time and I wanted Mrs. Miramoto's stoicism and strength and Maggie's youthful enthusiasm to be positive influences for Rosie. I thought they would be a good change to my moping and introspection.

The news that his mother and sister were not to join us in the assembly center was worse for Akio than for me. With Mr. Miramoto still in the Department of Justice camp, Akio felt responsible for his family. He worried himself sick speculating about their wellbeing. It would be several weeks before they could exchange letters between the camps and Akio could know for certain that Maggie and his mother were surviving just fine despite their heartbreak. Akio was a mess while he awaited word from his mother and sister.

We also had to deal with Henry. He was beside himself with grief over his separation from Maggie. He started to spend more and more time with us, asking if we had received any word from her. He was having trouble getting letters out to her since they were not related. We knew that something had gone wrong with them and Henry seemed desperate to get it right. I suggested that he start addressing her as "Cousin Maggie," but Akio warned that it wouldn't do anyone any good if Henry and Maggie got caught communicating under false pretenses. "Well," reasoned Akio to Henry, "on the other hand, you could go to 'visit' my father if you got caught and you could let me know how he is doing." For poor Henry, his grief began to manifest itself in anger. At first it was just at small things like the dirt or the food, but he began to fall in with the group of men who were voicing their general anger with the JACL and the injustice of the evacuation. Many of these were the men that Akio ate with when Rosie and I ate in our own room. From Akio, I knew that these men were becoming increasingly disgruntled with their internment.

Camp Harmony was unique in that it was completely self-governed by its own inmates who were, in turn, supervised by Army and government personnel. The supervisor of the inmate "government" was James Y. Sakamoto, a former head of the Japanese American Citizens League—JACL—of Seattle. James was charismatic but controversial. He had been a leader of the Seattle *Nisei* community and one of the local proponents of complying with the government's orders without complaint to demonstrate the Japanese community's patriotism. While many people shared in this idea and desire to demonstrate their willingness to follow orders, eventually grumblings of dissent could be heard throughout the camp. The grumbling got louder the longer we were there. I think many people initially assumed that the government would realize that they had made a mistake in interning the Japanese, especially the Japanese Americans. After months of being model citizens—writing anti-Japanese editorials, enlisting in the Army, packing up on a moment's notice and being moved to prison camps without complaint—the *Nisei* had hoped that the Army and the President would take a look and say, "Look at those people, those Japanese Americans. We were wrong about them. They love America."

But that didn't happen. Instead, after all those months of effort to prove themselves worthy of being American between December 1941 and May 1942, the *Nisei* and their Japanese parents found themselves in prison by the summer of 1942.

Worse, upon reflection they realized that they had liquidated their lives and gotten onto the camp-bound buses not only without complaint, but with smiles on their faces. They hadn't fought the evacuation at all. By mid-June, many people realized that their compliance hadn't made things any better.

I was able to hear both sides of the argument, debated in whispers, in the weeks before the camp vote that would bring the conflict to a head. Nearly every night Henry would come over to play cards with Akio and the two would discuss the situation. Like many of their mess hall companions, Henry felt that the JACL had betrayed the interests of the Japanese American community. Akio, ever the optimist—or able to predict the future—defended the JACL and maintained the position that cooperation was the best and only way to show patriotism.

"Henry," Akio would reason, "I know that you are frustrated. I understand it. I'm not happy to be here, to have my family here, to have the rest of my family away from me."

"You say that you understand," Henry would retort, "but you do nothing about it. Your father is in prison, your mother and sister are in California. God only knows where your other sister is. And what good was JACL? They worked the booths for us to register our families. They came ahead to the camps to "prepare" them. A lot of good that did! We live like animals!"

"Shhh! Keep your voice down, Henry!" Akio gently reminded our younger friend.

"Why, because I might get sent to prison if I get caught? Take a look around you, Akio. We are in prison already," Henry hissed under his breath.

"I know that it is bad…" began Akio.

"Bad?" interrupted Henry, incredulous. "This isn't *bad*, Akio. This is bullshit. Our own government put us citizens in prison because they don't like the looks of us."

"Don't use that kind of language in front of my family," said Akio, starting to get angry, which took a lot.

"What? The swearing or telling the truth about the U.S. government, Akio? Because if you ask me, if this is how the goddamn United States treats its citizens then it deserved to get bombed," sneered Henry, his anger at a breaking point.

"Out," said Akio. He stood up so fast that the chair that he had built out of scrap lumber went flying out behind him. "Get out of my house and do not come back if you are ever going to speak that way again. I will not have it."

"Fine," answered Henry, "but you'll see—someday you'll see that you did not deserve this, Akio."

Under his breath, as Henry went huffing out of the apartment, I heard Akio whisper, "I already know that I don't deserve it."

*****

The unrest in Camp Harmony only got worse as camp life grew more stringent. As soon as all the camp residents had arrived peacefully, the Army started to issue regulations. One of the regulations was no liquor, which we didn't have free access to anyway. That one was not too terrible as far as I was concerned because neither Akio nor I were drinkers, but I heard there were grumbling by the *Issei* about their *sake*. On the other hand, I was bothered by the curfew and fence regulations. Soon after we arrived at Camp Harmony we were told that we must be in the barracks by nine at night and lights out was at ten. Soon after that, a regulation went into effect strictly enforcing the area between the barracks and the fence. Meaning that anyone who went too close to the fence could risk punishment, or even death.

I know that my already low morale was not helped by the sudden onslaught of rules and regulations. I knew I had chosen to live in a camp with my family and I could accept that, but the new rules made life nearly unbearable. I did not like having to use a chamber pot in the middle of the night because I was no longer allowed to walk to the latrine at night. I did not like having to live in the dark past ten at night even if I had to get up to check on my daughter or if I couldn't sleep. Well, in honesty I could not have gotten up and turned the light on in the middle of the night even if there was no curfew—the light would have awakened my family and, most likely, would have seeped over the partition wall and bothered the family next door. No, these rules were problematic, but they were not the worst.

The regulation that I despised the most was the barrack-fence regulation. After a couple of weeks at Camp Harmony it was announced that we were no longer allowed to go anywhere near the fence that encircled the camp. This meant that we could no longer buy any candy or cigarettes from Puyallup locals through the links in the fence. I could live without the chocolate—barely—but I didn't think I could live without the little snippets of life outside the fence that I was able to find out while I made my candy selection. I could almost always get the locals to tell me what the latest headlines had been, what the status of the war was. We weren't allowed any news inside Camp Harmony and so I had no idea what was happening in the world but for the news from the girls who sold me a chocolate bar through the gaps. Once the regulation was put in place, anyone who came within three feet of that fence could be shot by the armed soldiers watching us in the guard towers. Shot dead for going too close to the fence. Once again, we were told this was for our own protection.

*****

Even after the argument with Akio, I saw Henry fairly often although not in our living quarters like before. I would often visit with Mrs. Fusaka when she came by to sit with me in my little barrack apartment. In time, in an effort to get out and about, I would go to the Fusaka barracks to have tea with Mrs. Fusaka and we would discuss "current events"—mostly camp gossip. I had liked Mrs. Fusaka from the moment that I met her and was happy to spend time with her. Mary Fusaka was unlike many *Issei* women in the camp. Henry's mother had been born in Japan where her parents, both Japanese, were Christian missionaries. Having become Methodists during the Meiji Restoration period, Mary Fusaka's parents traveled the island nation spreading Christianity to their fellow countrymen and women. When she was eighteen, Mary came to the United States through a

Methodist program in San Francisco. She had told her parents that she was going to America to study the Bible, but she told me that she really came to America "for adventure." From San Francisco, Mary traveled to Seattle with a church group, met Mr. Fusaka at a Japanese Methodist church service, married him, and later had Henry.

Much that I knew about Henry was learned from speaking with his mother. When we visited, Mary and I usually spoke of our children even though Henry was nearly twenty years older than my daughter. Despite the age difference of our children, I discovered that Mary Fusaka and I had a similar concern—the fear of what internment would do to our children's lives and spirits. I was worried that Rosie would be stunted academically, socially, and emotionally. Mary was worried that Henry was missing opportunities for education, career, and losing valuable years of his early adulthood. She was also worried that his newfound anger would get him into irreversible trouble. I couldn't help but agree that this last worry was not unfounded. I also have to admit that I was glad that Rosie was too young to be getting involved in the politics that were starting to ferment behind the scenes at Camp Harmony; it was certain to lead to no good end for those openly taking sides.

*****

About six weeks after taking up residence at Camp Harmony, the line was officially drawn in the sand: A group of dissidents versus JACL. Two *Nisei* attorneys from Seattle named Masuda and Ito openly challenged the JACL leaders of the camp, specifically James Sakamoto and his chief supporter, Bill Hosokawa. Masuda and Ito called for a new administration that would be elected by the population of the camp. Surprisingly, a vote was scheduled by the Army administration for mid-June. No one at the time seemed to think it strange that the Army would be so accommodating about such an issue. For many of us, the upcoming vote at least gave us something to do, something to focus on. Something to talk about while we waited in line.

As soon as the vote was announced, clear sides were quickly taken between the current leaders and the opposition and supporting arguments were circulated. Many people who had seen the logic in what the opposition had been saying changed their tune and went along with Sakamoto's unrelenting advice that cooperation was the most patriotic thing that any of the Japanese internees could do. Akio, always a staunch JACL supporter, explained to many fellow residents that it would do no good to fight or to cause problems. "Doing so will only give the government and the country the proof that they need to keep us here forever or send us all back to Japan, citizens or not," he would say. "If we cooperate it shows that we are not anti-American. Most importantly, it will show that we are not pro-Japan. No matter how unfair internment is, at least we can keep our heads held high and let the government know that we are willing to do what it takes to show that we are American."

The opposition was not convinced by this optimistic viewpoint and they went to lengthy efforts to convert people to their way of thinking. One day in early June, as I approached the Fusaka barracks I overheard Henry speaking to some pro-Masuda men. Rather, I heard one of the pro-Masuda men speaking to Henry. I was planning on simply walking past them and continuing on to call on Mary. However, what I heard stopped me dead in my tracks. I managed to duck behind a building where I could hear the conversation without being seen by the men.

"Why do what your friend Akio says, Henry?" said one of the men. "He's a sell-out to his people. Hell, he wants to be an American so badly he married a *hakujin*."

"Hey, Akio is an American, same as you or I," I heard Henry say.

"We are Japanese, Henry," said a man with a different voice than the first. "We may have been born here in this country, but the government has made it very clear that we are not welcome here."

"But maybe that is what Akio and Sakamoto are saying,"

continued Henry. "Maybe that is what we have to prove—that we are just as American as anyone else."

"We don't have to *prove* anything to anybody," said the man who had spoken first. "It's time that we took control of this camp and stopped kissing Uncle Sam's ass just to show what good little children we are."

"I just think that you are taking it too far," said Henry. "We should stand up for our rights, but it sounds like you guys are ready to fight for the emperor."

"Well, at least he wouldn't call us "Japs," now would he?" asked the second man.

"Hey, Henry, maybe you should go find your friend Akio and his little white wife and eat some apple pie together. And then, maybe you can marry his little half-white, half-Jap baby and have little diluted ass-kissing pansies like yourself." The first man's voice said this, I think. I was too scared to hear straight. "Oh, God," I muttered under my breath. "Oh, God help us."

"Yeah, you're right," said Henry. His voice sounded angry. "Maybe I should find Akio and when I do, I'm going to apologize to him and his wife. And guess what? I think I'll marry his sister, which will make his little white wife and half-white daughter my family. And if you ever speak that way about my family again, it will be the last thing you ever say."

"We'll see Fusaka," said one of the men.

"I knew you were worthless, Henry," said the other. "Do yourself a favor," he continued. "Stay low when we take over this camp. We don't like your kind."

I tried to make myself invisible as the men walked down the dirt road past me. One of them saw me out of the corner of his eye and turned around to Henry and yelled, "Hey, Henry! Here's one of your beloved *hakujin* now!" They laughed as they passed me. Neither said anything else or tried to approach me as they made their way down the road, which is all the better for me since I was so terrified that I could not move. Henry, who had come running up to me when he realized that I was standing just around the corner, snapped me out of my paralysis.

"Hey, Rose Marie!" he said as he put his hands on my

shoulders. "Are you alright? Oh God! Did you hear?" My face must have revealed the answer to his question for Henry continued, "Don't worry! I won't let them hurt you or Rosie. I'm so sorry about everything," Henry said, his words tumbling out of his mouth a mile a minute. He put his back against the nearest barrack and slumped down, his face in his hands. This war was trying real hard to defeat this young man's spirit. Henry was a good kid; despite the bad company that he kept and his argument with Akio, we all knew that it was likely he would come round. He had been kicked so many times in the past couple of months that nobody could blame him for being angry.

"Henry, those guys are trouble," I managed to say once I could speak again. I felt bad that I was scolding him like a child when he had clearly discovered that himself and had just stood up for me. "Thanks, by the way…" I said, nodding in the direction that the men had gone.

Henry nodded. "I was wrong about them," he said. "I mean, I don't think that it is right that we are here. We haven't done anything wrong, nothing to deserve this," he paused. "But this is not going in the direction that I would have hoped."

"I agree, Henry," I said. "So why have you changed your mind? I mean, have you changed your mind?"

"Yes, I've decided to support the JACL," he said. "I do not agree with everything that they have done, but I spoke to Akio again at lunch today and I see what he's saying. He's right: We have to face the truth. We are here, stuck in camps. We cannot change that and we probably could not have prevented it. If we would have tried to prevent it we probably would have faced fighting and people getting hurt or killed. Worse, we as Japanese Americans would have looked anti-American. We would never have gotten over that, never have been accepted. There is still hope to be accepted. If we just go along and try our hardest to show the country that we are Americans and willing to do what it takes, maybe it will get better." Henry stopped speaking and looked at me. "What do you think, Rose?" he asked. "Do you agree?"

"I hope so, Henry," I responded. "But even if you agree

with Akio about all of those things, don't you still agree that it would not hurt the camp to vote on its administration? Isn't that what Masuda and Ito want? By the way, was that them, those guys?" I asked.

"No, that wasn't them, just some of their supporters," said Henry. "That's the problem. The opposition to Sakamoto isn't just people who want a vote or who wish that we would have fought a little more before we got here. No, Rose, the opposition is filling up with *Kibei*—you know what that is, right?" he asked. I shook my head; I had a hard time grasping all the different characterizations of the Japanese in America. They seemed to have a different—and hard to pronounce—word for everything. Henry explained, "A *Kibei* is a *Nisei* who studied in Japan—like your sister-in-law. It also has a pretty big contingent of disenfranchised *Issei*. Rose, the opposition isn't just anti-JACL anymore," Henry exclaimed. "It's pro-Japan!"

"Pro-Japan? As in they want Japan to win the war?" I asked, astounded at the concept. I was even more astounded with Henry's answer.

"Exactly," he said.

"But they are Americans, aren't they?" I continued, having a hard time following.

"Yes, most of them are," said Henry. We paused for a second, watching people walk past us. How many of these people, I thought, have actually turned into what the government feared? How many people in Camp Harmony were actually hoping for Japan to win the war? Did that mean that the government was right for putting us here? No, it couldn't be, I thought.

"Henry," I wanted to ask him these very questions, but I was not sure how. "Henry, do you think that these people were pro-Japan before this?" I gestured to the camp around me. "Before the internment, I mean?"

"I'm not sure," he said. He seemed saddened. He reminded of the little boy that his mother often spoke of. "I don't think so."

*****

The vote took place in mid-June of 1942. The overwhelming majority of the residents of Camp Harmony who were qualified to vote cast their ballots to maintain the JACL-based administration led by James Sakamoto. Akio, Henry, both of Henry's parents, and I were amongst those who voted for the JACL administration. It is a good thing that we did; those who voted for the opposition were rounded up and sent to Department of Justice camps. It had not been a secret ballot. As anticipated by many, those who voted against the cooperative camp administration were seen as anti-government and thus put into prisoner of war camps, including the two thugs who had been bullying Henry the day that I walked up on them. The leaders of the opposition were labeled as traitors to the United States. It was no longer a mystery that the Army had so wholeheartedly supported an open show of dissent at Camp Harmony.

*****

After the vote, we settled into a pattern of life at Camp Harmony that would be the root for our life in the permanent camps. We lived in our tiny spaces with no privacy. We ate with no privacy. We bathed with no privacy. We stayed away from the fences. We went to the crowded mess halls at our designated times. We began to accept our fate. Even I began to feel less depressed as the routine of everyday life began to take over my emotions. Some internees got jobs and worked in the camp. Akio got a job with one of the maintenance crews and I stayed in the barracks with Rosie. Makeshift recreational activities were set up in each section of the camp. There was a baseball team from each section and they would play each other. There were dances for young people. A camp newspaper was set up for the seven thousand or more residents of Camp Harmony and we would eagerly read the weekly publication. It was actually pretty good— Henry wrote for it. Still, whether we were at musical events, games, or discussing the paper, the main theme of all camp conversations was the same: Where are we going next?

Of course, we internees were kept completely in the dark about our ultimate destination for the duration of the war. This lack of information led to wild speculation on the part of Camp Harmony residents. Some still hoped that we would be let out due to our cooperation and because it did not make economic sense to pay for the expense of moving over one hundred thousand people and continuing to house and feed them through the interminable war. Surely that money could be spent on weapons or feeding the troops, reasoned many. Others, including Akio and Henry, hoped that we would be moved to a camp in California where we would join up with the Bainbridge Island and Bellevue Japanese communities. For many weeks, it seemed that going south was likely; the camp newsletter even dedicated an edition giving information about the camp being built at Tule Lake, California in the belief that we would soon be heading to the new city-camp. I no longer held out hope that anything would happen as planned or expected. I left the guesswork to others and just did as I was told.

Finally, after weeks of speculation, we got the news. Of course, almost all speculations had been wrong. Camp administration called for volunteers to help ready the camp that would be our home. The volunteers were not sent to California or anywhere in Washington, but to Idaho. Idaho was to be our home for the duration of the war. We received the news in early August. By the end of the month we were put on trains, told to keep the shades drawn during the day so as to not scare the local residents who saw trains full of the "enemy," and transported from the lush green landscape of Western Washington to the dusty and harsh land near Twin Falls, Idaho. The Minidoka Relocation Center was to be my home for the next three years.

12 KIMIKO

From treason confession, continued.

I LEFT THE POLICE station with Ryuu. We went to the apartment that he kept in an old and upscale neighborhood of Tokyo. This was where he lived when he was in the capital and not being doted upon at the Miramoto compound in Hiroshima. Under any other circumstances it would have been a pleasure to stay in Ryuu's opulent city flat. In all honesty, I have always had to admit that Ryuu had exceptional taste in furnishings and artwork. He also, thanks especially to money earned during the Sino-Japanese War, had endless funds to procure Oriental antiques from both China and Japan. Thus, the Tokyo apartment was beautiful. If only that had been enough to make it pleasurable. As I stood there, just over the threshold taking it all in, Ryuu proceeded into the area just off the foyer that served as a sitting room and opened a small cabinet against the wall. The cabinet contained a small array of expensive liquors and crystal glasses.

"Watch carefully," Ryuu said. This was the first thing that he had said to me since we had left the station and he had promised loudly, seemingly to the entire station, that he would "take care of me." It was not reassuring that his comment elicited knowing laughs from the other men present.

"You will be mixing my drinks for me from now on," he continued, as I stood mute. "At the end of a long, stressful day, I prefer gin and tonic. This is how to mix it," he poured three shots of gin into a glass that contained one ice cube and filled the glass with tonic water. "I prefer these measurements. Do not be sloppy, Kimiko."

I was silent. Truly, I had no idea what to say to this man who was supposed to be my cousin and so I said nothing and waited for his next comment.

"It cost me quite a bit to bail you out, you know," he finally said after sipping his drink for several minutes. I was still standing awkwardly near the door. How I wished that I could just turn and leave. Sometimes I wonder what would have happened if I had just tried. I don't think I would be here to tell my story.

I knew even then that I was in survival mode. I gritted my teeth, clenched my fists so tightly that I could feel my fingernails draw blood from my palms. "Thank you, Ryuu," I said. "I am sure that my father, your uncle, will be pleased that you have helped me. When I get home I shall be certain to have him reimburse you for any expenses relating to this incident." I hoped that a reminder that we were family would spare me whatever might lie ahead, despite how sarcastic the delivery.

"Ha!" was the explosive reply. Ryuu's laugh echoed through the apartment as if the entire space was mocking me. "My uncle is no doubt in a prison camp and therefore penniless."

"Why would Papa be in a prison camp, Ryuu?" I asked worried that I had missed terrible news of a Japanese victory in America. And certainly my Papa was too old to be drafted so Ryuu could not mean that he was a prisoner of war.

"Ah, my poor dear," smirked Ryuu, "your precious America has put all of its Japanese subjects into prison camps. And guess what?" he was enjoying telling me this. "Even the citizens were imprisoned. So you know what that means, my darling? That means that America doesn't want any of its Jap citizens. You are meaningless to them." I exhaled the wind out of my lungs slowly, feeling as if I had been hit in the stomach. It could not be true. I had heard the rumors at my job, but it could not be true, I thought.

"No, it cannot be!" I exclaimed. Immediately I worried for my family; I had been so consumed with my own problems the last few months that I hadn't even thought that they too might be suffering because of the war.

"Now that you are not wanted at home, I suppose that you won't be needing this," Ryuu was prattling on as I thought about my family. I was so absorbed in my own thoughts that I didn't register in my head at first what I saw coming out of Ryuu's inner breast pocket as he said this. He had withdrawn a small, dark little book. No, not a book. A passport. *My* passport. My passport came out of Ryuu's pocket. The calculated gesture hit me as hard as any blow could have done.

"Ryuu," I cried when I realized what I was seeing. "I could have left, I could have gone home! Why would you do this?"

"Ah, my dear," he said, waving my passport back and forth, "What good would it have done? You would just be in prison if you had gone back. Look around you. Here you shall live like a queen."

I didn't understand. "Are you going to let me live in the family compound and help me until I can go home?" I asked. I was starting to panic. "Please, Ryuu. We are cousins," I said, dreading what this monster had in mind for me. When had he managed to get his hands on my passport? The only time would have been...the time that he attacked me on the bed. I had been packing and I left in a hurry. He must have grabbed my passport while we struggled; even in that moment of passion and fury he had been manipulating my life. He laughed as if reading my mind. "Live in the *family* compound, Kimiko? But that is only for family, isn't it. I notice that you have been reluctant to sign the registry."

"Ryuu, if I sign the registry, I will lose my American citizenship," I said. Obviously I did not add that I was not truly a Miramoto. I had no idea that my secret was out; I hadn't fully connected the dots.

"Is that the reason, my dear?" Ryuu asked me with the smirk

still stuck on his face. How I wished that I could smack that smugness right off his head. "Is it not for any other reason?" My mind raced. How could he know? What could he know? My passport! My passport had my true birthday, not the date that we had told the Miramoto family that I had been born.

"You seem to be a bit older than I knew," Ryuu was saying as I was thinking. So he had caught that. But that in itself did not mean that I was not a Miramoto I reasoned to myself so perhaps he did not know.

"Ah, Ryuu, you know how ladies are!" I attempted a laugh that sounded hollow and forced even to my ears. "We never want to reveal our age."

The blow was memorable for two reasons: The first was simply that I had never been hit before in any capacity for any reason. I had never expected to be hit, didn't know how to see it coming. Even though I had always had low expectations of Ryuu, even when we were children, I had not expected to be beaten by him. As I got up, dazed, I thought again about running away. But that option was going to be difficult and it didn't solve the next question: Then what? Best case scenario was to somehow get home where I would be put into a prison (although the internment camps would have been so much better than what I faced in Japan), worst case scenario was that I would walk out of Ryuu's door and he would have me put into prison as a prisoner of war. In the Japanese prison I was probably facing beatings and rape, no different than my future with Ryuu. At least with Ryuu I might not starve. Or, I found myself thinking as I picked myself up off the floor, if I didn't get sent to prison in Japan, I certainly would be reduced to begging or worse— prostitution—to survive. I slowly got to my feet and decided to face what came next.

"Well?" he said, leering at me.

"Well what?" I asked, slurring the words. My cheek felt numb. When I put my hand to it, it felt swollen. I hoped that I wasn't going to lose any teeth.

Ryuu raised his hand as if he were going to strike me again. "This is the first time, so I will give you a chance," he snarled.

"Apologize."

While it was degrading, I complied. Rather, I tried to comply. I wasn't sure what I was apologizing for. I couldn't even remember what we had been talking about before I had been struck. Passports, age, family...

"Ryuu, I'm sorry for my passport and my age," I stammered.

"Do not make me beat the truth out of you." Ryuu had his fist in the air again.

"What, Ryuu?" I cried out, cringing in anticipation of another blow. "What should I say? Please don't hit me again!"

"That's better." Ryuu's mood seemed to improve as he gained power over me. "How about apologizing for not letting me have my way with you when you were in Hiroshima?"

"What?" I stammered, completely taken aback. Blow two, not as bad as the first because I at least expected it this time.

"Apologize!" Spit streamed out of Ryuu's mouth he was so angry.

"Please! Please, Ryuu. I'm confused," I didn't know why I should apologize for not allowing a rape.

"Well, you know that you wanted me," he said. My blood chilled. "And you could have had me all along." What! Ryuu was such a narcissist. How to even respond to this?

Ryuu continued, "All you had to do was admit that we weren't family. We could have been together all this time." Ryuu had taken me into his arms at this point. He was looking at me with what may have been misinterpreted for love to a person who had walked in at that moment. If you ignored the blood dribbling out of my mouth.

"Ryuu, my mother is married to your uncle. He is my father."

"And yet he isn't, is he?"

How did he know? I never knew for sure. Ryuu was a very powerful man for a brief time period while Japan was winning the war. He knew people. He could pay people. And Japan had been watching the *Issei* and *Nisei* just as the FBI had been watching us. Maybe it was a guess. Maybe he knew exactly who my father was. I never asked. I did not want to give Ryuu the pleasure of thinking that I cared what he knew. I thought that only my mother and I knew the name of my biological father. My passport read Kimiko Miramoto. I would have to ask my mother if I ever made it home to her again.

"And so my little non-cousin," he continued, cooing in my ear as he rocked me back and forth, "we shall be married."

"Oh God," I thought to myself. "When Ryuu?" I asked him, hoping to buy time. My life would be made much worse if I were married to a Japanese man, especially this Japanese man. There was a knock on the door.

"Right now," he laughed. He opened the door, leaving me standing in the middle of the room in shock. In entered a handful of Japanese officials. One of the men—I'm not sure which—performed a marriage and the others witnessed. I don't recall consenting in any way. I remember thinking, as I was in the act of being married, that because of my time in the jail, I didn't even know what day of the year it was. I was married to Ryuu Miramoto on a day that is unknown to me in a geisha costume, with dried blood on my chin and a swollen cheek. It was September 1942 and Japan was winning the war.

THERESA LORELLA

13 ROSE MARIE

From archived interview, continued.

AT THE END OF the summer we moved to Camp Minidoka, a relocation center outside of the small town of Twin Falls, in Jerome County, Idaho. While we had been greeted in Puyallup by mud, dust was our welcoming committee at Minidoka. The government had hoped that we Western Washington residents would be able to turn Minidoka into a Garden of Eden of sorts. Literally: Minidoka was not only a relocation center, but an agricultural labor camp. Labor in the fields was optional; however, it was encouraged as a way to show patriotism to the war effort. Patriotism aside, it seemed that the work distracted people from the tedium of the camp. Even though many people in the Seattle Japanese community had not been farmers, it gave people something to do. So, with a newfound acceptance of our fate—there were no more open protests after the JACL-administration vote in Camp Harmony— most of us settled in with the goal of making the unknown future as comfortable as possible.

With this acceptance and subsequent release of anger came the foresight to realize that we had the power in our hands to make Minidoka as livable as we could. Personally, once we arrived in Idaho, my previous depression turned into a realization that I had a duty to my daughter to make her imprisonment as normal as possible. What a strange thing to say! "Make my daughter's imprisonment normal." She was still only three years old when we arrived in Idaho and already in prison. My heart broke for my daughter every time I thought about her future. So young and innocent and yet already so hated by the general population and her government.

Rosie had begun to realize that something was strange about our life right before we left Camp Harmony. While she had been fine—if a little confused—about our change of scenery, she obviously had no concept of the war or racism or internment. She certainly never sensed that she was perceived by her government to be a threat to national security. No, because she was so young, Rosie's primary concerns when we were evacuated were missing her toys and going to the park. My little one was also a creature of habit and it was strange to her to not be able to go about her usual activities in her little realm of the world. She missed her bed, she missed the yard. She was a tiny little gardener, even at that age, and she missed her grandmother's roses that I had told her were a special flower that I had named her for. I think that she thought that her grandmother and I had created Japanese roses just for her. She missed her grandparents and Aunt Maggie as well. She could not remember her Aunt Kimiko.

In absence of our family, Akio, Rosie and I became increasingly close with the Fusakas. Mr. and Mrs. Fusaka became surrogate grandparents to Rosie and continued to be a support for both Akio and I. Happily, the rift between Henry and Akio had been mended and the two became best friends, the brother that neither of them had had growing up. They took jobs together working the fields by day and spent the early evenings and weekends talking about getting out of the camp and showing their love for America. It was during this time period that Rosie began to call Henry, "uncle." Because we had no idea that Henry and Maggie were having any troubles communicating or otherwise, Akio and I assumed that this title would soon be true—just as soon as they could be physically present in the same state.

Henry never mentioned the lack of letters from Maggie, never explained what had happened between the two of them. Akio would at first ask if he had heard from Maggie and how she was; even we weren't able to communicate with the residents in Tule Lake very often so any news was welcome. Henry would brush off the question saying something like, "Yep, of course. She's good," and then he would change the subject. Not thinking that anything was wrong, I would fill my letters to Maggie with news of all of us, including the Fusakas. Her letters did not respond to this information that I could see, but the censors sometimes blacked out just about all of the substance of the letters so it was hard to say. I didn't realize that Maggie and Henry would go years before they were able to finish a conversation that began the night before Henry was evacuated.

*****

While the guys were out doing farm work together, I needed something to do. While I had not worked since Rosie was born, at least at home in Seattle I kept myself busy by keeping up the house and yard. Here there was little that I could do in our small barrack—the room was only about twenty feet square--here in Minidoka there was really only so much housekeeping that needed to be done in our little box home. Of course, there was always the dust, but that was a losing battle. I stopped focusing on it beyond what was needed for us to live in a semi-sanitary condition. I needed a hobby. Fortunately, many of the camp's residents were feeling the same restlessness and activities were actually starting to crop up.

After being encouraged by Mary Fusaka, I decided to take one of the adult education classes that had been organized by some enterprising internees. I looked through the camp newsletter and found a class in English literature. Before I had gotten pregnant, I had secretly wanted to go to college and study literature. And, to make it even more fun, my friend Toshi had organized the class. This, I thought, was a great opportunity to try my hand at a course and, as Mary said, get to know people in the camp. So, on the first day of class I left Rosie with Mary—my gracious babysitter—and set off for my class with only moments to spare before it was set to begin. Despite leaving the Fusuka's barracks at least ten minutes early, I was almost five minutes late by the time that I found the little shack where the class was to be held. I stood in front of the "classroom," took a deep breath, and went in.

Of course, I knew that I would most likely be the only non-Japanese person in the room. I even anticipated that many students would be older people who were not working in the fields or doing other labor. And, since I was running late by that time, I anticipated all eyes on me as I walked into the room. All of those things happened: I walked in and all eyes were on me. I took in the room as my eyes adjusted to the difference in light from the outside. I was the only Caucasian, non-Japanese person in attendance. And by "non-Japanese," I mean that I seemed to be the only person in the room who had not actually been born in Japan. The entire room was full of *Issei*—all except for my friend, Toshi, who I had met on my first day at Camp Harmony.

"Rose Marie!" she said as she recognized me. She seemed relieved to see me.

Toshi was standing at the front of the room, facing the class. I could tell that she was distressed. I thought maybe I had interrupted since I was late. "One moment," she said to the class followed by a phrase in forced Japanese. She came towards me at the door.

"Toshi," I said, "I'm so sorry that I'm late. Have I interrupted terribly?" This was much more embarrassing than I had anticipated. Toshi's response was not reassuring. "Let's go outside for a moment," Toshi whispered as she herded me back out the door. I felt like I was back in grade school, about to be scolded by the teacher. Toshi was taking this too far!

"Um, I'm sorry," I said, a bit confused. "I won't be late again." I hoped that Toshi wasn't planning kicking me out of class. It seemed strange that my friend seemed so upset because Toshi had always seemed so easygoing to me. I hoped that I hadn't upset her too much.

"Rose Marie," Toshi said again. "Something is wrong. There has been a misunderstanding."

"With the class you mean?" I asked. Obviously, I thought. What else could it be?

"Rose," she continued, "This is supposed to be an English literature class—a class where we read and discuss books. *In English.*"

"Of course, Toshi," I said. "That's why I'm here." What was I missing? "I thought maybe we could read something like Huck Finn; you know, what's right isn't always right and…" She was just staring. "Maybe that is too controversial? Should we not be calling into question the rightness of the law?" I laughed nervously. I was choking on the huge foot that I was sticking in my mouth here. Toshi looked at me with an amused look on her face before continuing.

"It is a good book," she agreed, "I would normally say let's do it, but did you notice anything about the class?"

"Well…" I began. How to best say, "They are all so *Japanese.* It just wouldn't sound right. "They all seem to be *Issei,*" I said, proud of myself for being so diplomatic.

"Yes," said Toshi. "This is fine, of course, although I was thinking that there would be at least a few *Nisei.* And you, of course, Rose Marie!" She squeezed my arm, genuinely happy to see me. I relaxed; she wasn't angry with me. "The thing is that none of them speak English…"

"Which makes it strange that they are here for a literature class," I completed the thought.

"Which they are not," said Toshi. "They are here because they think it is an *English* class. A learn-to-speak-English class."

"Oh," I said as I figured out what Toshi was saying. I had never thought of it that way, but I could see how the advertisements could have been confusing. Read and discuss English classics, or something that like. I was disappointed at first, but then it dawned on me that this could still be something for me to do, something more than just a passing diversion. "Well, that sounds like a good idea, actually."

"It does," agreed Toshi smiling. She and I seemed to be on the same page about this. "And it doesn't look like anyone was that excited about English literature."

"Hey," I laughed. "Except for me!"

"Okay," Toshi said after making a face and pointing at herself as if to say, "me too." "Well, what now?" she asked.

"Should we give it a shot?" I asked. "I mean, we might have to put off the Twain for awhile, but we've got plenty of time, don't we?" For the first time since the bombing, the unknown span of time of this evacuation didn't seem so daunting. I could use this time to do something.

"All the time in the world," she said as we linked arms and went back into the classroom and introduced ourselves as the new teachers.

Over the next three years, the English class would become my saving grace, a true calling for me while I was in the camp. After the first class, Toshi and I walked over to the Fusaka's barracks and enlisted Mary in our efforts. With her history with the missionaries, Mary had firsthand knowledge about ways to teach English as a foreign language. Mary would come to our class and help translate when absolutely necessary (we had an English-only policy). She would bring along my little girl who, besides being doted upon by dozens of grandmotherly ladies, acted as a "practice" conversationalist for beginning English-speakers. Rosie, after all, was fairly new to English herself. Through the years, Toshi and I taught several classes, eventually up to five days per week. After several months, the camp recognized our efforts and I was able to augment Akio's meager salary by earning a small teacher's salary. More importantly, I found a place amongst the *Issei* community. I felt like I belonged.

14 MAGGIE

From "The Roses of Minidoka," continued.

THERE WERE VERY FEW advantages to being interned at Tule Lake; I spent my time at the camp pretending I wasn't there, thinking about what my life would have been if I had not been sent there, and thinking about how to get out of there. The only real benefit of being stuck in that prison was being there with my mother. Prior to internment, I had historically had a complex relationship with my mother. I had always felt that she and I were at odds regarding our beliefs about how I should live my life; I was hoping to live my life as an American and my mother was hoping that I would live as a proper Japanese woman. Or so I had always assumed.

Before the internment, I had always thought of my mother as a prototypical Japanese wife, despite the fact that there was obviously a history that had led to the birth of Kimiko. She had always behaved so properly, helping my father with the house and farm. She was never subservient to my father, but my mother certainly doted on him. She was quiet and calm and reserved. In short, it seemed that such behavior came naturally to my mother and I thought that she expected it to come naturally to me as well. In reality, my natural behavior seemed to usually be the exact opposite—I was talkative and nosy and nervous and uninhibited.

Not only was I not the typical Japanese woman, I don't think that I was a typical American woman as far as women of my generation were concerned.

Because of her Japanese-ness, I was constantly in a state of embarrassment over my mother when I was a child. I rarely brought Caucasian friends to my house so that I didn't have to explain such cultural differences as my parents' foreign language or the use of chopsticks. I dreaded anytime that I had to have my parents involved in school functions and once went so far as to tell a teacher that my mother could not come to a mother-daughter tea party at the school because she had died. Of course, this caused quite a bit of confusion when the teacher to whom I told this lie actually came to our house one evening the next week to offer her "belated condolences" and my mother opened the front door. While this might have been bad enough in itself, the teacher, who had met my mother on several previous occasions, asked my mother if she was the new Mrs. Miramoto. Apparently my grade school teacher had difficulty telling Japanese women apart. In her defense, though, she did think that my mother was dead so her confusion was largely my fault. Unfortunately, I did not learn from this event, just perfected my lying skills. For years I would conveniently forget to tell my mother to come to the school and then tell the school that my mother was ill. I often did not tell my mother about events at all. After she showed up to one of my basketball games in a full kimono, I told her that I had quit the team and said that I was studying late at school when I had games.

Obviously, I didn't have to hide my mother in the camp— everyone had a Japanese mother. (Ironically, for kids like my niece, it was actually more of an issue to *not* have a Japanese mother than to have one in the camps. Everything was different during the internment.) It was also just my mother and me those first few months and we had to rely on each other to get through the ordeal of evacuating our home alone, being sent to a dustbowl in California alone and then to Tule Lake alone. We took our turns along the way of being the strong one and the weak one. When I could not control my fear or anger, my mother comforted me. When she could not control her despair over my father's incarceration in Montana or my sister's disappearance in war-torn Japan, I was her comfort. When I had cried about Henry or my fear of the future, she was my comfort. We really needed each other. Through this need came a deeper understanding and, I hope forgiveness, for past misunderstandings.

Our relationship took on a whole new meaning one day when we were newly arrived in Tule Lake. Mama and I were in the mess hall nearest to our barracks. We were both as giddy as young girls that day. We had just heard that the War Relocation Authority and whatever other pertinent powers that be had determined that my father was no longer threatening enough to national security to be held at Fort Missoula. My father was going to be coming "home" to us in Tule Lake.

After we got the news, Mama and I walked to the mess hall for lunch with our arms intertwined, planning a homecoming celebration for my father. We would invite our friends from Bellevue and pool together our stashes of cookies and dried fruit—party food. For once, the bleak conditions of the camp didn't bother me; I just wanted to see my Papa and have him fold me in his arms in a big hug. For the first time I felt the hole in my heart, the one right underneath the pearl ring that I wore around my neck, was filling back up. After the first few months of internment and separation, I still had no chance to speak to Henry. I had sent letters, but with no reply. Neither of us knew that our letters were being censured to the point of not being sent, or sent with so few words left that they were meaningless. My father's return would at least help heal the void in my mother's life and that was enough for awhile.

We were still rattling on about our party as we got our food and made our way to the long rows of tables in the mess hall we frequented. We scanned the benches for a place to sit; there was *never* a place to sit in the mess halls. This lack of space ended up breaking up the Japanese tradition of families eating every meal together. This was certainly true for large families in the mess halls. Nonetheless, there were just the two of us, so Mama and I pressed on, hoping to find a space for two.

"There's one, Mama!" I said, pointing to a table a couple of rows away from where we stood.

My mother's eyes followed my finger, saw where I was pointing, and she took off. While she was small and demure, my mother had a true talent for getting places quickly if the need to procure seating was involved. She was there before I was. As I walked up, she was already speaking to the *Issei* man whose back had been to us. I'm assuming that my mother asked the man if the seats next to him were taken. I had not heard, but what else could she have possibly said? I also did not hear the response, if there was one. When I arrived to the table my mother and the man were looking at each other, but each had an expression on their face like they had seen a ghost.

"Reiko?" the man asked looking up at my mother with his eyes squinted as if to see her better.

"No, sir," said my mother, in a voice that was deeper than her normal speaking voice. She sounded strange, as if she was purposely altering her voice. "You must have me confused with someone else."

The man said, "No..." as I said, "Mama?" My mother's response to both of us was to turn and walk away. Over her shoulder she gestured with her head for me to follow. Before I did, I turned and looked at the man who had turned around to face us. He was looking at me with curiosity, searching my face for the answer to an unasked question. "Um, excuse me," I mumbled to the man as I began to follow my mother. The man stopped me by putting his hand on my arm.

"What is your name?" he asked me.

I didn't really know what to do. In hindsight I probably should have kept walking, but it just came out, "Maggie Miramoto, sir."

"Ah," the man said. "I thought that you might be my daughter. You are too young though, I see."

"Excuse me, sir," I said again as I took my leave and tried to catch up with my mother. She had left the mess hall and seemed to be heading back towards our barracks.

"Mama," I called after her. She didn't respond. She was nearly running to get back to the safety of our little space. As I struggled to catch up with my mother I thought that maybe the man had said something rude or offensive; he certainly seemed confused, thinking I was his daughter. Maybe he was sick or something.

And then I stopped dead in my tracks, almost dropping the tray of uneaten food that I was still clutching. He had said her name. "Reiko," I heard him say: My mother's name. And he thought that I was his daughter, but too young. "Could it be?" I dared to ask myself. "Could that man have thought that I was Kimiko?"

*****

"I'm sorry, Maggie," my mother was whispering through her tears. We were back in our barracks, sitting on the cots that, when made for the day, acted as our living room furniture. I was facing my mother. She seemed so small with her hands tucked in between her knees rocking slightly back and forth to comfort herself.

"It's okay, Mama," I mumbled for the hundredth time, hoping that saying so would make it so. In truth, I wasn't sure if anything was going to be right ever again. How many things could possibly be turned upside down in my life? Was it only just a few months ago that I spent my days going to school, working the farm, and sneaking off to see my boyfriend?

I had known that my mother was married before; I thought she might be a widow for all she had ever spoken of her first husband. Clearly that was not the case. I realized that day that I had spent years thinking of my mother as nothing more than an embarrassment, a bundle of kimonos, foreign food, and old-fashioned concepts. Until a stranger had said my mother's name out loud, I had never thought of my mother as a person—a person with a life, a story of her own. My mother told me that story after we had sat in the dim barracks for several minutes in silence.

My mother, like my father, had been born in the prefecture of Hiroshima. Of course, Hiroshima was a big city, even then, and girls were not able to roam about freely. So my parents never knew each other in Japan, although they were originally in the same class and social station in their community. Each came from families of good standing both socially and economically. Each had ties to the ancient samurai class. However, around the turn of the twentieth century, the star of my father's family was rising rapidly while the star of my mother's family was quickly burning out. My father's father had made sound business investments that would only grow as the Japanese Empire expanded in the Pacific world. My mother's father, on the other hand, had inherited the family's fortune and quickly began to squander it.

Mama described her early childhood as happy, shielded from adult problems. Until she was older, there was still enough money for the family to live comfortably even while her father spent the family's money on liquor and gambling. For the most part, she had very few early memories of her father who, she later learned, spent most of his time living with his many mistresses in the capital. Her mother—my grandmother—had agreed to this separate living arrangement in order to protect my mother and her older sister from their father's volatile moods. My grandfather, apparently caring little for children who were not sons, showed little concern over his two daughters.

While my grandfather cared little for his daughters, Mama said that my grandmother adored her children. Mama and her sister—who I had never known about—would spend their days in the care of their mother who taught them to read and write in Japanese and even taught them a bit of the English that she had learned from missionaries as a girl during the Meiji Restoration. My grandmother would tell her daughters stories of the magical West where hills were made of gold and dreams came true. She made it sound enchanted and delightful—stories that she had no doubt learned from American missionaries who had embellished upon the attributes of their homeland.

More than any of these memories of her mother, though,

Mama's favorites were those of the times that she shared with her mother in the garden. My grandmother was an avid gardener. Her favorite flower was the rose. She loved all varieties of rose, but her favorite was the *Rosa rugosa*, or Japanese rose. She would gather my mother and my aunt around her Japanese rose bushes and point them out saying, "Look there at those roses. Of all the roses in my garden, those are my favorite," she said to her daughters.

"But they look different," said my Aunt Kimiko. "They aren't as pretty as the others."

"Look again, Kimiko-chan," my grandmother said to her oldest daughter. "They may look different, but that doesn't mean that they are less beautiful than the other roses in this garden." She turned to my mother and asked, "Reiko-chan, do you know what makes these roses special? Can you guess, Kimiko-chan?" When neither child answered, my grandmother gathered the girls in her arms and said to them, "The Japanese Rose is the most resilient and hardy of all roses. It survives."

My grandmother stopped speaking as tears welled in her eyes. When she had regained control again she smiled a sad smile and began speaking again. "My daughters, from now on, you two shall be my little Japanese roses. Kimiko, you are now Kimiko Rose and Reiko, you are my Reiko Rose. No matter how bad the conditions, you shall both survive. Like the flowers that you are."

Two days later, my grandfather arrived back to the family's Hiroshima home. Although my grandmother did not yet know it, he could no longer afford his Tokyo apartment, his fancy liqueurs, or his other women. The money was all gone and, thanks to his alcoholism and the syphilis that he had contracted from one of the women that he had kept in the capital, his mind was gone as well. He still, however, had managed to broker a last business deal, the engagement of Kimiko to a well known Tokyo family.

While he had never been a good father, Mama said her father had become a tyrant. What made this transformation more unbearable was the fact that my grandmother was clearly dying. Apparently her beloved missionaries had also brought along a foreign illness, tuberculosis. Perhaps because of this, my grandmother began to make the arrangements for the marriage of Mama; she must have hoped to have both girls married off before she died. My grandmother used her husband's name and began to make inquiries into suitable matches for my mother. She was able to access the family's financial information while her husband was too drunk or sick to get out of bed and discovered that he had lied to Kimiko's fiancé and there really were no assets left at all. In fact, the family was in debt to a degree that even selling the family home could not remedy. Also, after speaking to the local matchmakers, my grandmother discovered that her husband had sullied the family name in all of *Hiroshima-ken*. It was no wonder that Kimiko's fiancé was from Tokyo, where they may not have heard of my grandfather's failings.

Of course, news of failings travels faster than news of success. Not long after the announcement of my aunt's engagement, my grandparents received word from the fiancé's family that they were canceling the betrothal of their son to my aunt. They had been "led astray and lied to," they stated in the letter that my mother read when everyone in the house was asleep. They had no interest in marrying the daughter of a "debt-ridden, alcohol-weakened man who was more interested in visiting the pleasure women of Tokyo than in caring for his family." The words took the breath out of my young mother. Now that the family's reputation was tarnished, there would be little hope for her sister or her to marry well. My mother had no idea that she had already been married by proxy to a man in California.

When my grandfather read the letter later that day, once he had slept off a binge of drinking, he flew into a rage more violent than any the family had ever seen. Although the fault was all his own, he turned his wrath on Kimiko. "You dirty whore!" he screamed at her as his fists pummeled her body. "You have ruined this family!" For once my Aunt Kimiko stood up to her father.

"No, father," she spat back at him. "You have ruined this family. You are the failure." Her triumph was to be short-lived.

With my mother watching, my grandfather picked up his older daughter by her throat and sent her flying backwards. She landed with a dull thump, her head cracked open where it had hit the corner of the large wooden cabinet used to case the family's heirloom samurai sword.

My mother, not understanding what was happening and how it could even be happening, tried to cry out, but no words came out of her throat. She went towards her sister, to help her or to comfort her, but her mother was already there, standing at the cabinet looking at the face of her dead daughter. My mother described to me how my grandmother bent to the cabinet and removed the sword from its case. She held up the gleaming sword as if she was going to use it upon herself, but then, looking at my mother and then to my grandfather, she turned her wrist and lunged towards her husband. She killed him in one stroke. She then turned to her daughter, my mother.

"Reiko," she said, "Go to my room and look in the chest. In it you will find the papers that you need. My mother was motionless, no doubt in shock. "Go now, Reiko, leave now," my grandmother repeated. "And Reiko, remember that you are a Japanese Rose—you will survive this."

*****

By the time my mother had told me this part of the story, it was already nightfall at Camp Tule Lake. We still had not talked about the man in the mess hall, but I could see that my mother was exhausted, but she pressed on. It was dinnertime and we had not yet eaten our lunch. We were both hungry. "Mama," I said to her. "That is a terrible story. I don't know what else to say."

"It is a terrible story, Megumi-chan, my little blessing," she said with that sad smile she saved for moments of truth. "But there is also some beauty to it."

"Mama, you are telling me that your father killed your sister and that your mother killed your father! And then she killed herself?" I was in shock myself. "If I'm right, where's the beauty in that?"

"You are correct, my daughter," said my mother. "My father killed my sister and my mother did kill him. But she did so to avenge her daughter and to protect me. Once she had committed her crime, she had no choice but to end her own life. Besides, Megumi-chan, she knew she was dying anyway."

"Mama, how does the man in the mess hall play into all of this?" My head was beginning to reel; this was not the mother that served me *mochi* and tea at home in Bellevue when I was a child.

"He was the man in California that my mother had found for me to marry," she said. "I found the papers in her chest—the letters between the man and his family contracting for our marriage, my ticket to sail from Yokohama to San Francisco, and the picture of my husband. I was a picture bride."

"Mama" I asked meekly, my voice strangled by exhaustion, "is the man in the mess hall your husband?"

"Yes," she answered simply. "Rather, he was." She gave me a hug. "Don't worry, your father is my true husband; he and I were married in the courthouse in America—we are married." It was a little murky, but it was unclear if picture brides were married under the law. Mama and her first husband had never gotten married in a formal ceremony once Mama arrived in America.

"Does Papa know about the other man?" I asked. "Does he know all of these other things?" Please, God, I thought, let him know these other things. Knowing the history of my mother was enough of a burden on my young mind without having to worry about keeping it secret from my father.

"Yes, Megumi," she answered. "I was always very honest with your father. Before we married I told him everything. Certainly he knew that there must have been another man since I already had your sister…"

"Who you named for *your* sister," I realized.

"Yes," my mother continued, "so your father had some warning about that. And, I think to help him understand my actions regarding my first husband I had to tell him everything. Besides, it was only fair that he knew."

"Mama," I asked. "What happened with the first husband?"

"Well, I got off the boat in San Francisco with hope in my heart. I had time to heal while we crossed the Pacific. During the crossing I promised myself, God, and the souls of Kimiko and my mother that I would be a Japanese Rose; that I would survive so that they could live through me. I landed in San Francisco convinced that I would have a good life and not live in fear as we had in Japan."

She paused before continuing. "Of course, you have heard that the life of many picture brides was not what was expected, haven't you?" she asked me. I nodded. It was well known that many of the pictures used (by both the bride and the groom) in making picture matches were not accurate. The grooms were often quite a bit older than their pictures revealed. The brides often concealed defects of body or nature—or even the growing bump they had on their stomachs. The success of these marriages was varied, but, happy or not, most never broke up as the tradition of duty was stronger for most *Issei* than the more Western concept of "happiness."

"I was fairly lucky when I saw my husband," my mother had continued. "As you saw, he was not much older than I and he was not a bad looking man. He seemed pleased with me as well and I shyly sat beside him on the train to Oakland and the small house that he rented there."

"Was everything okay, Mama?" I asked. I was hoping to not hear any more morbid details, but I knew that something must have gone wrong.

"Come," she said, "let's go get our supper and I will tell you later."

"But what if we run into...*him*?" I asked her.

"Then we do," she said.

I am not sure which of the two of us was more worried as we walked towards the mess hall that evening. I suggested that we try a different mess hall altogether—preferably the one furthest from our usual hall—but my mother told me that we had to face this problem head on and she should not cower as she had earlier that day. Besides, she pointed out, he may not even be in this particular mess hall for dinner. After all, we had not seen him before and we had always eaten at the same hall. However, the man was not only at the mess hall that evening, but he was there waiting outside for us. When we saw him, my mother took a deep breath and walked towards him. They were close enough that I could hear.

"Reiko-san," said the man.

My mother answered simply, "Yes, Kenji-san. It is I."

"You look well," he said to her.

"As do you," she replied. "I am here with my daughter. My husband shall be joining us soon," she said. One would never have known that there was a history between them.

"Reiko-san," he said, apparently nervous by the situation. "What of the other girl—our daughter?" he whispered.

"Oh Kenji-san! Kimiko is stuck in Japan. I know nothing of her circumstances," said my mother. "She is a beautiful girl— smart and healthy."

"Ah," said the man—Kenji. "Then she is more like you than like me."

My mother seemed surprised. "You are different, Kenji-san," she said after appearing to give her words some thought.

"I am sorry that I hurt you," he replied. "I am sorry that I hurt our daughter. I hope that you may forgive me in this lifetime," he said earnestly.

"Leave me in peace and I shall try," answered my mother. Her first husband bowed to her.

"I shall," he answered. "Reiko-san?" he said suddenly as we had begun to walk away from him into the mess hall. "I stopped drinking after you left. I had always hoped that you would come back to me."

"It was not meant to be," replied my mother.

"I know that," he said in response. "I have also remarried. My wife is ill, but she is here with me. I will let you be. I wanted to let you know that."

"Thank you," said my mother.

"Reiko-san, please tell our girl to find my family if you are able to speak to her. They will help her while she is in Japan,"

Kenji continued. "Perhaps they can help."

"If I am ever able to speak to her, I shall do so," said my mother.

"I will bring you their contact information tomorrow and then not bother you again." My mother and this man bowed to each other and Mama and I entered the hall, where we ate dinner as if nothing unusual had occurred.

After dinner, back in our barracks, I told Mama how worried I had been when I saw Kenji standing outside the mess hall. My mother confessed that she, too, had been concerned. "You heard the comment about his drinking, no?" she asked me. I had. My mother continued her story, picking up where she had left off.

Soon after arriving in Oakland, Mama learned that, like her father, Kenji had succumbed to the power of alcohol. This, my mother said, had led to unexpected fits of violence early in her marriage to Kenji. While these rages were not always directed towards her—they were often caused by work or the discrimination that an *Issei* faced on the streets—the anger and results of the rage did often reach my mother. He did not hit her at first, she said, but he threw things. Often these objects would be heavy and hard and could easily have caused physical harm if they had hit my mother. While this was difficult and brought about memories of her family, Kenji's rages did not occur every day and only seemed to happen when Kenji had been drinking. Thinking that the problem could perhaps be easily solved, my mother began to sabotage her husband's drinking by watering down his beer and slowly pouring out his sake when he wasn't looking. She would only do a tiny bit at a time so that he would not notice a huge difference in his supply quantity all at once.

Despite the turmoil, after twelve months of marriage, my sister was born. My mother named her for her own sister and remembering her mother's words about the Japanese Rose gave her the middle name Rose. Unfortunately, if my mother hoped that she would now have a happy marriage, she was increasingly disappointed with her husband. Kenji's mood only grew worse when Kimiko was born—he was upset that she was not a boy and even more upset that his wife was now preoccupied with a baby. Having the child also made the small family's money problems worse as they now had to provide for three. It did not help, my mother said, that Kimiko was a colicky baby who kept both of her parents up at night with her screams.

When Kimiko was just a few months old, my mother began to see that things were getting dramatically worse with Kenji. His moods were darker and his anger towards Kimiko had seemed to grow into hate. One day, when he had come home smelling already of wine, he went to the cabinet where the sake was kept. He fumbled his hand to the back of the cabinet and brought out the now almost empty bottle. My mother had not been careful with her last pouring of the liquor and too much had come out. This time Kenji noticed. He began to scream and that made little Kimiko do the same. My mother, who was trying to plead with her husband to calm down, that he was confused, saw what was about to happen only a split second before it occurred. "Just shut that fucking baby up!" Kenji screamed, not to his wife, but to the room in general. In that split second, his arm went in the air and my mother ran towards her daughter. The bottle of sake hit her square on the back, blocking the clear aim at her baby's head. Kenji stormed out of the room, out of the house.

While Kenji was gone—probably at the tavern—my mother packed up her few belongings and those of the baby. She had been stashing money away under a rug in the bedroom, a penny or two left over from grocery shopping and the like. She raided that stash. Realizing that it was not enough to get her very far, she found some money that Kenji had left in his coat pocket. He had left the coat in his hurry to leave. Due to the large amount of money she found, it seemed that my mother's husband must have been paid earlier that day. My mother took only half of the money she said, not wanting her Kenji to not have enough to pay the rent. By the time that Kenji must have gotten home that night, my mother was already well on her way towards her new life and, eventually, my father. "I was on my way to find happiness," she finished her story with a happy ending.

*****

My mother's happiness was restored to her just days later: Papa arrived at Tule Lake after months of separation from Mama, first in immigration holding and then in a DOJ camp. Mama and I went to the gates with the other families who had the luck to be reunited with their husbands and fathers to form an impromptu welcoming party. I kept my eyes peeled on the bus door, anxious to see my Papa, day dreaming about running up to him in welcome. However, when my father walked down the stairs of the bus, I did not recognize him immediately. My planned show of love was thwarted as I stood there like a statue, not even recognizing my own father. Honestly, as Papa stepped into the daylight, I thought that he was there for one of the other families and I continued to stand on my toes and strain to see behind the man coming off the bus. But that man was looking at my mother and me and smiling. "Reiko! Megumi!" the man exclaimed.

"Papa" I yelped, more out of surprise than recognition. It was a question, not a welcome. Still, Mama and I ran towards my father as he moved slowly towards us. While he was nearing sixty at the time, before his imprisonment he had been healthy and strong—a farmer. This man who had returned to us was every bit his age. He could have been an even older man. His shoulders were more hunched; his hair grayer and thinner than I remembered. He had lost the spring in his step. My father was an old man.

Still, though his body may have caught up with his years, there was still a discernible sparkle in Papa's eye. I saw it as he looked at my mother. I can say with confidence that my father loved my mother. No matter what her family history or the fact that she had been married before, he loved her. She had told me that nothing seemed to detract my father from courting her when he met her in the boarding house in Seattle where he was staying and she was working as a housekeeper. Even the fact that she had a little girl by another man did not bother him. Rather, my mother told me that he had been enchanted with her pretty little girl and calling her his "Little Samurai" because of her self assurance and noble bearing. He had been more than willing to accept Kimiko as his own. My mother, too, loved my father. That I saw as I watched them together in Tule Lake and in the years that followed. My mother had always been a dutiful Japanese wife to her husband. When I was younger I had felt that her feelings for my father were based upon duty, tradition. I knew now that my mother did not let old-fashioned ideas of duty rule her life. She lived by her heart. And when my father took her in his arms that day at Tule Lake, I saw that my father was in my mother's heart.

The next few months at the camp were gloriously uneventful. Ever since meeting with Mama's first husband and hearing her story, I had been worried that Kenji would not keep his word to leave my mother alone. When I heard my mother telling my father about Kenji's presence, I had expected anger or jealousy to flare. But there was nothing. My mother, after all, had not kept any secrets from my father. Once, the two men did come face-to-face at a camp event. They simply bowed a general hello to each other and went on their separate ways, two men who were complexly tied to each other but who had no business with each other. They accepted that fate had brought them together on the peripheries of each other's lives and they respected the roles that their fates had dealt them in this lifetime.

*****

Letter from Reiko Miramoto, Tule Lake to Kimiko Miramoto, Japan, late 1942. Returned by camp censors, not approved for delivery.

My dearest Kimiko-chan,

I am having your sister write this letter for me as you know my English is not so very good. I am here in (portion redacted) with your sister and father. I think of you every day and hope to see you soon. Please forgive me for sending you to (portion redacted). I thought you would enjoy it. I miss you so much. If you need help, I am sending you the names of some people who may be willing; just tell them who you are: (Portion redacted.) I love you so much. Your father and sister are fine and send their love. I hope to see you soon my little Kimiko-chan.

Your loving mother.

15 KIMIKO

From treason confession, continued.

BY NOVEMBER OF 1942, I had settled into my life as the wife of Ryuu Miramoto. Of course, that is not to say that I was happy, just that I had accepted that I was married to my husband. I had not become complacent nor did I want to be married to Ryuu. By saying that I "accepted" my fate, I mean only that I realized that I was actually married to the man and denying that fact would not help me in any way. I still had the goal of making it back home. But that goal had to go onto the backburner and I had to focus on surviving: Surviving the war, surviving Japan, surviving Ryuu. While I was surviving, I figured that I had two priorities: One, I had to be crafty and try to use my situation to my advantage if at all possible and two, I had to try to minimize any future damage that my marriage might pose for my re-entry into America.

Unfortunately, in the balance of helping and hurting my chances of getting back to America, my marriage was already presenting huge dangers to my repatriation. I was now officially the wife of a man with ties to the Imperial Army. In fact, I learned right away that "we" were friends with many men of influence and rank within the Empire. These ties were certain to raise suspicion with United States officials when I managed to get away from Ryuu. However, possibly worse than the company we kept was my new citizenship status. When Ryuu and I were married, he had my name inscribed in his family's register. This is normally the goal in a Japanese marriage. For me, of course, my registry in the Miramoto family registry meant that I had declared my citizenship allegiance with Japan. In effect, I had renounced my United States citizenship. Or, more accurately, my husband did so on my behalf. "Now you are truly a Miramoto," he said when he broke the news to me. Ironically, I was now an official member of my father's family. I was truly a Miramoto.

My new associations and registration could not be changed, I told myself and I had to press on. I had learned from my first day of marriage that crossing Ryuu would not result in any sort of pleasant disagreement and I saw no benefit in being beaten more than could be avoided. While it pained me to do so, I decided that there was no need for me to cause fights that were unnecessary to the ultimate task at hand. I had to save my strength for the war and not waste it on meaningless battles of the will. And so I fell into life as Ryuu's Japanese wife. I mimicked the demeanor that I had seen *Issei* women adopt towards their husbands, but, assuming that the *Issei* were more Americanized than I might have given them credit for in my youth, I exaggerated that demeanor to an almost saintly level of devotion and wifely duty towards my husband—outwardly; he couldn't control my thoughts even if he controlled my body and movements. After two months of marriage, I had learned my husband's routine and tried to anticipate his every need. I did it to avoid any problems. I did it because I had nothing else to do during that time. More importantly, I did it to earn enough trust from my husband that I would someday be able to gain a bit of freedom. I had to work stealthily and with great patience.

Strangely, there were moments in those first few months of my marriage where I thought that, in another lifetime, I could have settled into my life with Ryuu. I did not love him, but he may have loved me. Or at least, he may have felt towards me a feeling that was as close as he could come to love as normal people know it. If he was happy with me, I would see his gaze soften and he would smile at me. At these times he reminded me of a little boy who was afraid of going through life not being loved. When he let down his guard, I felt differently towards him. Not love, but pity. Most of the time, though, he was just a bully. How he became this way, I did not know. Even though I was his wife, I knew very little of Ryuu's past and what could have made him the way that he was. All that mattered to me was that he was that way and I had to deal with it on a daily basis.

We spent very little time with Ryuu's family. I'm not even certain when he told the remaining Miramoto family that he had married me. By that point, though, there were not that many members of the clan left to tell. His parents were dead and most of the extended members of the family had left Hiroshima— some for America, others for Tokyo. However, despite our lack of family, Ryuu and I did not have a lack of people to entertain. Ryuu proved to be well connected in Tokyo thanks to his business dealings in this and previous wars. Ryuu had made his money on the success of the Empire and he was eager to use that success to continuously improve his financial and social position. Now that he had money, my husband wanted power.

And so I became hostess to some of the most notorious members of Hirohito's government. Generals, colonels, millionaires, and distant relatives of the emperor came to my table for tea or dinner. The crowning achievement was the day that I hosted afternoon tea for the wives of the Imperial military's generals and other officers. This was followed by a dinner for General Tojo himself. These meals were pure psychological torture for me. While I had nearly perfected my spoken Japanese by that time, it was still apparent that I was not a Japanese wife. Although I tried fervently to behave as a Japanese wife would while serving my guests, my mannerisms were still foreign. The very way that I carried myself screamed American.

As the months passed, I worked on this more than anything else—to pass as a Japanese woman. I was not doing so to be any less American, but to avoid putting myself in a situation where I had to explain my complicated life. Fortunately, my husband knew better than to give many details about our marriage and so our guests did not automatically know that I was *Nisei*. Until I perfected my way of moving and speaking and being, it was I who announced that I was an American. Once my guests guessed at my heritage, it inevitably unleashed a barrage of compliments for my loyalty to my true roots and how correct I was in denying my American citizenship and marrying a loyal citizen of the emperor. It made me sick.

For those who say, "Well, Kimiko, why didn't you stand up for your country? Why did you just put your head down and let your silence pass for modesty while the enemy spoke ill of your country?" I can say only that I did not want to die. While it may seem to be an overly dramatic statement now, I can assure you that you did not look a man like General Tojo in the eye and tell him to go to hell. It would have been a wonderful experience, but I would not be here today to tell you about it. And so that means that I am alive today to tell you that I served a beautiful dinner to General Tojo, the man who orchestrated the attack on Pearl Harbor, killing thousands of Americans, launching the Pacific War and causing the imprisonment of the people that I loved. At the end of that dinner, the general bowed to me and said that I was a testament to the loyalty of the Japanese people abroad. I did not take that as a compliment; I am not telling you this to brag.

Amongst the list of our illustrious guests, there was one that I dreaded more than the others. It wasn't that there was anything more disturbing about Colonel Shigetsugu Tsuneishi than the other officers and officials that I had met. All of them were the direct enemy of my country and all of them could have put me into prison—or worse—at the drop of a hat. But amongst all of these men, Tsuneishi caused a much more immediate terror for me. Tsuneishi was the head of Radio Tokyo. He produced programs in English that were broadcast throughout the Pacific. These programs, although they often had the opposite effect, were intended to demoralize the U.S. troops fighting in those regions. For Tsuneishi, there was no better employee than a *Nisei* living in Japan, or a *Kibei* as they were called. (While I had studied in Japan, I still always called myself a *Nisei*—I liked to think that I was still completely American, despite the facts.) He saw the *Kibei* as a major asset; not only did the *Kibei* speak English—which was a skill that Tsuneishi could have found elsewhere—but the *Kibei* were born and raised American. Therefore, he figured, they (or we, as the case may be) understood the American troops. And, you see, if we understood the troops we would be that much more effective at brainwashing them with our propaganda. We would know where they were the weakest and be able to attack accordingly. That was his thinking; he wasn't necessarily correct.

As with my husband's other acquaintances, at first Tsuneishi did not know that I was *Nisei* or *Kibei*. His dealings were primarily with my husband and I did not have to do much direct entertaining. As I slipped in and out of the room I would overhear Tsuneishi speak of his staff of *Nisei* men who had defected to Japan and were now in charge of his programs that were staffed by American and British prisoners of war. Tsuneishi had fished in the city's prisons and found the captured prisoners with radio or broadcast experience and put them to work. It was very clear that there was no choice in the matter for these soldiers. This was especially true with the soldiers Tsuneishi put to work on Zero Hour at the end of 1943.

Tsuneishi and Zero Hour would eventually cause me quite a bit of grief towards the end of the year and into 1944. In the meantime, though, I was feeling quite a bit of grief about the constant nausea that I started experiencing the first week of February 1943. I smiled through my days with my husband and I endured any dinner parties that I had to host, but it became increasingly evident that I was pregnant with Ryuu's child. I had not experienced my monthly courses since December, but I had been under a lot of stress and I thought that might have interrupted my cycle. Essentially, I denied all the signs of my pregnancy until almost March. By then I was three months pregnant.

Unfortunately, I have to say that I honestly was not happy to be pregnant. I had tried my hardest to prevent pregnancy the first couple of months of my marriage, but I certainly did not have access to anything besides the word "no" and that was meaningless in my marriage. Of course, there were options available to women who were desperate, but they did not work, sterilized you, or were hard to access. For a woman who never left the house, I had no means to even get my hands on such things should I have been willing to use them. Besides, I can only imagine what would have happened to me if Ryuu had found some type of crude birth control device in the apartment.

The pregnancy was therefore not only unwanted, but it plunged me into a vortex of depression that was so deep I was afraid I would be swallowed whole by my own sadness. I had dealt with my marriage to Ryuu by accepting it in the present, but by assuming that I would be free to leave in the future. I was clearly in denial. How did I truly expect to walk away from my husband one day and get on a boat or plane for America? What would I do when I got there? The fact of the matter is that things just don't work that way. But, my mother had left her first husband, my father, so I suppose I thought that I could do so, too. But that was in America.

My marriage had already potentially cost me my citizenship and put me at the dinner table with some of my country's greatest military enemies. Those hurdles were practically insurmountable in my hopes of returning home. But now I would have a child, a baby, to contend with. I could run away with my own self and risk my life to leave, but how could I risk the life of my own child to do so? And the child would be Japanese—how would I get it into the United States? I realized that the only way to save myself would be to abandon my own child. I knew that I would not be able to do that. So my unborn child became the true jailor who bound me to Japan. This thought led me to loathe my own baby. Try as I might, my depression only increased as I realized that I could not forgive myself for hating my own child so much.

Ryuu, of course, was overjoyed by the news that he was going to be a father so soon into his marriage. He began to speak incessantly of his "son" and how he would be a great general for the Empire. "Maybe," he would say to me as he rubbed my growing belly, "maybe our son will be a general in control of our new holdings in the West." When I did not respond, Ryuu must have mistaken my silence for misunderstanding. "He'll control America, Kimiko," he said to me with vigor. "Our son will bridge the divide between America and Japan and teach America to how to bow to the rising sun." How ironic, I remember thinking that *I* had been sent to Japan to be a bridge between the two cultures of Japan and America in the upcoming Pacific Era. Was this then the fruition of my parents' dreams for me?

*****

One of the positive aspects of my pregnancy was that it allowed me to slow down my marital and entertaining duties. I was sick for the vast majority of my second and third trimesters, losing weight at an alarming rate. The doctor who Ryuu hired for me ordered me to stay in bed. This way I was no longer expected to pour tea for Tsuneishi or other dignitaries. I was also excused—most of the time—from having to perform wifely duties with Ryuu. My only job for the long months of 1943 was to gestate Ryuu's baby. Still hoping for a great general out of the deal, Ryuu was a loving and doting husband as long as I kept my mouth shut. After a couple months of Ryuu asking if there was anything at all that I wanted, I held my breath and asked for some paper and some paint. I was able to paint my watercolors while propped up in my bed. This was the happiest time in my marriage. I even started to gain healthy pregnancy weight. I remembered that there was more to life than what I was dealing with. Thank God, I began to look forward to being a mother.

Because a doctor suggested early on in my pregnancy that I stay in bed and rest—mostly for my mental health, I think--Ryuu hired a girl to come in and wait on me and help me with everyday tasks. I suppose that I should have hated Hatsu, but I could not help but like her. In fact, I felt sorry for her. She was a young bride, already widowed by the war. While I knew that she was sleeping with my husband while I could not do so, I also knew that Hatsu was a kind-hearted girl who obviously had nowhere else to go than to be my maid and my husband's receptacle of punches and caresses while I was out of commission.

It was apparent from the start that Hatsu felt guilty for the sick relationship that Ryuu no doubt forced upon her, for she went above and beyond the duties of her employment to see to my comfort. While to a more cynical eye Hatsu's attentions may have seemed fawning and insulting in light of the fact that she was more kind to me after having slept with my husband, I knew that Hatsu's ministrations towards me were based upon a strange sort of mutual understanding between the two of us. We were both prisoners of Ryuu and the situation that Japan had created in the world. Because of the war, we were both deserted and penniless and left to survive in a world of opportunistic men. We were both just trying to survive and I could not hold that against Hatsu, try as I might.

Because I could see that she and I were in similar straits, I tried my hardest to befriend Hatsu. It took awhile, but she eventually realized that I was not her enemy, not worried that she was taking my place. (Of course, in many ways I was happy that somebody else had caught Ryuu's eye.) Still, I had to play my cards carefully because I was not sure at first whether Hatsu would use any of my attempts at friendship against me to barter for Ryuu's affection. I started by speaking of my home and how I missed my family. She would counter tentatively saying how lucky I was to have my husband. "Yes," I answered, "but I still miss my parents." One day, after several weeks of playing this game of feeling each other out, Hatsu responded to my statement about missing my family by saying, "I miss my husband." The ice was broken. We became confidants. In June, Hatsu confided that she was pregnant by Ryuu.

*****

I gave birth to a little girl on September 15, 1943. Present at the birth of my daughter was the doctor, my husband, and Hatsu, who was six months pregnant herself at the time. When Ryuu saw that the child was a girl, he was visibly disappointed. He left the room screaming to the doctor to shut up the baby and make sure that I was sewn up "as good as new." I was disgusted. I knew that my months of pregnancy had been a reprieve between a bad marriage and one that was surely going to only be worse. Finally, when the doctor and Hatsu had left the room as well, I held my daughter and looked down into her little face. All of the feelings of resentment towards my unborn child disintegrated as I held the living baby in my arms. "Kiyoko," I said to her. "You are called Kiyoko, the pure child. You will not be touched by the imperfections of your parents. You will endure. Kiyoko Rose."

16 ROSE MARIE

From archived interview, continued.

WE FINISHED UP THE year 1942 without much hope of leaving Minidoka. Instead of thinking about leaving, we spent the time getting used to our new life; I was suddenly so busy my life as it was that I didn't have time to think about the life I had left behind. I was focused on my teaching and my daughter, who was literally growing from a baby into a little girl in front of my very eyes. However, even though the war lingered on without an end in sight, things were starting to change. First there was the option of leaving the camp to work on sugar beet farms in places like Montana where the war effort was causing a shortage of farm hands as men joined the service and left to fight. Many people exercised this option and headed east. Although Akio and I wanted out of Minidoka more than anything and even though Akio had a background in farming, we decided that we would not tempt fate and opt for release through the farming program. We had enough of a problem with our interracial status in Seattle— we did not want to push our luck by going into the middle of the country where most people had never seen a Japanese American, let alone one with a Caucasian wife and mixed race child.

Around this time, however, while I was finally settling into life in Minidoka, Akio began to speak again of his desire to prove his loyalty to his country by being allowed to fight. Although we were not allowed unfiltered news in the camps, we knew enough of what was going on outside the barbed wire to know that the going was tough in the European theater and even tougher in the Pacific theater of the war. Goaded on by Henry and several other *Nisei* men in the camp, Akio became almost obsessed by his desire to join the U.S. Army and fight for his country. I was not exactly supportive of this obsession. Hadn't we learned in Camp Harmony to just keep our mouths shut and our heads down?

"Akio," I would often ask him when he was in one of his fervors about enlisting, "why are you so intent on fighting in the war? Men are dying everyday. As bad as it is to be locked in this camp, at least I know that you are going to survive."

"Rose," he would always answer with his characteristic patience, as if he was talking to Rosie instead of me, "the fact that other men are out there dying is exactly the reason that I should be there, too. I'm no different than any other American out there fighting for his country, for what's right. I should be there with them."

"But people are saying that the Army would probably keep the *Nisei* separate," I said, referring to rumors of an all-*Nisei* unit being formed. "Then you will not be with the other Americans. They won't get to see how brave and loyal you are." Usually by this point in the conversation, my desperation to keep my husband safe and sound with me was manifesting itself as anger.

"Just being there will show our loyalty," countered Akio. "It does not matter if we will have to fight in all-Japanese units or with any other type of unit. We just want to do our part."

Because of the lack of privacy in the camp, because anyone who wanted to could listen in on our conversation, and because I knew that would not be able to change Akio's mind, I would usually stop arguing with him at this point in the conversation. But even though I did not say it out loud, I wanted to shout to my husband, "What about your family, your child? Why do you want to go off to war and be killed and leave me and your daughter alone?" And, once I had worked myself into a proper fit of anger over the whole thing, I wanted to know how Akio expected to go off to war and "prove" his loyalty by dying for his country and leaving me as the widow of a *Nisei* man with a *Sansei* child to raise on my own. How would I raise a Japanese American girl without my husband in a world where Japanese Americans were put into camps for the crime of being Japanese American? How was I going to explain that to my child? I needed my husband to help me. I was afraid of losing him to the war that had already taken so many husbands from their wives.

Ultimately, though, once my anger subsided, I realized that I was proud of Akio for being brave, for being a big enough person to put aside the injustice being done to him and to his family and still wanting to fight for the country. Despite the feelings of personal loss and emotional upheaval that I felt at the time and for years to come, I look back now and realize that my husband was a hero in the truest sense of the word. He was everything that is good about America; he didn't need to prove it to me.

To my great happiness, it seemed that the government was fairly reluctant to let the *Nisei* out of the camps for any purpose except manual labor. Despite the desire of Akio and many other *Nisei* to fight in the war, that honor was not easily acquired and, for many months, seemed to be an almost unobtainable goal. Finally (and unfortunately for me), after months of speculation and hope, there was a breakthrough. In late January 1943, the government presented to the internees a "Loyalty Questionnaire." The proper answers to the questions in the questionnaire could be the *Nisei*'s ticket out of the camps, either to fight in the war or to go to university outside of the relocation camps and the exclusion zone. The improper answers led to an assumption that the person taking the questionnaire with such answers was not loyal at best, a traitor at worst. But, regardless of the strife caused by certain answers to the document, the questionnaire itself nearly caused a war amongst the camp populations. Lines were drawn in the camps once again, this time between the so-called "Yes-Yes" and "No-No" factions—lines that accentuated and brought to a head all of the differences of opinion and tensions within the *Issei* and *Nisei* populations in the internment camps.

*****

Although everyone in the camp was excited and talking about the impending Loyalty Questionnaire, I had other things on my mind. At the end of December 1942, my friend and co-teacher Toshi was due to become a mother for the first time. Her expected delivery was anticipated to occur the week between Christmas and New Year's. It's hard to say who was more excited for her, me or Toshi herself. Needless to say, when Toshi went into labor on the morning of Christmas Eve, we were all excited about her Christmas baby. We had all planned a Christmas Eve gathering for that evening with Toshi and her husband and the Fusakas, and we were going to attend our respective religious ceremonies in the morning. I was looking forward to Christmas that year; I had saved up some of the salary that I was receiving from the War Relocation Authority for teaching and had ordered Rosie a beautiful doll from the Sears catalogue. I made certain to order it well in advance of the holiday so that it would both arrive in the middle of nowhere, Idaho, and have time to be inspected for entry into the camp before Christmas. The doll was going to be perfect—it had a chubby little face and beautiful silky dark hair. It looked just like my little girl. I couldn't wait to see her face when she opened her sock on Christmas morning.

Rosie was just old enough that year to really understand the concept of Christmas presents and Santa Claus. This was somewhat unfortunately timing, however, seeing as how Akio and I had both limited resources for gifts and, even if we had had more money, we had limited opportunities for spending what we had. Because of this, I had hoped that Rosie would remain oblivious to Christmas traditions until we left the camps and we could resume with our usual dinner and get-together with family. Of course, we still did those things at Minidoka—but rather than eating in a decorated home we ate in a decorated mess hall and, while we could not be around our family, we were surrounded by our makeshift camp families. Even in that prison in the barren outback of Idaho, we still had a pretty hearty Christmas spirit.

But then, you have to enjoy the moments in life that you can, regardless of your circumstances.

Rather than being dissuaded by the surroundings, the camp's children had caught the adults' Christmas spirit. Rosie was not immune to that enthusiasm, nor was she immune to a concern that became very prominent for many of the children—the issue of Santa Claus. One night, not long after Thanksgiving, I picked up Rosie from her camp preschool class (we had gone from slats in the walls to preschools!). Even though she was getting heavy I had picked her up and, head bent down against the icy wind, was carrying my daughter so that we could get back to the relative warmth of our barracks as quickly as possible. With her little head next to my ear I could hear her saying something about Christmas. I couldn't quite make it out through the five layers of handkerchiefs that I had tied over my ears in an attempt to create earmuffs. I mumbled back a generic response such as, "Yes it will soon be Christmas, Rosie," but my daughter was adamant about her question.

When we got back to the barrack and I had a chance to unbury each of us from our copious layers of clothing, she began again. "Mama," she said, with all of the gravity of her little four-year-old self. "Mama, it is almost Christmas."

"Yes, I know, Rosie," I answered. "Aren't you excited?"

"Mama," she said again, getting exasperated that her mother clearly didn't understand the gravity of her news. "Mama," she was more to the point, "will Santa be able to find us here?"

This seemed simple. "Of course, sweetie," I answered.

"But we're not at home," my daughter pointed out.

"No, but Santa knows where you are," I said. Still, Rosie's brow was furrowed, her lips pursed in thought. "Don't worry, honey. He'll find you," I said, getting down on my knees to look into her eyes. "I'll bet he even has a great gift for you all ready to put into your stocking." Honestly, I was very excited about that doll. She was still looking upset.

"There's no chimbley," Rosie countered, clearly too old to simply believe me because I'm her mother. I was going to have to actually reason this out with her.

"*Chimney*," I corrected, "But not to worry—Santa can still get into fill your stocking."

"But, Mama," Rosie was insistent, "There's no chimbley because we're in jail camp. Jail is for bad people and Santa only comes for good girls." Tears were welling up in her eyes. She had been forced to spell it out for her slow mother.

"No, Rosie," I said, taking my daughter in my arms, "You are not a bad person. This camp is not for bad people. I promise." Although she was smart enough to be a little reluctant to accept this simple explanation—Rosie always reminded me of her Aunt Maggie that way—her tears dried. I knew that I had to make sure that Santa did not pass over my daughter's sock this Christmas.

I had the doll and Santa on my mind the morning of December 24, 1942 when Toshi's husband came to our barrack's door. His knock was more of a bang and I ran to open the door sensing that something was wrong. "It's Toshi," he said. "She's in the infirmary."

I left Rosie with Akio and ran over to the camp infirmary with my friend's husband. Toshi was in the early stages of labor. Why her husband came for me was at first unclear except that Toshi must have wanted me with her. I had, after all, given birth before (and, of course, we had become good friends). However, when I arrived to Toshi's bed, I discovered that her request for me was not completely centered on our friendship. "Please," Toshi said, imploring me with her eyes when I arrived, "please find a doctor." I said that I would, stepped into the hall and asked Toshi's husband, who had followed me back to the camp "hospital" unit why he had not found the doctor himself.

"Rose," he said, "You know as well as I that there is only one doctor assigned to this camp. I spoke to the nurse. She said he is in Twin Falls celebrating Christmas. Apparently this is not high on his list of priorities. I thought that maybe if you asked…"

"That he might come if a non-*Nisei* asked," I finished his sentence for him. "Well," I thought out loud, "I'm not sure that I have that much more influence seeing as how I'm pretty well known as a "Jap-lover," I could say it now without cringing, "But let's find out."

"Thank you, Rose Marie," Toshi's husband had tears of gratitude in his eyes. I set off to find the nurse.

The "nurse" was really just a *Nisei* girl fresh out of high school and not trained in nursing at all; still, nurse was her title at Camp Minidoka. When I found her, she was on the infirmary phone leaving a message that seemed to be for the doctor. "Please have him call me," she was saying. "Yes, I know it is Christmas, but a patient needs him." There was a pause. "Yes, I am calling from the camp." And then a plaintive, "Please!" And then she hung up the phone.

The nurse had her back to me. I did not want to startle her. She seemed to be crying, but I could not be certain. "He's not coming, is he?" I asked her softly.

"I can't find him. I don't know what to do," she said as she turned towards me. "I'm not a nurse." She put up her hands plaintively, as if to show that she had no tricks up her sleeves. "I've never done this before." I was about to let her know that it was okay, as in not her fault, but our conversation was interrupted by screams from Toshi's room. The baby was on its way.

There was no time to think. The nurse (it's not her fault that she wasn't trained and so I'll call her a nurse) and I went into action. The nurse ran to find rags. Toshi's husband went to find hot water, which, even in the infirmary was hard to come by. I went to Toshi and found her on the floor. I got her into a squatting position, but could not get her back into the bed. She was red in the face and screaming in pain. She laid herself back down on the floor and refused to get up.

By the time the nurse and Toshi's husband got back, it was clear that the baby was ready to come at any minute. Trying to find a spot in my subconscious were I could remember exactly how I gave birth to Rosie, I did my best to guide my friend through her delivery. Pretending that I was not averse to blood and fluids, I stuck my head up under my friend's nightgown as she pushed and hoped to see the head of her baby. What I did see made my blood run cold.

"It's upside down!" I screamed out to anyone who could hear.

"Breach?" screamed back the nurse.

"No, thank God," I responded, "but the head is turned the wrong way. It can't ease itself out this way. It's stuck on the bone. It needs to be turned." I had learned this from my own obstetrician when I was pregnant with my daughter.

Of course, since we were not medically trained, none of us knew how to turn a baby in the birth canal. Just before my calm gave way and panic set in, the phone rang. It was the camp doctor. His wife had given him the message that his nurse had called. He was on his way. It would take at least an hour for him to get to us, he said. "What do we do?" asked his nurse into the phone, frantic. She nodded solemnly as the doctor spoke to her and then she came back into the room where Toshi's screams had turned to low moans.

"We have to find a doctor," said the nurse.

"I thought the doctor was on his way?" asked Toshi's husband.

"He may not be here in time," Toshi managed to gasp. She had gone white, like a ghost. Please don't let my friend die, I prayed.

"There has to be a doctor here!" I exclaimed. "Come on, think!" I demanded. "Who was a doctor in Seattle?" The Seattle Japanese community had been comprised of doctors, lawyers, shopkeepers, bankers. Professionals and business owners. There had to be a doctor within the barbed wire walls of our camp.

Toshi's husband thought for a minute, nodded to himself and, taking his leave, said, "I'll be back as soon as I can." He kissed Toshi on the forehead and turned back to the nurse and me on the floor beside Toshi on his way out the door, "Please don't let my wife die," he whispered so his wife wouldn't hear.

"Go fast," I said, attempting to smile in reassurance.

The makeshift nurse and I did what we could while we waited. At one point I stuck my fingers inside of my friend and attempted to turn the baby with my own fingers. I was so desperate that any fears of hurting the baby's little head or my friend's body took a backseat to my fear that Toshi was dying in front of me. Her screams and moans had died off. She had no energy left to express her pain. She had been losing quite a bit of blood during this ordeal and I knew that it was just a matter of time. The baby had stopped moving altogether.

Toshi's husband and a *Nisei* doctor from Seattle arrived at the infirmary before the camp doctor made it to us. The Seattle doctor pushed us aside, and examined Toshi and the baby inside the birth canal. "Holy God," I heard him mutter. He stayed calm. The Seattle doctor got up calmly and turned to the nurse and me.

"You have done the best that you can," he said. "Where the hell is the doctor?" he asked, trying to control his anger.

"He was not at the camp today," answered the nurse apologetically. "I'm sorry," she whispered.

"You are the not the one to be sorry," the Seattle doctor answered. "When is he getting here?"

"Any minute now," answered the nurse with more hope than certainty.

"We don't have minutes," answered the Seattle doctor. "Here's what we are going to do…"

By the time that the doctor arrived to the camp infirmary, the Seattle doctor had done an emergency caesarian on Toshi. He did not have the time or the drugs available to give her any anesthetics, but she had lost so much blood already that she remained unconscious through the procedure. The Seattle doctor had to push the baby back out of the birth canal in order to extract it from Toshi's womb. It had gotten caught on its own umbilical cord as it had descended. It had strangled to death long before it had even begun to live. Discovering the loss, the Seattle doctor's goal was to save the mother.

When the camp doctor arrived, he banished the Seattle doctor and closed up Toshi's belly himself. As he did so, the camp doctor, whose breath had a distinct odor of Christmas-time eggnog and rum, threatened the Seattle doctor with having his license revoked for performing surgery in the State of Idaho and for doing so without permission from the War Relocation Authority. "The mother could have died," said the camp doctor with an air of superiority.

His anger finally getting the better of him, the Seattle doctor said, "I hope that you do make that complaint, because then I can explain how, if you had been here, this mother would not be fighting for her life and there would be a healthy baby in his mother's arms right now. A life was unnecessarily lost today, *doctor*!"

"Get out!" screamed the camp doctor as he turned a deep shade of crimson. To the nurse he said, "Please indicate in this patient's records that she lost much blood due to her attempt to give birth to a deceased fetus."

"Doctor," began the nurse, "The baby was not deceased when labor began…"

"Write what I tell you," said the doctor.

By the time that I returned to my barracks it was the evening of December twenty-fifth. I had missed the Christmas celebrations that we had all planned. Akio greeted me at the door.

"We heard," he said, taking me into his arms. The Fusakas were in the barracks as well. I looked around and saw my Rosie—my healthy little girl—playing with her new doll. Akio had remembered.

"Look, Mama!" she said, proudly showing me her doll. "I'm good! Santa found me!"

I went to sleep that night with Rosie in my arms, the doll in hers.

*****

In the weeks following Christmas, I spent most of my time helping Toshi recover. I sat with her daily when she was still in the infirmary keeping her company and acting as a nurse (I was just as qualified as the poor girl who still worked the infirmary). More importantly, I tried to keep up her spirits. During this time, I also helped Toshi and her husband, who was beside himself with grief, to prepare for the burial and funeral of their little son. We had the service two weeks after the baby's death with the camp's Methodist congregation. All of the *Issei* from our classes, even those who were not Methodist, attended. Once Toshi was able to move back to her barracks, I helped her keep her room warm and fetched her food while her husband was out working. She was recovering from a serious abdominal surgery and could not even lift the wood to go into the little stove that each barrack used for warmth. In addition, because there was no refrigeration in the barracks, none of us could keep an adequate supply of food in our barracks and we had to go to the mess hall three times a day to fetch food. However, Toshi was not supposed to walk, especially not in the frigid cold of the Idaho wastelands. The barracks were not an ideal place to recover from surgery.

When I first went to Toshi's apartment I was always left Rosie at home with Akio or with Mary Fusaka. I had made the mistake of bringing Rosie only once to help keep my friend company. The sight of my daughter reminded Toshi of her loss and she broke down into tears. This served only to frighten my daughter who also started to whimper, on the brink of crying herself. I had hoped that things would get better, but by late January I could see that Toshi's mental health was only getting worse as she stayed holed up in her eighteen by twenty foot barracks. It was time, I told her, to get back into the classroom.

All of the other classes were already back in swing after the winter holidays and our *Issei* students were anxious to resume as well. Although I had not been certain about this decision to push Toshi back to teaching, my instincts were correct: Starting class again proved to be the best thing for Toshi as all of the *Issei* wisdom in the class were ready and waiting to share their experiences and wisdom with her about the loss of a child and how to recover. I was amazed to hear the women recount the hardships of coming to America and settling either in the poorest parts of the city or in the unrelenting wildness of the Pacific Northwest. While the pain and learning of these other women could not take away Toshi's pain, I think that it helped connect her to a larger picture of suffering and that made it easier to deal with her loss. Toshi later told me that, after speaking with the *Issei* women, she no longer felt that God had singled her out, but that pain happened to all people for no rhyme or reason. Just as she was coming to this conclusion and getting back on her feet, Toshi and I became aware of the fact that the whole camp had been abuzz with news: The Loyalty Questionnaire was finally on its way to the internment camps.

*****

One day in early 1943, Akio came home to the barracks, bounding in like a child declaring, "Now's our chance!"

"Our chance for what?" I asked laughing despite my efforts to keep a straight face at his openly child-like energy.

"Our chance to show our loyalty," said Akio. "They've confirmed that we get the questionnaires. And did you hear the news?"

"No, what news is that?" I asked, still laughing.

"Roosevelt's finally going to allow an all-*Nisei* unit!"

My laughter stopped. So this was it I thought, my foreboding coming true. The government needed troops in the tough wars being fought in both Europe and the Pacific and now that things weren't going so well they needed *Nisei* soldiers. Fresh blood. I did not say any of this to my husband. Instead, I mustered a smile and said, "That is what you have always wanted."

"Oh, Rose Marie, I can't wait!" Akio said, nearly jumping for the joy at the thought of it. I waited until he had left to break the news to Henry to break down and cry.

The rumor was true and my husband's wish was fulfilled. President Roosevelt activated the 442nd Regimental Combat Team on February 1, 1943. This unit would join with the Hawaiian *Nisei* unit, the 100th Infantry Battalion that had been formed in 1942. The Hawaiian Japanese population had not been interned. The government had decided that, although the Hawaiian Japanese were actually closer to Japan, and despite the fact that Hawaii had been the site of the Pearl Harbor attack, it would essentially be too difficult to mobilize the large population of Hawaiian Japanese and Japanese Americans into camps. Because the Hawaiians were predominantly of Asian ethnicity, the government felt that the other Islanders were not as enthusiastic about removing their Asian neighbors to camps. Besides, without the Hawaiian Japanese and their children--the group that made up the majority of the Hawaiian sugar cane workers--who would cut the Hawaiian sugar cane that was shipped to the mainland?

Men like my husband and Henry surged to join the new unit. In fact, the 442nd was so successful at attracting Nisei volunteers from the ten relocation center internment camps that there would be no need for the military to institute a draft for the Nisei unit until January 1944. Once I heard about the 442nd, I knew that my husband would be leaving me soon. However, first we had to complete our loyalty questionnaires. In February of 1943, the much-anticipated questionnaire arrived at the internment camps courtesy of the War Relocation Authority. All internees age seventeen and older were ordered to complete the questionnaire. Because I was officially an internee, I also received my mandatory copy of the questionnaire.

For me, the questions were easier to answer than I think they were for many of the internees. Overall, I think that the questionnaire was the most difficult for the *Issei*. The older generation had been born in Japan, come to America as young adults, and, despite having lived their entire adult lives in America, had been denied the right to naturalize as citizens. That meant that they were still technically citizens of Japan. While the loyalty of most *Issei* no doubt rested with the United States, there were two questions on that questionnaire that were particularly difficult for these members of the camp populations. One day in February, not long after the questionnaires had been passed out, the *Issei* in my class chose to practice their English by discussing the questionnaire. It was through this language practice session that I learned how difficult the questionnaire was proving to be to the camp's *Issei* population.

"It is just two of the questions that are bad," said one of my female students.

"Which two" I asked, forgetting in my interest in the conversation that I was supposed to just listen as my students practiced.

"Twenty-seven and twenty-eight," answered several students in unison.

I knew the questions well. In fact, they had sparked some interesting discussions in my barracks as well. Even for the *Nisei* these two questions were almost insulting in light of the fact that the government had interned United States citizens into prison camps without any thoughts about due process rights. "Can someone please read Question Twenty-Seven to the class?" I asked.

"Question Twenty-Seven," an older female student began to read. I was truly impressed with the progress that my students had made with their language skills. "Are you willing to serve in the armed forces of the United States on combat duty, wherever ordered?"

This question had been no problem for Akio and Henry. They eagerly answered the question, "Yes." For us women this question was a little confusing. Women did not serve in combat duty in 1943 so we were not certain how it applied. Women did, however, serve as nurses in combat zones, so Question Twenty-Seven was not completely inapplicable to us women. But even if I was asked to serve in a nursing capacity, what about my daughter? The truth was that I could not very well say that yes, I would be willing to drop everything and serve on combat duty. But the reason that I wanted to answer in the negative was not that I did not want to serve my country or our soldiers. It was more complicated. I realized that day in class, that the answers to the questions were complicated for many reasons to many of us.

"We are too old to serve," said one of my students—a truly ancient elderly man. "What do I say? No? Yes?"

"And we are not citizens," said another. "Does the Army allow non-citizens to fight?"

"The answer to that is, yes, they do," informed another. "But I do not know about age."

"The Army will be full of little old ladies!" exclaimed yet

another student—one of my favorite ladies in the class thanks to her good humor and energy. "We'll fight really good!" she continued.

"Really *well*," I corrected. "And I have no doubt that you would, Mrs. Yoshida."

"What is the right...no, *correct*...answer, Teacher-san?" one of the students asked. My students had affectionately called me "Teacher-san" ever since I explained that they could call me "teacher" instead of "*sensei*."

"I believe that the question that declares loyalty to the United States is a yes," I hesitantly explained. I also took that opportunity to describe my own issues with that question and an answer in the affirmative. "I mean, if that is what you believe." I shouldn't be giving the answers, I realized.

"I think that the WRA did not think well before making this question," said Mrs. Yoshida once I had explained my situation.

"I think that you are supposed to think, if I was a young, strong man, then yes I will fight," said another student. We all nodded agreement. It seemed to be the only logic that made sense.

After discussing that question, I asked for a volunteer to read Question Twenty-Eight. Mrs. Yoshida began to read the question that came to be known to the internees as the "loyalty oath" question. "Question Twenty-Eight," she began. "Will you swear unqualified allegiance to the United States of America and faithfully defend the United States from any and all attack by foreign or domestic forces, and forswear any form of allegiance to the Japanese Emperor or any other foreign government, power, or organization?"

"Well, that one isn't so difficult, is it?" I asked. The class had fallen silent after Mrs. Yoshida read the question. "Of course everyone is loyal to the United States, right?"

An uncomfortable feeling settled into the room and I saw the students looking at each other. Finally Mrs. Yoshida explained. "Teacher-san," she said. "Of course we are loyal to this country. We came here to build and live a life here as Americans. We had our children here and they are Americans.

But we are not Americans. This is not by our choice, but by the choice of America. And now, here we are in a camp. *We* have been loyal to America, but America has not been loyal to us."

"I believe that many *Nisei* have that same frustration," I began, recalling a conversation that Akio and Henry had whispered to each other over our barrack table one night.

"But for us," continued another student, a dignified older gentleman who had been a doctor in Kyoto before coming to America, "But for us *Issei* it is different than for our children."

"How so, Dr. Hasegawa?" I asked, ashamed that I had not thought of the pressures that faced my *Issei* students while I had been worrying so much about myself. I was reminded that this war was touching the lives of everyone, not just my family and me.

"For the *Issei*," continued Dr. Hasegawa, "We have no country. We are not wanted here. Our only other option is our country of birth—Japan. Now, this country that does not want us *Issei* seems to want us to belong to no country at all."

"You see, Teacher-san," continued Mrs. Yoshida, "If we forswear any allegiance to Japan, then we have no country at all. We wanted to be Americans—most of us still do—but this is a sacrifice that is being asked from us."

"But you do not support the Emperor," I stated more than asked. "Do you?"

"We do not support the actions of the Emperor," was the answer that I received from Dr. Hasegawa. "What more can you expect us to say?"

*****

For several weeks following the news and distribution of the questionnaire all ten of the camps were caught up in a flurry of excitement over questions twenty-seven and twenty-eight. Debates were held in public and in the privacy of individual barracks over willingness to serve, ability to serve, loyalty to the United States and loyalty to Japan. Factions began to grow. For many, such as the *Issei* in my classes, the issue was one of a practical nature—if they could not be ultimately loyal to the country of their still-current citizenship, then where would they belong? Would anyone want them once the war was over? For others, the questions had become complicated philosophical questions that required a deep reflection of what the word "loyal" meant from inside a barbed wire fence.

For many families in the camp a division of thought appeared between the opinions held by members of the *Issei* generation and the opinions held by the *Nisei* generation. Many of these *Nisei*, American citizens, were both willing to serve and willing to swear their allegiance to the United States. Most *Nisei* had no problem forswearing any loyalty to Japan, as they had never felt any allegiance to the land of their parents' birth to begin with. In these families, many of the *Nisei* answered affirmatively to each question (yes-yes) while their parents answered (yes-no). Some of the *Issei* though, were confused by the request to serve in the military and simply answered "No" to each question (no-no).

For the majority of families, the *Issei* understood that answering either or both of the loyalty questions in the negative would not make life any easier. Concerned that his parents might have the same concerns as many of the *Issei* in Minidoka, Akio attempted to correspond with his parents and sister down in Tule Lake regarding the questionnaire. Of course, this was difficult because of the censors and the vast potential for saying anything that could be misconstrued. Akio wrote: "Hope all is affirmative with all of you. Maggie, please see to it that Mama and Papa are as well and positive as we hope that you are. All up here are yes." Maggie must have known exactly what her brother's letter was meant to imply and responded with the simple response: "Affirmative here, for all. We understand and are all yes and positive." Poor thing, that was all the more she could tell us. The fact was, things were not that positive at Tule Lake.

17 MAGGIE

From "The Roses of Minidoka," continued.

TULE LAKE WAS NEVER at any point a great place to live. It was big for one thing, over eighteen thousand residents at its peak. Essentially, Tule Lake was a temporary city in the middle of nowhere. Not unlike any regular city of its size, there were problems at Tule Lake. There had always been issues of violence, especially as the traditional Japanese family unit broke down and teenage boys and young men roamed wild and free to do whatever they wanted. The issue of gangs continued to increase as the internment dragged on. As the gang problem increased, so too did our fear of violence. To think that we were put in these camps for safety!

What had been the most disturbing aspect of these gangs was that the boys and men who formed them were overwhelmingly pro-Japan. Many of these groups were comprised of *Kibei*. Based upon what I saw and heard at Tule Lake, it seemed that much of the overseas "education" of these young men consisted of bowing to the emperor. The introduction of the Loyalty Questionnaire into this already-tense atmosphere created unimaginable problems for the residents of the camp. When the questionnaire was introduced, Tule Lake became a war zone.

While it never really crossed the minds of Mama or me to answer questions twenty-seven and twenty-eight with anything but "yes-yes," that thought was not as popular as I would have expected. But by 1943 people were tired of living in prison camps. We had been evacuated, assembled, relocated, and interned and did so without complaint to show our loyalty. However, with no end in sight to the wars in Europe or the Pacific and, therefore, no end in sight to the end of Japanese and Japanese American imprisonment, tempers had run short. Loyalty and patriotism became more difficult in light of the fact that, especially for those of us American citizens who were interned, no respect had been given for our constitutional rights. And Tule Lake was not as cohesive and well, pleasant, as Minidoka. By February 1943, the answer of Yes-Yes seemed almost anti-intuitive to many internees. Even for people who eventually answered Yes-Yes, the initial reaction to the questionnaire was not so affirmative. My father was one of these people.

While Papa had always dreamed of one day being a naturalized citizen, his faith in the United States seemed to wane with every year that passed behind barbed wire. I think for Papa it was even more difficult to keep a stiff upper lip after being arrested and held in Fort Missoula for all those months. My father had looked terrible when he arrived at Tule Lake and his physical appearance was a reflection of his weakened morale. His initial imprisonment had taken a toll on my father from which it would take years for him to fully bounce back to his old self.

Perhaps some of the change in my father's attitude was due to the fact that the time at Fort Missoula had affected his physical health. Or maybe his body gave up a little once his mind started to let in depression. Whatever the cause, the result was that Papa had left us a middle-aged but strong truck farmer and he returned to us as a rickety old man. His hair, once only peppered with gray, had become silver. His back, once held up so tall and straight, had stooped. The pride that he once expressed for his land, his home, his family—all these were absent inside the fence at Tule Lake. When the time came for him to express his willingness to declare loyalty to the country that had betrayed him, my father was not overly enthusiastic to answer yes. Seeing the writing on the wall, Mama and I set out to convince my father that the loyalty questionnaire was simply not the proper forum to express his dissatisfaction.

"Hiromi," my mother would say to Papa as they sat at their makeshift table, the questionnaires before them, "You cannot tell the government that you are angry. That is what they are looking for, what they are hoping for."

My father, sitting there with an impassive look on his face, responded, "then perhaps I will not answer at all."

"Ah," my mother answered, beginning to get angry. (Yes, even my passive mother showed anger after being stuck at Tule Lake!) "Then you might as well answer 'no,' because the WRA will know that is what you mean!"

"No, Reiko," my father answered soothingly—he always disliked upsetting my mother. "I would answer with nothing because that is the easiest answer. How do I give up my citizenship? How do I become a person with no country?" he asked. Then, in almost a whisper, he continued, "How do I pledge loyalty to a country that took me away from my family in the middle of the night like a common criminal? They accused me of being a spy, Reiko!" he exclaimed, his own anger flaring.

"But, Hiromi," my mother continued patiently. "Do you want to go back to Japan?"

"Not after what they have done to my country," my father answered. As soon as he said it, I think he realized his true feelings. Thank God. In the end, my father's loyalty to the ideals of America won over his frustration and anger at the treatment he had received. My father answered Yes-Yes. My mother's instincts about leaving questions twenty-seven or twenty-eight blank were correct—a lack of answer was interpreted as a "no" and thus a failing answer to the loyalty questionnaire.

Oddly, after the debacle over what he would answer on the questionnaire, my father seemed to bounce back to life from his depression. He would tell me that he was invigorated with a new sense of his longing to be an American and that meant, according to him, that he had to live long enough to get out of Tule Lake and show his country that he was happy to be in it. His back began to straighten, his mood started to lighten, and he became more active. He even became socially active. For many *Issei* the internment camps provided the only opportunity that they would ever have to relax. After a hard life of labor or farming, many *Issei* were able to spend their times in the camps playing cards, learning English and hobbies, and enjoying a well-earned vacation from non-stop physical work. It was one of the many ironies of the camps. Around this time my father began to build his rock garden—a garden that he would later reinstate in Minidoka after the move. That was the father that I knew and loved, the man who could plant a garden in the middle of a barren wasteland and turn nothing into something beautiful.

*****

Once my parents were no longer a concern, I turned my attention to answering my own loyalty questionnaire. While I had no problem answering Yes-Yes, there was significant influence at Tule Lake to answer in the negative to at least question twenty-seven. Even I got my fair share of this influence. I was lucky to have a few friends from Bellevue in the camp, including my former schoolmate, Mitzi. I was visiting her family's barracks one day when her brother, Horu, caught us talking about the questionnaire and our plans to answer in the affirmative.

"How," Horu asked rhetorically, "can the government truly expect you—or us men—to risk our lives for them after what they did to us, to our parents?" Horu's patience with the government had run out. After several months in Tule Lake— suffering the infamous work shortages, bad pay, substandard living conditions, and, of course, the barbed wire and armed guards--it seems that the *Kibei* had found an apt listener in my friend's brother.

"Horu," I asked him in return, "how can you say that? Saying "no" is the same as wearing a big sign that says, 'Look at me, I'm a traitor.'"

"No, Maggie," answered Horu, "What it really means is that I'm saying hell no I do not want to be drafted to fight in this war and leave my family behind in a prison."

"But there's the new regiment—the 442nd," I interrupted Horu's rant. "You would fight in the all-*Nisei* unit. Like my brother and..."

"I know, like your brother and your boyfriend up in Idaho." Horu was jealous of Henry I had realized as of late-- along with the realization that Horu perhaps had feelings for me. I certainly did not let Horu know that I had not spoken to Henry in some time. Although I still had hopes of seeing Henry someday, I was certain that he had by now forgotten me. I never received a response to any of my letters. I instinctively pulled on the ring around my neck. Before I had a chance to respond, Horu continued his rant. "Why should the *Nisei* be segregating into their own unit? Why can't we just fight in the Army and Navy like every other American? Why not?" he asked when I was silent.

"I don't know, Horu," I admitted. This fact had bothered me and many other internees as well.

"I'll tell you why, Maggie," Horu went on, "because they still don't trust us *Nisei*. We're still just a bunch of Japs to them. They are going to put us into a unit together so that we can make easy targets. All they have to do is just send the entire damn unit off on some half-ass mission and the whole bunch of them will be blown to bits. You see? It's ingenious. Now they're not just putting us in prison. Now they're taking our young men and sending them off to their deaths. They get some suicide soldiers and they get to clear out the camps a little and get rid of the next generation of Japs. Lucky them, but not me. No thanks, I'm not going."

"So you are going to risk saying no-no just to avoid service?" I asked, incredulous. "But they are taking volunteers. They won't even need to draft *Nisei*."

"Trust me, Maggie," he responded, "They will need to draft *Nisei* once the volunteers start dying."

"Horu," I said after a pause to think of the best response.

"I answered yes-yes. I still believe in this country. *My* country."

"Change your answer, Maggie," Horu responded, unaffected by my patriotism.

"There's talk of sending the no-no's to Japan, Horu," Mitzi piped in. She was scared of her brother, I think, but probably more scared of being called a traitor. The camp had ears; you had to put on a show of your loyalty (or lack thereof).

"And so we'll go together," he replied, grabbing my hand. So there it was, I remember thinking; he's finally put it out on the table.

"No, Horu, I cannot go to Japan. I am an American. I already turned in my questionnaire." I paused. "And I love someone else." Horu dropped my hand and stormed out of his family's barracks.

Horu and the other *Nisei* who answered in the negative to questions twenty-seven and twenty-eight became known as the No-No Boys.

*****

Following the stress of the loyalty questionnaire, I knew that I had to get out of Tule Lake and back into the world. I had work to do, I had decided. I wasn't sure what it was, but I knew that I had to get out and prove that I was worth it, that I deserved to be an American. I decided that this meant that I had to follow my dreams. I wanted to make up for lost time by living life to its fullest. I wanted to go to school. Ironically, the War Relocation Authority, the very government organization who had stripped me of so many of my dreams and anticipated plans for the future, was now offering me the one thing that I had always truly dreamed of but then took away. The WRA was offering students release to go to college.

Of course, there were conditions to the War Relocation Authority's drive to have college-age *Nisei* leave the camps for school. Like the announcement and lists that we received regarding our evacuation from Bellevue, there was also a list of conditions that I needed to comply with if I wanted to evacuate

JAPANESE ROSES

Tule Lake for educational purposes. The first requirement was that I had to be accepted academically to the school of my choosing while I was still in the camp. Second, the school that accepted me had to be accepted, or "cleared," by the WRA. Third, I had to be able to provide for myself financially outside of the camp for at least one year while I was at school. Fourth, I had to be assured of a welcome in the community that housed the school. Finally, fifth, I had to provide an autobiography to the WRA. Ironically, the easiest aspect of the WRA's process was the one that was normally the most difficult: Being accepted academically. The rest was the hard stuff.

I was in pretty good standing regarding the first aspect of the educational release. My grades were great—I had officially graduated in the Pinedale Assembly Center from Bellevue High, where I had a straight A average (in absentia, of course). That wasn't the problem. My problem was that I had to choose to a school to which I would ask for acceptance. While over five hundred institutions throughout the country would eventually accept over three thousand *Nisei* students, none of these schools were those along the West Coast. The West Coast was still an excluded zone for Japanese Americans regardless of the allowance for school. What this meant was that nearly every school in the nation was open for my application except for the one that I had always wanted to attend, the University of Washington.

I had always wanted to attend UW. The campus overlooked Seattle's gorgeous Lake Washington and the view was absolutely stunning. Even more so, it was the academic pride of the State and already had a history of accepting Japanese American students; there were even *Nisei* clubs on campus—before the internment. In fact, the school even had a few Japanese American professors who were interned during the war along with my family at Minidoka. I had always hoped to be accepted into the UW and live in Seattle. But beggars can't be choosers and, ironically, I was now faced with the possibility of heading east and going to an old, established school, which is a possibility that I would have never even considered back home when I was

197

in Bellevue. But then, back in Bellevue, I would have never imagined that I would spend a year or two in California, imprisoned and with my life on hold.

So once I made the choice to go to school, the first big question was where and which one. For this decision my parents were a great source of help. Both of my parents were incredibly supportive of my decision. Nonetheless, before I knew that they would be so enthusiastic about the idea, I was nervous to tell them. Despite my reluctance, time was short and I shared with them my plans not long after turning in my loyalty questionnaire. One night after dinner (after risking my life by walking a few laps around the camp by myself and thus tempting the gangs that beat up—or worse—raped young people walking alone), I went back to the barracks and sat down with my parents at the little table that comprised the center of our tiny apartment. "Mama, Papa," I began, "I have made a decision that I would like to discuss with you."

"Oh no, Maggie!" exclaimed my father. "Are you marrying Horu?"

This took me off guard. "Papa, no! Of course not!" I exclaimed. I was upset by my father's question for a variety of reasons, especially because my parents had obviously realized that I was no longer speaking to Henry. Because of this, I had stopped speaking of him; I thought that I was forgotten. The pain of being away from him was so intense that I tried to convince myself that I did not need him. Especially now that I had the opportunity to go to college.

"Why do you think that I would marry Horu?" I asked, momentarily put off track due to my surprise.

"It is not that Horu was not once a polite and helpful young man," my mother said. "We just do not want you to get caught up in this anti-American business." I had to smile at my mother's use of the term "business." She had been studying her English in the camps and was actually speaking like a true American now, slang and all. "Horu is a No-No," she continued, "and he is not Henry."

"I hadn't realized that Horu was so involved with the No-No

Boys," I responded. In truth, I had been avoiding him since our parting, doing my best to not know what he had been up to since submitting his no-no questionnaire.

"Mama, Papa," I said again. "Horu and I are certainly not together. Even though Henry isn't here, I haven't forgotten him. What? Do you guys think that I just switched from one boy to the other?" I laughed.

"We just wanted to make sure that our daughter is not 'slack-happy,'" my father cut in, bursting into uproarious laughter.

"That she is not 'khaki-wacky,'" added my mother, also laughing.

My mouth literally hit the floor it opened so far in shock. Who were these people that used to be my parents, I wondered. These terms that they used were phrases that you heard high school age *Nisei* drop around the camp. They each meant "boy crazy." Both the *Issei* and the *Nisei* had picked up or created slang words in the camps. For the *Issei* most of the words were a mix of English and Japanese, or English words pronounced in an easier to say manner for native Japanese speakers. For example, *besu boru* was a common *Issei* pronunciation for "base ball," *kyampu* for "camp," and so on. It was a hybrid language that could maybe called, "Japanglish." As for the *Nisei*, we just said crazy things that had some basis in reality and some basis in the fact that we were teenagers.

"Is this what you two are learning in English class?" I asked, joining in their laughter. "How to speak like *Nisei* teenagers?"

"Well, we are trying to be more American," said my father with a serious face.

"So, Maggie," my mother said, getting us back on track. What is it that you had to tell us?"

Okay, here it goes, I thought. I took a deep breath. "I wanted to tell you and Papa that I have decided that I would like to try to use the WRA's program and get accepted into a college. I want to go to school."

"Maggie..." began my mother.

"Mama, hold on please. Let me say this," I interrupted her mid-sentence. "I've been thinking about this and you know that I have always wanted to go to school." When they didn't respond, I continued. "I want to go to school to be a writer or maybe a teacher. I think that it is important that I succeed at this so that I can help show that the *Issei* and *Nisei* are good Americans. And I think that I can get accepted and promise that I will try to find a scholarship or a way to pay for this myself. Also, I am sorry to leave you here alone, but I promise to come back to Bellevue when we are allowed to and make sure that you are taken care of. I promise." I was rambling now. I wanted to convince them before they turned me down. Still, my mother was interrupting me.

"Maggie!" my mother said, a little more firmly this time. "Slow down and let us speak."

"I'm sorry, Mama. I'm sorry Papa," I just had to get all of that out before my nerves got the better of me." I paused. "Well...what do you think?" I held my breath.

"How amazing!" said my father once I finally stopped speaking. "This is exactly what we want for you. Your mother and I were just speaking of this possibility earlier today after hearing of it from other *Issei* parents."

"We're so proud!" said my mother.

I was stunned. "Well," I said, "I haven't even been accepted yet. I don't even know where I want to go. I need your help with that."

"Do you have any ideas, Maggie?" asked my mother.

"Well, I wish I could go to the University of Washington, but that zone is still off-limits. So, basically, I can go anywhere I can get accepted on the East Coast or the Midwest—provided I can pay and assure my welcome. I could also apply to Washington State University." Eastern Washington had not been included as a West Coast restricted zone. A few Japanese had decided to voluntarily move out to Spokane for the duration of the war. Most chose to ride out the war in the camps. Washington State University was outside of Spokane in Pullman, Washington. There was also Gonzaga University in Spokane. There was the possibility of going back to my home state.

"Do you want to live in Eastern Washington?" asked my

father. The two halves of the State are like night and day in their differences.

"Papa," I replied, "Honestly, if I have to go east, than I would like to go as far east as possible."

"Why not?" asked my mother again pleased with her own use of colloquial English.

"Right, Mama," I said, "Why not?" Except there was a why: What about my parents? I couldn't leave them here alone.

"Do you have anything in mind," my father asked me.

"That's the problem, Papa," I said. "There are so many choices and I don't really know anything about many of the schools."

"Perhaps you can ask other people your age about different schools," suggested my mother. "Or possibly the WRA has information."

"Well, they do have some information and I've heard a bit about a particular school, but it may be too difficult..." I trailed off.

"It sounds like you are trying to talk yourself out of something," noted my father. "What school are you thinking about, Megumi-chan?"

"Well, there is a school that I have heard about that might be good. It is an all-girl school, which is not necessarily my first choice..."

"Because you are khaki-wacky," interrupted my father.

"No!" I laughed, "Just because it seems strange to not have any men around to beat at debates," I joked back.

"What is the name of this school?" asked my mother.

"Vassar," I responded. I noticed my parents exchange a sidelong glance at each other.

"Maggie," said my mother. "Mrs. Smith, the priest's wife went to Vassar I am almost sure. She spoke about it because Mrs. Roosevelt is very involved with the school. It is close to her home." Eleanor Roosevelt had become the talk of the camps for openly speaking against her husband's decision to intern the Japanese Americans. She even visited a relocation center and visited with the internees.

"You must speak with her," my mother had continued, referring to the Episcopalian priest's wife. The couple had actually moved into the Tule Lake facility when their Japanese parishioners had been evacuated from Oakland, California. They were good, kind people who seemed to truly practice what they preached.

"I will speak to her tomorrow," I promised.

*****

I spoke to Mrs. Smith the next day. I went to the church (which was conducted out of yet another barrack, of course) and she was there. Mrs. Smith had indeed gone to Vassar and she was more than happy to assist me in my quest to attend her alma mater. I will be eternally grateful to Mrs. Smith, as her intervention on my behalf was nothing short of miraculous. Not only did she personally recommend me to the admissions staff of the university, she also arranged for a scholarship to be awarded to me from monies collected by her wealthy fellow alumni in the Poughkeepsie and New York area. My tuition was going to be completely paid out of these funds with just a bit left over for living expenses. The kindness did not end there. Mrs. Smith also arranged for me to stay with the family of a local Episcopalian pastor close to the university. I would stay there in exchange for helping out with simple household chores. I nearly fell over myself thanking the woman when she came to my parents' barracks to tell me this final piece of good news. I swore I would work harder than I ever had before.

"Maggie, I want you to remember that you are not the Gilberts' maid, you are their guest. Don't work too hard," Mrs. Smith said to me as she told me about the Gilbert family. "They won't treat you like a maid, don't worry," Mrs. Smith said in response to the look of worry that had settled on my face. "I just don't want you to feel guilty while you are there. I know how you are a hard worker, Maggie. Just relax. Spend your time studying. Oh, and Father Gilbert will provide a letter saying that your welcome is assured in the town of Poughkeepsie. In fact, I believe there will even be other internee women attending the school."

"I don't know how to thank you, Mrs. Smith," I said with tears in my eyes when this kind woman came to my barracks to tell my parents and me this good news.

"My only concern is that you will not have enough money to buy clothes or other necessities," said the priest's wife. "You will need time to study and help with chores and I don't want you to have to work a menial job while you are in school."

"Don't worry, ma'am," I said. "If I need anything I will find a way to earn it."

"And I have saved a bit of money over the years," said my father. "You know, there are no finer strawberries in the world than the ones grown in Bellevue. I had some good years."

"Papa," I was shocked. "You do not have to give me any money. You and Mama will need that money to live on after the war."

"Maggie," said my mother, "It is our honor to help our youngest daughter go to school. We will help you however we can."

After a small party consisting of tea and crackers, Mrs. Smith took her leave of our barracks. As she left, I excused myself and ran out the door after her.

"Mrs. Smith," I said as I caught up with the priest's wife, "You have already done so much, but I'm afraid that I have one final favor to ask of you."

"Of course, Maggie," laughed Mrs. Smith. "What is it?"

"Can you please keep an eye on my parents once I'm gone? They don't really have anyone here—my brother and his wife are in Minidoka. I'm so worried to leave them. I feel like I am abandoning them here just when Tule Lake is turning into a nightmare."

"Don't you worry about that, Maggie," answered Mrs. Smith. "Father Smith and I will keep an eye on all members of our congregation, but I would be honored to watch over your parents personally. Perhaps there will be a way to have them join your brother and his wife. I will help them with that. You go to school. Make them proud."

Over the next several months, Mrs. Smith kept her word and took care of my parents. As life at Tule Lake deteriorated, she made sure that they were not being persecuted by the No-No Boys for answering yes on their questionnaires. She wrote to me and let me know that she thought that Horu, who had become very active with the anti-government faction at the camp, had actually been protecting my parents from being the target of his group's wrath. If this was indeed true, I am forever grateful to Horu for not allowing his group to beat or terrorize my parents. My fear of these occurrences was very real as violence had become a staple of life at Tule Lake in the wake of the loyalty questionnaire.

As tensions rose, the violence that arose was not only aimed at inmates. Many camp residents—No-No's as well as those who had answered Yes-Yes—were increasingly dissatisfied with living conditions at Tule Lake. Inadequate housing, unsafe working conditions, lack of food, as well as camp administration's inability to protect its residents from gang violence had led to general unrest. During the summer and autumn of 1943 the camp experienced work stoppages, labor disputes and demonstrations. I left in the middle of this, leaving my parents to face this alone.

After I was already gone, on November 1, 1943, a demonstration was held in front of the War Relocation Authority's administration offices. Somewhere between five thousand and ten thousand inmates, depending on the source, protested the white camp administration's failure to hear their needs. The WRA camp administrators got scared and built a barbed wire fence between the camp administration center and the camp proper and the United States Army was mobilized and poised to intervene if necessary. On November 4, another dispute broke out in the camp over missing truckloads of food. This time the Army rolled into Tule Lake in tanks complete with machine guns. Martial law was declared and it lasted until January 15, 1944.

Eventually the WRA would declare Tule Lake the official residence of those who had responded no-no on their notorious questionnaire. Those residents who had answered in the affirmative were allowed to transfer to one of the other nine relocation centers. With Mrs. Smith's help, my parents were able to transfer to Minidoka in time to spend New Year's 1944 with their daughter-in-law and granddaughter. Akio was already in Europe by then. However, unlike my parents, many people would not leave Tule Lake because, despite the unrest, they felt that they had built something of a home at the camp and did not want to start anew in yet another new camp environment.

I am glad that my parents left when they did. From what I had heard, Tule Lake took on a somewhat surreal quality once it became designated as a camp for "non-loyal" *Issei* and *Nisei*. Although the Army had imposed stricter security measures, those measures were really meant to protect Caucasian camp staff from the camp residents, not the residents from the violent factions in the camp. Tule Lake was a little pocket of animosity and violence, tucked along the Oregon-California border. When FDR allowed citizens to renounce their citizenship with the signing of Public Law 405 on July 1, 1945, of the five thousand five hundred eighty-nine Japanese Americans who renounced their U.S. citizenship, over fifty-four hundred of those citizens were housed at Tule Lake. In fact, of all the families sent to Tule Lake, over seventy percent had at least one member renounce their U.S. citizenship by the end of the war. After the war, there was a roundup and mass deportation for these "Native American Aliens." They were sent to Japan—many for the first time in their lives. Horu was amongst this group of people.

Most of those who renounced their citizenship were allowed to regain it and reenter the United States. However, they did not win this victory without a fight. After years of fighting the courts and the government, civil rights attorney Wayne Mortimer Collins regained citizenship for many of these people. In 1971, Nixon repealed Public Law 405. An American citizen can no longer renounce citizenship in a time of war. Mr. Collins and his colleagues also assisted in regaining citizenship for *Nisei* who had lost or renounced their citizenship while stranded in Japan when the war broke out—unless they made the mistake of "confessing."

But as I said, I was not at Tule Lake for the majority of the events that enfolded in late 1943 and after. While the camp had never been very safe and demonstrations had begun before I was accepted to school, the military occupation occurred months after I left. August 4th, 1943. That is the day that I left Tule Lake. I would never again set foot there. I was free.

18 KIMIKO

From treason confession, continued.

MY DAUGHTER WAS A completely unexpected source of joy to me. While I had worried that a child would only make it more difficult to leave Japan after the war, I loved Kiyoko so much that that worry faded away when I held her for the first time. Rather than see my daughter as a liability to my repatriation, I saw her as an inspiration to survive and get home. I was also relieved to discover that I loved Kiyoko completely and entirely. I had been afraid that I would look at my child and see only the face of her father—a man who was a mean, unhappy little tyrant of a man. I did not love Ryuu and I never would, but he had helped me create the most perfect little thing in the universe and for that I was appreciative.

Ryuu did not seem to be as smitten with Kiyoko as I was. He never held his daughter and he became disturbingly angry whenever her cries interrupted the serenity of his home. And, most confusing to me, he seemed to be jealous of the attention that I was giving to our baby, presumably because he wanted that attention himself. However, even if I had the time for my husband, my attention towards him was only out of a need to survive and not out of love as they were when I cared for Kiyoko.

In those first months after Kiyoko's birth I still had a wonderfully convenient basis to excuse myself from relations with Ryuu. He did not seem to care while Hatsu was still able to service him in this manner. That poor girl, I could see the pain on her face as the child inside her stomach grew larger with every passing day. In her room, Hatsu had a small shrine to her deceased husband. She kept the picture of her husband hidden under the bed. I only knew about it because one day, when I went to Hatsu's room needing her help with the laundry, I walked in to find her on her knees, rocking back and forth. Her back was towards me; she hadn't seen or heard me enter her small sleeping space. She was holding a picture of a young man—her husband she told me later. Very softly she was saying, "I'm sorry, I'm sorry," over and over. "I'm so alone," she said to the picture in her hands. She then took a drink of something. "Tea," I remember thinking, "Hatsu is having a tea ceremony with her dead husband."

Maybe I should have said something to the girl. I could have said, "You are not alone, Hatsu," or even "I understand." Instead, I backed out of the room and let her take her time to find me when she was ready. Why didn't I reassure Hatsu? Because she was correct—she was alone. She and I may have developed a friendship of sorts, but we were each alone. We each may have wanted to get away from Ryuu, but thought that we had different destinations. I really knew very little about the woman with whom I was sharing my husband. Maybe I was a little jealous of her, or even scared of her. Whatever it was, rather than reach out and connect with Hatsu, I backed out of the room and left her to her ceremony.

I wouldn't have necessarily thought twice about what I witnessed if Hatsu had not collapsed later that evening while serving dinner. I was up holding Kiyoko, who had begun crying as soon as Ryuu and I sat down. "Shut up that damn brat," Ryuu had warned me. I was walking back and forth across the bedroom space when I heard the commotion from the dining area. It was a crash followed by a scream of agony. Or maybe the scream came before the crash. I ran towards the dining area with my baby in my arms. Hatsu was lying on the floor, dinner splayed out all around her, uneaten. She was lying in a pool of her own blood.

Hatsu survived, but her baby did not. Doctors had to be called into our apartment to remove the dead child within her. She was nearly nine months pregnant at the time. I never confirmed my suspicions, but to this day I believe that the "tea" ceremony that I observed was actually an abortive or suicide ritual.

*****

Following Hatsu's miscarriage and recovery, my husband seemed to be freshly interested in me. When I turned down his affections because I had to care for Kiyoko, he took the baby from me—literally from my arms—and took her down the room to Hatsu. "Make yourself useful," he said to the girl, "Care for this baby." He turned to me. "Now that that is taken care of you, my dear wife can turn your attentions to more important things." To him, he meant.

"But I need to feed her," I said. I was breastfeeding my daughter.

"Hatsu," asked Ryuu turning back towards the maid, "You are still making milk, correct?" It made me sick to think of how he knew this. But, it made sense that Hatsu's body was still reacting as if she had given birth to a healthy child.

"Yes," she whispered, our eyes making contact briefly before she looked away, down to the floor.

"Then you shall feed this brat." Ryuu grabbed me roughly and pulled me back to our bedroom. "It is time that we have a son," Ryuu said to me, as if in explanation for his behavior. The joy that I had felt being with my daughter vanished. My despair was complete once again.

*****

Of course, one of the wifely duties that I had to resume was that of perfect hostess. As 1943 drew to an end and 1944 dawned on a new year, I was graced more and more often by the presence of various members of the Radio Tokyo team. Ryuu seemed to have an almost obsessive fascination for the radio in general and this station, dedicated to propaganda, was the light of my husband's life. Indeed, he certainly seemed to donate quite a bit of money to help keep the pro-Japanese programs running.

Ryuu's favorite program was the famous "Zero Hour" with "Orphan Annie." We learned all about the behind-the-scenes of this program from none other than Colonel Tsuneishi himself—military head of Radio Tokyo--who had begun to frequent our table once again. Radio Zero had premiered on the airwaves in November 1943. Its purpose was to demoralize the American and British troops fighting in the South Pacific. Recognizing that propaganda could not be completely effective across cultural differences, Tsuneishi had once again searched the ranks of the Japan's prisoners of war for soldiers from the United States or the United Kingdom with broadcasting experience. He was successful. I overheard him telling Ryuu that he had assembled a team of POWs who were able to put on a well-produced, English-speaking program. Although I usually kept my mouth shut at such gatherings, I was horrified to hear that Allied POWs had defected. "Why would they do such a show?" I gasped out loud (in Japanese, of course), instantly regretting my outburst. "Why, Madame Miramoto," replied the colonel, "I do not recall giving them a choice." He and Ryuu laughed at this as if it were the most hilarious joke in the world.

"Of course," continued Tsuneishi, "Since I can't truly trust the POWs, they are watched over by a couple of *Nisei* boys from America. Just to make sure that the message of the program doesn't get off-track."

"*Nisei*," I asked. "Are they also POWs?" I forgot that the longer I spoke, the greater the chance of revealing my American identity. As it turns out, the Colonel had a keen ear.

"No, not these boys," answered the colonel. "These two had good parents who knew where true priority lies. They were studying here and, once the war broke out they chose to claim their true citizenship. They are now members of the Imperial military."

*Nisei*s who had defected to the Japanese military! Niseis who, like me, were studying in Japan when the war broke out, but unlike me, *wanted* to be in Japan. They had wanted to renounce their U.S. citizenship. They were willing traitors. Not like me, I told myself. I never wanted to betray my country.

"And what about the girl," Ryuu asked Tsuneishi, interrupting my thoughts. "Who's this Orphan Ann?"

"Ah, she's the best out of the mix," replied Tsuneishi. "Another *Nisei*. She was stranded here at the onset of the war. She worked for Domei News as a typist. Ince and Cousens—those are two of my POWs, hand-chose her."

"Did she give up her citizenship, too?" I asked, my curiosity getting the better of me. Did I know this woman? Had we worked side-by-side?

"The Thought Police have been working on her, but not yet," responded Tsuneishi. "I don't know what the hold-up is—after all she spends her day creating propaganda for the Emperor. She is one of us now."

"What's her name?" I asked.

"Iva Toguri, a Californian," replied Tsuneishi. I had not known her at Domei. "The soldiers throughout the South Pacific call her Tokyo Rose." Another Rose; the name caught my attention. Obviously, "Rose" is not a common name in Japan. I felt an immediately affinity with this woman.

I didn't know what Iva went through after the war; I've been busy trying to keep my own head afloat. If I had known that she had been impoverished and desperate, I would have tried to help her. I would have come forward earlier if I had known that she sold her story to American journalists as the "one and only Tokyo Rose" to try to earn some money. I don't care that she took that credit (which she deserved despite the fact that many people filled in at Radio Zero for Orphan Ann); but who would have known that it would have been used against her in a trial for treason? I would have helped. I am trying to help now, to make people see how it was.

Only after the fact did I hear that Iva was imprisoned in Japan awaiting trial. She was separated from her husband, Felipe D'Aquino—a Portuguese citizen of Japanese and Portuguese descent. She gave birth to a child in jail in Japan despite her hope to give birth to the child in America. The baby died. Then, in 1949, Iva was shipped to San Francisco, California and stood trial on eight counts of treason. She was convicted on one count. Iva Toguri was the first woman ever convicted of treason in the history of the United States. God willing that I won't be the second.

From what I heard, the trial was a joke. The witnesses included none other than Colonel Tsuneishi and the two *Nisei* defectors who helped run Radio Tokyo. Those who testified and hoped to assist Iva were the POWs who worked the show. Unfortunately, they were unable to present any evidence that indicated that their life was in danger if they refused to broadcast. And, it was argued, Iva was not a prisoner of war, so her life was not in danger. In other words, the jury believed that the only reason that Iva Toguri broadcast for Radio Tokyo was because she wanted to help Japan. I wasn't a POW either, not in the military sense. But I also made the choice to broadcast in Iva's shoes on Radio Zero. Of course, like Iva, I had my reasons.

*****

The call came in late spring 1944. I heard Ryuu speaking to Colonel Tsuneishi over the telephone one afternoon. Although I could not hear the colonel's end of the conversation, I had an immediate sense of dread when I heard that man's name on my husband's lips. When Ryuu began to nod his head and say into the receiver, "Yes, yes, of course she will. No problem, Colonel," I knew what lay ahead even before Ryuu spoke to me.

Ryuu hung up the phone and turned around. Seeing me he began to speak, but I cut him off before any words came out of his mouth. "No, Ryuu," I said. "Whatever it is, the answer is no."

Ryuu responded with a quick, hard slap to my face. "Do not speak to me like that," he said, his voice level and calm. "Put on your coat, we are expected at Radio Tokyo immediately."

"No! I cannot go there!" I yelled, not caring if I received another blow. In fact, I hoped that Ryuu would hit me so hard that I would be knocked out or my teeth would loosen and fall out and then I would not be able to go with him. However, my husband was planning to hit me with a different type of blow. "Besides," I added trying to buy time, "the baby is sick and I need to care for her."

"Very well, my dear," he said. I always knew that when he stayed calm like this it meant that he was at his diabolical worst. He began to walk towards the room that was shared by Hatsu and my daughter. "Hatsu!" he screamed.

"Yes, Ryuu-san?" Hatsu said breathlessly as she came running from her little room. Kiyoko was in her arms. More than anything in the world I wanted to grab my baby girl out of her arms and run as far away from Ryuu as I could.

"Hatsu," continued Ryuu, "please pack your bags and those of the child. You will be going away from here."

Hatsu glanced up and met my eye. For a brief second I saw a compassion and pity so deep that I knew that I could trust the girl with my child. The second passed and Hatsu steeled her glance and looked up at my husband. "Sir," she said, "as you wish."

"Where are they going?" I asked, clinging to my husband's arm. "Why are you doing this?" I was the only person in the room who had not maintained her cool. My world was reeling.

"My dearest wife, if the girl is no longer here then you will not need to concern yourself with her care. She will be gone within minutes. Within that same time we shall be at Radio Tokyo."

"No," I cried, "please. She doesn't need to go away. I'll go with you. Please don't send her away." I knew that there was a very real possibility that if Ryuu took Kiyoko out of my sight I might never see her again. Even without having to worry about my unstable husband, the country was at war and babies should not be traveling at such times without their mothers. In order to keep my daughter, I sold my soul. I just hoped that someday I would be able to get it back.

"Very well, then," said Ryuu smugly. "Let's go."

*****

We arrived at the radio studio just minutes before Zero Hour was supposed to go on the air. My husband, firmly steering me with a steel grip on my arm, ushered me into the studio. He plopped me down at the microphone and went to acquaint himself with the defector *Nisei* who was overseeing the program that day. After a moment, the two came over and spoke to me.

"So you are from Washington?" asked the *Nisei*. He spoke to me in Japanese.

"I am American, yes," I responded, my heart pounding. I hated this man and it showed. Fortunately, I was saved from any further opportunities to cause trouble for myself.

"Please excuse the interruption," said a non-Japanese man with an accent that was either English or Australian. He spoke to us in English. "I need a minute with this evening's star," he continued as he shooed the *Nisei* and Ryuu away. I thanked God that my husband and the overseer actually let me be with this man long enough for us to speak in private, hushed tones.

"I can't do this," I whispered to the man—one of Tsuneishi's prisoners of war, I realized. "Please," I said, "I can't turn against my country."

The man answered loudly, obviously for the sake of prying ears. "Have you ever listened to our Orphan Ann on the show?" he asked, referring to Iva. When I said that I did he responded, "Just do it exactly like she does and you'll be fine. Remember, exactly like she does it. I'll give you the script and try as hard as you can to read it the way you think that Iva would." Out of eyeshot of the *Nisei* and Ryuu, the POW winked at me. "Don't worry," he said to me under his breath. "We all have the same goal."

I had just enough time to look through the script that the

POW handed me before we went on the air. I tried to conjure "Orphan Ann's" voice in my head as I read it through. Holding the paper in my hands I realized what had always seemed strange about Zero Hour when Ryuu made me listen. I hadn't been able to put my finger on it before, but now it seemed obvious that the script was odd. It was in English, but the words were arranged and stressed in odd ways. Certain phrases were repeated several times in a way that made the repeat sound halfhearted or even ludicrous. I realized as I read through the script that to the ears of thousands of my countrymen in the Pacific I was not putting on a pro-Japan propaganda show, but actually putting on a parody of Japanese propaganda. Zero Hour, unbeknownst to Tsuneishi and his goons, had turned into entertainment for the GIs stationed in the South Pacific. How nobody at Radio Tokyo figured this out was beyond me since it did not seem to be a secret with the boys who listened. They loved Orphan Ann, or, as Iva called herself, their "favorite enemy."

I felt so much better after I had actually filled in for Iva that evening that I was almost pleased that I had done so. However, as the high of being a radio personality wore off on my ride home it dawned on me that my participation with the program may not be seen by the United States government as pro-American despite the effect of the show on soldiers and the POWs' best intents. Please, God, I said to myself as Ryuu and I neared home, please don't let this hurt my chances of getting home with my little girl. I had taken to including Kiyoko in my prayers for homecoming. I was concerned that if I asked only for God's help in getting me back to Seattle, He might forget to include my daughter as well. Sometimes, for good measure, I prayed for Kiyoko to make it to Seattle even if I could not ever return. My daughter's well being was my new goal in life.

It was Kiyoko that I was thinking of as I walked back into the apartment. Even though it was not unusual for the apartment to be quiet, there was deafening silence that struck me as immediately eerie as walked through the door. I ran to Hatsu's room and, upon opening the paper door, I let out a little scream. I fell to my knees as the realization hit my body in waves of disbelief. Kiyoko was gone. Hatsu was gone. They were not there. Their personal belongings were not there. I was the only person in the little room.

Ryuu did not come to me. He made me come to him once my shock had passed. He was sitting at a desk looking at his financial ledgers when I came into the room.

"Why?" I managed to say, trying my hardest to keep my voice level. "I did what you wanted."

"I wanted a son," he responded. I was taken aback by this answer. Of course, I was speaking about going to the radio station and doing the show. He must have confirmed his orders to Hatsu before we left for the radio station when I had been in my room grabbing my coat. I expected my daughter to be here when I returned. To Ryuu, however, the whole episode had gone beyond the evening's events and had somehow served to remind him of the undesired gender of his child. My heart was broken, but it was also chilled by the apparent emptiness in the soul of the man who I had married and with whom I shared a child. Please God, I prayed once again, please let my daughter be safe in the hands of Hatsu.

"You may go and prepare for bed, Kimiko," Ryuu was saying to me. "Wear something nice. Tonight we will be trying for a son." We would have to try very hard, I thought in silent response. After having my daughter ripped from my breast I had been too depressed to eat much. That, coupled with the stress that continued to course through my body, had finally resulted in the complete cessation of my monthly flow. It was my silent protest against Ryuu—I had done my best to become infertile after the birth of my daughter.

19 HENRY

Personal interview with RLM, October 2002

AKIO AND I LEFT Minidoka in June 1943 for Camp Shelby, Mississippi to begin our basic training. We were both so excited—this was the opportunity that we had been waiting for— to serve our country. Sure, I was sad to leave Mom and Dad but I knew that Rose Marie, Rosie, and the Miramotos would help keep them company and take care of them. In fact, I was and remain eternally grateful to Rose Marie for her promise to help care for my parents if anything were to happen to me while in combat. I knew that I was being selfish volunteering to go to war since I was my parents' only child. In Japanese culture, the children care for the parents in old age. If I didn't return, there would be nobody to see to their needs as they grew older. Except that, when I voiced my concern to Rose Marie and Akio one night, Rose Marie said, "Of course there will be somebody to care for them, Henry." At first I didn't understand what she meant.

"Who," I asked without thinking. "They have no family except for me."

"Henry," Rose Marie replied patiently, "We are family, no

matter what." No matter what happened with Maggie, who I still had my heart set on. "Don't you worry about your parents; they have me. They will have Akio. They will have little Rosie, who adores them. We'll take care of your parents." I actually cried I was so grateful. I was not used to crying in public, but Rose Marie and Akio always seemed to see the extreme sides of my temperament. However, not even they had seen the tears that I had shed over Maggie.

The truth was, Maggie Miramoto had broken my heart in a big way. As I left her house that night in early 1942, I literally wanted to die. But, at the same time, I was too macho and young to show my emotions to anyone. I was also too young to realize that I should have written to her immediately—put a letter in the mail before I even left for Camp Harmony--and told her that I would wait as long as she wanted, do what she wanted. I didn't care if she wanted to go to school and get a job. I just thought that if she did, it would mean that she would be too busy to love me. I was selfish. I was wrong. I should have told her that I would wait forever; that my love would outlast the war. And, I thought as I rode the train next to her brother to train for war, I was too late. I had lost her. She was going to school. I was going to war.

Thank God that Akio was there with me because, truth be told, I was scared to death. I knew that Akio was scared too—scared of not coming home to his family. But Akio was much better at controlling his emotions than I was. He was so much better at seeing the bigger picture. Akio was better at being a hero than I was. Deep down, I was just a kid going off to war to take my mind off of my girlfriend. Akio, though, he was going to war to prove that Japanese Americans were loyal Americans, to get his parents out of prison camps, to make his daughter's life better. He fought for America because he wanted to make the world a better place. I really needed his influence. Thankfully, Akio stayed by my side until the end. I just wish that doing so had not turned out so tragically for him.

*****

When we got to Shelby, we joined up with the 100th Infantry Battalion—the boys from Hawaii. "One Puka Puka," they called themselves. The 100th had been formed the year before and, thanks in part to their success, the Army decided to create a unit for mainland *Nisei* as well. Of course, the Hawaiians were not interned and did not have to answer any loyalty questionnaires. But they were still segregated by ethnic heritage. When the 442nd was created, the Army decided to just lump us in with the 100th. You know, keep all the "Japs" together.

Guess what? Just because we all had dark hair and slanted eyes, those of us in the 442nd and those in the 100th did not get along at first. Later on we would join together and fight unlike any other unit in Europe. At first though, at Camp Shelby, the Hawaiians became the "Buddhaheads" or, depending on your pronunciation, the "buta-heads," "buta" meaning "pig" in Japanese. So we called the members of the 100th, the "pig-headed." In turn, they liked to refer to us mainlanders as "katonks" or "kotonks." Presumably this is the sound that a coconut makes as it hits an empty head. In other words, us mainland *Nisei* were the "empty-headed." Suffice it to say, the welcome we received at Camp Shelby by our Hawaiian brothers was not that enthusiastic.

The Army picked up on this discord and organized tours of the internment camps for the members of the 100th. Once they saw what we were going through on the mainland, we all got along pretty well. So, when I talk about the 442nd, we were also the 100th and if I don't list the two together it is only for the sake of efficiency. We were a team, a unit. When I say one or the other, I mean both. We were the Japanese American soldiers of the 100th and 442nd.

And what a team we made. We were the most decorated unit in the history of the United States military based on our size and length of service. The 442nd earned over eighteen thousand awards. We had seven Presidential Unit Citations, twenty-one Medals of Honor, and fifty-two Distinguished Service Crosses to name but a few. We also earned nine thousand four hundred eighty-six Purple Hearts. The 100th also had so many Purple Hearts that they were nicknamed the "Purple Heart Battalion."

For those of you who don't know, the Purple Heart is awarded to soldiers who are either wounded or die in battle. We had a lot of hurt boys and boys dying in battle even though we were really good soldiers. It can be argued that our commanders sent us into no-win situations. This made some of us angry—we figured it out right away. That's actually how we got our motto. One of our soldiers—who was already facing potential court martial for bringing up this very observation about our missions—determined that one of our orders from on high was very nearly battle suicide. This soldier, being very pragmatic and very brave, decided that, since we had nothing to lose, we might as well "go for broke." And that became our motto—"Go for Broke." I like to think that our history in that war was pretty illustrious. We did a lot in the short amount of time that we were allowed to fight.

Let me give a brief idea of how the 442nd spent the Second World War. Since the 100th had been training longer than the 442nd, they got shipped out first. In early September 1943, they landed in Algeria. They were attached to the Army's 34th Infantry Division and over one thousand members of the 100th took a boat trip up to Salerno, Italy with that unit. They lost their first two men to combat in Italy on September 29, 1943. Later that year, the 100th joined the forces fighting at Monte Cassino. Those buta-heads were quite the fighters. They lost a lot of good men in those first few months. By February 1944 there were just over five hundred members of the 100th left in Italy. Still, those five hundred plus men joined the troops at Anzio and there they stayed until May 1944. Some members believe that the 100th was purposefully held back so that the non-*Nisei* units could go into Rome and successfully liberate it. Whatever the case, Rome was liberated.

Akio and I were amongst the members of the 442nd who joined up with the 100th in May 1944 at Civitavecchia, Italy. Some of our unit had remained in the United States to train replacements; in Italy, the 100th was officially joined to the 442nd.

They would remain a separate unit, though, in order to properly reflect their previous distinguished service. Attached to the 88th Infantry, we pushed up Italy and fought in the battle to liberate Bruyeres, France. In southern France we became attached to the 36th Infantry and helped rescue the "Lost Battalion" from the Germans in the Vosges Mountains. That was our "Go for Broke" campaign.

After the Vosges campaign, we went back down to the French-Italian border, did some training and got back to some battles. In April of 1945, we returned to heavy combat and seized Monte Belvedere and Carrara in Italy while attached to the 552nd Field Artillery Battalion. After those battles, members of the 552nd were some of the first troops to liberate Dachau concentration camp. Following the declaration of victory in Europe, those of us who survived returned home or stayed on for further service.

*****

I didn't return home right away. I was not looking forward to what faced me when I arrived. I did not want to look Rose Marie Miramoto in the face and say, "Your husband was my best friend. He saved my life. I'm so sorry." I didn't know how to say those things to that woman. I didn't know how to say those things to Akio's parents or to Maggie, should I ever speak to her again. Akio had died saving my life and I felt like it was my fault that he was dead. I was so afraid that the people that we held in common would turn against me. I couldn't bear to see the pain in their eyes.

It happened during the "Go for Broke" campaign in the Vosges. The battle lasted five days, from October 26th, 1944 to October 30th, 1944. We had been sent into the mountains to free the "Lost Battalion," the two hundred and eleven American soldiers who had been surrounded by the Germans. We did it—we went for broke. During that campaign we suffered over eight hundred injuries and one hundred twenty-one deaths. On the second day, Akio and I found ourselves isolated from our unit and under fire. He and I were good shots, but my gun jammed. As I looked down at my weapon for just a second to free my bullets, I felt myself flying towards the ground away from my friend. I hit the ground pretty hard. It took me a minute to figure out what was going on.

At first I thought that I had been hit. My hands went to my chest checking for bullet holes. I was clear. I looked up. Akio was on the ground, face down. I crawled over to him and turned him over. Oh God, what I saw! My friend, my brother had been hit. The German sniper had hit his mark.

"Akio! Akio, come on!" I said to him, staying low to the ground. "We gotta get out of here. We need to get you help."

"Henry." Akio's response was feeble, strained. "I'm done. I'm going."

"No," I said. "No."

"Stop, let me speak, not much time," Akio responded.

"Yes," I knew it was inevitable. "Yes."

"Please watch over my girls. Tell them I love them," Akio whispered.

"Of course," I responded. "I'll take care of them. Please, let's get you to the medic." I just couldn't believe this was happening. Akio was so full of life, so much larger than life.

"You saved my life," I said after a moment. I didn't know what else to say.

"That's right," Akio smiled. "I guess that means that you owe me one."

"Anything," I said. "Anything at all."

"My sister," Akio answered. "Please try to help my sister."

"Maggie?" I asked, not sure what he meant. Akio knew that I loved Maggie.

"Hey, you owe me one, but I'm not expecting any miracles," he smiled. Even dying Akio had a good sense of humor. "I wish you all the luck in the world with Maggie. I wish you all the luck in the world without her," he paused to catch his breath. "Kimiko. Please find out if she's okay. Please try to help her get home."

"I will find her, Akio," I answered. "I promise."

"Henry?" Akio's voice was barely more than a whisper. "I want to tell you something, but no laughing."

"Of course."

"No, really, no jokes about old Akio being a pansy."

"What is it?" I asked.

"Henry, I love you. You're like a brother."

"Me too," I answered, tears coming to my eyes. I don't know if he heard me. Private First Class Miramoto died on October 27, 1944 taking a bullet from a German sniper that was meant for me.

20 AKIO

Letter sent to Minidoka, 1944. Personal collection of RLM.

TO MY DEAR ROSES,

How are my girls doing back at summer camp? I hope that you're eating well and having fun. I am writing to you from the Italian countryside on the way up to France. Can you believe it? I always wanted to see the world but never thought I could afford it. What luck!

I'm happy to be here, happy to finally be doing my part in this war but I miss you and Rosie dearly. I carry in the pocket over my heart the picture of the three of us in front of Mama's roses in our little backyard on Beacon Hill. What I wouldn't give for us to be together back home. I hope that those of us fighting in the 442nd and 100th will prove to America that we are worthy and the WRA will close the camps for good. Truly, you should see these boys fight—like their lives depended on it. I think that we are doing our country proud, I really do.

This war is nasty. I won't trouble you with the details, but this is so much worse than I ever could have imagined. It's a worthy cause, don't get me wrong, but there are days when I just want to stand up and shout over to the enemy, "What the hell are we all doing here trying to kill each other? Can't we all just go home and let each other be?" But, if I did that, I would be shot down by about ten German snipers. If I lived, I'd probably be discharged for insanity. So far I haven't done it!

Rose Marie, I miss you more than I even thought I would. I didn't know that I could miss a person the way that I miss you and our daughter. I know that it wasn't easy for you to marry a *Nisei*—even your own family was against it. But you loved me and you were so brave. And then, when they started putting us in camps, you were still brave and stayed right by my side. I know that it has been hard, but I am so proud of you. I'm proud not only because of your courage and conviction, but I'm proud that you are my wife. You being with me—you being with me at Camp Harmony and Minidoka—shows that you must love me. And I love you so much.

I don't want to scare you, but I want to say something just in case I don't make it back. I want to apologize for leaving you alone with a child that is half-Japanese in a world that seems to hate us. I know that you aren't ashamed or anything, please do not worry that I think that. I just know that it will be hard and I'm sorry if I can't be there to help you. I have confidence that you are the best mother in the world and that our daughter will be loved. My one regret is that we did not give Rosie a little brother or sister to keep her company. There are few things in life that I have treasured more than my own sisters.

So, my dear, if I don't come back, please don't let any feelings of fear or guilt stop you from leading the best life that you can. You are beautiful and young and if I couldn't give Rosie a brother, maybe someone else can. Don't worry about hurting me. You have made me so happy that is all that I want for you. I also hope that you will try to patch things up with your family. They are a product of their society and not necessarily bad— especially your grandmother. Being separated from my family has reminded me that we need to spend as much time together as possible because we never know what may come along tomorrow to separate us. I guess what I mean to say is please don't cut off ties with your family on my behalf. I understand.

Finally, and forgive me for being a little selfish, please don't let Rosie forget her Daddy. I'm going to include in this letter two little rings that I bought on the Italian coast for my little ladies. I hope to see each of you wearing them soon. I love you both with all my heart. No matter what, I'll always be there with you. Please don't forget me.

Love,

Akio (Private First Class Miramoto)

PS. Not to scare you, but should I decide to stay over here in Europe indefinitely, promise me that you'll transfer the farm in Bellevue into my parent's name if it's ever legal for the *Issei* to own land.

21 ROSE MARIE

From archived interview, continued.

THE DAY THAT I heard was just like any other day at Camp Minidoka. That is something I've noticed about the days that change everything; they start just like any other. I had spent the day doing laundry (which never ceased to be a terrible time-consuming activity in the camps), teaching an English class, and practicing reading with my daughter. It was autumn, but it felt like winter. It was early November 1944. I was looking forward to an evening with my in-laws, who had arrived at Camp Minidoka earlier that fall. I had become much closer to my mother-in-law in particular since Akio went off to the war. I would have liked to have seen Maggie, too, but we were all so proud of her, off at school. Still, our gatherings were populated with the absence of so many loved ones.

The events of that day have played out so many times in my head it is like a movie reel that I can rewind and watch over and over again. In the late afternoon, just before dinner, Mrs. Miramoto and Mrs. Fusaka were in my barracks fussing over me.

I was pregnant; I had discovered it just after Akio had left for training. I had tried to contact Akio by letter to tell him the good news, but from the content of his letters home to me, I'm not sure that he ever knew—he was moving so much and in the middle of so many battles, it was hard to pin him down long enough to get mail through. Although it bothered me that he didn't know, I comforted myself with the thought that it would be such a surprise it would be for him to come home to a new little son or daughter. In the meantime, I had to focus on getting through this pregnancy without letting my concern for my husband complicate matters. I had determined to just go about my daily routine for as long as I could without focusing on the pregnancy and my fears.

Of course, my mother-in-law and Mrs. Fusaka wouldn't let me think of anything but the baby. "Rest," they would say as they took Rosie over to the Fusaka barrack. "Eat," they would say as they tried to force down my throat the cookies and dried fruit they had saved up for and purchased at the camp store. It was all very sweet, really. It was just that their attention and worry stressed me out even more because it was so obviously to keep my mind off of my husband. It was as if their best efforts only worked to cause me to think more of the possibility that Akio might not return. If I stopped and thought about my situation I was seized by a sadness that I couldn't even begin to fathom. From the moment that Akio had been scheduled to leave for training, I had a sense of dread. Please God, I prayed ten thousand times every day, please let my husband come home alive. Please God.

So on that November afternoon when the two Caucasian men in Army uniforms stuck their heads into my barrack, I knew. I had been expecting them from the first time that Akio had said that he would like to serve. I had known that it was just a matter of time before I heard the news. Still, when the time came, I found myself praying that the soldiers were at my door not to speak to me but to ask for directions, maybe to a neighbor's barracks—just about everybody at Minidoka had a husband or son serving. I hoped for a moment that maybe they were there looking for someone else, Mrs. Fusaka maybe. It was a terrible thing to hope for, especially considering that Henry had become like family to me. I was immediately seized with not only a feeling of fear, but also one of terrible guilt towards my friends. I knew then that a person as terrible as I could only expect to hear the worst of news. I deserved it.

When the officers walked up, I remember my mother-in-law was combing Rosie's hair. She dropped the brush when one of the soldiers said, "Mrs. Miramoto?" The brush was heavy and it hit her foot. She had a huge bruise for weeks but she said that, at the time, she didn't feel a thing. Mrs. Fusaka, who had been prying open a can of sugar cookies turned and looked at the soldiers with the look of a deer caught in the headlights. Time stood still.

Both my mother-in-law and I answered in the affirmative to the officer. The two men looked from my mother-in-law to me and then down at their papers. "I'm his wife," I said, reading their minds. "That is his mother." Please God, I thought, let him just be injured. Give us time to say goodbye, in the very least.

"Mrs. Miramoto," the second officer said nodding towards me. "Mrs. Miramoto," he said acknowledging my mother-in-law. "I regret to say that I bring news of your husband and son, Private First Class Akio Miramoto."

"Is he alright?" gasped Akio's mother. Perhaps she hadn't caught the word "regret." What good news would be regrettable? I remained silent, not wanting to hear the soldier's reply.

"Ma'am," he said, choosing his words carefully. "Your son was a pride to his unit, a hero amongst heroes. He fought bravely and valiantly. I am sorry to have to tell you that your son died defending his country. He was a true and good American." My mother-in-law looked as if she were going to faint. Mary Fusaka had come up behind her and grabbed her before she fell.

"Where is he?" I asked the soldiers. They seemed confused and taken aback by the question.

"He is in Europe, ma'am," the second soldier replied. "He will be returned to the States soon. If you like, he is eligible to be

229

buried at Arlington." A hero's burial. He would have liked that, I thought. It would be very far from Seattle, but Akio deserved to be buried in the National Cemetery. Also, selfishly, I thought that if Akio were buried far from me I wouldn't be able to go to his grave often. It would be easier to forget that he was dead if I didn't have to look at his grave on a weekly or even yearly basis. He would be in the nation's capital with the other American heroes and I would visit his grave occasionally, when I had the means to go to Washington, D.C. I didn't want to be married to a piece of stone and a plot of land. I wanted to remember my husband as a person. As a living person. I didn't go until the year 2000, when President Clinton awarded many posthumous awards to the all-*Nisei* units. Maggie and I stood at the grave that now bore the inscription that my husband had been awarded a Medal of Honor. "You know," Maggie said, putting her arm around me, "Akio means hero in Japanese." I hadn't known that. But it certainly fit the man. Akio Miramoto was an American hero.

*****

In December 1944, just days before Christmas, the U.S. Army held a small ceremony at Camp Minidoka, Idaho. Four mothers were being presented with their sons' Purple Heart medals. Like Akio, all four of the men being honored that day had been killed in the Go for Broke campaign. There had been some hope that the medals would be awarded in Twin Falls, but it the WRA did not deem this occasion to be momentous enough to allow the Japanese parents of the fallen soldiers leave to temporarily exit the camp.

I was present at the ceremony and so was my daughter. When the officer presented the medal to my mother-in-law, with my father-in-law standing behind her with his hand on her shoulder, I saw her look up at the young man. "And where is my son?" she seemed to ask. I don't think that my mother-in-law had allowed herself to understand that Akio was dead until that very moment. She put her head down and did not say a word.

Both of my in-laws slightly bowed to the officer as he moved on to the next couple. After the ceremony my father-in-law asked if he could keep the medal until his death, at which time he would give it to Rosie. "Of course," I said. "You deserve the medal, too. He was your son," I replied. From that moment until the day he died my father-in-law kept that medal pinned on his body and would proudly show it off to anyone who noticed it. "You see this?" he would say, pointing to the medal. "This was my son. He was an American soldier. He died fighting for his country."

*****

After I received the word of my husband's death, time both stood still and sped up. It was all I could do to keep my head above water every day. I tried to take care of my in-laws, who were also clearly in pain, but I am afraid that they were more helpful to me than I was to them. My mother-in-law and Mary Fusaka helped care for my daughter during those days when I was too crippled by disbelief and despair to get out of my narrow Army cot to respond to Rosie's cries or questions. The questions were the worst: "Where's Daddy?" she asked over and over again. "Why isn't Daddy coming home?" When none of us could adequately explain the situation to her, my poor little girl became silent. For three months she said very little, if anything at all. She was even more confused when Akio's letter arrived along with our rings after we had received news of his death. I had to explain once again that Daddy wasn't coming back and there hadn't been a mistake with the officer's news. Thankfully, Rosie eventually snapped out of her self-imposed catatonia, but only after I began to seriously worry about her.

There was also serious worry about the baby that I was carrying at the time that I heard of Akio's death. My mother-in-law especially seemed to push aside her own grief over the loss of her only son in order to help me carry to term that son's child. Following my initial shock and grief, that baby was a source of strength not only for my in-laws, but also for me. Thanks to my children, I had to get up and make sure that I was taking care of myself. It became my mission in life to care for my children—especially once I received the late-arriving letter from Akio asking me to do so. If only he would have known about his second child.

I was able to carry that child to term and I gave birth to a healthy little boy on February 14, 1945. On that day, in Minidoka, Idaho, my son was born, healthy and strong. I named him Akio Henry Miramoto. I named him for two good men, one that he would never meet and one that he would meet because of the heroic acts of the other. His father would have been so proud of him.

22 MAGGIE

From "The Roses of Minidoka," continued.

IN NOVEMBER 1944 I received a phone call from Mrs. Fusaka. When I was called to the phone, I was hit by a sense of dread. It was not the usual day for my telephone call from my parents. Once I heard Mrs. Fusaka's voice on the line, my blood ran cold. I thought that something had happened to Henry. Please God, I thought, let Henry be okay. I missed him. When I got to Vassar, alone and far from my former life, I had a lot of time on my hands to reflect. Away from my loved ones, I began to realize what I really wanted: More than anything, I wanted to go back in time to December 6, 1941. I wanted to be back at home on the farm in Bellevue with my parents, with plans to see my boyfriend and my brother and his family the next day. The more I thought about it, I realized that I wished that I could go back even further to a time when Kimiko was still in America and we were all together. Except that I didn't know Henry then, so I really wanted to go back to a time that did not exist. Maybe it was a time in the future. But, as I was about to learn, the future would never be the same.

"Maggie?" asked Mrs. Fusaka when I answered the phone. Henry's mother had always used my American name. "Maggie, is that you?" she asked.

"Yes, Mrs. Fusaka. I'm here," I responded. "Is Henry okay?" I asked before she could get another word in edgewise.

"Maggie," she continued, "I have some bad news for you."

"No. Henry?" I was already crying.

"Maggie, Henry is fine."

"Thank God." I thought for a moment; who then? "My parents?" I asked through my tears. It dawned on me that something could have potentially happened to a variety of people that I knew and loved. I was so far away from them all, carrying on with my life. Something terrible could be happening to my family and I wouldn't know it. Something wonderful could happen and I wouldn't know it. I had left.

"They are fine, Maggie," she responded. "I need to tell you something, Maggie."

"Yes," I said and I waited for what I knew would be news that changed my life.

"Your brother was injured in the war, Maggie."

"Akio," I whispered. He was the last person that I thought was hurt, even though I knew he was fighting in Europe. In my mind my big brother was invincible.

"He saved Henry's life," she paused. "He didn't make it, honey."

I responded with complete silence. The last time I had seen my brother was the day over two years before when I saw him off to Camp Harmony; I thought that I would be seeing him in just a couple of weeks. If I had known that I would never see him again, what would I have said that day? Surely more than "see you later."

"I'm so sorry, Maggie," Mrs. Fusaka broke into my thoughts.

"I have to go," I said. "I'm sorry, Mrs. Fusaka. I need to go."

"I understand, Maggie."

"Mrs. Fusaka?" I managed to remember myself. "How are

my parents doing…and Rose Marie and Rosie? Oh God, poor Rose Marie!"

"They are doing as well as they can. We are trying to keep Rose Marie focused on the baby." The baby that would never know its father.

"Did Akio ever know about the baby?"

"Your sister-in-law is not sure if he ever received her letters with the news. She hopes that he did."

"Mrs. Fusaka?" I asked, embarrassed by my behavior towards her son and wishing that I could say so much more. "I'm sorry. Thank you for helping my family."

"Of course, Maggie. Please take care of yourself."

"Mrs. Fusaka?"

"Yes, dear?"

"I'm happy that Henry is okay. I…well, please tell him that I am happy that he is okay."

"I will, Maggie."

It wasn't until I hung up the telephone that I noticed the tears that were running down my face.

*****

That moment remains suspended in time for me. I think back to it and it is as if I am right there again, telephone to my ear, tears running down my face. It is one of those moments that still haunt my life, a pivotal moment. As I hung up the phone, my heart was broken for the loss of my brother. It was broken for the loss of a life that I could now, truly, never return to. It was also broken for my family. I looked around the home in upstate New York where I was staying and thought to myself, my parents are in a prison camp. My brother is dead. My niece and her unborn sibling are fatherless. My sister-in-law is in prison camp, a war widow and pregnant. My ex-boyfriend is still in the military and doesn't know how sorry I am. My sister is lost in Japan and I haven't heard from her in years. And, after listing the tragedies of the Miramoto family, I realized that I had left; I had avoided it all at my first opportunity. I was living three thousand miles away from Minidoka, living the life of an average American student. But that is not who I was, no matter how much the WRA may have hoped when they relocated us *Nisei*. While it was an honor and an opportunity of a lifetime to be in school at Vassar, it was not where I was supposed to me at that moment in life.

I was unable to tell anyone at school what had happened for almost two days. I simply hung up the phone and went upstairs to my little room. I didn't leave it for the next day and a half. I didn't come out for meals, chores, or school. I may have stayed in there forever if my host mother hadn't gently knocked and let herself into my room on the second day. I still remember that the first time that I said the words, "My brother is dead." It was in explanation for my behavior. It came out sounding like a confession of a crime that should never have been committed. It sounded so horrific to my ears that I could barely utter the words out loud.

In order to take my mind off the pain, I swung into a flurry of action. I knew that I had to go back to my family; I could not leave them alone at a time like this. But I also knew that I couldn't abandon school without at least attempting to finish up the term. It would be one thing to come home without graduating, but I knew that my parents—and my brother—would not want me to come home without getting any credits that I had earned. How odd that I say "home." Of course, I am referring to the camp. I hadn't even been in Camp Minidoka which is where I requested to be placed since my whole family was now located in Idaho. When I say "home," I meant where my family was. My home was wherever my family was, be it our farm in Bellevue, a little house in Seattle, or a tiny barrack room in Idaho. The thing was, though, I couldn't just go. I had to get permission.

I wasn't sure who at the school I should go to first to help me wrap up the term so that I could get back to my family. Obviously, I had already told the family with whom I was staying. They were supportive and even ending up giving me some money for the train. I had discovered that I did not have enough to make it to Idaho and I had offered to do some quick work for them to earn some extra money. When I refused to take any money without work, my host family paid me at least twice as much as what I had earned. I accepted this generosity with gratitude.

Next, I tackled my professors. I was overwhelmed by the sympathy I received and the overall willingness to allow me to finish the term. My professors, along with the school administration, agreed that if I stayed until early December, I would be able to sit for early examinations and get full credit for the current term. I would also receive letters of recommendations for any school that I may apply to in the future as well as an open invitation to return to Vassar. While I had enjoyed my time back East, in my heart I knew that I would not be coming back. I was more determined than ever to finish up my university schooling at the school that I had wanted to go to since I was a teenager: The University of Washington. I knew that it wouldn't happen immediately, but it was confident that it would happen someday. I could wait.

After clearing up my school credits, I had to speak the New York office of the War Relocation Authority. I took a train down to the city with a group of Vassar students traveling to visit their families. After meeting with a WRA worker, I knew that my hopes of getting back to school in Seattle would be delayed for some time. While I was at Vassar, I had almost managed to forget that the Japanese and Japanese Americans were still so hated in the West. I had focused on my studies and involved myself with a small group of people who did not find my presence shocking or offensive. In my daily life at school I did not encounter the racism and paranoia that was still in full effect on the West Coast. It all came rushing back to mind as I entered the WRA's offices. Oddly, the people at the War Relocation Authority office presented the least support and biggest obstacle to my return to the internment camps.

There is a theory that I heard later that the WRA's attempts to send *Nisei* students to the East Coast and allow *Nisei* farmers to move to the Midwest was based not in altruistic hopes of providing a better life to internees, or even the more pragmatic benefit of lessening the economic burden on the government by emptying the camps of many residents. Some say that *Nisei* students and farmers were sent east to further break up the Japanese family unit; to separate the two generations of *Issei* and *Nisei*. I do not know what the WRA's motives were and I will not attempt to speculate after all these years. All I can say is that the WRA field office in New York did not seem to see any logic to my statement that I had to be re-interned with my family at Camp Minidoka. A variety of "options" were presented to me, including that of staying at Vassar, or, if I wanted to go west, to relocate to Spokane. "No," I said to each of these suggestions. "I need to be with my family." When they looked at me blank faced, I tried to explain. "My brother died." At one point I was so frustrated by the WRA workers' lack of willingness to just send me back that I threatened to show up at the gates of Minidoka so that they would have no choice but to put me back into the camp.

"Miss," an exasperated WRA worker responded to my impertinent threat, "if you show up in Idaho without permission, you could potentially be arrested as a national threat or a traitor. You would probably be sent to a Department of Justice facility or Tule Lake. Please do not be rash."

"Please," I tried to explain again, exhausted. "My brother died in the war. I need to be with my family. Do you really think that I just want to go back there? Please, tell me why I would want to send myself back to a prison camp?"

Finally, after repeating myself many times, one of the WRA men who had been called to assist with my case was silent for a moment. He turned his back on me and grabbed a form from a shelf behind his desk. As he began to fill it out, he said to me, "Miss, it is not a prison camp, but an internment camp. It is meant to be temporary so try to get yourself out of there as soon as you can." He handed me the paper, keeping the carbon copies for himself. It was an order allowing me to be re-interned, my school privileges temporarily revoked. "My son died last year," he said in response to my whispered thanks. "It is important to be with your family."

*****

The train came to a stop in Twin Falls, Idaho in mid-December 1944. I had to meet my scheduled transport to the camp at Minidoka immediately so as to not cause a security situation. How odd it was to have the freedom I had gained in self-exile taken from me; as I saw the military transport I immediately dreaded what lay before me. I had hated Pinedale and Tule Lake. I could barely stomach the thought of spending more time behind the barbed wire and guard towers of a third internment camp. I had been free, I thought to myself. I could still be free at school and not being escorted to prison—*camp*—like a common criminal. Of course, I quickly reminded myself, had I really been free during my time in Poughkeepsie? I had moved there only under the conditions of the WRA and that authority monitored me even while I was in school. I had not been free to go to the school of my choice. I had not been free to travel to the states of my choosing. I had not been free to return to my home. Even though I had been out of the camps, I had not been truly free. As I was escorted into Camp Minidoka by armed guard I realized that I would not be free until the war was over and prejudice towards my ethnic heritage was abolished. Until that happened, I knew that I wanted to be exactly where I was: With my family. As I walked through the gates of Minidoka, I tugged the ring around my neck for luck and looked for the welcoming faces of my family members, waiting for me with open arms.

23 KIMIKO

From treason confession, continued.

AFTER MY INITIAL EXPERIENCE filling in for Orphan Annie, I had to do it two more times. Once I understood that Zero Hour was not a pro-Japan propaganda show, I was happy to help the POWs and broadcast a show out to the troops in the Pacific; it made me feel a bit connected to my own country's soldiers when I thought of them listening to my voice. Of course, my real problem was my husband. When Ryuu told me that I was to do the show a second time I protested; he would know something was up if I just willingly agreed. My mock unwillingness led to a terrible fight, one black eye, and a night locked in a closet. I had to do it though. Ryuu was a smart man and if I was willing to do the show he might be suspicious. I could not let my sudden change of heart lead to any sort of realization by Ryuu and Tsuneishi that Zero Hour was not the powerful propaganda powerhouse that they thought it to be. However, the third time that I was told to do the show I said nothing, feigning to be the ideal submissive wife. Thankfully,

Ryuu bought it and I was spared another beating.

Most likely the reason that Ryuu fell for my submissive acceptance to go back to Zero Hour a third time was because I had once again thrown my energy behind trying to appear to be a proper wife. With the birth of Kiyoko I had forgotten that apparent submission was the key to getting along with my husband. Following the loss of my daughter to Hatsu and their departure to Hiroshima, I had no energy left to focus on pretending any compliance with my husband. For quite some time, I engaged in open hostility towards Ryuu. That only resulted in increasing punishment for me and thus less chance of a reunion with my baby. I realized that I had to see my daughter and the only way to get Ryuu to agree to let me go to Hiroshima would be to convince him that I was his ideal wife. However, this was still difficult at first because Ryuu seemed to have no plans of leaving Tokyo and the center of action. Without Ryuu accompanying me, there was no hope of me going to Hiroshima. Thus, not only did I have to convince Ryuu that I was a good wife, but I had to convince him that a move would be in his best interests.

Thankfully, after just a bit of time the Allied Troops helped me to convince Ryuu that Tokyo was no longer safe. As 1944 pressed on, it had become clear that Japan was losing the war in the Pacific. Although it had once had the clear upper hand in the war, since the Battle of Midway in June 1942, the tides had changed for Japan. The Allies were making slow but steady progress in the Pacific Theater. Of course, those of us in Japan had no idea that the Imperial military was losing the war—the propaganda remained strong and consistent in the emperor's favor. I, however, had learned the secret of the radio announcers and could hear what they were really saying. Even I began to look forward to hear the famous Tokyo Rose come on and mock her captors by listing successes that no longer existed. It seemed that for many months my husband, along with his countrymen, chose to believe what they heard; they thought victory for Japan was imminent.

However, once Tokyo began burning it became very clear

that Japan was not as safe or as strong as the propaganda machine claimed it to be. From February through March 1945 the Allied powers fought for and eventually took the island of Iwo Jima. By June of 1945, the Allies had taken Okinawa. They now had land holdings close enough to the mainland of Japan that they could send their fighter planes over the capital city to drop bombs of fire and have enough gas left to get back to their base. Once the Allies had Okinawa, it was over for Japan (although you wouldn't know it from listening to the radio).

Still, Japan did not give up despite the fact that the city was in flames. Bombs were being dropped like leaflets from the sky, and there was little, if any, hope that the Empire would be able to stage a counteroffensive. The pride of the nation was hurt and most of the populace was confused—they were supposed to have won this war. But Ryuu was too well-connected to be confused: To my relief, Ryuu finally, after more than a year of my games and pleading, had determined on his own that Tokyo was no longer safe enough for his presence. Ryuu and I were on our way to Hiroshima and I was on my way to Kiyoko.

*****

Getting to Hiroshima was easier said than done. People were swarming out of the devastation of Tokyo, trying to get out before the next bombing, and many roads were in disrepair. It took three times as long to get back to the Miramoto compound as it would have before the war, but we made it. Compared to Tokyo, Hiroshima was a peaceful and tranquil city—as if there was no war at all going on. No bombs or fires had erupted this far away from the center of power. I had always thought Hiroshima was a pretty city and I was glad to be back, away from the overwhelming non-stop hustle and bustle of Tokyo. And I was so very excited to see my little girl. I could almost have given Ryuu a willing hug for finally bringing me back to my daughter. He, of course, made no mention of Kiyoko.

As we drew up to our family's home, I knew immediately that something was wrong—the house seemed too empty, too quiet. I ran in the door, to the obvious dismay of the servants who were used to the women of the family being subdued and calm. "Hatsu!" I screamed. "Kiyoko!"

"They are not here, Madame," said Sakura, one of the housemaids, who had come up beside me from a side hallway. Ryuu, who had been taking his time coming into the house, was standing in the doorway behind me, silent. I glared at him before turning back to the poor girl, and not more than two inches from her face, screaming, "Where is my baby?"

"Yes, where in the hell are they?" asked Ryuu, surprising me.

I turned at the sound of his voice. "Did you send them away from here?" I accused, too frantic to care if I was angering him. "In the middle of a war did you send your own child away just to spite me?"

Surprisingly, this did not spurn the wrath of Ryuu. "I do not know where they are, Kimiko," he said to me. He seemed confused, not as in control as normal. Perhaps even a bit concerned if I am being judicious.

"Madame," said Sakura, her eyes down. "Sir." The girl was shaking as she faced the firing squad that was the gaze of both Ryuu and me, for once united. "Miss Hatsu had to leave to help her mother. Firebombs hit her family's house and Miss Hatsu's parents were hurt. She brought the child with her to ensure her safety."

"She brought my baby *into* the zone of fire bombs to keep her *safe*?" I was incredulous at this logic.

"She said it was her job, Madame; that the master forbade her to leave the child with anyone else."

I felt myself slip to the floor, unable to hold myself up on my own feet. Please God, I thought to myself, Please keep Hatsu and my child safe. I turned towards Ryuu. "We must go back," I said.

"We must wait," said Ryuu. "You will see your daughter again, Kimiko-san." For a brief moment I saw a flicker of compassion in my husband's eyes.

*****

Ryuu was correct: We spent our time in Hiroshima waiting. We waited for word of the war to end; we waited for word of my child's safety. By late July, I was waiting for word that my child had died. But, despite our patience, we received word of nothing. By this point, the situation was so bad in Tokyo that Ryuu would not allow me to leave. After his brief moments of concern, he apparently did not feel the need to risk even my life to go find his child. I spent my days praying and thinking of ways to, in the very least, get word to Hatsu. Finally, in the first couple days of August, we received two breakthroughs. On August 1, 1945 I received a hurried note from Hatsu giving the location of her family's home in Tokyo, her apologies, and her word that Kiyoko was safe. She had not known that Ryuu and I were coming to Hiroshima. She thought that she would speak to us at our apartment in Tokyo. "I will protect your child with my life," she assured me. The letter was dated July fifteenth. I just hoped that they were still safe. I was upset that Hatsu had brought my daughter back to the city, but I realized that she had thought that I was still there and she likely didn't know what to do when she heard about her mother. I knew she cared for my daughter; I just had to hope that her affection would guide her choices and she would stay safe until I could be reunited with Kiyoko.

At this time, there was also word regarding the war. Ryuu had found out through his connections that the new president of the United States had issued an ultimatum to the Japanese on July 26, 1945 outlining terms of surrender. This became known as the Potsdam Declaration. If Japan did not accept the terms of the Potsdam Declaration, President Truman promised "the inevitable and complete destruction of the Japanese armed forces and just as inevitably the utter devastation of the Japanese homeland." Just how this complete destruction was to be carried out was not mentioned in the Declaration.

"Japan will never surrender," Ryuu had said when I asked what he thought of the declaration and the threat of destruction. I was surprised that the Japanese were not taking the declaration more seriously. After all, the Allies had already all but won the war—Japan was surrounded, Tokyo was in flames. I also could not help but think that Hitler had also claimed that he would never surrender but he was now dead in an underground bunker and Europe belonged to the Allies. Surely America would win this war. Surely Japan wouldn't push them to follow through on this blatant threat of destruction.

"My dear American wife," Ryuu continued, "I know that you want your precious United States to win, but it will never happen."

"Ryuu," I patiently argued, "It already has. Only a miracle would save Japan now."

"Well, perhaps the Emperor has one up his sleeves. After all, he has connections to the heavens." The emperor was seen, even in 1945, as being a demi-god and so his actions were thought to be directed by the divine.

"All right then, Ryuu," I was starting to understand that Ryuu, too, had been taught to never accept defeat. "Let's say it's the U.S. that has the miracle. What could Truman be talking about? What is the extreme measure that will ensure utter defeat and destruction?"

"There has been talk of a bomb, more powerful than any other," Ryuu said. "This is not the official theory, but one that I have discussed with a few of my connections. Both the Americans and the Germans have been trying to create a bomb that can wipe out entire cities. It is to be a bomb that harnesses the very forces of the universe to create havoc and destruction where it is detonated. I am certain that this is the inherent threat that we are supposed to assume in Truman's declaration." I could tell by Ryuu's sarcastic tone that he did not have confidence in the U.S.'s warning. "Nothing more than an empty threat," he continued, affirming my thoughts.

I remained silent. America would win this war, of that I was certain. I was also certain that the Japanese would not admit defeat easily. How do you win against an enemy that will not surrender? "They will have to annihilate them," I whispered in response to my own question. My blood ran cold thinking of the possibility. If I were a general and I had a bomb that could destroy an entire city, where would I drop that bomb? I asked myself. Tokyo. I knew then that I had to get to Tokyo and save my daughter and Hatsu.

While I had come to this conclusion, Ryuu had continued speaking about Truman and his "empty threats" and how Japan was surely using apparent defeat to lure the Americans onto their soil so that the Empire could "destroy them." I was only half listening. I had no time to spare and I wasn't going to waste it listening to the delusional drivel of my husband.

*****

In order to get out of Hiroshima, I would need help. The problem was that I had very few people that I could trust and, thanks to my husband, I was only allowed to speak to the servants at the family compound. Sakura was the only servant that I had every really spoken to beyond simple sentences; I had apologized to her after my outburst the day we arrived and she had readily told me that there was no need to apologize. She had been a child when I had first visited Japan with my family; her mother was the family's maid before her. She seemed sympathetic to my situation and I hoped that she had not already fallen victim to the interest of my husband. Sakura liked to hear stories of America when nobody was within earshot. She even wanted to learn English. She was my only hope.

"Sakura," I said to her on the night of August first, after my conversation with Ryuu. "I think that the United States may be planning to drop a bomb on Tokyo."

"Pardon, Madame Miramoto," answered Sakura bowing deeply as if to counteract her contradiction, "but they drop bombs on Tokyo everyday."

"This one will be different," I said. "It will kill everyone in the city."

"But…that's terrible," she said. "Your daughter is there," she whispered with a look of horror. I know that she had enjoyed helping Hatsu care for my sweet little girl. Since I hadn't seen Kiyoko for months, Sakura would treat me to stories about

8:13 a.m.

A boy answered the door to the little house. I had knocked without stop until the door was answered. I must have terrified the poor child. He looked up at me as if I might be a madwoman.

"Kiyoko," I said by way of explanation. "The child; I am here for the child."

"Please wait, madam," the boy was polite beyond his years. He ushered me into the small foyer and went into a back room. I heard voices. It was definitely Hatsu. And then, yes, it was my little girl.

8:14 a.m.

"Mama!" my little girl cried as she wobbled towards me on her toddler's legs. "Thank God!" I exclaimed as I swooped down to take my daughter in my arms. I held her tight and said a prayer of thanksgiving to all that is good in the universe.

8:15 a.m.

A small plane called the Enola Gay flew over the city of Hiroshima. At 08:15 local time, the U.S. fighter plane dropped "Little Boy," the world's first nuclear bomb.

8:15:15 a.m.

I came back to attention when I sensed the presence of Hatsu in the room.

"I am so very sorry, Madame," she said, eyes downcast. "I thought you were still here in Tokyo. I did not mean to scare you."

"There is to be a bomb, Hatsu," I answered in a frenzied panic. "We must leave immediately."

"I cannot move my parents, I'm afraid," she answered.

At that moment a moan came from the other room. My little girl looked up at me and said, "Help, Mama." Hatsu had been a good surrogate mother. Someone needed help. I just prayed to God that we would be able to leave the city in time.

8:15:50a.m.

"Little Boy" took his time coming down—fifty seconds passed before the bomb detonated at approximately two thousand feet altitude. At that moment, "Little Boy" transformed itself into a huge ball of atomic fire. The bomb hit Hiroshima with the power of all the forces of the universe, just as Ryuu had described. Those who survived suffered atrocious and unheard of injuries. In the wake of Little Boy, not even death was normal. Eyes melted from their sockets; clothing disappeared after burning its patterns into the skin of its wearer; people seemingly vanished as their bodies were completely obliterated by the force of the atom bomb. In many cases those who survived were less fortunate than their friends and family members who had not. The injuries of the survivors were painful and life threatening. Even those who did not bear any apparent injury would later discover that their inner bodies had been destroyed in the blast. Cancers and birth defects still plague Hiroshima.

8:30 a.m.

Hatsu and I had spent several minutes in her parents' backroom caring for her father, who was very badly burned from the recent fires in the neighborhood. While trying to ease the pain of my friend's father, I noticed that there was a commotion out in the streets. My first instinct was that I had somehow been too busy with the old man to hear or notice the bomb dropping on Tokyo. I excused myself and ran out onto the street to see what was happening.

"What is it?" I tried to ask people passing by.

"A bomb!" cried one person. "The whole city is gone!" cried another. My blood ran cold, thinking that my predictions had come true. But then it dawned on me—I was standing in the middle of Tokyo and it appeared that the city was, in fact, still there.

"Hiroshima is gone!" cried another.

"Hiroshima?" I tried to stop someone else walking by.

"Yes, Madame," answered a teenage boy. "A bomb hit

Hiroshima. The whole city is gone."

"When did this happen?" I asked.

"At 8:15, madam," the boy answered. I felt faint. "Oh God," I whispered.

"Why Hiroshima," I asked, not expecting an answer.

"I don't know," answered the teenager. I noticed that his arm was bandaged. He was wearing an tattered Imperial Navy uniform. He must not have been more than fifteen.

"Is the war over?" I asked.

"Japan will never surrender," answered the boy defiantly.

*****

Japan did not surrender following the atomic bombing of Hiroshima. On August 9, 1945, the United States dropped a second atomic bomb on the city of Nagasaki. On August 10th, Japanese officials said that they would accept the terms of the Potsdam Declaration and accept defeat, but negotiations faltered. Japan still had not surrendered. Bombings resumed, although not atomic. Finally, on the 14th of August 1945, President Truman announced victory in the Pacific. Japan had done the unthinkable; Japan had surrendered.

The surrender came after losing over eighty thousand civilian lives in Nagasaki and over one hundred forty thousand civilian lives in Hiroshima. Listed among those who lost their lives in Hiroshima was the Ryuu Miramoto family—Ryuu and Kimiko. The survival of the "Miramoto child" was unknown, as was the fate of my friend, Sakura. As far as the uncertainty about my child and the mistake about my survival, I did not rush to correct the information. In many ways I had died the day that Japan dropped its bombs on Pearl Harbor. How fitting, I thought, that the day of my death would be listed as the day that the United States dropped a bomb on Japan. After the bombing of Hiroshima, I allowed my name to die as my hopes for a new life slowly rose from the ashes of Japan.

24 ROSE MARIE

From archived interview, continued.

NEWS OF A BOMBING, especially one as horrific as the one used at Hiroshima, is never good news. Hearing reports of the destruction of an entire city and of the terrible, atrocious injuries of the bombing survivors was not a cause of celebration for anyone that I know who lived through the Second World War. Certainly as we came to learn that the bombs in Hiroshima and Nagasaki that ended the World War, in effect, began the Cold War, we realized that the use of the atomic bombs would only mean fear and paranoia for future generations. However, it would be untrue to say that, for Americans, there wasn't a sense of relief that the war with Japan had finally ended. There may have even been a feeling of sweet revenge, however inappropriate that may seem.

For the people interned in the internment camps, the news of the bombings and surrender of Japan was especially bittersweet. The end of the war meant that the camps would be closing and the West Coast would be re-opened for the Japanese and Japanese Americans to return to their homes. Of course, for many internees, especially the now elderly *Issei*, going "home" posed many difficulties and stresses. Many of these older folks refused to leave the camps until the War Relocation Authority forced them out. This reluctance did not necessarily reflect a love for the camp, but a fear of leaving. Most *Issei*s did not have homes to return to and those who did were often too old to start anew as labor intensive truck farmers. Sadly, many of the *Issei* who had once provided the coast with its lettuce, peas, and berries, would live out their lives in hastily constructed tenement apartment houses in Seattle, San Francisco, or Los Angeles. The life they had led for nearly forty years was gone.

For some in the internment camps, the news of the bombings of Hiroshima and Nagasaki brought a very real fear about family members in the bombing. Many people in the Seattle Japanese community were originally from the *ken*, or prefecture, of Hiroshima; many of those interned at Camp Minidoka had possibly lost family and friends in the bombings. My heart went out to these people when we heard of the use these horrific weapons. While they, like my in-laws, had to maintain their joy that America had won the war, I know that their smiles masked a sadness about what had been lost in the home of their childhood.

When the Miramotos heard of the bombing in Hiroshima, there was only one thing that they thought of: Kimiko. My mother-in-law was beside herself as she was convinced that her daughter must have sought out the aid of her family in Hiroshima. Maggie, who had surprised us all by joining us the previous Christmas, tried to assure her mother that Kimiko was almost certainly in Tokyo and not in Hiroshima. "She would never have gone to the Miramotos for help," Maggie had said with certainty. When her parents asked her why, she answered, "Because she really disliked cousin Ryuu." When they tried to get more information from her, Maggie simply said that, when they had met him as children, she and Kimiko had decided that there was "something wrong with him." Obviously, their intuition had been correct. While we waited for word, the Miramotos held onto the hope that Maggie's assumption was correct; that Kimiko had stayed away from the Miramotos and was thus far, far away from Hiroshima the day that the bomb fell

.

*****

While the world started to come back to normal life, we needed to leave the camp; how odd to say "needed" instead of "were able to." But in August 1945 I was a young widow with a small child and an infant. I was still too shocked about my husband's death to even fathom what I was going to do when I left the camp. Oddly, Minidoka had become a sort of security blanket for me while I recovered from the loss of Akio. Although I was free to leave, and probably could have received special permission to remove my children at that point since the tides of the war had changed, I had stayed. In the camp I did not have to worry about where I would live or how I would support my children. More importantly, in the camp I had my family— the Miramoto family. Although my in-laws and the Fusakas had treated me like a true member of their families during the war, I was terrified that once I left the camp I would no longer belong to them. Not that I feared that they would abandon me. I guess I feared that once I left, society wouldn't allow me to be a family with my in-laws. It had been hard before, wouldn't it be even more difficult now? More than anything in the world, I wanted to stay with the Miramotos.

I suppose because of my reluctance and feelings of being overwhelmed, most of the work involved in getting us all ready to leave Minidoka fell on Maggie's shoulders. Because Henry had decided to remain in the Army and was on his way to do some "confidential" work in Japan, Maggie had volunteered to help the Fusakas transition back to Seattle as well as her parents and me. I still didn't know that Maggie hadn't communicated directly with Henry for years. Poor girl, she was trying so hard to be forgiven for drifting away from Henry. In hindsight, if only they would have just *spoken* to each other, I'm certain that they would have discovered that they were still in love. Maybe I would have been more persistent in urging such a conversation, but I was still too tired and heartbroken to play matchmaker. For the time being, we all had to focus on getting our lives back on track. Once we were home, we could start living again.

*****

Maggie and I left Camp Minidoka in late August 1945. We had heard rumors that people were welcomed home by signs of vandalism and hatred and we wanted to see what lay ahead before we brought out the rest of the family. So, leaving Rosie with her grandparents--the Miramotos and her "other" grandparents, the Fusakas--I packed up little Akio and Maggie and I set out to see what was left of our world.

We were able to board a train in Twin Falls where the population had, in the very least, grown accustomed to seeing Japanese faces. We stayed to ourselves on the journey back to Seattle and were pleased to not encounter any open hatred. Of course, I was—am—Caucasian, but I was worried about Maggie and I was worried about the baby. Still, most people paid no attention to us or even avoided us completely. This was a relief because we had heard that there was suspicion and anxiety about the re-introduction of the Japanese American population to the West Coast. For some there was outright disagreement about the end of the exclusion and many people made those feelings painfully clear. While we did not encounter this on the train, we did speak with a *Nisei* young man in the uniform of the 442nd in the dining car. The young soldier had visited his family in Minidoka before heading for Seattle. He wore his uniform with pride and had obviously been wounded in battle. He was still using his Army-issue crutches.

The soldier caught our eye not only because he was *Nisei*, but also because he instantly reminded Maggie and I of Akio and Henry. He also caught our eye because he was struggling with some food in one hand while trying to navigate the moving train with his crutches. Except for Maggie, the soldier, and my child, everyone in the dining car was Caucasian. Maggie ran up and grabbed his food from him, helping him to find a place to set his meal. We ended up sitting with the soldier and sharing stories. Awkwardly, I attempted to apologize on behalf of the other people in the car who had not come to his aid.

"In some ways I prefer to be ignored," he responded. "Sure beats the lady earlier who looked at me and told me that every time she sees one of us 'Japs,' she thinks how 'one of us' killed her son in the Pacific." I gasped.

"What did you say?" asked Maggie, her hand covering her mouth in horror.

"What could I say?" said the soldier. "What can you say when a person is so ignorant?"

"I don't know," responded Maggie, "But someday I hope to have an answer for you."

The soldier smiled at her, partly at her naiveté and partly, I think, hoping that she would someday make good on that promise. "Well, let me know when you come up with something good, kid."

✳✳✳✳✳

We had a plan for what we would do once we arrived in Seattle: First we would go take a look at the Fusaka's apartment. It was close enough to the train station that we could walk. We wanted to get this part over with quickly; in many ways we were terrified to go into the International District. The dislike of many of the Chinese residents of that neighborhood towards the Japanese had been intense during the years of the Sino-Japanese War and many residents had gone out of their way after Pearl Harbor to draw a big line in the sand between the Chinese and Japanese communities. Fortunately, however, as Maggie and I walked through the streets there were no jeers, no names being called towards my sister-in-law. In fact, the neighborhood was completely different than the one we had left behind just a few years before.

It wasn't just the attitude: The part of the neighborhood that had been predominantly Japanese before the evacuation was now completely different. The Japanese businesses were almost completely gone. Where there had been Japanese teahouses, banks, and shops, there were now storefronts in English and Cantonese. Japantown was gone. Even the names of streets had changed. Japanese names gone and replaced with Anglo names. We actually got lost trying to find the Fusaka's building since all the businesses that we had formally used as markers were gone. Fortunately, when we finally figured out that the building we had walked past at least three times was in fact the correct one, and all looked well. Using the Fusaka's key, we were able to enter the apartment and, thank God, everything appeared to be untouched, albeit covered in three years' worth of dust. Exhausted, we cleaned the apartment enough to settle down and get some rest. We still had quite a bit of work ahead of us, but we felt that we had accomplished much for our first day back.

*****

Early the next morning I made a phone call to my grandmother. I didn't know what to expect, but I knew that I wanted to hear her voice. I was expecting Ethel to pick up the phone, but when the line was answered, it was my grandmother's voice that greeted me. She sounded different. She sounded old.

"Grandma," I said, "Grandma, are you alright?"

"Rose Marie?" my grandmother practically screeched with delight. We had not heard each other's voices in years. I had written one letter to my grandmother that was intercepted by my grandfather who wrote back to me saying that he would not accept any letters from the "Jap camps" at his address.

"Is that you?" my grandmother continued, "Where are you? Where is that precious little great-granddaughter of mine?"

"Grandma," I said, so happy to hear her voice. I hadn't realized how much I had missed her. "Rosie is still in Idaho; she'll be back soon. But, Grandma," I continued, "I have another baby, a boy. He is here with me."

"Where is 'here?'" she asked.

"I'm in Seattle with Maggie and my little boy. We are staying at a friend's apartment at Main and Fifth."

"May I come and visit you?" she asked. She was excited, but it sounded like she expected to be turned down; it broke my heart to hear her ask permission like this.

"Yes, Grandma," I said. "I can't wait to see you. Please come as soon as you can, but you'll have to excuse the mess. The Fusakas haven't been around to straighten up for years."

"Of course," she said. "Of course I will. Rose Marie?"

"Yes, Grandma," I asked. There was something about her voice that made me that she was saying much more than her words alone.

"I have missed you so much."

"Me too, Grandma," I said. "I've missed you, too."

As I hung up I started to cry. Maggie came up and gave me a hug.

"How about I leave and let you and your grandmother have some time alone?" she asked.

"Maggie, no," I said. "What would you even do out there? You are not going to wander the streets alone. Besides," I said with a smile, "You're my family, too."

"But will it cause a problem for all of you," she grimaced. "You know, because..." What she didn't say out loud was "since your family hates mine so much."

"Maybe it's time they got over that," I said. And for the first time I realized that I meant it. I had nothing to be ashamed of and it was high time that I surrounded myself with people who agreed.

*****

My grandmother made it from Capitol Hill to the International District in record time. She looked as if she had hastily put on her clothes and makeup—a sign that she was truly excited to see me considering that she normally never left the house with a hair out of place. When I opened the door she practically fell into my arms embracing me. After a few minutes she stepped back to get a better look at me. She cupped my face in her hands and looked me straight in the eye. "Rose," she said through her tears, "I'm sorry about all these years."

"I know, Grandma," I said. I did know that she did not share the views of her husband or son. She had been good to me. She had been better to me than the rest of my family, anyway.

"Your grandfather passed away a few months ago," she said before I could even usher her into the dusty apartment. I thought of the imposing man who had been my grandfather. I had loved him at one time with a child's adoration, but his love for me—at least the part that he had showed to me—was conditional. I was sorry, but the fact was that I had lost my grandfather years before his death.

"Oh Grandma," I said, feeling sorry for her loss, "Are you alright?" They had been married nearly fifty years.

"I've been so lonely," she said. "Even before he died. He wasn't an easy man." I was surprised by this candid admission. I think that she surprised herself, too, and she immediately collected herself. "Where's that baby of yours?" she asked.

I showed her into the apartment and reintroduced her to Maggie, who she also embraced, and then led her to my little boy. It was love at first sight. "He's beautiful!" she exclaimed. "Just like his wonderful sister who I cannot wait to see again." After a moment's thought she turned to me and asked, "Rose, I've been reading about the bravery of the Japanese troops. I thought of your husband. Is he...?" She didn't know.

Now it was my turn to cry. Maggie joined in. "He was wounded in battle, Grandma," I stuttered. "He didn't make it." The words were barely out of my mouth and she was up and embracing me once again.

"I have a proposition to make to you Rose, and I'm sorry that I'm doing it under these circumstances," my grandmother said. "I have inherited enough to be quite comfortable for the rest of my life. I would now like to spend what is left of my life making up for the things that I have not done in the past. And that includes spending more time with you. Life is too short and fragile to not be surrounded by those we love."

"I would like that, Grandma," I said, taking her hand.

"And I want you to know that you will always be alright, too, Rose Marie. There will always be enough for you and your babies," she said. "You don't need to ever worry."

"Thank you, but you know that I was never interested in your money," I said.

"I know that you aren't, but you must be worried now," she responded. The truth was that I was terrified. I had no skills other than teaching in the camps and I now had two small children to care for. And those children were half Japanese. I did not know what life had in store for me. I had imagined the worst. "Well, in the very least I would like you to know that I have a gift for you." She pulled an envelope out of her purse and handed it to me.

"The deed to my house," I said as I looked at the document. I owned my little house on Beacon Hill. She must have transferred the deed into my name after my grandfather's death. It was in my maiden name; Japanese were not allowed to own in that neighborhood. Still, this was quite a gift. "I can still pay you back the amount of the loan," I stammered as relief washed over me.

"No, you most certainly cannot," Grandma answered. "A gift is a gift. I have been given my own house, why not you have your own, too?" She smiled. "Besides, there is something I need to tell you."

"What is it?" I asked, alarmed. Had my house burnt down since I left, had vandals destroyed it?

"Do you know who rented your home when you first left for Puyallup?" she asked me.

"Well, I knew that it was a woman, but everything happened so quickly." Maggie and Mrs. Miramoto had mentioned it in a letter from Tule Lake, but we had been cut off for so long that it didn't even matter by the time we were all in Minidoka together.

"It was Ethel," said my grandmother. "She had been saving money and decided that she could help you while helping herself move on. She has been taking wonderful care of the home, even tending for the roses."

"That's wonderful," I said, not quite understanding where my grandmother was going with this.

"Well, I know that you need a place to live and the house is yours, do not get me wrong..."

"But..." Clearly my grandmother did not want me to kick Ethel out of the house. Of course, I had always cared for Ethel myself so that was the last thing I wanted to do.

"Ethel has a son, I don't know if you knew that," she said.

I thought for a second. "You know, it makes sense," I said. "She just never said it outright to me." Ethel had made comments about children in the past that I had been too young or too self-involved to care about.

"She got pregnant when she was young and her sister helped raise the baby," said my grandmother. "Well, I say "baby," but he is a man your age."

"What does he have to do with all this?" I asked, not rudely, just not quite following.

"He was injured in the Pacific. He lost a leg. And he came home for Ethel to help care for him," she continued. "He is in the house with her now."

"How sad," I said, my heart going out to good, kind Ethel.

"I just. Well, I just..."

"You don't want to kick her out, especially now that she has her son," I finished for her.

"I was going to make a proposal to you when I saw you next," my grandmother began, nervously. "I would like to give you my home. I was going to sign over the house to you for you and Akio and the child—children to live in. An early inheritance."

I was astounded. "What about you, Grandma?"

"I was hoping that I could live there with you. It would give me time with the children. I was hoping to get to know Akio, as well," she replied. "And I will help with the bills, anything you need."

"Grandma," I said, overwhelmed, "You do not have to buy my love. I would love to come and live with you. You do not need to put the house in my name. We can deal with all of that when the time comes."

"Well, you can certainly put it in my name," Maggie piped in. "I'm just kidding!" she exclaimed when my grandmother looked at her with a funny look on her face. "I was trying to lighten the mood. And it sounded like a very nice house was up for the taking!"

"Well, maybe we better put it in my name now—before someone else tries to snatch it up," I joked.

"Done," said my grandmother.

"And I want Ethel and her son to be able to stay in the Beacon Hill house as long as she needs."

"I will let her know," said my grandmother. "She has been so worried. She can't afford anything else but she did not want to impose."

"It is a pleasure," I said. "It will be good for the children to grow up in your neighborhood." I paused. "Unless, I mean, what about…."

"What is it?" my grandmother asked me.

"What about their ethnicity, Grandma? What will the neighbors think?" I stammered. "They are Japanese American." As if she didn't know.

"What about it?" she responded. "This is Seattle. There are people of Asian descent everywhere you look. People will learn to deal with it. We will deal with close-minded people together, Rose Marie. And while we do so, we might as well live in one of the nicest homes in the city."

"She's right about that, Rose Marie," Maggie cut in again. "It doesn't matter where you live—there will always be close-minded people. So you might as well live in style!" I have to admit that I couldn't see the harm in it myself; my children and I moved in with my grandmother on Capitol Hill. I was very lucky. My life could have been very different. I have always been a person whose life has relied heavily on the goodness or lack thereof of the people around me. I have been fortunate to discover that there are more good people in the world than I would have previously believed.

25 MAGGIE

From conclusion of "The Roses of Minidoka."

I'LL NEVER FORGET THE day that we went back to the farm for the first time after the evacuation. After meeting with her grandmother, Rose Marie and I used Mrs. Lundgren's car to drop off the baby and Rose Marie's grandmother at the Capitol Hill home before we set out over the bridge to Bellevue. Mrs. Lundgren confirmed that there were rumors that most of the farms in Bellevue had been neglected or abandoned and that there were reports of vandalism and unrest about the return of the Japanese citizens. We were worried and did not know what to expect when we arrived at my childhood home. Rose Marie tried her hardest to keep my mind off of my worries on the way over the bridge.

"Maggie," she said. "It's going to be alright. My father rented the land, remember? And what does he love more than anything?"

"Money," I asked, hoping that this wasn't a blatant insult to Rose Marie. It wasn't. Secretly I asked myself "But doesn't he hate the Japanese even more than he loves his money?"

"Exactly," she responded decisively. "If he could have made money, then he would have. I'm sure everything is fine."

"But Rose, don't you know how hard it is to truck farm?" I asked. "There is no way that your father—or any of the other non-Japanese men in Bellevue—actually pulled off an operational truck farm. It's too labor-intensive."

"I agree," said Rose Marie, "But apparently many of the people who took over the farms hired Filipino workers to come onto the fields."

"I heard that, too," I answered. "But the whole structure was gone. You can't just hire farmhands and nothing else. There had to be someone to drive the produce to Everett or to Pike's Place Market at five in the morning. There had to be people willing to work six days a week with the knowledge and pride that this was their life's work. There had to be a family. That is what made it work."

Rose Marie smiled sadly. "I'm concerned about it, too," she said. "I also heard how the people in Bellevue couldn't even hold together the cooperative that was run by men like your father. As soon as the Japanese were gone, so too were the berries and lettuce and other produce that had been shipped all over the country." She was silent for a moment.

"What is it, Rose Marie?" I asked.

"Well, it's all so stupid that it makes me angry," she exclaimed. "You know, wouldn't it have made more sense to keep the farmers here, producing their fruit and vegetables? Wouldn't that have made more sense than locking up the farmers and letting the farms and their crops go to waste? We could have sent food to our troops. What was the point in all of this waste?"

There was no answer to that question, at least not a good answer. Nor was there a good enough answer to explain what had happened to my parents' farm and home when we finally arrived. My mother and I had left the farm three years earlier. It had been a prosperous and tidy little farm and the house had been impeccable. We had left the house boarded up and completely secured with our large household goods secured in back rooms. We had rented the farm out to Rose Marie's father so that the land would be continuously used and would not lay dormant. The farm that stood before Rose Marie and I stood before the day that we returned in the summer of 1945 was not the same farm that I had left behind in the spring of 1942.

"Good God," I heard Rose Marie whisper as we approached the house. She looked as if she was going to be sick.

I didn't feel sick. I felt angry. The front door of the house was opened. It looked as if it had been kicked in. Pasted on the door itself were a variety of signs, similar to those we would start to see throughout Bellevue after the war. "Keep out Japs," said one. "Don't come home, Japs," read another.

"How dare they?" I said through clenched teeth. Rose Marie tried to comfort me, but I shrugged her off as I ran towards the back of the home. Sure enough, the locks on the back bedrooms had been pried off. The house was empty. Everything was gone.

I was still growling threats and obscenities through my teeth as I went out the back door and out to the farm. It had run completely wild. Nothing had grown on it for at least two years. Before going back to the car, where Rose Marie was waiting for me, I checked the shed. The farming equipment was gone. Everything that my parents had worked for their entire lives was gone.

When I got to the car, Rose Marie was crying. "I'm so sorry, Maggie," she whispered. "I hoped that my father wouldn't let this happen. I would have never suggested that he rent the farm if I had known."

"Oh, Rose," I said, seeing my sister-in-law's embarrassment. "This is not your fault. And a lot worse was done here than just letting the farmland go wild."

"Shall we go and ask my father how this could happen?"

"No," I answered. "Why bother?"

As we were speaking, we had not noticed that a man had come walking towards our car. "Excuse me. Maggie Miramoto?" he asked, peering in our window.

"Mr. Collins?" I asked, recognizing one of our neighbors.

"I thought that was you," he said. He asked how my family was and I gave him a quick update on my parents and siblings. I asked how his family was doing and I was sad to learn that he had lost two sons in the fighting in both Europe and the Pacific.

"I'm sorry about your house," he said after we had made small talk. "It has happened to all the Jap...enese farms in town."

"When did it happen?" I asked.

"When they found out that you were coming back," he said.

Rose Marie and I cut short our conversation and left. We stayed the night with her grandmother on Capitol Hill, trying to forget what we had seen in Bellevue.

*****

Once I knew the condition of their home, there wasn't much that I could do except let my parents know what awaited them upon their arrival back to Bellevue. Rose Marie was adamant that my parents not see the violent and destructive aftermath of the vandal's work on their home and so she and I cleaned up the farm as best we could. Seeing us hard at work, Mr. Collins came over and helped us clear some of the weeds that had grown on the once-pristine farm. Although we couldn't replicate what had been taken from the farm, Mrs. Lundgren very generously helped us purchase some furniture and kitchen items to make the place immediately livable for my parents. She also offered my parents and me a place to stay in her own home if we felt that we could not stay on the farm. I thanked her, but I was certain that my parents would not cower and avoid their own home.

My predictions were correct: My parents insisted on being brought to their farm immediately when we picked them up from the train station. My heart had already broken so many times for Mama and Papa that I thought I wouldn't be able to handle the look of disappointment on the faces of my parents when they saw the present condition of their home. But, in true Miramoto fashion, they seemed only relieved and proud when they arrived back to their home after three years absence. As they walked through the house and farm, I couldn't help but make a mental list of all that was gone, all that was different. They, on the other hand, seemed to see what was still there. I was confused by their refusal to succumb to anger or frustration and I told them so.

"Maggie," said my mother, who had developed a habit in Minidoka of calling me by my American name (finally!). "Both your father and I came to this country with nothing. We have known what it is to start over when life goes unexpectedly wrong. We can do it. Besides, we look around and see that people who love us have made an effort to clean and provide for us. We look around and see that we are home."

*****

My parents stayed in their home in Bellevue despite the obvious preference from the community that they find housing elsewhere. They were one of only three families who returned to Bellevue. Despite their contentment to return to their little farm, my parents soon accepted that they were really too old to begin truck farming from scratch. After a couple of years of trying to regain what was lost, my parents faced the facts of their situation; they sold off the farm land a few years after the war to a developer who converted the fields into a several family homes. My parents were able to keep their own home and watched as a city grew up around them. While this was heartbreaking in many respects, my parents were able to live off of that initial money until my father passed away and my mother sold her house to another developer at a huge profit. My mother spent her last years of life at the homes of her surviving children and grandchildren before she joined my father.

Before their deaths my parents were able to realize a life-long dream. In 1954, the United States government lifted the ban prohibiting *Issei* from becoming citizens and my parents, as well as the Fusakas, became naturalized citizens of the United States of America. As a present, Rose Marie presented them with the deed to their farm.

*****

We did not know anything about Kimiko until well after the war ended. It took time for the lines of communication to re-open and my sister had her own issues to deal with in Japan. In fact, so much time had passed without word from Kimiko that I believe that it is fair to say that we all assumed the worst: Kimiko, we felt, must have died in Hiroshima or the bombings of Tokyo. Or, if that was not her fate, we feared that she could have been taken prisoner by the Kempetai Secret Police at the outbreak of the war and had endured years of torture. With so many bad possibilities to choose from regarding my sister, my parents and I didn't dare get our hopes up about Kimiko until the day that the letter arrived.

Perhaps "letter" is not the correct word for what arrived in the mail to my parents' home in early January of 1946 was really nothing more than a cryptic note that raised more questions than it answered: "I am fine, so is baby. Name no good. Letter will come when able." It was not signed, but it was definitely Kimiko's handwriting; it matched the handwriting in the letters she had sent before the war that I had etched into my memory the moment, just a few years before, when the FBI had confiscated them and had taken my father.

I was the one who brought in the mail that morning. I had walked down the driveway to the mailbox on the street and was thumbing through the assorted bills and official mailings when I saw the Japanese postmark. It had come through the U.S. Army. "Henry!" was my immediate thought. I had given up on receiving letters from Kimiko and I knew that Henry was now stationed in Japan doing intelligence work. I had even overheard my mother asking Mrs. Fusaka to pass on information to her son about Kimiko's biological father's family in case they knew something about their daughter. I tore open the letter, hands trembling. I didn't know what to think when I saw the note. And then it sunk in.

"Mama! Papa!" I screamed as I ran towards the house. "A

letter! We received a letter!"

"Maggie-chan," my mother greeted me at the door, my father close on her heels. "What is it? Why are you so excited?"

"A letter," I said again, out of breath and words failing me in my excitement.

"Yes, it does appear to be so," observed my father seeing my flailing arm, letter clutched in my hand.

"Papa," I panted, "Take it! Read it!" He stepped past my mother and took the letter from my hand. His eyes scanned the words quickly and then once again more deliberately.

"Praise God!" he exclaimed under his breath. "Reiko, our daughter is safe!"

Rather than explain, my father read the letter to my mother. Not believing the words in English, my mother asked my father to translate the words into Japanese. As the words took meaning to my mother, she fell to the floor of the porch in tears of joy.

"Thank God," she said softly. "Thank you God."

*****

Further news from Kimiko was not immediately forthcoming. Still, just knowing that she was okay was enough to lift the spirits of my family. Every day we ran out to the mailbox hoping for another note. When we didn't receive a second letter from my sister, we sat on the porch, or the kitchen table as the weather cooled, speculating about the mysteries contained in my sister's note. In many ways, we had reverted to our pre-war conferences about Kimiko and her letters. However, now it wasn't so much that we tried to figure how to get her home, but we tried to figure what she had meant. "What baby?" I would ask, never expecting an answer (but always getting one nonetheless).

"Maybe she has had a child!" my mother would always say with tears in her eyes. "Can you imagine?" she continued. "A little grandchild that I have never met!" My mother lived for her grandchildren.

"What did she mean about her name?" my father would

always ask.

One day I couldn't take the tension of not knowing another second. Despite my previous vow to the contrary, I found myself saying, "I will go and find her. I will go to Japan and find Kimiko myself!"

"You cannot go to Japan, Megumi-chan," said my father. "It is still dangerous."

"And you certainly cannot forget that you said that you would never return," my mother said with the sparkle of hope in her eye. She was desperate for news of Kimiko.

"For Kimiko, I would go," I said. "I will speak to the Fusakas. Henry is there, maybe he can help."

"Ah," laughed my father, "now I understand why you would consider going back to Japan—you are still khaki-wacky!" I flushed with embarrassment; my father was correct, I would do just about anything to have an excuse to see Henry again. To have the opportunity to apologize to Henry for not responding to his letters. I tugged at my ring as my father teased me.

"No, Megumi-chan—Maggie," said my mother. "You are going to the university this autumn. You have worked so hard and waited so long to be accepted to the University of Washington and you have succeeded. That is your priority. Kimiko said that word would come when possible. We will await that day and you will get on with your life. It has already been interrupted too many times."

"But, Mama…"

"No buts, Maggie," my mother cut me off. "Go back to school. It is your dream. Kimiko will make her way back home in her own time."

"Yes, Megumi," my father added. "Go to school. Live your life. Kimiko will come home. So, too, will Henry." He winked. "Just be patient, my blessing."

"Patient," I scoffed. "I am the epitome of patience." I was silent for a moment. "Mama, Papa," I said, my voice thick with tears. "Thank you." There was nothing more that I could say.

I began studying at the University of Washington the autumn of 1946. I had been able to transfer my Vassar credits and I began at that school as a sophomore. Although I entered as a journalism student, I ended up graduating with a degree in Sociology. My focus was the study of Asian Americans in the United States. As I learned the history of my people and the struggles that we had overcome, I came to embrace my Asian heritage. Later I would use my degree to help the JACL bring attention to the internment of Japanese Americans in the quest for reparations. And, believe it or not, but I told the university to have my degree printed with the name Megumi. That is the name that I used for the rest of my life—Megumi Rose Miramoto. And, following my marriage, Miramoto-Fusaka.

*****

Henry showed up at my parents' door on Christmas Eve, 1947. He was home on a surprise leave to visit his parents. He had not told anyone that he would be coming. I was caught totally unaware when the doorbell rang that afternoon. I was in the kitchen helping my mother prepare food for the Christmas dinner we would be having that evening. I was wearing an apron and was covered in flour. A piece of my hair kept falling into my face, but I could not move it because my hands were covered in the cookie dough. I was a mess. I certainly was not looking as I would have hoped for the moment that awaited me.

When I heard the doorbell, I was irritated. Who, after all, could possibly be at our door at three p.m. on Christmas Eve? I knew that my parents were busy with various tasks so I yelled, "I'll get it," as I huffed towards the door, muttering my annoyance under my breath.

The bell rang again as I approached the door. "Coming, coming," I mumbled as I opened the door. "Yes, what can I do for you," I said as I swung open the door. I wanted the person standing on the other side to understand that I was being inconvenienced. "What is it, what can I do for you?" I repeated in an irritated whine as I opened the door. As I did so, I was looking down, hoping to avoid a long conversation by actively ignoring the person on the other side of the door. Thus, the first

271

thing I saw was the boots. Army-issue. My heart jumped—I thought instantly of my brother. Slowly I lifted my eyes to meet those of the visitor.

When I made eye contact with the soldier at the door my heart stopped. "Henry?" I stammered, my hello both a welcome and a question.

"Hello, Maggie," he said, taking in my dirty apron and messy hair. And the hand at my chest, gripping my good luck ring for dear life. He smiled.

"I'm thinking of going by Megumi, now," I responded. This, I thought, *this* is what I say to Henry when I see him again? No apology, no hello, but a snide correction about my name?

"Well, that is also a lovely name," Henry responded. "Nice to meet you, Megumi. I thought you might be a girl named Maggie who I once proposed to," He smiled again. He didn't take his eyes off mine. Had he thought that I had changed, that I had moved on? A new name for a new life? "I was hoping she might still be here." Still, I didn't say anything. I just stared back at him.

Suddenly he seemed shy, like his bravado had left him. "Well, I have come with a gift for your parents. Tell them Merry Christmas for me, will you, Maggie—Megumi?" He pulled an envelope from his breast pocket and put it in my hands. As I looked down at the package in my hands, Henry turned and began to walk down the stairs towards his car. I dropped the envelope in my distress.

"Henry," I said, starting to cry. I couldn't let him go again. "Henry!" Why wouldn't the words come out of my mouth? I normally couldn't stop myself from talking too much and now nothing. But he had stopped. This time I had another chance. "Maggie," I said to his back. "I'm still Maggie." He turned slowly back towards me. Don't walk away I wanted to shout. "I'm still Maggie and I would love more than anything to put this ring on my finger like I should have years ago." Still his back. "Can I do that Henry?"

"No," he said slowly. I almost reeled backwards the rejection was so painful. I had done this to him once. I closed my eyes, feeling faint. When I opened them, he was there, in front of me. "Whoa. I'm sorry; I didn't mean it like that." He took me in his arms, steadied me.

"I'm sorry. I'm so sorry," I began to chant as I rocked back and forth on my heels. The tears were pouring down my face at this point. "I should have kept writing. I should have..." I didn't know what more to say.

"Maggie," he said, pushing the loose hair behind my ear. "No you cannot put the ring on because I should do that for you. May I put the ring on your finger?" In response I unclasped the chain that I had worn around my neck for years and let the ring fall into Henry's outstretched hand. This time I said yes. It happened on what had started out as an ordinary day in December. A cold day in December. "Come inside," I said to Henry. I picked up the envelope as we walked into the house, hand-in-hand. "Welcome home."

*****

From the estate of Megumi Miramoto-Fusaka

November 17, 1947
Tokyo, Japan

Dearest Mama, Papa, and Maggie,

It has broken my heart to have been unable to speak to you since the outbreak of war. I look back and cannot believe how much has changed; how unexpected turns have arisen in our lives. I certainly did not expect to live in Japan, running a tea house for American GIs in Tokyo. However, it was because of this that I met Lieutenant Fusaka. He was a customer in my tea house and we were speaking about America. I was so excited to see a *Nisei* that I couldn't resist being nosy. I had heard stories about how the Japanese Americans were treated in America that I had to confirm this. Lo and behold, this Lieutenant Fusaka could not only tell me about the internment camps, but about my own family. What a small world this really is! It was through my new friend that I also learned of Akio.

Mama, Papa, Maggie...I do not have the words to express my pain at hearing about my little brother. My heart goes out to all of us, but especially to Mama and Papa and dear, sweet Rose Marie and her children. How sad to grow up without a father. That, unfortunately, will also be the fate of my own child. I have a wonderful little girl named Kiyoko. I was married during the war. It was a bad situation, one that I will tell you about in person someday. Because of this, I have been using my birth name, Kimiko Saito. Amazingly, the lieutenant knew of this possibility through his mother who he said is friends with you, Mama. The lieutenant, as it turns out, was looking for me as a promise that he made to Akio. He offered to bring this letter to you in person when he takes his next leave. I had not written before in depth because, after hearing about the camps, I was not sure if you were at our home. I was so worried that you were displaced somewhere. The lieutenant has assured me that you are well and at home in Bellevue.

I miss home so much. I miss the life that I had before I left for Japan. I miss the world before this terrible war. Mostly I miss all of you so very much. I have planted Japanese roses in my garden here in Tokyo to remind me of Mama and your story about enduring. You were right: I have made it through this ordeal and I am certain that I will make it home someday, but in the meantime I will live my life as it is. And it's not all bad. I have my daughter, I have my business, and I have my friend Hatsu and her family. Perhaps, since it will take some time for me to get back home, you might come and visit me and meet Kiyoko? Of course, this would mean that Maggie would have to come back to her favorite place. But, I have a feeling that the lieutenant might be willing to accompany my little sister if she would allow him to do so!

There are things that I have done during this war that I am

not proud of. I hope that you will find it in your hearts to forgive me when I tell you these things about me. Please know, though, that I have never lost my faith in my family, my country, or my heart. Even after hearing about the treatment that I would have endured at home, I still have faith in America. I still have faith in the world. We may fight and drop bombs on each other and hurt one another, but deep down I believe that there are more good people in this world than bad. Life will go on and, someday, maybe we'll get it right. At least, for the sake of my daughter, and all the children in the world, I hope that we will learn from this war. Perhaps we can even make the world a better place than it was before the bombs fell on Pearl Harbor.

With all our love,
Kimiko Rose and Kiyoko Rose

FURTHER READING

My thanks and recommendations for further (non-fiction) reading about this time period go out to the following:

Azuma, Eiichiro. *Between Two Empires: race, History, and Transnationalism in Japanese America.* New York: Oxford University Press, 2005.

Cao, Lan and Himilce Novas. *Everything You Need to Know about Asian-American History.* New York: Penguin Group, 1996.

Duus, Masayo and Edwin O. Reischauer, translated from the Japanese by Peter Duus. *Tokyo Rose: Orphan of the Pacific.* New York: Harper & Row Publishers, 1979.

Fiset, Louis and Roger Daniels. *Imprisoned Apart: The World War II Correspondence of an Issei Couple.* Seattle: University of Washington Press, 1997.

Gordon, Linda and Gary Y. Okihiro. *Impounded: Dorothea Lange and the Censored Images of Japanese American Internment.* New York: W. W. Norton & Company, 2006.

Gunn, Rex. *They Called Her Tokyo Rose.* Rex B. Gunn, 2008.

Heresy, John. *Hiroshima,* New York: Vintage Books, 1989.

Houston, Jeanne Wakatsuki and James D. Houston. *Farewell to*

Manzanar. New York: Dell Laurel-Leaf Publishing, 1995.

Howe, Russell Warren and Ramsey Clark. *The Hunt for '   Tokyo Rose.'* New York: Madison Books, 1990.

Kitano, Harry H. L. *Japanese Americans: The Evolution of a Subculture.* Englewood Cliffs: Prentice-Hall, Inc., 1976.

Lawson, Fuao Inada, editor. *Only What We Could Carry: The Japanese American Internment Experience.* Berkeley: Heyday Books (with California Historical Society, San Francisco), 2000.

Matsuda Gruenewald, Mary. *Looking Like the Enemy: My Story of Imprisonment in Japanese-American Internment Camps.* Troutdale: NewSage Press, 2005.

Murray, Alice Yang, editor. *What Did the Internment of Japanese Americans Mean?.* New York: Bedford/St. Martin's Press, 2000.

Nakano, Mei and Grace Shibata. *Japanese American Women: Three Generations 1890-1990.* Berkeley: Mina Press Publishing (with Nat'l Japanese American Historical Society, San Francisco), 1993.

Neiwert, David A. *Strawberry Days: How Internment Destroyed a Japanese American Community.* New York: Palgrave MacMillan, 2005.

Niiya, Brian, editor. *Encyclopedia of Japanese American History: An A-Z Reference from 1868 to the Present.* New York: Checkmark Books, 2001.

O'Brien, David J. and Stephen S. Fugita. *The Japanese American Experience.* Bloomington: Indiana University Press, 1991.

Sone, Monica. *Nisei Daughter,* Seattle: University of Washington Press, 2002.

Sosnoski, Daniel, editor. *Introduction to Japanese Culture.* North Clarendon: Tuttle Publishing, 1996.

Tateishi, John and Roger Daniels. *And Justice for All: An Oral History of the Japanese American Detention Camps.* Seattle: University of Washington Press, 2001.

Thomsen, Harry. *The New Religions of Japan: A Spotlight on the Most Significant Development in Postwar Japan.* Rutland: Charles E. Tuttle Company, 1963. Uchida, Yoshiko. *Desert Exile: The Uprooting of a Japanese-American Family.* Seattle: University of Washington Press, 1991.

ABOUT THE AUTHOR

Theresa Lorella is an author and practicing attorney. She lives in Seattle with her husband.

Made in the USA
Lexington, KY
10 August 2019